USA Today *bestselling author Megan Mulry takes readers from the sun-washed coasts of Florida to the cobbled streets of London, exploring the fresh, messy course of real love—and the courage it takes to keep it . . .*

A beautiful stranger

It's something about his eyes: the intense, searing blue; the focus on her—not just her body, but on Ellie herself. Those eyes hint at passion, determination, the scars of grief. But when she asks the handsome mechanic to meet her for coffee, Ellie knows nothing about him—not even his name.

What she does know is that after three years of building a decent life out of the shrapnel of tragedy, she's ready to open up again. Ellie is a survivor. She's willing to fight for a new happiness.

But the unforgettable Luke McCormick has wounds and contradictions of his own. He's a maddeningly patient lover, and an insatiably passionate soul; an aristocrat and a cowboy; a man with the mark of violence on him, more gentle than anyone she's known. And yet as Ellie and Luke unfurl the pleasures of a second chance, the terrors of the past lurk just beneath the surface.

Also by Megan Mulry

A Royal Pain
If the Shoe Fits
In Love Again
R is for Rebel
Roulette

Bound to Be a Bride
Bound to Be a Groom
Bound with Honor
Bound with Love
Bound with Passion
The Wallflowers

MEGAN MULRY

Published by Megan Mulry
www.meganmulry.com
ISBN-10: 0-9899975-3-7
ISBN-13: 978-0-9899975-3-9

"My bounty is as boundless as the sea,
My love as deep; the more I give to thee,
The more I have, for both are infinite."
-Shakespeare, *Romeo and Juliet*

Chapter 1

Ellie Sinclair pulled into the parking lot of the BMW repair shop and looked down at her wedding ring. She wondered how much longer she'd wear it.

It'd been more than three years since Rob had died in the small prop plane he was flying back from their vacation in the Bahamas. Ellie had returned a few days early to finish getting everything ready for her mother's sixtieth birthday party. She'd been standing in her kitchen chatting with her mom and the florist about gerbera daisies versus peonies in the centerpieces when the phone rang. The Coast Guard asked to speak to the owner of tail fin number sierra-india-nine-two-eight-seven and Ellie, wet daisy stems in one hand, stiff peony stems in the other, told him impatiently that her husband was not at home and would he mind calling back another time.

The rest of that day and week remained a murky collage in her memory. Her mother's birthday party never happened.

Obviously.

A quick double-knock on the driver's side window snapped her back to the present. She pressed the black button and watched the glass slide with Bavarian precision down into the door. The Florida summer heat was a blistering assault and she couldn't see the attendant's face for the glare.

"Hi," she said, squinting up at him.

He held a clipboard and a pen. "Hi. Do you have an appointment?"

"Yes, I spoke to Bill yesterday and he said to bring it in. The air conditioning is faltering again."

He wrote a few notes then paused to look at her. "How many years have you had it?"

"Oh . . . I don't know. About eight years I guess. I don't even know what year it is exactly."

He returned his attention to the clipboard and made a few more notes. "Can you leave it?"

"Yes. My father's pulling in now to give me a lift back to my place. Keep it as long as you need it. Do you want me to leave it running?"

"Sure. I'll move it into the shop."

She looked back into the car to make sure she hadn't forgotten anything, then bent toward the passenger side floor and grabbed her bag. Ellie got out and turned to see the mechanic standing just to her left. She could see his face clearly now. Hard, tanned planes framing diamond bright blue eyes. All she could think was: piercing. His eyes were piercing. His whole being was piercing.

Weird. Why would she think such a thing?

She must have stood there an awkward beat too long because he murmured or cleared his throat or made some similar guttural sound to disturb her.

"Oh, sorry." She was blocking his access to the car. "I didn't mean to stand in your way."

"No worries." He smiled briefly as she moved away and then he slid easily into the car. He adjusted the mirror slightly and revved the engine a tiny bit before thrusting the gearshift firmly into place and heading down the row of garage doors.

Her father pulled up to where she was standing and gestured for her to get in the car already. He wasn't about to roll down his window and let any of that 99-degree heat get in.

Two days later there was a message from Bill at the repair shop on her answering machine saying the car was fixed but she was probably looking at a full overhaul of the heating and air conditioning system within the next six months. He also left the usual offer to buy the car in case she wanted to get rid of it once and for all.

She put her cell phone down on the white marble kitchen counter and stared at the Atlantic Ocean, wide and free, seemingly infinite outside the wall of windows at the back of the house. She and Rob had bought this place during a lull in the Florida real estate market about five years ago. A year or two after Rob bought the BMW. The house and property were very small by Palm Beach standards, but it was on the ocean and that was all that had really mattered.

Rob and Ellie had met their first week at the University of Virginia and never really parted after that. They'd created their own software company while they were still undergraduates; they were best friends with the same bizarre loves: writing code and moneymaking and each other. Rob did most of the tech development and Ellie secured the angel financing and eventually ran all the marketing. Her parents called them the dynamic duo, shaking their heads from behind their very placid, conservative lives in rural Virginia, then later in Florida.

After seven years, they sold Sinclair Systems to Oracle in an eight-figure deal and an obscene amount of stock. At the ripe old age of twenty-seven, the two of them were completely free.

Since it looked as if babies were not on the docket—many years of unprotected sex and zero interest in hormones and turkey basters had made that discussion moot—they decided to take the money and run, as it were, and live the life that everyone else always talked about but never got around to. She and Rob had laughed at all those people who said they would never retire no matter how much money they made.

Uh. Duh.

Why not?

It wasn't as if retirement meant atrophy. For Rob and Ellie, it meant whatever they wanted it to mean. So with money in the bank, they sublet their apartment in New York, shuttered the house in Palm Beach, and decided to take the Rob-and-Ellie show on the road. They chartered a boat and sailed around the

Caribbean for a few months. They spent five months in Southeast Asia and Australia. They lived outside of Madras for another eight months. They read and wrote and painted and Rob invented imaginary machines in notebooks full of blueprints and Ellie began taking photographs in earnest. After nearly three years of acting like Bedouins, they decided to return to Florida to spend time caring for Rob's ailing parents and, a few years later, her parents moved there as well.

The phone rang again and she saw it was her best friend Lotta calling from San Francisco.

"Hey!" Lotta trilled before Ellie had a chance to speak.

"Hey, you."

"Want to come out to Sonoma in a couple of weeks?"

"Sure. Why? What's going on?"

"Well . . . I think I might be getting married?"

Ellie's coffee cup hit the counter harder than she'd intended. "What?! To whom?"

"I love that even in a pique of excitement and disbelief you use the object instead of the subject!"

"Who is marrying you? To whom will you be married?!"

"Oh, Ellie, it's the craziest thing, but it's Philip . . . "

"Philip . . . ? Philip Bennet, my cousin Philip?"

"I know, yes, isn't it the wildest thing? It was like the most ridiculous Harry-met-Sally moment at the Fourth of July party in Burlingame a few weeks ago." Lotta's voice was gentle and sweet in a way Ellie couldn't ever remember hearing it before. "There we were, being our embittered selves, mocking every ridiculous baby-chasing parent who'd foolishly given the nanny the day off, and then we just sort of looked at each other and I kind of wanted to jump his bones right then."

"I'm speechless."

"I thought you would be. I wanted to wait a little bit—you know, make sure it wasn't a one night stand and all that—before letting you know." Lotta laughed quickly, almost a bark. "And then he asked me to marry him—of all things—and I thought that pretty much ruled out the one night stand theory, so I'm calling you to see if you will come out and be my maid of honor, or matron or whatever the fuck it is."

Ellie was laughing over Lotta's rendition of her courtship and wedding plans. "Of course I'll come out to California. When are you guys going to do it?"

"I think eight weeks is enough time to get everyone together, don't you? I was thinking we could all meet up at that great little inn near Mendocino, in Elk. Remember?"

Lotta knew perfectly well that Ellie remembered. She and Rob had been a dozen times and it was one of the places she'd avoided since his death because it was all Rob . . . every pine needle on the narrow path down to the beach, each scent wafting up from the kitchen garden into the cool room where they slept.

"Yes, I remember."

"Oh, Ellie, doll. It's all going to be good. We all miss him still." Lotta's voice trailed off when she realized the empty meaning of that.

"I think I looked at another man the other day . . . for the first time in forever," Ellie said.

"Oh, that's great! I mean, that *is* great, right?"

"I don't know. At least it didn't feel like treachery or adultery like I thought it would. He was just this sort of interesting-looking person, you know?" Ellie almost sighed aloud then caught herself. "Really intense blue eyes that had a bit of sadness I could relate to, not maudlin or anything. Just like he had seen it all and there it was. Nothing any of us could do about it, but keep on."

"Where did you meet him?"

"That's the funny part. He's this new guy at the BMW repair shop where I always go to take Rob's old car. I don't even know why I still have that car."

"Maybe it was so you could eventually meet Mr. Blue Eyes."

"You are so Northern Californian—I'm not going to dignify that with a response."

"Since when is Northern Californian a veiled insult?" Lotta's voice took on a jovial if defensive edge.

"You know what I mean—hidden meanings, fate. Next you're going to tell me Mars is in retrograde and I'll have to hang up on you."

"Well, it is, but I'm certainly not going to tell *you* that. I just meant, everything is connected, and I know you know what I mean. I won't go all spiritual on you, but try to let it all flow for a while. I know you have improved, but try not to, you know, have to understand everything."

"Now I really am going to have to hang up on you. I know what you're implying is that I shouldn't fall into my typical bad habits of over-analysis to the point of paralysis."

"Nice rhyme."

"It was, wasn't it? Enough about me. I want to hear more about you and Philip." Ellie took another sip of coffee and hoped Lotta would take the hint.

"What's to tell? You already know both of us, now it's just both of us together."

"Where are you going to live? Are you going to have babies? What's he like in the sack? You know, things like that."

"We are going to keep both places. We're going to live in my apartment in town during the week, then his place in Mill Valley on weekends. We are going to have babies. Quickly. And none of your business."

"So he's totally twisted and you can't even tell me because he's so off the charts wild in bed that you might freak me out? Like that badass?"

Lotta laughed. Hard.

"Oh. My. God. He really is?! I was just joking and I hit it, didn't I? You two must be like a pair of minks. I don't even want to think about the stuff you and your dirty minds get up to."

Lotta was laughing so hard, Ellie wondered if she might be choking.

"Actually I do want to think about it, but not you two doing it. Gross. All right, catch your breath, I don't want to have to call the SF Fire Department and tell them you need to be resuscitated."

"Oh, Ellie. I have missed you."

"I know. I have missed me too."

They were both quiet for a few seconds.

"Ellie?"

"Yeah?"

"Why don't you bring Mr. Blue Eyes to the wedding?"

"Because I've never even met him." Ellie snorted a quick laugh. "I saw him for two seconds. I probably won't ever see him again. End of story."

"Of course you'll see him again. You have to go pick up the car, don't you?"

"Yes, but the owner usually deals with the bill and giving the car back. For all I know that other guy has already quit and resumed his life as a homeless wayfarer."

"Well, if he is still there, would you at least talk to him? Consider it *spiritual work* from your *Californian* friend. Tell him it was an assignment from your life coach."

"Then I really would never see him again. Because if I were him, I would certainly run from any woman who said that to me!"

Lotta laughed. "I know, but seriously, for me, as a little wedding present, will you just talk to the guy for a few minutes? You know, strike up a conversation. Nothing weird. You used to be able to talk the bark off a tree. Remember?"

"Barely."

"Fine. Do what you can. I'll be sending out blast emails from here on out. Mark your calendar. Elk. September 15. That has a nice ring to it, don't you think?"

"Yes. Oh, speaking of nice rings, did Philip get you one?"

"I hate to admit it, but yes," she whispered with conspiratorial glee, "And I love it!"

Ellie laughed at her artsy, anti-establishment, anti-materialistic best friend marrying her preppy, strait-laced, venture capitalist cousin. "Describe it to me."

Ellie could picture Lotta turning her hand at that very moment across the continent.

"Well, it's . . . just perfect really. He's kind of great in that way, you know?"

"He's my cousin, not my fiancé, Lotta. In what way is he great?"

"He kind of knows exactly how far he can go, you know? He knew I would despise some vicious diamond from some horrible mineshaft. He found this beautiful piece of red turquoise and well, you'll see it soon enough. But it's kind of earthy and sexy and fiery and all these metaphors that he was sweet enough to say made him think of me. So I love it."

"Oh, Lotta. You're in love. I'm so happy for you. For you both."

"Thanks, sweetie. I am too. I have to go, but I'll be back in touch soon, probably crying about my mother, but in the meantime, go talk to Mr. Blue Eyes. Love you. Bye."

"Bye."

Luke McCormick leaned against the frame of the open garage door and wiped his hands slowly with the dirty rag. He kept his breathing deep and steady, out of years of habit, and tried to feel the texture of the cloth as he pulled it the length of each finger to clean off the motor oil. The humid, stagnant heat reminded him of Southeast Asia, and the memory briefly conjured Desmond and Kate and so many dark memories he'd buried for years. He watched as the beautiful woman from last week got out of her father's car and walked slowly over to Bill's office to pay for the repairs on the perfectly maintained 740iL.

Her long red hair was loose and had a careless beauty. It was shining in the brutal July sun, but only from having been brushed, he thought, not from hours at a salon. Her long legs were smooth and bare, tan against the white shorts. The only other things she wore were a simple gray tee shirt and flip-flops.

He forced his mind, and eyes, back to the cloth in his hands. He'd been celibate for years, because the alternative had become unbearable. Stay on task and be present, he reminded himself.

She is *very* present, some other (long dormant) part of his mind taunted.

He looked up from his hands to see she had stopped, one hand on the door to Bill's air-conditioned office and one hand shielding the sun with her gaze on Luke.

She turned away from him for a second, looking over her shoulder at the sound of her father's car accelerating out of the parking lot and onto Dixie Highway, then turned back to look at him. She let her hand fall away from Bill's door and started walking toward him.

He was particularly grateful for years of meditation and breathing. Months of isolation. Practice. This was just one more simple moment in an infinite string of simple moments. Or at least that's what he tried to tell himself.

Then she was standing a few feet in front of him, still in the sun's glare while he stood in the shadow of the hot garage, and he knew there was nothing simple about her.

"Hi," she said, with far more timidity than he would have imagined.

He smiled. "Hi."

There was a rich, long silence as they stood there looking at one another. He kept breathing. She kept looking, one hand angled at her forehead to block the ferocious sun, the other hanging limp at her side.

"So. I have this friend I was talking to the other day," she started in, as if they were already in the middle of a conversation, "and she told me I should say hi to you if I ever saw you again. So . . . so now that I've done that I guess I'll go get my car."

But she didn't go get her car.

She just stood there.

And so did he.

"Would you like to come in out of the sun?" He gestured with one hand, his motion controlled but gentle. She stepped into the shade, let her hand come away from her face, and then lifted her sunglasses up onto her head.

"I can't see very well in here."

"Let your eyes adjust for a second." He looked right into her eyes as they got accustomed to the shadows. She was exactly his height, he supposed they were both just under six feet. Her eyes were a misty, faraway green; specks of yellow and brown were flaring to life near her pupils.

She was quite good at silence.

He looked away from her eyes for a few seconds, at the turn of her long neck where it met the edge of her gray T-shirt, then back to her eyes.

She smiled, a small closed-mouth smile. More with her eyes.

"Hi," she whispered.

"Hi."

"Would you like to meet for a coffee sometime?" she asked.

"Yes."

"Okay. That sounds good. Do you have a phone number? I mean, do you want to make a plan now, or should we talk later?"

"I'm off tomorrow. Do you want to meet at that Starbucks in City Place? At ten tomorrow morning?" he asked.

"Yes."

"Okay."

"Okay," she said.

And then she was turning back toward Bill's office to pay for her repairs.

He looked down at the dirty gray rag in his hands and realized he had never stopped rubbing it methodically into his fingers.

Ellie spoke normally to Bill. Paid for the repairs. Laughed softly when he offered to buy the car.

"I think I'll keep it. Sentimental reasons and all that."

"I hear you. It's a beauty. But it just doesn't seem like you drive it very often. A shame to keep a car like that in the garage. Why don't you take it out a bit more?"

"I will. I think I will."

"All right. See you in a couple of months then. I mean," he laughed a bit, "I'm not *hoping* it needs any work, but you know, it probably will."

"Thanks again, Bill. See you soon."

She left his office and the car was running and waiting for her just outside the thin, metal door.

He must have driven it up and left the AC running for her. She felt a bubble of nervous laughter.

He.

She hadn't even introduced herself. She didn't even know his name!

She put the car in gear, slid her sunglasses back down over her eyes and turned on the Blaupunkt stereo. She had never taken out the twelve CDs that Rob had last put in the changer before the accident. It was like his embalmed little world in that car. The car itself. The smell of the leather, the feel of the powerful engine, the music: Red Hot Chili Peppers, Andres Segovia, some angry California surfer punk shit that he had loved and she had hated, Aerosmith, Nirvana, Mozart, Pearl Jam, Black Sabbath, Liz Phair. Ellie had always loved that he loved Liz Phair. She cranked that Liz Phair so loud she felt it in her major organs.

She drove the car around for about two hours, heading out to 441 with the strawberry fields on one side and the Everglades on the other. She floored the accelerator a couple of times and reveled in the feeling of speed, escape, immersion. Then she set the cruise control and tried to appreciate the benefits of adhering to the rules.

The comfort in conformity.

It felt safe. She switched to the Mozart CD and spaced out, letting the car do all the work.

She pulled into her driveway a few hours later and slid the car into the garage, turned off the ignition, and sat there for a while in the cool silence. The car had its little clicks and hums, like a horse after a long ride, she thought, feeling the mechanical life drain out of the beautiful machine.

She went into the house, fixed herself a drink, and sat out on her back porch. All in all she felt pretty damned proud of herself. Later that night, she fell asleep brimming with optimism.

Chapter 2

Saturday morning was a disaster.

The rain that had been threatening for weeks finally broke, coming across from the Bahamas and slamming into the east coast of Florida around three in the morning. The lightning bolts crackled and thunderclouds boomed as if they were all gathering directly above Ellie's house. She and Rob had always shared a childish fear-love of violent passionate weather. They would sit in their living room and watch the menacing clouds build on the horizon and roll toward them, trying not to flinch as the power and chaos began to let loose.

Now, with Rob gone, the thunder and lightning made her feel around for the memory of that shared joy, because there'd been no firsthand joy for a long time. Then it got better, just sitting on the couch and trying to be present.

She tried not to think about thinking, as much as that was possible without a degree in Eastern mysticism. She tried not to think about why certain things always reminded her of Rob. She tried to let things simply be whatever they were: thunder, the slow roll of the tide. These were meaningless, or at least meaningless as far as they were related to two random humans who had once experienced them together.

The past three years had been good practice.

From four a.m. on she lay in her bed listening to the pounding rain and the intermittent flashes of lightning that threw lurid shadows across her ceiling.

She didn't think of Rob. It was just noise.

She supposed that was progress.

The lack of sleep was *not* progress. She loved her sleep. She craved it like some people craved food. And when she didn't get the necessary eight hours, well, she tended to be a little peevish.

So she was irritated sitting there at Starbucks: wet from not being able to find a parking spot nearby and having to run through the rain, and prompt because, well, she was always prompt, and feeling like an idiot with every few minutes that passed, and cursing the fact that she didn't bring a book, because she always brought a book wherever she went but not this time of course, because she was meeting someone. Someone whose name she did not know. Someone who was now fifteen minutes late and made her get out of bed on a dark and stormy Saturday morning, the kind of morning that whispers all sorts of promises about how very right it would be to stay in bed all morning, or maybe even all day, and maybe take a bath and get right back into bed. It was that kind of wonderful day that demanded absolutely nothing of you.

Instead.

Instead, she was sitting in a Starbucks, which she kind of hated on the principle that they, whoever the evil corporate *they* were, had created a product that she was becoming entirely too fond of. And she resented that.

And she resented the piercing blue eyes that came in the front door just then and scanned the length of the coffee shop. She resented those eyes a little less when she saw the hint of eagerness or worry when he was looking for her, for that second before he saw her, and then she hardly resented anything at all at the moment those eyes landed on her. Because he was a picture of relief and gratitude and something else, something gentle.

And then he was walking over to where she was sitting.

And then he sat down and started talking.

"I am never late. I despise when people are late." He had his hands clasped loosely on the table in front of him. For a second she had a strange feeling that he was going to grasp her hands in his and start preaching to her, which would have been impossible because she had her arms crossed in a display of defensive-body-language-101 that silently screamed this-better-be-good. He continued, "I think it shows a complete lack of consideration for another person's time and efforts, and their very soul."

"Luckily I don't have a soul, so we can dispense with that portion of the apology. Because I also despise when people are late. But bad things happen to good people, I hear. So what happened to you?"

"I never met anyone without a soul. How does that work for you?"

"We can broach my missing soul after. Why were you late? Do you want a coffee?"

"No, I don't drink coffee."

"Then why did you suggest we meet at Starbucks?"

"It came to mind."

"I feel a bit tricked. I thought it was something we had in common. A shared interest."

"A shared interest in Starbucks? A kiss to build a dream on?"

"I—"

But he smiled just then, really smiled, and all the words flew out of her head. Everything flew out except that smile. The impatience and the paranoia and every other spurt of adrenaline that had been fueling her for the past few hours just—pffft—and the world, or at least the part of her brain that was able to reflect upon the world, was only interested in that smile. The turn of his lips. It wasn't a big toothy grin, it was just a knowing look. And his eyes crinkled at the edges, with humor but also with wanting to connect. Ellie could feel it perfectly. He had a desire for a shared interest. But a real one.

And it was funny, to think that Starbucks was something they would share. She got the joke, but only because he was able to slow time and hold it out to her in the palm of his . . . soul.

She leaned toward him, uncrossed her arms and rested them on her side of the table.

"I bet there are thousands of people who have built their dreams on a kiss and a shared interest in Starbucks. And then, when they can't have children, or one of them dies, or their best friend tries to commit suicide, they can always walk into Starbucks. And remember that good time. That shared interest."

His humor vanished. "Has any of that happened to you?"

Ellie didn't want to look at him anymore. He was too intense. Too tender. She looked toward the street, out the front window, "I don't know. Yes. No. Some of that." Then she reached for her big, delicious, reliable, corporate coffee and took a grateful sip.

Maybe all of that would send him running.

Or worse. He would want to talk about all of that and she'd be stuck there for hours listening to some sob story. He would be empathic.

What a nightmare.

But he didn't do any of that. He was an excellent bider of time. He knew how to wait. Perfectly.

She finally gathered the courage or the curiosity or whatever was required to look into those eyes again. And he just kept her gaze. And held it. And she wanted him to pet her.

That's all she could think. She wanted him to rub his hands on her like a dog or a cat, to soothe her and praise her and lo—

"Okay then!" Ellie slapped the palms of her hands against the bare flesh of her thighs, readying herself to stand up and walk away.

"Have you ever been skydiving?" he asked.

"No. Have you?"

"Sure. A bunch of times. It's great. You want to go do it?"

"Right now?"

"I don't have to be back at work until Monday morning. Do you need to be anywhere?"

Ellie tried to remember some prehistoric dating rules about not making yourself totally and completely available lest you appear easy or something. "I never need to be anywhere."

"Lucky you."

"I haven't thought of myself as lucky in quite some time," she said.

"Why is that?"

"Because I used to think of myself as really lucky all the time. I was proactively grateful. I was practically stunned sometimes at how lucky I was. I'm not necessarily smarter or nicer or better than anyone else, but lots and lots of good shit kept happening to me."

"And then what happened."

"And then, I guess it's still good, but something really bad happened that made all the other good things kind of pale. You know what I mean?"

"Yeah. I totally know what you mean," he said. "Not the details, obviously. Do you want to talk about details or should we just stay in the abstract for a while?"

"Either way. I get this feeling I'm going to dump every bit of my story out at your feet at some point in the next few days of you-not-needing-to-be-anywhere-else, so I guess it's just a matter of whether you are one of those people who like to have lots of information right out of the chute or if you like things to unfold."

He was smiling again. "I think I like the unfolding."

"I figured that. You seem like a patient sort of person. I guess I have been forced into patience." Her lips quirked at the irony. "But I wouldn't say it's my natural setting. Hey, what's your name by the way? I'm Ellie." She reached out her hand to shake his and he looked down at her slim, bare hand hanging there and she thought for a second that he wasn't going to touch her or that she was being overly formal.

Instead, he took her hand in both of his and held it like a gift, turning it over and running the pads of his fingers over her palm while the back of her hand rested in the palm of his.

"My name is Luke. It's a bit anticlimactic when I say it like that isn't it? Just Luke."

"Hi Just Luke."

"Hi Ellie. What is that short for?"

"Eleanor." She had to force herself not to sigh when she said it, distracted as she was by his touch.

"I like Eleanor. It's formal."

"You like formal?" she asked, losing her concentration.

"I suppose, in a way, yes. I do like formal. I like structures and machines. Engines. They are formal, aren't they?"

"You are not just a mechanic, are you?"

He squeezed her hand. "I don't think any of us are just anything, do you?"

"Sometimes I think I'm just a girl." She couldn't look away from his eyes.

"That's something else altogether. From the inside looking out, I'm just a lot of things. From the outside looking in, I might very well be just a mechanic."

"It's a good word mechanic," she said, trying to follow what he was saying through the dreamy haze of his voice. "It's more than it appears."

"It's a great old word," he agreed. "It really just means to work with one's hands."

He was still holding Ellie's hand in his and she refocused her attention on the feel of his hard strong fingers. He started massaging the muscle at the base of her thumb.

"I feel brittle compared to you," she said softly.

"In what way?"

"Your hands feel wonderful against mine, but mine feels stiff. A bit." She wasn't quite sure how to explain it, so she stopped babbling.

All of a sudden Ceci Rehnquist was standing next to the café table looking from Ellie to Luke, to their clasped hands, then back to Ellie.

"Ellie! What are you up to? I haven't seen you in ages! Where have you been?"

Ellie slid her hand away from Luke's hold and rested it around her paper coffee cup. "Hey Ceci. How are you? Ceci, this is Luke. Luke, this is Ceci."

Ceci shook hands with Luke and gave him a warm, brilliant smile. Ellie did a quick double-take and looked at Luke with new eyes. Was Ceci flirting with him? She had been so lost in his eyes she didn't really take in the rest of him. He was wearing an old white oxford shirt, clean and probably good quality, but a bit frayed at the collar and rolled up at the sleeves. He had a great tan and was clean-shaven, but there was a roughness to his skin that made him seem like a workingman.

Ceci was rich, and thin, and blonde, and at a quick glance, probably wearing and carrying $5,000 worth of Prada, Gucci, and Pucci. And she wasn't even dressed up. She was just coming into Starbucks to get a coffee. Her sunglasses and her purse alone were worth a fortune. She had on cute piqué-cotton white shorts and a colorful fitted tee shirt. Ellie wondered if she herself looked like that. So polished. Buffed. Not in a muscle-building way, but buffed like a piece of old silver. Ceci had a patina.

Ellie looked from Ceci to Luke and saw how he was talking to her. Listening to her. Lots of people ignored Ceci. She talked too much so it seemed as if she wasted her words in the torrent. If she had so many words to spare, the thinking went, they probably were not that valuable. But Luke was making her feel valuable. Ellie loved that. Then she felt a shiver of insane desire shoot up her spine and gooseflesh raised on her upper arms.

Luke turned instantly to face her. "Are you okay?"

"Sure," Ellie replied, then turned to look up at Ceci. "Do you want to sit with us for a bit? We were just talking about going skydiving."

Luke got up quickly to pull another chair over to the small table. Ellie stifled a grin when she realized he was glad because it afforded him the opportunity to move his chair next to hers, and Ceci would be across from them.

"Sure," Ceci said, "Let me just get my latte. I'll be right back. Thanks." She was grateful in a way that gave Ellie the brief impression that no one had ever in her life asked her to sit down for an impromptu coffee.

Luke reached for Ellie's hand under the table and gave it a momentary squeeze then pulled his hand away. "I wasn't really done holding your hand."

"Yeah, about that. I'm out of practice on the hand-holding."

"Excellent. We'll have to practice, practice, practice then." But he didn't reach for her or touch her again.

Ceci returned to the table and launched into a veritable interrogation. "So Luke. Tell me all about yourself. Ellie holding hands is big news!" She was mischievous, but there was nothing mean about her.

Luke turned to Ellie and asked with his eyes.

Ellie lifted her chin and said, "Yes, Luke, tell us all about yourself." Then she put her elbows on the table and rested her chin in her hands, like an adoring fan eyeing her teen idol.

"Not much to tell I guess. Ellie and I met a few days ago and then yesterday decided to meet for coffee."

"How did you two meet?" Ceci asked.

"At the BMW repair shop."

"Ellie, I thought you got rid of that car when—"

"No," Ellie interrupted. "I never got rid of it."

"Well, that's good," Ceci said. "So were you there having your car repaired too, Luke?"

"No, I work there," Luke answered.

Ellie watched the wheels turning inside Ceci's perfectly coiffed blonde head. She wasn't a snob, but she wasn't a liar either. A mechanic would not be an easy story to tell at tennis on Monday. Words like slumming and dalliance came to mind. But Luke didn't look like slumming to Ceci.

"Really," Ceci continued slowly, "have you always been a mechanic?"

Luke looked totally at ease with her line of questioning. "I guess in a way I have. But not always with car engines. I've worked in a lot of different . . . capacities. I'm kind of retired now. I'm 43 in case you are wondering." He looked at Ellie for a second, just to check in, then turned back to Ceci.

"Really? A retired mechanic. I'm intrigued. Please tell," Ceci prodded.

"I was uninspired with what I was doing, I guess," he continued, "and I always wanted to see how simple I could get my life to be, so I sold my house and my car and most of my possessions and moved into this little place by the beach about fifteen minutes south of here and got this job at the BMW repair shop because I've always loved engines and now I just get to play with engines all day. And then I met Ellie. So," he gestured with both of his hands palm up, "Right place right time and all that."

Ellie felt her heart at that moment, or more precisely, she felt the negative space that her heart usually occupied, because her heart was somewhere down near her stomach.

"Charming!" Ceci said. "Well, you two enjoy the rest of the day. I have to go pick up the boys from soccer practice. Very glamorous. Nice meeting you Luke."

He stood up and shook Ceci's hand. "Nice to meet you too, Ceci. Have a great day."

"I think I shall." She waved and left with a cheerful step.

They watched her go then turned to one another.

"So where were we?" Luke asked as he sat back down.

"I think we were talking about skydiving."

"And I was holding your hand."

"And you were holding my hand." She slid back into his eyes. It was comfortable there. Warm and safe. But she kept her hands flat between her thighs.

"What were you thinking just then? I like that look in your eyes."

"I was thinking how I felt warm and safe . . . " She felt shy and ridiculous all of a sudden, and looked away.

They sat in the quiet for a while after that. Ellie was really starting to appreciate how Luke could be open and honest and forthright without prying. After a few minutes she took the last sip of her coffee and looked to the street. "Do you want to go for a walk or something? Where did you park?"

"Sure. Where do you want to go?"

To bed with you, she thought. Then she was momentarily convinced she had said it out loud or he had read her mind and she blinked away her confusion. "Uh. I know it's really hot outside but I'd love to go out to the Everglades. Do you want to do that?"

"Yeah, let's do that." His eyes were full of pleasure. "Can you leave your car here or do you want me to follow you back to your place to drop it off?"

They were up and walking out to the sidewalk. "I thought you just said you didn't have a car?"

"I sold my car and got a motorcycle. Is that okay? Or we can go in your car. I know some people don't like motorcycles."

"I used to love motorcycles. When I was 12, I once spun out on my cousin's 750 cc—which he had strictly forbidden me to ride—and nearly took out the front porch of my parents' house."

"Were you scared?"

She stopped in the middle of the sidewalk and stared at him. "You know, you're really something. I don't think I've ever met anyone like you, who clicks so easily from reality to feelings."

"Don't you think feelings are real?"

"I guess. But I—" She looked into the middle distance to buy some time. "I was sort of raised to think of them as separate or private or irrelevant or—you know."

"I know what you mean. I used to think that feelings were separate, the way you mean, but then, time passes and things happen and I don't feel or think separately anymore."

"Interesting." Ellie tried to process that. "Because for me, when 'things happened' my feelings became even more disconnected. I mean, I was connected to them—" Her smile was weak. "—but I certainly didn't want anyone else wandering around in there."

They were walking again.

"I guess when my 'things happened' I was more afraid of being alone in there." Luke tapped the side of his skull.

"Yeah, I've heard that. I know what you mean. But, something about the particulars of my husband's death—" She looked to make sure he heard. "—that was my 'thing that happened' by the way, my husband died three years ago, but my point is that I didn't want to share my grief because it was like everyone wanted a piece of it, so they could have a piece of him. And it was mine, you know?"

"My wife, Kate, committed suicide. That was my 'thing that happened' and I didn't want that to be mine alone."

They had turned down a quiet side street in West Palm Beach. They were the only two people. Cars were going by, down on Dixie at the far end. The sun was shining with cruel intensity, but nothing out of the ordinary. It was nearing midday and the heat was blistering. Just a sweltering summer day in South Florida. Regular.

Ellie felt like she couldn't breathe. The air was too thick, there was no oxygen in it.

"Luke." She leaned against the side of an old building and looked down to see random shoots of grass forcing their way through a crack in the sidewalk near her feet.

"Yes."

She turned to look at him. He stood close, but wasn't crowding her. Crossing some invisible boundary, she reached out and put her hands on his cheeks. She wanted to feel him on her skin, to stroke his dark brown hair, to rub her hands along his back. She wanted so many things. She tried to convey some small expression of that through her eyes.

He knew.

He brought his hands up to her neck and she reveled in the contrast of her smooth, moist skin and his strong almost-rough palms. His thumb traced the tense cord of muscle along the column of her neck. She wanted to collapse into him. Her eyes drifted shut, then opened.

"I want to feel you and look at you at the same time. It's hard." She smiled and he smiled back.

"I know. It's a toss up. I want to feel you . . . " He looked at his hands as they moved down her neck and gently across her collar bones then back up to her neck. " . . . but I want to see you and hear your voice. I want to taste you."

Her breathing hitched. The heat of the bricks at her back, the feel of his skin under her fingertips, his cheeks. His lips. She traced one thumb along the edge of his mouth. He opened his lips a fraction, as if to catch his breath, then the tip of his tongue was touching the tip of her finger. His lips closed around her thumb and he held her in his mouth, sucking gently, holding her eyes with his. He slowly released his hold and her thumb slid out.

"Oh my," she whispered.

He brought his thumb up to her lower lip then, sliding it back and forth across the tender inner skin. She couldn't do anything but stand there and absorb the heat of the day, the sidewalk, the heat of this man. Even in that small touch of his thumb, she felt a wave of the power that was being contained inside him. She wanted to take everything in—to burn. For the first time in years, she wanted to consume and be consumed by life.

She felt the tears down her cheeks before she realized she was crying. "I'm sorry." *For everything*, she wanted to add.

"So am I." He leaned in and kissed at her tears, one of his strong legs settled between hers, holding her steady.

Her hips tilted toward his thigh as if it was the most natural thing she'd ever done. She felt natural with him. "I don't know why I'm crying. Maybe from joy," she added with a small laugh, as the tears kept coming.

"Maybe," he breathed, as his kisses became more determined, moving toward her ear and her neck, then back to her temple and hairline, "I can't tell anymore either. I want everything. I'll take it all, the joy, the misery. You."

She took a deep breath and pulled his face back and away a few inches so she could look into his eyes.

"I want to go on the motorcycle now," she said.

He looked at her to make sure she was okay. He wiped her remaining tears away with the side of one hand, then let his hands trail through her long auburn hair, using his fingers like a loose comb. "Your hair is . . . "

She nearly purred, and he watched as she simply enjoyed the feeling of his hands in her hair, the intimacy and the tenderness.

"Are you always so gentle?" she asked.

"Not always. Sometimes not at all." He gave her a sly wink that caused a shudder of anticipation to roll through her. "Let's go for a ride."

He held her hand as they walked the rest of the way down the empty street and turned into the shade of the public parking garage.

His motorcycle was a classic 1969 BMW.

"Oh, it's beautiful," Ellie whispered. She let her hands touch the smooth black paint along the tank and the old leather of the seats. "Is it safe?"

"I think so. I've taken it apart and rebuilt it a couple of times so I know everything is as safe as possible. But, let's face it, motorcycles are not really about safety, right?"

"Yes."

"So do you want to go in your car instead?"

"No."

"Do you want to walk?"

Ellie burst out laughing. "It's 93 degrees outside and it's about ten miles straight west."

Luke shrugged his shoulders. "I've walked ten miles. Have you?"

"I think once, maybe I did for a charity walk. But it was in Virginia in the spring and I was a teenager. I mean, I probably *could*. Is that a dare?"

"Why? Would you be more likely to do it if I dared you?"

"Maybe. I like a challenge." She looked around the empty garage and had a wave of memory. "Oh my god, the funniest thing happened to me in this garage. We'd come to the movies and had dinner after and then when we started walking back to the car, Rob—that was my husband—" She made an awkward face, to somehow acknowledge that Rob was important but she couldn't stop to indulge in that tragedy every time his name came up in conversation. "—and we start to get near to where we parked the car and Rob reaches into his pockets and can't find the car keys and he starts to freak out that he left them in the restaurant or they slid out of his pocket in the movie theater and how we're going to have to go back and retrace our steps and it was almost midnight and then we are standing there next to the car. And it was still on. The engine running. We had left the keys in the ignition and raced to get to the movie on time—because I'm obsessed with getting to movies on time, and the bridge had been up and we were running late—and we just sprinted out of the car and down those nasty industrial stairs at the back of the garage that come out right here. Where I'm standing. And the car had been on the whole time. No one had stolen it. No one had taken anything out of it. So weird." Ellie was lost in the memory for a few seconds before returning her attention to Luke.

He watched her, then asked, "What do you think? Motorcycle or no motorcycle?"

"I think yes."

"I like the sound of that." He handed her the extra helmet and helped her get the strap adjusted to the right tension under her chin. She liked the feel of his fingers against her skin and the look in his eyes when he was adjusting the strap. He looked like he wanted her to be safe, but he also had a look that suggested he simply enjoyed when things were done properly—the way he slipped the buckle into the hasp—his movements were deft. "What are you smiling about?" he asked.

"I like how you look when you're concentrating."

He finished with the strap and touched her cheek. "You are beautiful."

Then he turned with no gravity whatsoever and opened one of the saddlebags and took out his own helmet and gloves.

Ellie stood there, the weight of the helmet making her feel like her head was too heavy for her neck, and wondered at the last time anyone had paid her that compliment. Rob had always told her she *looked* beautiful, when they got dressed up to go out, or even at the beach or at random times, and maybe she was parsing words, but the way Luke said it, it almost had nothing to do with her appearance.

She looked at his fingers while slowly finished the adjustments on his helmet, and then she saw he was staring at her.

"What?" she asked.

"I suppose that sounded canned. 'You are beautiful.' I'm a bit out of practice, too," he added. "I seem to just say whatever pops into my mind. I can't be bothered to censor myself anymore. I feel too old for it. You know?"

"Yes!" she said, delighted. "And no, it didn't sound canned. What a funny choice of words. I wonder why you'd think that. Or . . . was it canned? Do you often tell people they are beautiful?"

"Never." He turned and made himself busy with the kickstand and the key and then straddled the sleek machine with his strong legs. She realized now why he was wearing jeans when it was burning hot outside.

"Is it okay that I'm wearing shorts?" she asked, her voice louder than normal since the engine was revving and the helmet padded her ears.

He looked at her long tan legs, and then smiled up at her and gave her a thumbs-up. "I'll show you how to put your legs so they're not near the exhaust pipe."

She thought for a moment that she might not even mind getting burned, having a scar to remember this day. Something permanent and irrevocable. She would be able to look at the mark for the rest of her life and think *that* was when she first met Luke.

He waited for her to come closer, then showed her where to put her feet, and he adjusted her to get her settled into the seat, her abdomen flush up against his back. He reached behind and guided her hands around his waist, pressing his gloved hand over her bare one, silently telling her to hold on tight.

She squeezed him hard to show she understood. His abdominal muscles flexed in response. Turning to rest her helmet against his upper back, she shut her eyes in sheer bliss.

He drove like he spoke, like he moved: patiently and confidently. He was so smooth; regardless of other drivers cutting them off or driving too close, he maneuvered the bike with simple grace. Within fifteen minutes they were out of the snarl of downtown traffic and larger tracts of undeveloped land started interspersing with new shopping centers, mostly vacant. The occasional cows were grazing and then an enormous sporting goods store. It was like a schizophrenic viewfinder. Urban. Rural. Suburban. Rural.

And then they were surrounded by green. They shot down one of the old highways that used to be the end of the known world, and within a few years would probably be littered with housing developments and strip malls. The tall grasses and river reeds were dense with birds. Egret, heron, ibis.

Ellie sighed against Luke's back. The smell of his shirt, the heat of his skin beneath the fabric, filled her. She felt like she could stay there, holding him, forever.

Luke slowed down and turned into a narrow gravel road that led to one of the parks along the edge of the Everglades. He pulled the bike into a shady spot and killed the engine. He turned to look at Ellie, but her face remained against his back, as if she were sleeping.

He undid the clasp of his own helmet, hung it from one of the handlebars, then turned more fully to see her, lifting his left arm up and over her head.

"Hey, you okay?"

She looked up at him with a powerful mix of desire and joy and fear. He slowly undid her helmet strap, methodically hung it from the other handlebar, then swung one of his legs effortlessly over the front of the bike and then re-straddled the engine so he was facing her, inches apart, on the warm seat. The hot machine was settling and cooling between their legs.

Ellie reached her arms back around his waist and rested her head against his chest. Their knees were knocking at an awkward angle so he helped her lift her legs up and over his, loosely straddling him. She looked up and he rested his forehead against hers.

"Did you like the motorcycle ride?" he asked softly.

"Yes. Very much." She licked at her dry lips.

Every hint of sound was overloud after thirty minutes of the engine droning in their ears and through their bodies. The razor palms scraping against one another, small animals in the scrub around the empty parking lot. A bird called a harsh screech in the distance. Her voice.

She tilted her head a notch to the side. Her eyes slid down to his lips. She put her lips against his as if he were offering a first sip of water after a long journey in the desert. Just her lips against his. Then she pulled away slowly and licked her lips again. Trying to taste him on her.

He stretched out his back, extending his neck so his face was looking up to the tropical canopy, the trickle of hot sunlight mixed with prehistoric plants, dripping moss, cedars. Ellie ran her hands down his hard, flat stomach and he gasped when she reached her hand under his shirt.

His hand flew to cover hers. To prevent her from going any further.

"Not yet, Ellie."

She looked at him, hurt and embarrassed that she had been so carried away, that she had violated him somehow. Or as her mother would have said, *she was fast*.

"Oh God, I'm so sorry. That was wrong. I didn't mean to . . . " She tried to squirm away from him, but he held her in that damnably intimate position.

"It wasn't wrong."

She looked back up at him. Calming. That's what he was. He had a calming effect on her. She stayed silent for a while. "Then what was it?"

"Just too much I guess. What next? I lay you down in the nettles over there by the sidewalk?"

She grinned, as though the rasp of the nettles against her bare back might be worth it. And then he laughed and it was like a physical pleasure coursing through her veins. His laugh was strong. And then he pulled her close in a sweet, affirmative, fortifying embrace. "Let's go look for alligators." He swung his right leg over the bike then stood to one side and lifted Ellie effortlessly off her seat. She squealed for a second at the unaccustomed weightlessness. "I'm not a wisp of a thing!"

Once she was back on the ground, he hugged her again, the full length of his lean, strong body pressing up against her chest and stomach and thighs. She wanted to sink into him so badly, to just dive into his strength and fade completely away.

Her therapist would hate that, she thought. The dreaded fading away again.

"What is it?" Luke asked, sensing the tension in her body.

She retreated but he kept her hand in his. They strolled toward the boardwalk that led through the swamp.

"Oh, nothing I guess. I just have a bad habit of wanting to disappear."

"What do you mean?"

He didn't seem inclined to get that crazy worried look that so many of her friends did when she tried to be honest about her feelings, about this desire for nothingness. He just looked interested. Like an interviewer on PBS. Concerned. Engaged.

"I mean, after all the crap, sometimes I just wish I could shut life off for a while, you know? I'm not suicidal or anything—" She winced a little at the thought of his wife, then plowed on. "I guess philosophically it might be technically suicidal, or nihilistic, or whatever, but the way I mean it, it's just, I want to turn it off sometimes."

"Go on."

"And when you were hugging me then . . . " Just saying the words made her stomach do a happy flip. "It made me want to dissolve right into you. And then I thought my therapist would just hate that, you know, that my desire . . . " She caught herself, but there it was, so no point beating around the bush. "That I was sort of tied up in wanting to lose myself in those good feelings. Is that nihilistic, do you think?"

They had been walking for a few minutes, into the heart of the cedar swamp, the Spanish moss hanging lank and hot above them, the occasional sound of something small and frightened skittering through the watery undergrowth beneath the boardwalk. In a slant of sunlight against the railing, a small lizard breathed, perfectly still except for his red flap expanding and contracting beneath his chin in a showy, methodical beat.

Luke watched as Ellie took a contemplative breath.

"No, I don't think that's nihilistic at all," he said. "I think it's life-affirming. Just the opposite of all that loss of self."

"I'm overwhelmed with wanting to dump my life story at your feet again, to just sit you down and tell you every detail, I want you to know me, so I don't have to explain myself. And then I breathe and I think it might be beautiful to just be still, like that little lizard . . . and wait."

"Either way. I'm right here."

"I like that. Takes the pressure off. No rush."

"Exactly. No rush."

He looked at her then and she felt a whip-crack of desire slam through her. *No rush my ass.* She wanted him in her bed as soon as possible. Their hot skin against the cool white sheets, the reflection of the ocean in the late afternoon flickering across the ceiling, her hands all over him. His rough hands against her soft pliable flesh. His adept hands.

"Ellie . . . "

"Yes . . . "

"You can't keep looking at me like that or I'll go nuts."

"Like what . . . " But she liked that her desire was obvious. She wanted him to feel it like the heat of the sun. Unavoidable. Like summer in South Florida, you could either fight it and bitch about it, or just give yourself over to it, to the burning consistency of it. Her lips were slightly apart, her lower lip dry. "I'm not sure I've ever felt this kind of raw . . . wanting . . . " Her stomach clenched at the insanity of it, like falling off a cliff. "I don't know you, or about you I guess, but I know I want you, I want to feel your skin against my hands. It's so unexpected. I don't know what it means. This isn't really like me."

Luke laughed softly again, and led them on through the path of overhanging, languid foliage. "What would be more like you?"

"Oh, you know . . . " Her voice was lighter again, the sexual tension back in check. "I'd meet you at a dinner party of mutual friends. You'd call me a few days later, or the next time you were back in town, because you probably live in New York or Dallas or California, and then we'd go out to dinner and you'd kiss me goodnight. And then we'd be seated next to each other at a few more parties, and then we'd exchange some mildly amusing emails. And then I'd realize that I didn't have any genuine interest in pursuing anything, you know, physical—which would soon became sort of obvious to both of us—and then you'd meet someone charming and probably younger than I am, and fall madly in love and thank me for being a good friend during your time of post-whatever transition. Like that. That would be much more like me."

"Whewwwww." Luke breathed out slowly. "That's pretty brutal."

"I guess. But not really. I have lots of friends who have tried to protect me or whatever. It's kind of sweet in a way."

"Except . . . "

"Yeah, except . . . it leaves me with a lot of alone time." She shrugged. "Which is fine, don't get me wrong. I read probably five books a week, I'm a photographer—or I take photographs at least—*photographer* sounds a bit self-aggrandizing."

"No it doesn't."

"Well, you like me I think, so it wouldn't sound that way to you."

He smiled and brought her hand to his lips and kissed the back. "I do like you."

"I'm glad."

They walked for another hour, mostly in quiet shared solitude, with the occasional burst of lust that Ellie tried to tamp down. The afternoon clouds started to roll in and Luke suggested they get back to town.

"Do you want to come to my place for a late lunch?" Ellie asked. And a late roll in the hay, she thought, unable to stop the idea.

"You know I do, but should we try to pace ourselves?"

"Why?"

"I don't know."

"Do you have other plans? I'm sorry I'm being way too forward. You're right. Let's make a plan for another time. We can meet up next week, or whenever. I'm kind of notoriously bossy, so just tell me what works for you and—"

He pushed her up against the side rail along the boardwalk and kissed her. *Finally*, she thought. She was so juiced from just holding his hand she was practically throwing her legs around his waist. And that kiss . . . she could see now why he was bent on holding back earlier on the street, then later in the parking lot, and all afternoon really. Just holding hands and holding her at arm's length.

Because once he started kissing her, it really was nearly impossible to put a halt to it. There was no beginning and, consequently, no end. His tongue was tentative then thrusting; he toyed with her mouth, he did things with her mouth that blatantly foreshadowed other things they would do, and how it would feel. For a moment he would just nip at her lip, and then he would be plunging in again, and sometimes she felt like she was racing after him, following his tongue with hers, tracking his rhythm, and sometimes he followed hers, inviting her deeper into him, sucking at her, devouring her.

She pressed her chest against him, doing whatever she could to relieve the tension in her breasts. Her nipples were hard and taut. She gave in to the urge to rub up against him.

"Stop!" He pulled away, breathing hard like a referee who really participates in the sport, like hockey or basketball. "No rubbing up against me," he panted, half laughing.

Chapter 3

He looked at her then, her shimmering green eyes glowing with pleasure, her lips wet and swollen from all that kissing. She blinked once, slowly, then held his gaze.

Luke took a deep breath then rubbed Ellie's upper arms, as if he were trying to help get her blood circulating again. "Let's get out of here. Your place for lunch sounds great. I'm starving."

The two of them started running. They suited up quickly—helmets, sunglasses—and rode the motorcycle back into Palm Beach and to her house, just beating the afternoon rains. Ellie fumbled with the front door key, her hands shaking from the exhilaration and the heavy moisture in the air that made everything feel like it was slipping through her fingers.

"Here, let me." Luke took the keys out of her hand and slid the lock open with a steady turn. He held the door for her to precede him into the house, then pulled the door closed behind him and turned the bolt. The sound of the metal sliding home echoed through the small front hall.

"Let's go into the kitchen." Ellie turned to her right.

Luke put the keys down on the Plexiglas side table next to the front door, where a dish of keys sat next to an antique silver toast rack with a few pieces of opened mail and post cards tucked into the slots. He let his fingers trail across the smooth edge of the clear, thick plastic.

"What are you doing?" Ellie had poked her head back into the front hall from the kitchen.

"Just feeling how smooth the edge of the table is. It's an interesting process . . . it's a petroleum product, you know. This kind of plexi. I like how it seems weighty and weightless all at the same time."

"Aaah. I'm relieved you like material objects."

He smiled and followed her into the kitchen. "Why wouldn't I like material objects?"

"All that about getting rid of all your possessions, when you were talking about simplifying your life this morning. I figured you were on some sort of anti-materialism quest or something. My enlightenment will never veer toward deprivation, I'm afraid." She glanced over her shoulder as she flipped a switch and the vintage French medical lights that hung from the kitchen ceiling illuminated. "I love objects and things . . . heavy, permanent things." She gripped the edge of the two-inch-thick slab of white marble that covered the large island in the middle of the room. "I like things I can hold onto in a storm. Corny, I know, but it's true."

She turned to open the refrigerator and Luke tried to take in what was happening. He knew he needed to back off, slow down, take it easy, all the things he had been trained for, wished for, hoped for over the past few years. But Ellie was something else altogether. Unexpected, yes, but he also felt as if he had been preparing for her his entire life.

He watched as she took a few packages of cheese out of the refrigerator, a bag of fresh arugula, a couple of chicken breasts, and a bottle of wine.

"Do you drink?" she asked as she began to remove the metal seal at the top of the bottle. She uncorked it with a speed and dexterity that showed a happy familiarity with the task. "My friend Lotta thinks you're in recovery because you suggested we meet at Starbucks on a Saturday morning." She smiled as the cork came free of the bottle with a satisfying pop.

"Yes, I drink. No, I'm not in recovery. From alcohol at least."

"Oh no, were you a heroin addict? A sex addict?"

"Ellie, do you have any concern for your own safety?"

She looked momentarily frightened, then she must've caught the serious concern in his eyes. "Not really." She poured two glasses of rosé and handed one to him. "I don't think I'd feel any more or less safe with a strange man in my house, whether or not he was a recovering addict or just some guy. *Just Luke.*" She raised her glass and he picked his up and tapped it against hers.

"Cheers."

"Cheers." She kept her eyes on his.

He watched as she took a small sip and then she closed her eyes to enjoy it. "Mmm, perfect. I love that wine. It tastes exactly like the town in the south of France where I first tasted it. The whole environment in one tiny sip, you know." She opened her eyes and gazed at him. "The sycamores and the village square and the cicadas and the church bells and the sleeping cats. Just perfect."

With that, she turned and began preparing lunch. She worked efficiently and within fifteen minutes she had grilled the chicken, sautéed some chanterelle mushrooms in a bit of the wine, whipped together a shallot rosemary dressing, and tossed it all together with the washed arugula. She set up two placemats at the scuffed round table between the kitchen and the living room. The table still had some crumbs on it from her breakfast.

She was totally comfortable in her own home. Luke kept looking at how she moved through the space, as if she had really created a world in which she was happy, never frustrated.

She put her cell phone into a speaker system and switched on some music, a collection of Flamenco guitar. "Is that okay? Do you like music when you eat?"

Standing with her hands resting on the back of the chair she was about to sit in, she surveyed the table, making sure she had everything. He watched as she did a mental inventory: coarse salt, pepper mill, extra dressing, baguette.

"It sounds great. Not too loud. Perfect."

"Yeah, I eat alone most of the time so music has become kind of *de rigeur* for me when I have a meal. If it's too quiet I feel like someone is about to jump out from behind the couch or something." She smiled when he came behind her to pull her chair out, helping her scoot it back in once she was seated.

"Thank you," she added, as she opened the sky-blue linen napkin and settled it onto her lap.

She poured them both a bit more wine, then stopped and took a deep breath, her wineglass poised in mid-air, her elbow resting on the table. "Welcome to my home. Here's to you."

Luke felt the weight of her words. Good. Strong. The resonance of *my home* and *you* all in one sentence. "Thank you, Ellie."

"Thanks for coming over and not making me feel like a grasping lecher. I shan't attack you, I promise."

"I don't know if that's really a promise I want you to keep," he added between bites. "This is delicious by the way. You're a great cook."

"Thanks, I love it. I don't think I'm great, though, because I can't really take the time to use my imagination or be too daring, but when I find things I like, I really, I don't know . . . " She gestured with her fork then stabbed at her salad for another bite, embarrassed that she was rattling on.

"You have a great voice, by the way. Really firm."

Ellie laughed. "Some people call it strident. My mother in particular has given me numerous suggestions for what she calls 'toning it down a bit'. She thinks it's not lady-like."

"She might be right," Luke raised one shoulder, "but I think it suits you really well. You seem gentle, but certain. Does that make sense?"

She finished chewing then took a sip of wine and thought about her answer. "I never thought of myself as gentle, I'm kind of fierce really, especially in business, but then, after Rob . . . " She brought her napkin up to her lips then continued, "I suppose I mellowed a bit. Can't fight the tide and all that."

Luke smiled his understanding and took another bite.

Ellie finished her food and rested her fork and knife in a neat line across her plate. "I'm going to get a glass of water, would you like some."

"Yes, please."

Ellie returned to the table with a bottle of water and two thick hand-blown glasses from the south of France.

"Are these from Biot?" Luke asked.

Ellie looked at him askance. "Why? Have you been there?"

"Yes. A really long time ago. It was a strange situation. Ages ago, really."

"Hmmm. Yes, you'll see I'm a bit of a shameless parvenu when it comes to most things French. And these thick bubbly glasses are one of them. I love them. So heavy and satisfying. It's like they are militantly certain of their purpose. Glass. Drink. Like what a glass would look like in a child's vocabulary book." She held it away from her as if she were showing it to an audience. "Glass."

He smiled again.

Ellie laughed at herself. "See what I mean? I like things that keep me grounded. Even my glassware."

They finished the wine and Luke brought the plates over to the sink and washed them along with the silverware and loaded it all into the dishwasher. He wiped the counter with one of the kitchen towels he had been using to dry off his hands, following years of habit of cleaning up after himself.

"Don't worry about that. I'll do it."

"I like to do it," he added as he finished getting the last bit of splattered water from the edge of the sink, then folded the towel in a trim line and let it hang over one of the long drawer pulls.

"Ship shape. Were you ever in the military?"

Luke turned to look at her: she was all long and lean and easy, holding her glass of wine in one hand, the other hand supporting her elbow, her hip against the white marble kitchen counter.

"I guess," he answered.

"Doesn't seem like the type of thing one would guess about."

"I'd like to skip over that part if you don't mind."

"Well, of course I mind. Now I mind. I mean, before it didn't matter, but now that you've been all mysterious you've piqued my curiosity and I want to know. Were you a spy? A *saboteur*?"

She had a lovely French accent. He stayed quiet.

"All right then. Can't tell me or you'll have to kill me? I get it." She smiled.

He didn't. Smile, that is. Or *get it*, for that matter.

"Oh." She put the glass down on the counter with a bit too much force.

"It's nothing terrible," he said, "Just high-level security clearance. I've been out of this country for a long time. No one's after me or anything." Almost no one, he amended to himself.

"Well. That's not quite what I expected, but okay. I mean, you're still you, right?"

"Whatever that means. Yeah, I'm still me. I am *me*," he added quietly.

The wine and the food and this beautiful man Luke standing there.

Ellie walked across the kitchen and stood in front of him, her hands hanging at her sides. "I think you should probably take me back to get my car at Starbucks." She stepped closer, almost touching him.

Yael Naim was singing in the background and Ellie stopped to listen to her silly la-la chorus about being a new soul. Then Ellie was kissing Luke—with total abandon, with something indescribable she'd never recalled feeling with Rob, or any high school crush, or anyone ever, really. The light melodic vocals wafted through the kitchen as she raked Luke's hair through her fingers, grasped the hard muscles of his back, pulled him in.

"Oh God, Ellie."

She forced herself away and looked at him, her hand still holding onto the waist of his jeans. "Luke."

A new song strummed in the background, going on about loneliness and desperation.

"I'll take you back to your car," he said.

"That's probably the right thing to do," she agreed, running her hands along his shoulders.

But going upstairs and spending the rest of the weekend in bed together might be a feasible alternative, she thought to herself. Perfectly feasible. The right thing to do? Damn it. She had to bite down on her lower lip to refrain from speaking the words aloud.

They walked out of the kitchen, Luke holding her hand as they moved through the house toward the door. Ellie grabbed her keys from the front hall table where Luke had left them. They put their helmets on with a touch of grim determination. For whatever reason, Ellie gave in to Luke's decision to dispense with any heated sexual continuation of the day's visit. They rode in silence back to City Place. Ellie's car was sitting alone, forlorn, at the end of a quiet street, a wet parking ticket splayed against the rain-soaked windshield.

"So. I'll see you soon," Ellie tried, hoping it didn't come out sounding too much like a question.

"Of course. Are you free tomorrow?"

"Look, Luke, I'm free right now. I can't pretend to have other plans, because even if I have other plans I'll cancel them if you call, and I just can't bring myself to act as if I'm too busy to see you. So just . . . " She inhaled and then sighed. Stupid girl. "I mean, I really like you and I haven't really liked anyone, well, in a very long time, so . . . you have my number. Just call me when the CIA lifts the kill-on-sight order, or whatever." Ellie smiled and leaned in to kiss him on the cheek.

He was still sitting on his motorcycle and faltered for a second when her lips touched his face. He took a hard slow breath, then exhaled and looked up after her face pulled away.

"I'll see you soon, Ellie. It was a great day. You are . . . you're a really good person."

It was a strange thing to say, but Ellie appreciated what he was trying to convey. She fiddled with her car keys, looked down at her fidgeting hands then back up at Luke.

"It sounds dumb after a single day, a few hours really, but I think I'm going to miss you when you drive away." She felt the strangest mix of happiness for having the courage to say that out loud and misery for having to actually feel it.

He reached up and touched her cheek, just like he had earlier in the day after putting on the helmet. "It won't be long. Really." He leaned forward and gave her a too-chaste kiss on the lips. "Bye, Ellie."

"Bye, Luke."

He watched to make sure she got into her car okay, then pulled away and headed west on Okeechobee, then south onto I-95 back to his house.

Ellie drove home in a daze. She had no idea what had happened there at the end. She thought for sure they were going to end up in bed after all that kissing out at Loxahatchee. Instead she was alone and making her way back into her house, the car parked safely in the garage. The house an empty shell.

She double-checked the locks, a habit Rob had instilled that she'd never given up. She re-flipped the bolt to the garage, re-fingered the switch-lock on the sliding glass doors out to the ocean, re-locked the side door to the yard, and then doubled back to the front door to make sure everything was shut. She turned on the perimeter alarm, then stepped out of her canvas sneakers. She left them in a neat side-by-side pair at the bottom of the stairs, and then headed up to her bedroom.

A few hours later, she was in bed reading the latest book from a local author who specialized in gory murder mysteries. Not the right thing to soothe her nerves, but the compelling, page-turning menace helped. It was a mental scourge of sorts. Impossible to think of anything else when the threat of decapitation and/or psychotic serial killers loomed at every paragraph.

She nearly flew out of her bed—*Exorcist*-style—when she heard the firm triple-knock at the front door just after midnight.

She tried to calm the frantic beating of her heart, grabbed the bathrobe she'd left in a pile next to the bed, pulled out the loaded .357 magnum she kept in her bedside table, and started down the stairs. The rain had resumed in earnest. She peeked through the narrow side window to the right of the front door and saw Luke standing, soaked, on her tiny front porch.

She opened the door and he remained standing there, completely oblivious to the rivulets of water that streamed down his face and neck.

"I thought since it was officially tomorrow we might—"

She yanked him into her house before he could finish the sentence, then she set the gun down next to the dish of keys and shut the door behind him.

"What is that?" He stepped further into the front hall, dripping water all over the coquina tile, and grabbed the weapon off the table. From what appeared to be years of habit, he flipped the carousel open and emptied out the bullets. "What are you doing with a loaded gun? Any robber could disarm you in seconds."

"No they couldn't. I like guns, believe it or not. One of my inexplicable quirks. Especially when I started living alone, I decided to become rather proficient at handling a gun. I like knowing I can at least hurt someone who might try to hurt me."

Luke stood in front of her, soaked, holding the cool, weighty revolver in one hand and the bullets in the palm of the other. "Show me. Load it." He held his hands out to her, his palms offering the weapon and ammunition for her to piece back together.

Her hands were shaking from the idea that this fierce, hard, beautiful man was standing wet and ready in her suddenly too-small front hall. *He was here!* Her fingertips grazed his palm when she took the gun from his right hand. Then she trailed her index finger slowly long his other palm as she delicately picked up each bullet individually and slid it into its perfectly honed chamber. When she had finished loading all six bullets she flipped the cylinder back into place and gave it a quick spin, just to show off a little.

She kept it pointed slightly down and toward the hall that led to the kitchen as she double-checked the safety, closed one eye and admired the mechanical perfection of the small device, then she opened both eyes and lifted Luke's right hand and placed the gun back into it.

"There."

He didn't look down at the gun but kept his eyes on her face. "How many guns do you have in the house?"

"Wouldn't you like to know?" she asked with a coy bat of her eyelashes.

She started to turn, thinking he would follow her up to her bedroom, so she gasped when he pulled her back to face him, his grip strong on her upper arm. "Ellie. You just handed me a loaded gun and you don't even know me. You let me into your house in the middle of the night. What version of safety are you practicing?"

"The I-feel-safe-with-Luke version." She looked down at her arm where his hold remained fast, then dipped her head to kiss the knuckle of his middle finger there.

"Ellie . . . "

She moved closer to him. "I'm so glad you came back."

"Watch out for the gun!"

But she laughed and he shook his head at her carelessness. "Do you have a safe where you keep it?"

"Well, no, obviously. It wouldn't do me any good if someone broke in and I had to say, 'Hey, hold that predatory thought while I get my gun out of the floor safe over there under the carpet next to the piano.' I mean, I do have some in the floor safe over there." She tossed her head in that general direction. "But I like to keep a couple of others, you know, handy."

She was starting to quite like the firm hold he kept on her upper arm. Like she could relax into him.

"Well, let's put this one back where it belongs." He let go of her, emptied the chambers again, slipped the bullets into the front pocket of his jeans, and held the empty gun as if it were contaminated—dangling from two fingers—and followed Ellie upstairs.

Ellie tried to see the house through his eyes, for the first time. It was pretty small. Just the open-plan kitchen and living room and front hall downstairs, and three modest rooms up. Luke peered toward the office at one end of the upstairs landing, then briefly into the guest room with two single beds. She gestured toward the hall bathroom in case he needed it, then led them toward the east. Her bedroom wasn't very large, but it had room for a king size bed, two small bedside tables and a single, small, upholstered chair in the corner opposite the foot of the bed.

The east wall had a large window with an unobstructed view of the ocean. The rain had stopped again and the clouds were parting to show bright swaths of night sky. It looked as though moonlight dripped across the black sea.

"Amazing view," he said.

She turned from looking at his profile to looking out the window, and felt as if she'd never really seen the view. "It is good, isn't it? You'd think it would get boring after a while, but it never really does. The colors, the light, the subtlety, the birds, the moon." Her voice trailed off, then, "Do you want to get out of those wet clothes?" She couldn't help smiling at the age-old offer. "There's a big robe in the bathroom. I have lots of books all over the house . . . what do you like to read? Mysteries . . . "

Bizarrely, she was suddenly trying to behave according to some version of polite society.

"Ellie?"

"Yes," she answered with too much brightness as she adjusted the small pillow in the single chair.

"Come here."

She walked toward him and he simply took her into his arms. She didn't care that his wet clothes were seeping through her thin cotton robe and nightgown. In fact, she loved it. She started undoing the zipper on the rain jacket he must have picked up at home and worn for the night ride back to her place. She finished unzipping it then ran her hands along his shoulders and down his upper arms as she guided it off his body. Catching her breath, she went into the bathroom and hung the jacket loosely over the glass door to dry.

When she came back out he was taking off his shoes and socks and starting to unbutton his pants.

She rested against the bathroom doorframe and watched the pull of his back muscles as he completed the familiar, simple task. Her heart pounded in a steady, yearning beat. He was intense and determined, but most of all he was entirely without superfluity. His movements were spare and direct. He was precise.

She felt a rush of heat in her belly and lower down as she contemplated the possibility of how that heightened sense of focus would feel when it was directed entirely toward her. He turned then and must've caught the nature of her thoughts, giving her a slow smile. He finished taking his jeans off and walked towards her, in his underwear and the old white oxford shirt he'd been wearing earlier.

She loved that they stood precisely at eye level. Ellie started unbuttoning his shirt. He grabbed her wrist and pulled her toward the bed.

"I don't want to sleep with you, Ellie," he said.

"What?"

"I mean—" They both looked down at the straining fabric of his boxer briefs. He laughed, more of a short croak really. "—obviously I do. But, I just want to be with you for a while first, okay? To curl up in bed together, you know? To be together."

"That sounds heavenly." She resumed unbuttoning the placket of small white buttons.

He reached toward her and slid off her bathrobe while tracing the skin along her shoulder. She gave a happy shiver then the two of them crawled under the covers and she kicked a gust of air into the space under the comforter by her feet.

At first she thought the nearness of his powerful body would prove too disconcerting for her to actually fall asleep. They faced each other at the center of the bed. His arms were still cool from the rain and the night air against his skin. She ran her hands along his upper arm muscles and watched as his eyes slid nearly closed. She'd been so focused on taking her own pleasure earlier in the day, she'd forgotten how lovely it felt to give it. His muscles began to relax and she rubbed the tension at the base of his neck with more depth and pressure.

"God, Ellie. That feels so good." He let his eyes shut all the way.

"For me too."

"I'm glad."

"I was so set on getting my hands on you today, for myself I suppose—" She kept rubbing his neck and reached around to bring her hands into the base of his skull where the muscles ran up into his hairline. "—that I forgot how luscious it is to watch, to see you in a state of pleasure."

"Mmmmm."

"I haven't been with anyone in a really long time," she whispered.

"Me neither. Let's go slow, okay?" He reached for her soothing hands and brought them to his lips. "Let's just sleep."

"I'll try." She laughed softly as she reached for the bedside lamp and switched it off, then rolled back into his arms. After a few minutes she swiveled around so her back was against his front. "I was never able to sleep face-to-face, all that hot breath is too distracting."

He squeezed her more securely against him. "I like you this way, too."

She felt his erection against her bottom and resisted the urge to push herself closer up to him there. "Are you sure you just want to sleep?"

"My body has a mind of its own, but yes, in my rational mind, I'm sure." He kissed the nape of her neck and she felt herself finally begin to settle. "That's it. Just relax into me."

She started to breathe in sync with him, the two of them joined in this tentative, warm beginning. The ceiling fan turned a lazy circuit overhead. Ellie gave a grateful exhale and fell into a deep, embracing sleep.

Luke woke up as the first shafts of a bright, new dawn came over the horizon and cut into the room. He hadn't noticed all the details last night when he'd first arrived, but the space was a study in tranquility. The pitched ceiling was old Florida pecky cypress that had achieved a lovely faded gray color from years of exposure to the sea air. The simple white fan gave the room a lazy tropical feel. The walls were the faintest blue, almost like cool air. On the wall opposite the bed, a row of black and white photographs with wide white matting and thin black frames, rested on a long strip of white trim molding. The single chair in the corner was a feminine touch with a small round upholstered seat and busy floral patterned fabric. Luke thought he'd probably break it if he ever sat in it.

He turned his head to the right and watched as the sun rose over the edge of the world. His senses were nearly drunk with the simple pleasure of dawn. The light, the color, all of the metaphorical possibilities. Added to that—the smell of Ellie's hair, something like chestnuts or honey—she smelled like the south of France in the fall.

And the different textures of her body near his, the silk of her soft red hair against the pillow near his face, the skin of their intertwined legs. Luke shut his eyes and tried to take her in with all of his senses. He listened as the soft lilt of her breathing and the rhythm of the ocean wove together.

Going slow with her was going to prove much harder than he'd anticipated.

As if her body sensed that he was awake before her mind did, her backside pressed closer to him, and she moaned a small sound of burgeoning pleasure.

"Mmmmm."

He had tried to keep his hands in the less incendiary regions of her body, her upper arms, the length of her thigh, but that small groan was more than he could resist. He let his hand reach around to the gentle, low curve of her belly. Her nightgown was still on, but the fabric was thin and soft.

He rubbed his hands over the fabric and felt the warmth of her skin beneath.

She reached her own hand out from under the pillow where she'd had it curled, and placed hers over his in an encouraging gesture.

"Good morning," she whispered.

"Good morning."

"You feel quite nice in the morning. Sorry I forgot to put down the shutters last night. Did the sun wake you up too early?"

She reached for the bedside table drawer and he noticed another gun sitting there and tried not to wince. She pulled out a small remote control and pressed a button that set the electric hurricane shutters into a slow downward motion.

He smiled and kissed her shoulder. "How decadent."

"I know. It was a guilty pleasure. Sometimes I am so lazy I think I should get one of those clappers so I don't even have to open the drawer and press the button on the remote control."

The accordion slats of white plastic touched the bottom of the outside window frame then started to stack firmly against each other. Ellie hit the button again, stopping the process, and turned to Luke. "Do you want it totally dark, or a little light coming in?"

He kissed her cheek. "I like it like that. So I can see you."

"I like that too." She tossed the remote control onto her bedside table and turned back to face him as she leaned up on one elbow, her head resting in the palm of her hand, her hair hanging down in a cascade.

"I love your hair."

"Ooooh. Do we get to say what we love about each other?" Her eyes twinkled. "I love how your body moves."

"I love how you are not afraid of me."

Something wary crossed her eyes. "Why would anyone be afraid of you? What a strange thing to say."

"My daughter is afraid of me."

"You have a daughter?" she asked.

"Yeah. I have a twenty-four-year-old daughter. She lives in northern California."

"Are you close?"

He smiled, liking the angle of her jaw as he looked up into her eyes. "I'd say we're about as far apart as two people could possibly be."

"Aw, that's too bad."

"I don't know. I don't think she thinks it's too bad."

"Of course she does."

"No, Ellie. I really don't think she does. And it's okay. I mean, of course I want her to come around and at least be able to tolerate me, but in the meantime I can handle it if she wants to blame me for her mom and all that."

"Well, you're a more patient person than I am. I'm a terrible fixer."

"Really?"

"Yes. Consider yourself warned. I tend to take it upon myself to organize . . . people."

"I'll try to stay alert." He reached his hand up and wrapped his fingers around the base of her neck and drew her toward him.

He stayed gentle, brushing his lips against hers, then cautiously dipped his tongue into her mouth. He kissed her forever. He had to willfully restrain his hands from pawing her like a mad beast.

He wanted to go very gradually. Maybe if they took their time they might be able to deal with any obstacles or disappointments; that's what Kate used to call them . . . disappointments.

Ellie pulled away. "What happened just then? It was like you were there—" She licked her upper lip absent-mindedly. "—and then you were gone."

"How did you feel that?"

"Your mouth was against my mouth . . . what do you think, I wouldn't notice if your mind wandered?"

"Well, I guess I . . . yeah, for a second I remembered something my wife used to say and it kind of took me away from the moment."

Ellie punched up her pillow and settled her head back into it, as she clasped her hands in front of her. "So tell me."

"Tell you what?"

"Tell me what your wife used to say."

"Here in your bed you want me to talk about my wife?"

"Well, would it really make a difference if we talked about her over breakfast or on a walk on the beach? I never really bought into any of that site-specific emotional logic."

"I guess you're right. Especially if just yesterday I was going on about how seamless and integrated my emotional and mental worlds are. But still, there's something to be said for keeping certain discussions contained."

"Contained, huh? I was never very good at containment. I tend to spill all over." She reached across the small span between them and rested her hand on his cheek for a few seconds then put it back under her pillow. "So, what were you thinking?"

"About disappointment. About how Kate, that was my wife, used to have this really bitter sense of humor and when something legitimately atrocious would happen, she would say how *disappointing* it was in that offhand way that made it all seem meaningless."

"So . . . was our kiss disappointing?"

He laughed. "You're joking, right?"

"It never hurts to check in." She grinned.

"No. Obviously not disappointing. I was just thinking that I really want to go slow—or some rapidly dwindling sliver of my rational mind really wants to go slow—because then maybe we'll have the wherewithal to recognize pitfalls or *disappointments* as we go along. Instead of blazing wildly into this and then realizing there are all sorts of—"

Her gleaming smile interrupted his train of thought.

"What?" he said.

"You are so much *worse* than I am. It's such a relief."

"I am?"

"Yeah. I mean, I'm bad. I'm a projecting, hypothesizing, organizing, plotting type of person, but you're really ten moves ahead and I'm probably only about four moves ahead. So, relatively speaking, compared to you I'm practically living in the now. It's great!"

He kissed her forehead then settled back onto his pillow.

"So," she began, "how slow should we go? I totally agree it's for the best."

He smiled but didn't answer.

"I mean, I've been out of the loop for fifteen years. What is slutty these days? I've always wanted to be slutty."

He laughed and kissed her neck as she kept talking.

"Let me see. We made it through the first night, so at least I don't have to say, 'Oh yeah, that guy I slept with the first night I met him.' But I have to confess I'd even done a little forward-recon-rationalization on that and came to the conclusion that *technically* I met you the first day I brought the car in, then again on Friday, and then we had coffee on Saturday. So, *technically*, I've almost known you a week. Is that slutty?"

"Yeah, probably." But he smiled as he said it, teasing her.

"Here's the deal," Ellie kept on. "I'm good at managing known commodities. You wouldn't know it from this little haven of peace I've created here in the tropics, but I used to be one tough bitch when it came to running my business. And the way I did that was by being super clear about expectations—my expectations for others and their expectations for me. As long as everyone is really clear about expectations, great shit can happen and everyone wins. So, just expectation-management-wise, are we talking a week? A month? A year?" She rolled away and slid off the bed. "I have to use the bathroom while you think that over. I'll be right back."

She shut the door gently behind her then returned to bed a few minutes later. "So, what's the timeframe?" Her breath smelled of mint and she'd washed her face with something herbal and pungent. She looked young and fresh.

"You smell amazing." He pulled her toward him.

"Stop hedging. I'm not even pressing for firm answer, I just need to get my mind around it. Approximately. How long?"

"Let's say a month. Or around a month. Is that okay?"

"Sure. I mean, of course it is terribly, horribly, miserably *not* okay. But, yes." She gave him a winsome smile. "Everything about you is very okay. I think a month feels wise. Or solid. Or something."

Then she just breathed him in and started to feel herself slipping into a gentle doze.

"I think I might be able to fall back to sleep after all," she said on a yawn. "What with all this postponement and all." She reached for his hand and wove her fingers through his. "Fall asleep with me."

He watched as her eyes became glassy and her tongue made that gentle, newly familiar pass across her bottom lip.

"I'll see you there," he whispered, as he let the sound of the ocean and her breathing steady his too-fast heart.

Ellie's cell phone started ringing at ten. She'd set it to vibrate, but she was close enough to waking on her own that she picked it up and checked the caller ID.

Lotta.

She tapped the talk button but didn't say anything since Luke was still sound asleep. She slipped out of bed and walked out of her bedroom, closing the door quietly then walking down the hall toward her office.

"Hey," she whispered. "What's up?"

"Oh my god! You trollop! The mechanic is there, isn't he?"

"Shhhhh! Your voice is booming."

"I'm in California! How booming could it be across thousands of miles?"

"It's really quiet in the house right now and trust me, it's booming," she whispered. "Let me get into my office and shut the door . . . Okay, now I can talk."

"What. The. Hell."

"I know! I'm a total whore. Can you stand it?!" It felt delightfully thrilling to be whorish.

"Ellie! Who is this guy? Is he safe? Are you sure you're okay having him with you alone in the house?"

"Jesus, you sound just like him."

"What?!"

"He came back last night and I met him at the door with my .357 and he freaked."

"I can barely continue this conversation. You know how I feel about you having all of those ridiculous firearms. It's a part of you that I'll never understand. I'm glad he's equally opposed."

"He's not. Opposed, I mean. He just wanted to make sure I knew how to handle it and wouldn't let some burglar wrestle it from my hands and get shot by my own gun."

"What is he? An ex-cop or something?"

"Or something."

"What do you mean?"

"I don't know what he used to do, but I'm pretty sure it was dangerous and secret and I'm kind of turned on by that."

"Oh my God. I can't believe this! I'm supposed to be the wild one! And instead I'm about to marry the preppy reliable Eagle Scout and you are about to—whatever it is you are about to do—with James eff-ing Bond."

"Good things come to those who wait," Ellie laughed.

Lotta sobered quickly. "They really do, El," then she lightened her tone, "So was he like an international man of mystery in bed, all dark foreboding and throaty whispers?"

"As if I would tell you after your scrimping on all the details of your own escapades with Philip."

"Come on, just a morsel. I'm about to sleep with the same man for the rest of my life. Throw me a bone here."

So might I, thought Ellie with a ping of unexpected hope.

"You still there?"

"Yeah, I'm here. The thing is, he wants to wait awhile until we, you know, do the deed."

"What!?" Lotta barked, then continued with a deprecating sigh. "He's gay. Or he's a recovering sex addict. There's no way a guy could spend the night in the same bed with you and not screw you."

"Thanks. I think. But I'm quite certain he's not gay as far as his dealings with me are concerned, and if he's a recovering sex addict and the thirty-day holding period is part of his program, then I'm totally okay with that."

"Thirty days? Are you crazy? When Philip and I realized what we might have going, I don't think I could have waited thirty minutes, much less thirty days. What's the point Ellie? If the two of you have the hots for each other, just go for it. You're consenting adults . . . aren't you? How old is he? Is he even legal?"

Ellie started laughing. "Of course he's legal. He's forty-five."

"Oh."

"Do you think that's old?"

"Well, I don't know. I mean . . . it's ten years older than you."

"I really like him." Ellie's voice was soft and vulnerable to her own ears.

Lotta exhaled. "Okay. Tell me."

"I don't know. At first I was a little frantic with wanting to jump his bones—his body is obscenely hot—but you know, now I'm kind of excited to drag it out a little bit. Think how great it will be when we actually do it."

"Yeah, right, as long as you haven't killed each other in the interval. Seriously." And then as an afterthought Lotta asked, "What about masturbation? Orgasms? What are the ground rules? Genital contact?"

"Lotta!" Ellie was laughing. "I swear, you sound like a PSA for sexually transmitted diseases. Cut it out!"

Ellie heard the door to her bedroom creak open and the floorboards in the hall squeak as they gave way under the weight of Luke's steps.

"Gotta go," Ellie whispered. "He's awake."

"Oh my. This is unbelievable."

"Goodbye!"

"Go fuck him! Run!" Ellie heard the words in the distance as she had already pulled the phone away from her ear and cut her friend off right before Luke tapped on the office door.

"Come in."

"Hey," he said as he opened the door and peered in.

"Hey, how'd you sleep?"

"Great. Seriously." He walked into the room and looked down at her. "I haven't slept like that in ages. That falling-back-to-sleep sleep is some of the best stuff going."

She smiled up at him, her knees tucked up under her nightdress, her arms hugging her shins, the cell phone still held loosely in one hand. His bare chest was making her brain feel fuzzy.

"Did I interrupt you?" he asked.

"No. Just my friend Lotta in San Francisco. She was calling to find out what happened with the blue-eyed mechanic at the coffee shop."

"And?"

"And when I answered the phone in a whisper it wasn't much of a mental leap for her to figure out that you were still here."

"Is that okay?"

"Is what okay?"

"You know, that she knows I spent the night."

"Look . . . " She gestured for him to join her on the small love seat where she was sitting, and she continued when he'd settled in next to her. "I meant it when I said—I don't need to be anywhere or show up for anyone but myself. My parents live nearby, but they're pretty self-sufficient, and I usually end up needing their assistance far more than they need mine. I can have sleepovers, motorcycle rides, dirty stay outs, you name it. It's no one's business but my own."

"I'm listening."

"Lotta's main concern is the pace we're setting."

"See! She agrees. It is best to wait."

Ellie burst out laughing. "No! She's concerned about the fact that you haven't slept with me already!"

Luke let his head drop into the palms of his hands and gave a low, growling laugh. "You did not tell her that," he said through his fingers.

"Well, it wasn't like I volunteered it or anything. It's not as if I'm going to run and call her about every little detail, but she was getting all excited on my behalf. I mean, seriously Luke, like

Ceci said yesterday, Ellie holding hands is big news." She rested her cheek against her knees and looked at him sideways.

He watched her carefully, then brought his hand up to her cheek and slid his fingers through her hair to get it out of the way—to touch it *and* get it out of the way—to get a better look at the smooth elegance of her face. "What else?"

"What else, what?" she quipped.

"It sounds like there's more to this. What else did Lotta say?" he asked

"You're persistent when you want to be, aren't you?"

He came in close and kissed her neck. "Absolutely."

"Very well." Ellie took a deep breath. "Lotta thinks you're either gay or a recovering sex addict, otherwise you would have had sex with me by now."

"After one day?" He laughed through the words.

"To be fair, I started talking about you a week ago. And I tried to tell her it was not terribly out of the ordinary." Ellie smiled. "But apparently she has a high regard for my . . . allurements."

His face turned serious. "I'll have sex with you right now if you want to get it over with."

"Gee, thanks." Ellie closed her eyes, mortified.

"I didn't mean it like that. I just meant, I thought it would be great to really get to know each other without all of that . . . what I suspect will be pretty distracting, consuming, what have you. That's all. If it's going to be more distracting or annoying or whatever *not* doing it, then let's just do it."

"Wow. Your offers just get better and better. I can hardly wait."

His expression was adorably pained. "You know exactly what I'm trying to say, you're just enjoying watching how far into this hole I'm going to dig myself before you offer me a kind hand to step out."

"You're right. I don't care at all what Lotta and her perverted mind think. I am fully on board with the thirty-day plan."

"If you're sure."

"I'm sure." But then she hesitated. "I mean, you're not gay or a sex addict are you?"

He grabbed her body to his. She nuzzled her face into the warm, firm skin of his chest. He was sitting there in close-fitting cotton-knit boxer shorts and nothing else. He seemed perfectly at ease in his own skin. "No. And no."

After a few minutes, she slid her legs out from under the bottom of her nightdress and repositioned herself so she was sitting on his lap. "So what should we do today?"

He breathed her in and tried to steady the pace of his heart, which had accelerated when she slid onto him. "Actually, a friend of mine works at a hunting plantation about two hours from here and invited me to come check it out. The owners are away for the summer and he said he's allowed to have friends come and shoot with him. I wouldn't have mentioned it, but now that I know you're a modern-day Annie Oakley I thought it might be fun."

"Ooooh! So much fun! What do they have? Quail? Wild turkey?"

He tried to ignore how her bottom squirmed into his thighs in the midst of her excitement.

"Listen to you, all bloodthirsty. I think wild boar. Would that freak you out to go after something that big?"

She thought for a minute, then imagined the heat and the waiting and the long time spent in very close proximity to Luke in the blind or the scrub and she shook her head. "Not at all. If we're going to be hanging out together, I don't think I could have a bad day."

"I like the sound of that." He gave her a quick peck on the cheek and then a quick slap on her behind. "Up and at 'em!"

She leapt from his lap and laughed. "You are unpredictable Mr.—oh my god. I don't even know your last name!" She started laughing even harder. "Here! Take my gun! Sleep in my bed! And by the way, what's your name?"

He watched her joy and felt it flow over him like the ocean had flowed over his sleep all during the night before.

A salve.

When she quieted down, he stood up and reached out his hand. She marveled at how he was able to redefine his stance into something aristocratic and formal, even though he was still nearly naked, standing there barefoot in his underwear. Through some trick of posture or practice—his shoulders firm, his spine long—he had transformed himself into something quite formidable.

"Luke Asquith Powlett de Rothschild McCormick."

She gasped, then slowly gave him her hand. He leaned down and kissed it with courtly perfection.

"That's quite a lot of names . . . for a mechanic," she added. "If you don't mind me saying. I'm Eleanor Sinclair. Period. My mother thought middle names were wasteful."

"I think I like your mother already," Luke said with a touch of self-deprecation, relaxing his shoulders back to their normal, easy angle.

"I think you will. She doesn't like waste, whether it's words wasted in conversation, effort wasted in useless endeavors, or time wasted in life. It sometimes comes off as impatience, but she's really just avid."

He was still holding her hand, lightly rubbing her knuckles. "If I ever meet your mother, I'll be sure to introduce myself simply as Luke McCormick."

"Don't be silly! First off, if you're sticking around for thirty days, you'll definitely meet her. Second, she'll love all that aristo stuff. Give her the full deck of cards. In the meantime, I'll be the one trying to get my mind around Luke blah-blah-blah Rothschild blah-blah-blah McCormick . . . the mechanic. About a hundred questions are now pinging around my head on the heels of that . . . that laundry list." She pulled her hand slowly away. "Why don't you shower in the hall bathroom, just there? There are plenty of clean towels, soap, shampoo, and all that. Take your time. I'm going to take a swim. Probably a half hour or so. Did you bring a change of clothes?"

"I did actually, but they are most likely soaked or moldering in the side-bags of the motorcycle."

"I'll go get them and throw them in the dryer. You hop in the shower. I'll meet you downstairs in a bit."

"Okay. Thanks." He kissed her lightly on the lips again and then watched as she made her way down the short hall and back to her room. The beams of morning sunlight through the partially closed shutters cast a beautiful silhouette of the curve of her hips and the length of her legs through the fine white cotton of her nightgown.

Ellie walked into her bedroom and shut the door, then leaned up against it for support.

What was he, she wondered, some lord on the lam? Running from the law, or more likely his responsibilities? So typical. Everyone seemed to wash up in south Florida. She chided herself for liking him more when she didn't know his name . . . or rather, *names*, she corrected herself.

She hated to admit it, but she liked him better when he was *just* a mechanic. She pulled off her nightdress, pulled on the sporty black bikini she usually wore for morning laps and walked downstairs. She disarmed the security system, went to his motorcycle, and retrieved his change of clothes.

A single cardinal trilled in the palm tree to the left of her small driveway. Ellie looked up and gave him a little salute, then turned back into the house.

The clothes were only slightly damp so she threw them into the dryer on a short cycle then walked through the kitchen and living room. She pulled open the sliding glass doors and stepped outside toward the narrow lap pool. Ellie stretched her arms as high above her head as possible then dove into the pool in one long, smooth motion. She normally did a hundred laps each morning but she figured, what with her visitor and all, that if she got twenty-five in she'd be fine. She wasn't too preoccupied with exercise or nutrition, but, especially after Rob had died, she had come to rely on the routine. For a while after Rob's death, she'd also needed to rely on sheer physical exhaustion to ensure at least a few hours of much-needed sleep, and would often resort to long-distance swims to guarantee her rest.

Thirty minutes later she came out of the pool feeling invigorated. She stepped into the partially concealed outdoor shower that was one of her favorite parts of living in Florida. She took off her bikini, rinsed it in the shower water then hung it over the wood slats that shielded her from prying eyes on the beach, and proceeded to wash her hair and body. She was quick about it, hoping to be back upstairs before Luke came downstairs.

She realized too late (or maybe not) that she'd miscalculated the timing, when she stepped, perfectly naked, out of the shower enclosure to see Luke standing at the back door with a white towel around his waist and a stunned look on his face.

Ellie had a moment of thinking she should cover herself, one hand above, one hand below—like Eve being expelled from the garden, she always thought—then, instead, she put her shoulders a bit straighter and put her arms out away from her body, as if to say, here I am, take it or leave it.

Luke gave her a brilliant smile then covered his eyes as if the sun was too bright. "I'm blinded."

Ellie grabbed her towel and wrapped it efficiently around her body, folding and tucking it so it stayed secure over her breasts. She tried not to think too hard about how good it felt to have his eyes on her.

He opened his eyes slowly, looking at her, warily, as she walked toward him. She stopped a few inches in front of him.

"Your clothes are in the dryer; the laundry room is through the door to the left of the sink. I'll be back down in a couple minutes." She leaned in and gave him a warm kiss on the lips.

He smelled of soap and the ocean and tasted of the promise of something delicious. She pulled back to look at him, then licked at the corner of her lip and smiled for a few seconds. She looked out to the ocean, then back into his eyes, and slowly turned into the house. The next thirty days were going to be fascinating. Suddenly, she was looking forward to the protracted foreplay with genuine pleasure.

She made her way up to her bedroom and smiled when she saw that Luke had made the bed and hung her bathrobe on the hook at the back of the bathroom door. She threw on a pair of old khaki pants, a tank top, and a long-sleeved oxford shirt of Rob's that would protect her from the sun and any stray branches or brambles out at the ranch. She tied on a pair of sturdy, lightweight, waterproof boots, put her hair back in a sensible ponytail, and went back downstairs.

A few minutes later, she walked into the kitchen and saw that Luke had fixed a pot of coffee for her and a cup of tea for himself. He had taken the butter and jam out of the refrigerator and was toasting a few slices of the baguette leftover from yesterday's lunch.

"Well, aren't you resourceful!" Ellie exclaimed.

"Yes . . . it was the strangest thing," he answered slowly, turning to look at her. "I stepped outside to enjoy the view of the sea and I was overcome with a vision of The Birth of Venus, all wet and divine and arising fully formed out of the surf, as it were." He took a sip of his tea and held her gaze over the rim of the mug. "I needed a cup of tea and some toast to help me recover my senses."

She walked toward him and rested her hand on his cheek. "I kind of like this idea of your senses being overcome. I think you might be far too sensible, despite all your talk of skydiving and motorcycles and gunplay . . . and other mysterious adventures." She gave his cheek an extra pat, then went to the coffee maker and poured herself a cup.

Just as when she'd made lunch the day before, Luke watched her as she moved around the room and she felt it like a touch—how his gaze followed the tension in her arm when she pulled on the refrigerator door, or the way she poured milk into her coffee.

She swiveled to face him. "What?"

"You're really a joy to behold."

"Is English your mother tongue?"

"I think you're supposed to say something like, 'Why thank you for the lovely compliment!' and then I'm supposed to elaborate on your many lovely attributes."

"Is that right? Okay, thanks for the compliment and is English your mother tongue?"

"You're welcome. And not really."

"Are you being coy? What language did your mother speak?"

"Her father was French and her mother was American. She grew up in France. But I never heard her speak. She died shortly after she had me. So I guess the idea of a mother tongue doesn't really apply to me."

"Oh no." Ellie felt instantly despondent and walked around the island in the middle of the kitchen so she could be closer to him. "I'm so sorry, Luke. How horrible."

"You're sweet, but it was so long ago, and such a matter-of-fact part of my life. I never really give it much thought."

Ellie pulled away a bit at that. "You don't have a mother and you never give that much thought?"

"I mean, of course, I got to school and realized everyone else had mothers—most of them alive and, well, mothering—but I think children are entirely adaptable . . . and since I never really had a mother to lose, I don't know, it just *was*."

"What about your father?"

"What about him?" The quick, cool reply said it all.

"Ah, that bad, huh?"

"No. He's just not what I'd consider a decent person. He's more along the lines of . . . a total ass. So I—" He paused suddenly and took a deep breath. "So, he and I don't really spend much time together. But I'm a grown man and it's not like I need my father's approval or input or whatever. These are, or were, all relationships that informed my past. Not my present."

"Ha! Nice trick. Yesterday you said how seamless your emotional landscapes have become, but you don't think your relationships with your parents inform your present?"

He looked out to the ocean to think through his response. "I know what you mean. But I think I have a healthy disdain for my father as a separate individual." He turned back to face her. "As a father, he was not present. As a person, he is uncharitable and, perhaps, even cruel. I am a pretty strong adherent to the blank slate school of thought when it comes to child development. So, I see it as a sort of boon that I was not learning to be like him."

"So then, who raised you? Were you raised in a Skinner box?"

"Hardly!" He laughed over the word. "For the first eight years of my life my father . . . well, I wouldn't say he raised me, but he had me in tow. And I had a wonderful Scottish nanny and a French tutor, and they spoke to me in English and French."

Ellie took another sip of coffee. "Mmm-hmm. Where were you?"

He did not look like he enjoyed talking about it, and she wasn't going to press him *too* hard, but she craved a bit more knowledge about his childhood.

"All around Europe, mostly."

"And then what happened when you were eight?"

"I thought you were the one who was going to dump your life story at my feet, remember?"

"I guess I'm just prying, but I thought we were in the getting-to-know-you stage of . . . whatever this is . . . so I thought a little background conversation wouldn't go awry. No need to elaborate if it makes you uncomfortable." She took another sip of coffee and raised her eyebrows in a silent dare.

"I'm not uncomfortable talking. I'm just not in the habit of talking about myself."

"No worries." She shrugged noncommittally, but he got the hint that he was a bit of a coward for not continuing.

"All right. You win. When I was eight I went to live with my uncle in Wyoming. I spent my summers in France with my mother's parents. I went to school out in Wyoming until I was sixteen, then went to college in California. After I graduated, I moved to Asia. Then I . . . retired a few years ago . . . moved down here about a year ago . . . started working for Bill. And that brings us up to date."

She smiled at that. "Nice. Okay if that's how you want to play it. I grew up in rural Virginia, went to University in Virginia, started a software business and then sold it. Then I moved here a couple of years ago." She raised her coffee mug in a silent toast. "And now I like to take pictures. A pleasure meeting you."

He smiled back.

They ate breakfast and talked about the day, then straightened up the kitchen and got ready for the two-hour drive out to the ranch.

"Do you want me to make sandwiches or bring a cooler or anything?" Ellie offered.

"No, I think Sam will take care of all that when we're out there. Do you want to bring your own gun?"

"Sure!"

He watched as she walked across the living room and knelt next to an oval hook-and-eye rug with various nautical knots depicted on a weathered blue background of worn wool. It looked like some long-dead colonial ancestor had made it two hundred years ago. She pulled it back to reveal a flat floor safe about two feet by two feet square. She adjusted her position so she was sitting cross-legged on the floor and began putting a series of random numbers into the digital locking mechanism.

He listened as the bolts slid through the thick steel cover and she pulled at a recessed handle that normally lay flush against the metal.

"Come check this out." She could hardly conceal her eagerness.

Luke walked across the living room and peered down into a safe about four feet deep that had what looked like about a dozen shotguns and rifles in individual nylon or leather cases.

"Which one should I bring?" She was as bright and cheerful as if she were asking which boogie board to take to the beach.

Luke looked from the safe into Ellie's sparkling, mischievous eyes. She gazed up at him from her position on the floor. "Jesus Ellie. Are you planning to start a revolution?"

She looked a little crestfallen and he regretted saying anything that made that childlike glimmer fade from her eyes. He squatted down so he was closer to her face. "Sorry. I didn't mean to put a damper on it, but seriously. This is an arsenal."

She looked into the safe with new eyes, her hands resting in a loose clasp in her lap. "I guess it does look a bit excessive. But Rob and I just bought a few here and there and then, well, since I've been on my own I didn't see the point in getting rid of his, but they're really just pairs for any occasion." She gave him a winsome smile that made his heart crimp. "So . . . I think probably the .45-70, don't you?"

He stared at her. "Ellie. I don't know whether to laugh or cry. I don't think I could have dreamed up a more perfect you."

She tilted her head away from him, suddenly embarrassed by the sweet compliment.

He brought his hand to her chin and turned her face back toward his. "I think the .45-70 is perfect."

"I have two. Do you want one?"

"Sure. Bring the pair." He stroked her chin and jaw then let his hand fall away. He stood up from his crouching position with easy grace.

She reached into the dark hole in the floor and pulled out two identical Orvis cases, hunter green canvas and well-oiled rich brown leather, and handed them up to Luke. He set his coffee cup down on the piano, taking care to make sure the mug was dry on the bottom, then took the two weapons from her outstretched hands.

He brought the shotguns into the front hall and set them against the wall next to the door then returned to the living room.

Ellie had finished closing the safe and re-setting the alarm and was in the midst of replacing the carpet over it. Luke got his coffee cup and reached down to help her up with his free hand. She rose and then stood for a few seconds in front of him. She squeezed his hand in hers.

"Thanks for the hand up."

"Any time."

"Shall we just stand here in my living room staring at each other or is your friend expecting us?"

"I'm fine just standing here," he answered slowly.

"Me too." She leaned in and kissed his neck. "But I don't think I'll be able to honor our little agreement if I stand this close to you for very long. Honestly, it sounds like a cliché, but you do something to me." She nipped at the skin of his neck where it met the strong muscles of his shoulder.

Luke groaned and thought the handle of the coffee mug in his left hand might snap off in his grip.

"Ellie . . . "

She stopped what she was doing and looked up at him, her eyes glassy and wanting, her lips moist and waiting. "Yes?"

"Let's go."

"Okay."

"We should probably take your car. Two hours is a bit much on the bike, especially if it rains on the way back. Sound good?"

They collected the guns, Ellie set the house alarm, and they stepped out into the small driveway.

"Why don't we take the BMW? It's got more room than my TT—and if it breaks down you'll be able to fix it." She winked at him. "Here, give me the guns and I'll put them in the trunk, then you can move your motorcycle into the garage when I pull out."

Chapter 4

Two hours later they were in the middle of nowhere. They parked the car in the shade of a group of overgrown slash and sabal palms at the end of an unmarked dusty road. The crackling heat and slow purr of insects combined to make the entire place feel utterly abandoned, prehistoric. Luke got the guns out of the trunk and led Ellie through a wooden gate to the left of the parking area. They walked quietly down a sandy path, Spanish moss hanging overhead in the canopy. Cypress, pines, and all variety of palm trees formed a dappled, sweltering glade.

After a few minutes, they emerged into an open grassy area, with a few buildings scattered around a central lawn. A long ranch house stretched away to the right, a wide shaded front porch running the full length of the rustic log structure. The wood beams were dark with age, though the green tin roof looked like it had been replaced more recently. A few large shade trees stood perfectly still at either side of the house, and behind, creating a natural shelter from the oppressive sun.

To the left were three outbuildings. One looked like a stable, the next like some sort of grain storage, and the third was a small cottage or shed with two small windows and a charming chimney.

"Have we travelled back in time?" Ellie whispered.

"I know, it feels like it, doesn't it?"

"Yeah, I'm kind of waiting for a family of Seminole Indians to come wandering out of the brush over there."

"I think we're okay," he said as he squeezed her hand in encouragement.

Luke led her toward the stables. Before they had reached it, a tall, lean man, probably a few years older than Luke, emerged from the building to greet them.

"Sam Grinnell. Nice to meet you."

Ellie suspected that Luke's friend Sam was, like Luke, probably far more worldly than his working-class appearance might suggest. He looked from Luke to Ellie with an approving, if clinical, eye.

"Hi, I'm Ellie Sinclair. Thanks so much for letting me tag along."

"I'm looking forward to it. Anyone who thinks hanging out in a hundred degree swamp with two codgers is more than welcome."

"Where are the codgers?" Ellie asked, all innocence.

Sam looked at Luke and smiled, "She's beautiful and an exquisite liar. How perfect for you."

"Don't forget she knows her way around a .45-70," Luke added.

"Is there such a thing as too perfect?" Sam asked.

"You two better wait to see me shoot before you fly off the handle complimenting me like that. What if I can't hit a tree at five yards?"

"Why don't we do a little target practice, then?" Sam suggested. He grabbed one of the two guns that Luke had carried from the car and led them around the stable.

On the other side of the building, a split-rail fence was set back about ten yards, beyond which tall grasses and swamp were in a permanent state of encroachment.

"Why don't I set up a few cans and we can just see how we do?"

"That sounds great," Ellie said. "I haven't actually fired this one in ages so it will be good to give it a whirl before we head out."

Sam gave Luke a wide-eyed quick look behind Ellie's back as he headed off to one of the storage sheds to get a few boxes of ammunition.

Since moving to Florida, Ellie had become accustomed to standing perfectly still in the heat of high summer. There was no use fanning or fretting or swatting, as that only made for more sweating. It was sort of a game she played with herself, to see how long she could remain perfectly still, regardless of the occasional mosquito. She probably could have stood there for hours, observing the minutia of the plants and insects, taking in the tiny sounds of birds and small creatures in the nearby rushes, breathing in the thick, hot air, nearly burning her nostrils. She could, that is, if Luke hadn't come up behind her and wrapped his arms loosely around her waist. She felt a totally unfamiliar tightening in her core that bloomed into a tension in her lower abdomen, and then spread heat and jolts of pleasure to her fingertips. Desire was distracting. She leaned back into him and let the air out of her lungs.

"This is quite something." She rested the back of her head against his shoulder and rested her arms over his in front of her. "So wild and peaceful all at once."

He stood there holding her for a few more minutes until they heard Sam returning from the shed. Ellie was still skittish from the past few years of solitude and her instinct was to pull herself quickly away from Luke's embrace. Instead, he held her gently next to him—almost absorbing her nervousness somehow—and slowly turned both of them to face Sam's approach.

"I thought we could do some target practice with these and then graduate to the .45-70's. Does that sound good?" He was holding a couple of rifles and a couple of handguns, lifting them slightly.

"Sure. Let's start with the rifles," Luke said.

Ellie took one of the lightweight rifles and flipped open the barrel to check if it contained any ammunition, then left it open and safely draped across her forearm. She looked up to Sam and held her hand out for some bullets. "I'll go first."

"She's such a shy little lady, Luke. You'll have to try to encourage her to be more forthcoming."

Ellie smiled. "I am about to be holding a loaded gun. Let's keep the little-lady claptrap to a minimum, shall we gentlemen?"

Luke laughed. "You'd better do what she says, Sam."

Ellie gestured impatiently, flicking the tips of her fingers. "The bullets, if you please?"

"Have at it." Sam smiled and gave her a handful of bullets.

She loaded two into the chambers and snapped the barrel shut with easy confidence. "What's the target?"

"Do you want to go beyond the fence?"

She looked at him and rolled her eyes. "Duh."

"Okay," he laughed, "Just there to the left is a yellow wildflower . . . do you see it?"

"Yes, I've got it."

Luke watched as she took a moment to contemplate the target, the loaded gun still facing the ground, loosely hanging over her arm. She kept her eye on the tiny yellow blossom as she slowly lifted the butt of the gun and fitted it neatly into the waiting curve of her right shoulder. She relaxed the muscles in her neck and face with a gentle subsiding. Exhaled. Paused. And fired.

He didn't bother looking to see if she'd hit the mark. It was clear from every muscle in her body that she had perfect aim. No tension, no flinching. A natural.

"Jesus, Ellie. Where did you learn to shoot?"

"I'm a country girl. " She turned to him with a beatific smile. "Liked that, did you? I think it's one of my best attributes. I have great aim." She said it in a way that made it perfectly clear she'd set her sights on him.

Luke thought the heat might have gone to his head because he was unable to breathe or think, just caught in a voluntary prison of wanting her to look at him like that for . . . well, forever.

"All right you two," Sam said, clearing his throat to get their attention. "Obviously, we don't need any rudimentary lessons. Let's fire the handguns a couple of times in case we need to do any quick clean-up while we're out there and then we'll be on our way."

They made sure all the guns were firing properly, including the .45-70's, then packed everything into an old Willys Jeep. Ellie noticed a large white cooler in the open rear section right behind where she was seated in the back seat.

"Help yourself if you want a soda or a snack or anything. I packed a few sandwiches into the cooler."

Ellie realized she was pretty near famished and opened the cooler to grab a sandwich and a soda. "How far out do we drive?"

Sam looked at Luke. Luke shrugged his shoulders.

Ellie's mouth was full of ham and cheese and white bread, so she had to mumble around the food, "What are you two up to?"

Luke looked over his shoulder and smiled. "Apparently there's a really big, pissed off boar about four miles out. Do you want to go for it? Lions and tigers and bears and all that? Might even be dark by the time we get back." But his voice sounded far more gleeful than cautionary.

Ellie chewed more slowly, contemplating her answer, then swallowed and took a sip of soda. "Sure. Let's go for it. We've come this far, right?"

Sam was shaking his head right and left, but smiling.

"See, I told you she'd be up for it," Luke said.

Ellie had a momentary panic that she was in the middle of frickin' *Deliverance* and Sam and Luke were going to carve her into bits and leave her for boar breakfast in the middle of a Florida swamp.

Luke saw the fleeting thought cross her face. "Hey, you okay? I only meant . . . I was telling Sam earlier how fearless you are. We can stay closer in if you want . . . "

He was so tender and empathic in that moment that the passing paranoia evaporated.

Still, she thought, as she polished off the ham and cheese sandwich, that even though *she* wasn't at the end of his bloody sword, that someone, somewhere, at some point in time, had been looking into Luke's piercing blue eyes when they held no compassion whatsoever.

He held her gaze through her silent litany of judgment, watching over his shoulder as her mind rolled past the possibility of his lack of humanity. He lifted his chin, almost imperceptibly, as if to say, yes, that was also me.

Sam was starting to drive away from the homestead, down a well-kept trail that led deeper into the swamp. Luke put his hand on his friends shoulder to get him to stop the vehicle, then he turned back to Ellie.

The Jeep slowed to a stop.

"Are you sure?" he asked.

She knew he was questioning a whole lot more than whether or not she wanted to ride out after an angry, wild pig.

Her throat felt dry and her voice cracked a little on her reply. "I'm sure."

He smiled again, reached his hand between the two front seats and back to her leg to give her an encouraging squeeze on her thigh.

"I'm really glad."

The rest of the trip was bumpy and the engine noise made it difficult to talk. Ellie wished she had brought her camera, but hoped that a future visit to shoot pictures instead of wild animals might be in the offing.

They spent four hours tracking the big old angry boar. By three in the afternoon, they had bagged a couple of quail, let a few deer go, and only seen a bit of scatological evidence that the mythological boar even existed. Ellie had her doubts. She'd been hunting enough times with her parents and uncles and cousins to know that longed-for prey could take on monumental, and often imaginary, proportions.

Late in the afternoon, they parked the Jeep at the top of a narrow trailhead and started walking into a particularly lovely glade. Sam was several paces ahead of them, Ellie in the middle, and Luke trailing behind her. They were all hot and tired from the heat and the waning adrenaline of hours spent in pursuit. Luke had touched Ellie throughout the day, small caresses every now and then. Checking in. His fingers at the nape of her neck. His hand at the small of her back.

As the setting sun cast golden spears of light through the ancient scrub forest, Luke came up behind her and wrapped his left arm around her waist, pulling her up against his hard stomach. He leaned into her neck and kissed just below her ear, then whispered, "Walking behind you all day is a delightful torture. I can't stop looking at your hips."

They were standing still, Sam walking further away from them. Ellie closed her eyes and turned her head slightly so she could kiss Luke's temple, tasting the sweat of the day against his skin. She opened her eyes slowly.

Paused.

Then froze.

Two prehistoric beady black eyes stared at her with empty malevolence through the thick low branches. With the sense borne of years of tracking, Sam had also stopped where he was, about twenty feet ahead of them and almost around a slight bend in the trail.

Luke held Ellie around the waist, his grip tightening as if his single arm could protect her from what looked like 300 pounds of feral animosity. Ellie knew she was the only one in position to shoot. She could feel the tension in Luke's body as he realized the gravity of the situation—that he was behind her, his gun at an awkward angle over his forearm—then, with military control, his body eased with acceptance and he transferred his strength into her.

In barely a whisper, he apologized, "It has to be you."

Something about the blank indifference of the pig's stare made it easier than she thought it would be to pull the trigger.

She raised her gun very slowly and brought it to her shoulder, putting her cheek carefully against the smooth wood of the butt. She had to undo the safety before firing and knew that the click would sound thunderous in the unnatural quiet that surrounded them, as if every animal knew to stay perfectly still or risk attack.

Luke moved with her, the two of them moving in tandem. She flipped the safety and remained perfectly steady as the beast charged—sprung from his reverie by the small snick—and hurled himself right at her face. She pulled the trigger and watched in super-slow-motion, while the enormous, brutal, beautifully hideous beast collapsed and rolled to a stop about nine inches in front of her perfectly still body.

She moved the barrel of her gun so it was a few inches from the side of the boar's huge head, and watched as the life drained out of the one black fathomless eye that stared up at her from the collapsed pile at her feet.

"Did I get him?" she whispered to Luke.

As if to prove he was not so easily destroyed, the pig grunted his dismay and anger, rolled his head away from the barrel of her gun, and shut his eyes as his legs spasmed three times and frothy blood started to come out of his mouth. His life left him completely as the dark, hot blood oozed from his fatal chest wound in a steady stream that was starting to pool near her boots.

Sam approached them from Ellie's right, a cocked handgun in one hand and a rifle strapped over his back and shoulder.

He whistled, a long, low sound of appreciation. "Nice shooting, Ellie. I'd say you got him."

Ellie wasn't sure she could move. She felt as if she might need to stand there, her gun trained on the beast's dead head, until someone forcibly removed the weapon from her frozen grasp.

Luke could feel the tide of adrenaline as it began to well up inside her. He knew she'd be shaking uncontrollably in a matter of seconds. He handed Sam his gun then pulled Ellie's out of her grip and handed that one to Sam as well.

"Give us a minute, will you Sam?"

"Sure. I'll bring these back to the Jeep and see about some rope to get this guy trussed and transported."

Sam walked off, leaving Ellie staring at the huge animal she'd killed. Every bristle of hair on his back was etched in beautiful relief. The strange contour of his bizarre, curled, horn-like teeth. She could feel the heat of his body, so near to hers. She thought for a moment that she might like to bend down and touch it, to tame it. Or apologize.

But it was wild and raw and brutish. And dead, she thought sadly. She had killed it.

Luke turned her into his arms and held her tight, through the waves of shock and terror and a sick glee at being alive and a flood of tears that coursed down her face and into the soft, old cotton of his shirt. He held her so closely he had the impression he could feel the bursts of adrenaline coursing through her muscles.

He murmured simple, soothing words like "it's okay" and "you're going to be fine" and "you did great" and "you're all right" and she finally let the emotion pound through her in a few final racking sobs then subsided.

He moved them to a felled log a few feet away from the boar, and helped her settle in next to him. She rested her head on his shoulder and reached her arm around his back. He kept kissing the top of her head and inhaling the scent of her, the lovely cinnamon was mixed with something pungent and terrifying, or terrified. The hint of that smell made Luke want to kill the boar all over again for having made Ellie afraid, for having put her through that.

He must have shuddered as well, because Ellie looked up at him, eyes wide, and used one of her shirttails to dry the edges of her eyes and wipe away the tearstains along her cheeks. "Are you okay?" she asked softly.

"God, Ellie. A goddamn charging wild animal almost just killed you. Of course I'm not okay." But then he looked from her stunned eyes to her sweet, waiting mouth and kissed her with enough ferocity and blatant, erotic desire, that Ellie thought he might be perfectly fine after all.

She moaned her pleasure and bent her body into his, pulling him toward her with the hand at his back and gripping his thick brown hair with the other. She had a vision of the two of them as part of some prehistoric tribe, clinging to each other after the proximity of death had temporarily receded once more. She wanted him so badly, but not for some titillating erotic exercise. She wanted him in the most primitive way, a wild joining that would overcome fear and starvation and war, an urge to rut that must've been the original act of humanity's defiance, albeit momentary, against encroaching death. Ellie felt viscerally connected to that woman she would have been five thousand years ago, grateful to the point of tears for the man in her arms: both for the shared joy of his presence and the selfish joy of how he existed for her own survival.

"Ellie." Luke sighed her name in answering gratitude.

"I know," she added softly between heated, desperate kisses. "It's probably just the adrenaline . . . right?"

"Right." But his strangled tone suggested it was far more.

The business of gutting and transporting the boar seemed to help Ellie feel a lot calmer. Luke offered to walk her back to the Jeep while he and Sam saw to the bloody mess of eviscerating the enormous creature.

"No, I feel like I owe it to him to stay." Her smile was weak. "Does that make any sense?"

Sam nodded. "Makes perfect sense to me."

Luke agreed reluctantly, his desire to protect her—from everything—battling against his respect for her wishes to close the circle on the experience.

Why had he even suggested they go hunting? Served him right for being such a cavalier idiot.

Sam had returned from the Jeep with a black nylon bag filled with the necessary knives and ropes. Ellie watched as the they handily slit the abdomen and the organs slid out onto the dry earth. The strange smell and heat of entrails wafted around them as they worked. After draining as much blood as they could, Sam and Luke tied the carcass to a long pole that Sam had brought for that purpose.

From that first glimpse of those eternal, black eyes to the trussed up beast swinging gently from the pole as they carried it along the hot dim path back to the Jeep, not more than half an hour had passed.

Luke glanced at Ellie and felt like it had been a lifetime.

Once they were back at camp, they sat in the living room of the main house sipping some very old, very good scotch.

"So, not a bad day, huh?" Sam asked.

Luke didn't share any of the rising joy that Ellie and Sam seemed to be experiencing. He stayed quiet as the other two spoke.

"How old do you think he was, Sam?" Ellie asked.

"Oh, I don't know. Probably eight or ten years."

"Was he big or about average?"

"Pretty big. And pretty crafty, didn't you think? I walked right by him. How did you catch his eye?"

"I'd just turned my head—" She looked at Luke, reliving the moment of him kissing her neck. "—and my eyes sort of locked with his. And then it was all kind of slow-mo and really fast all at the same time. Do you know what I mean?"

"Yes." Sam took another sip of scotch and looked at Luke for a second, then back to Ellie. "I know exactly what you mean. In that moment of intensity, everything sort of expands and contracts in different ways. It's over before you know it, but while it's happening you are in this soup of protracted movement and thought. Right?"

"Yeah, exactly. The soup. I felt Luke at my back and it was as if my body began to move in some elemental way, thoughtless almost. Instinctual, right?"

Luke was bordering on fury. He hated this talk of instinct and the elements and protraction—this artistic abstraction of his terror. Ellie had almost died in his arms and no one seemed to acknowledge the severity of it.

"Luke?" Ellie's voice jarred him out of his brooding.

79

"Yes?"

"Do you think we should head back?"

"Yes. I guess we should." He was passive, but not in an accommodating way. He shook the ice in his glass and then got up to leave it in the kitchen across the room.

Probably thinking he was out of earshot, Ellie whispered to Sam, "What's the matter with him?"

"He's not really into the thrill of the kill, Ellie. I know you two have just met, so—" He looked briefly toward the kitchen. "—it's best if you let him explain it."

"All right. I guess." She rattled the remaining ice cubes in her own empty glass then stood up to join Luke in the kitchen. She found him leaning against the worn Formica countertop, staring blindly out the window over the sink. The last remnants of summer sun were glowing orange and purple and peach against the black silhouette of palms and pines.

"What is it?" She put her glass down on the counter and wrapped her arms around his waist from behind, leaning her cheek against his back.

He hung his head, reluctant to speak. "I hated today."

"What do you mean?" She watched the tension in his grip at the edge of the counter.

"I hated everything about it. The stalking, the killing, the carving it all up. I was disgusted. And trust me, this is not the first time I've done it. I've probably hunted every creature on earth at one time or another. I'm not squeamish." He turned to face her, letting his hands rest carefully on her hips. "I hated that you were here."

"I loved being with you," she whispered.

"Ellie." He reached up and laced his fingers through her hair, then gripped the base of her skull, tilting her face to his. "I loved being with you, too, which is why I don't ever want to do this again. It was insane. What if something had happened to you?" His voice was a harsh, hoarse reprimand, as if he were punishing her.

Which, she supposed, in a way he was. Punishing her for being foolish with herself, now that *herself* needed to be protected by him.

She imagined that parents felt this way when their children escaped from a car accident brought on by their own foolishness, something along the lines of *I'm so glad you're alive and now I'm going to kill you.*

Ellie turned her lips into the palm of his hand to give him a reassuring kiss. "It's okay. I won't let anything happen to me." She hoped her quirky smile would force him to lighten up.

He leaned in to kiss her, holding her neck and jaw steady in his strong hands, tilting her to the angle he chose. The kiss was brief and firm. He was letting her know . . . something. That she was his, probably.

He released his hold, took her hand in his, and led her back into the living room to say goodbye and thanks to Sam.

They drove home in a meditative silence and he followed her into her house to make sure everything was safe once they got back to Palm Beach. She invited him to spend the night and she was so relieved when he agreed. They showered in separate bathrooms and fell asleep after nothing more than a chaste kiss on the lips. After all the fire and drama that afternoon, they were both relieved to slip into a peaceful lull.

He headed out just after five the next morning, with a promise to call her in a few hours. He gave her a peck on the cheek and she reached up sleepily to grab him for a real kiss. They both moaned in pleasure, but he eventually pulled away.

"I have to get to work, beautiful. Have a great day." And then he was gone.

Chapter 5

The hardest thing to get used to was that he didn't have a cell phone. Ellie was the type of person who liked to touch base. A lot. She and Rob had hardly ever been apart. They had worked together in the same office, lived in the same house, gone on the same vacations. Some friends had questioned the wisdom of spending so much time with each other—that they'd burn out—tire of one another's company.

In hindsight, Ellie felt like some grand cosmic clock had been ticking all along and they'd spent a lifetime together in the relatively short fourteen years they'd had with one another. No commuting, no lengthy separations for business. No wasted interstitials.

But she realized she'd been spoiled. Anytime she'd had a random thought or a stray observation, Rob was usually within earshot, or at least on the other end of a very quick phone call. She'd never had to stockpile her conversations. Everything was in real time.

Luke was another concept altogether.

She suspected that his job at the BMW shop had nothing to do with fulfilling financial obligations and some capitalist, supply-and-demand part of her resented that he chose to do that instead of spending all of his time gazing into her eyes. The rational part of her knew that his occupation was an integral part of who he was. The irrational part of her was simply . . . irritated. Why wasn't he *with her*, for goodness sake?

He was regimental. After those first immersive days, he called her at seven in the morning before he left for work, noon when he was taking lunch, and at seven when he got home from the gym or running on the beach. Technically she didn't need to wait by the phone, hers *was* a cell phone after all. But it still *felt* like she was waiting by the phone. Even if she was at Publix or the gas station or the dry cleaners. She was always waiting at those three times of the day. And she didn't like it.

By Thursday at noon she told him flat out to cease and desist with the crazy scheduled phone calls. "I think you should stop calling me."

"What? What do you mean?" he asked, sounding hurt.

"I mean, stop calling me at precisely the same time. It's weird. I am not a stop on the City of New Orleans. Just call me when you feel like it, otherwise I feel like I'm some sort of chore."

"Chore? Are you kidding? I'm calling you like this because if I don't pace myself I want to call you every five minutes."

Funny how that made her feel so much better. "Really?"

"Yes. Really." But it didn't sound like it made him as cheerful as it made her, the wanting-to-call-every-five-minutes business.

"It felt like you had sort of scheduled me into your day planner or something. Sorry. Why don't you come over for dinner tonight?"

He exhaled through his teeth. This was not going at all how he'd hoped. Slow. Thoughtful. That was what he'd hoped for. Instead, he felt like he wanted to hop on his motorcycle and break every speed limit and rip her front door off when he got to her house and then throw her down right there on the entryway floor. And be very, very quick and thoughtless about it. And then, afterward, maybe, he would be slow and thoughtful. Repeatedly.

"Ellie?"

"Yeah?" He could hear her walking around her kitchen, pushing her glass under the ice dispenser in the front of the refrigerator.

"I'm trying to be patient."

"I know. I want to be patient too."

He laughed. A short, quick smack.

"Really!" She laughed, a little defensively. "I do. I'm completely won over to this crazy idea of prolonged, anticipatory pleasure. Seriously."

He hummed skeptically.

"I mean it, Luke. All saucy joking aside, I think it will be much better this way. You're going to be the first man in my bed since my husband died, and I want to . . . acknowledge that. I think it's the right thing to do."

Something twisted inside him. He didn't like the way she said *first man* as if there would be a string of others after he broke the mold, the first in a long line of future lovers. He had to be so damn careful. "That's good to hear. I'm glad."

"Good. Okay, so we're on the same page about that. But the regimental phone calling is just . . . not me."

"I suppose I am sort of regimental. I like order. Sorry."

"Don't be sorry. It's just a quirk of your personality, right? I don't want to have to apologize for *my* weirdness and quirkiness."

He found it pleasantly unnerving that all of the things for which Kate had berated him—his stodgy, old-fashioned peculiarities, his need for order—were summarily, breezily swept aside by Ellie as simple quirks of his personality.

"What weirdness would that be?" he asked with a silky, suggestive tone in his voice.

"Wouldn't you like to know?" He heard the smile through her words. "I certainly won't let you see any of the real crazy until well into month two. A girl's gotta do what a girl's gotta do to seal the deal."

"Just one more thing to look forward to, I guess."

"So no dinner tonight?"

"Can we play it by ear? I told Bill I'd go to a karate class with him."

"Of course. No worries."

"How about a movie tomorrow night for sure?"

"That sounds perfect."

"Okay." He sounded reluctant. "I have to get back to work. I'll call you . . . soon. At some random time."

She laughed and wished she could kiss him. "All right, that sounds great. See you soon."

"Bye, Ellie."

"Bye."

Ellie spoke to her parents later that afternoon and ended up inviting them over for dinner. She'd grilled some salmon and they were just opening a second bottle of wine when the doorbell rang around eight o'clock. She'd never heard back from Luke so she'd assumed he was going to the class with Bill.

"Who could that be?" her mother asked, reaching for her glass of wine.

"Um." Ellie stood up, setting her napkin carefully on the table. "I think it might be a friend of mine."

"Who would come by unannounced at eight o'clock at night?" her father asked.

"Let me go see."

Each step toward the door made her heart beat faster. She didn't know why she hadn't mentioned Luke to her parents, but she just hadn't. There was no point in getting them all riled up. They were overly protective of her since Rob had died, and she didn't want their input one way or the other. Either they'd be incredibly hopeful that it would lead to something permanent, or incredibly wary that it would lead to nothing at all.

She put her hand on the doorknob and took a deep breath. When she pulled it open all thoughts of her parents and their expectations flew out the window, because it was just Luke, and he was windblown and gorgeous and tentative. And holding what looked distinctly like an overnight bag.

Damn.

He crossed the threshold and pulled her against him, kissing her neck and rubbing his cheek against her skin. He hadn't shaved in a couple of days and he was kind of sweaty and *god* he felt so delicious.

"Um . . . " She tried to keep a grip on the fact that her parents were probably craning their necks to get a better look down the dim hallway that led from the kitchen to the front door.

Luke pulled away quickly. "What is it? Is everything okay?"

He was so adorably concerned, as if she might be in real danger.

She took a deep breath and whispered, "I'm fine, but you're about to be grilled. My parents are here."

He smiled and pushed the door shut behind him. "Good." He gave her another peck on the cheek and dropped his gym bag near the front hall table. "I want to meet them."

She was a grown woman in her own house. She kept reminding herself she was not a sixteen-year-old introducing her first boyfriend and looking for her parents' approval. But maybe the hint of that was always there.

Luke peeled off his tight leather biker jacket and hung it in the front hall closet. "All set," he said, extending his arms out for inspection. He'd obviously come straight from the gym, and was wearing a sweaty grey T-shirt and a pair of black karate pants. Ellie thought he looked sexy as hell. Her mom would probably think he looked like a felon.

"Okay." Ellie sighed. "Come face the inquisition."

Ellie's mother couldn't conceal her surprise. Her father looked plain old puzzled: a man in Ellie's house simply did not compute.

"Mom. Dad. This is Luke McCormick. He and I . . . " Her voice trailed off as she looked from her parents to Luke and back again.

" . . . started dating a few weeks ago," Luke filled in easily. He reached out his hand to shake each of theirs. "It's such a pleasure to meet you both. I'm so sorry to interrupt."

Ellie's dad spoke first. "Nice to meet you, too. How are you?"

"Fine thanks."

Ellie gestured for him to have a seat. "Let me make you a plate of salmon. I'll be back in a minute."

Oh god. If you were thinking of having sex with someone, he was probably exactly what you would imagine in your best fantasies—dark, handsome, a bit rough around the edges, gritty . . . *hot.* If you were thinking of someone dating your daughter, he was probably exactly what you would imagine in your worst nightmares—scruffy, unpredictable, predatory . . . *old.*

She tried to breathe evenly while she fixed a plate of food for him. She listened to the conversation at the other side of the room with half her attention—the other half playing out all sorts of horrible scenarios involving her mother calling her in the middle of the night, crying into the phone about how worried she was for Ellie's safety. *Motorcycles, you know!*

She set a plate of food in front of him and he looked up from the conversation he was having with her mom and whispered *thanks* with the most delicious smile. She blushed and turned back to the kitchen to get him a glass for wine.

When she sat back down there was a brief silence, the four of them looking at each other and eating quietly.

"So," her mom said with a smile. "What a small world."

Ellie looked up from her plate. "How's that?"

"Such a wonderful coincidence that Luke's uncle in Wyoming was a few years ahead of your father at St. Paul's."

Ellie swung her head around to stare at Luke. "Yes, such a coincidence."

Oh, but he was a clever boy. He knew just the thing to put her parents at ease. That comforting connection to the WASP establishment that would obliterate any fleeting concerns about grey T-shirts or motorcycles or showing up at one's daughter's house unannounced for what was most certainly a booty call.

"When was the last time you saw Grant?" her dad asked, referring to Luke's uncle.

"About four months ago. He just turned eighty and we had a big tent and everything to make him grumpy. But he put up with it."

"Sounds like the Grant I remember," Ellie's dad said. "He always was anti-social."

"Yep, he still is," Luke agreed.

They finished dinner and Ellie's parents made a quick exit. "No coffee, thanks. Nice to meet you, Luke."

Lots of superficial chatter about looking forward to seeing each other again and that sort of thing, and then they finally left. Ellie waved goodbye from the doorway until they'd pulled out of sight. Her hand dropped and she shut the door, then leaned back against it for support.

"Your parents are great," Luke said, pulling her close.

"That was stressful."

"Well." He kissed her neck. "At least the awkward first meeting is over." He kissed higher up her neck. "Why didn't you tell me they were going to be here?" He kissed her cheek. "I might've showered." He laughed a little. "I've been known to make a good first impression when I set my mind to it."

She finally softened into him. "I didn't expect them for dinner. It was just a last-minute thing. We see each other a lot. And when I didn't hear from you, it didn't occur to me to give you a heads-up. But they liked you, I could tell."

"I'm glad. But they're not really the ones I'm after."

She hummed into him. "They're not?"

"No." He kissed her full on the lips, tracing the edge with his tongue, and seeking entry. "Let me in, Ellie," he said softly against her lips.

She opened her mouth to him and they kissed like that, up against her front door, just holding each other and making out, for what felt like hours.

Luke spent that night and several more over the next few weeks, always tender and affectionate. Always (almost) chaste. They talked for hours, mostly about superficial things—their favorite foods and favorite places to travel, movies, books. It was also getting easier for Ellie to talk about Rob without feeling like she was betraying him or dwelling on him. He'd been an integral part of her life for nearly half of it. Luke totally respected that.

Emotionally, it was all good.

But physically, Ellie was about to combust. Luke seemed so contained—well, more able to contain himself than she was—through that iron self-will of his. She loved it, actually. It wasn't that he was playing a game, resisting her, it was more like he was letting the desire build over a slow flame. The two of them were becoming totally accustomed to each other's bodies. Swimming, eating, lounging on the couch watching a movie.

It sounded trite, but they were actually getting to know each other, the shape of each other.

Chapter 6

Thursday afternoon they were chatting on the phone and Ellie suggested a little mini vacation. Their thirty days were almost up and she was about to expire from lust. "So I was thinking it might be fun to go away this weekend. Do you have to work?"

"What did you have in mind?" he asked.

"There's this great little place near Islamorada that's simply heaven in the summertime. Kind of like going to the Bahamas without having to hop on a flight. Really quiet. Swimming in the ocean. Reading. Swinging in a hammock."

"Sounds great," he said. "Do you want to go down Friday night or Saturday morning?"

"I think Saturday morning is easier. Friday night we might run into traffic around Miami."

"Do you want to go on my motorcycle or in your car?"

"We should probably take my car so we can bring a couple of coolers with supplies." Then she lowered her voice to a throaty whisper. "Though I love the idea of spending hours with my legs wrapped around your hips . . . from behind." She heard a clatter on the other end of the line.

"Luke?"

"Yes," he answered quickly. "I dropped the phone."

"Oh," she said, sounding contrite, then pleased. "Good."

"What time shall I pick you up Saturday?" he asked.

"Why don't I come to your place?" she asked, then felt like she was prying, and sped up the pace of her speech. "I mean, to save you the trip twenty minutes north, then twenty minutes south. But not if you don't want me to see where you live—"

"Why wouldn't I want you to see where I live?"

"I don't know. It's not like you've ever invited me over. You . . . it . . . I . . . thought you seemed like you wanted to keep it sort of private or apart or something."

"Yeah, I guess you're right in a way. But certainly not apart from you."

Well, that made her feel almost as good as all of his repressed desires to call her every five minutes. "Oh. Okay then. I'll be at your house . . . or apartment . . . or whatever . . . on Saturday morning at 8. Does that sound good? Not too early?"

"It's a house. And yes, that sounds perfect." The way he said *perfect* made her shudder. They both breathed into the phone for a few seconds longer. "I have to get back to work. I'll call you . . . soon. And I'll see you Saturday."

"Okay. See you then. Bye."

She hung up the phone and felt the silence settle back around her. Her perpetual companion: the gentle silence. She spent a couple of hours checking email, making reservations at the place in the Keys, and then reading a new monograph about the Parisian photographer Valérie Belin.

Around three o'clock she went back downstairs, made herself a sandwich, then picked up her camera and walked out to the beach to eat and take a few shots. She hadn't shown any of her pictures since Rob died, and she didn't have any plans to do so, but lately she'd been feeling inspired to create a new body of work. Something intimate. Something like Luke, she thought ruefully.

The roar and crash of the ocean was such a part of her recovery, or grief management, or transition. She was never quite sure what to call it. The need to name things was perfectly human. Biblical, really. But there never seemed to be the right name for what she had gone through—was going through—after Rob died. It never seemed to fit into some named experience.

Lamenting, maybe.

Of course, there were entire sections of the bookstore dedicated to identifying and naming it. She wasn't being egomaniacal in thinking her experience was unique or indescribable. She just felt that no one ever really got the actual semantics quite right.

She finished her sandwich as she sat on the hot sand, then leaned down to photograph a small tidal pool. A group of shells had become trapped in a little world of isolated seawater. She got to her knees to frame the small universe in her lens. She watched as the sun sparkled against the six- or seven-inch circle of water, a couple of bubbles at the edge. There were several orange shells, and two small white shells resting just below the shallow surface.

Were they parts of the same shell . . . finally separated after a lifetime of joined purpose? Or just random? Thrown together in a moment of violence?

Ellie sat there for nearly two hours.

The sun warmed her back and neck as she shot about two hundred frames of that small pool. The light changed from second to second. The drying sand changed tone. The occasional wind added a little ripple to the surface.

She'd been happily shooting wide frame landscapes for most of the past eight years. All her time wandering, especially on the boat with Rob, had led her toward expansive, open portraits of nature. She'd gone in for vistas.

Was creative change so easily effected by a new man in her life? she wondered to herself, almost ashamed. Rob had been expansive. Open. His laugh. His worldview. The spread of his arms when he wanted her to enter his embrace.

Even in the short time she'd known him, she'd seen how Luke was specific. Finite. Intimate. Precise. He held small things in the palm of his hand and really looked at them. He was patient.

Oh, lord. She was getting way too into her own head. She needed a big glass of wine and a long conversation with Lotta to set herself straight.

When she looked up, an unfamiliar man was walking toward her along the beach. Not toward *her*, she corrected, since it was a public beach. But living this far north, nearly at the tip of the island, she rarely saw people she didn't know, or at least vaguely recognize.

He seemed sort of unnatural. He was wearing a pair of black swimming trunks and a black rash guard that looked more suited to a Navy Seal, rather than someone taking a stroll on an empty beach in mid-summer.

Ellie remained in a low squat, her camera tucked unseen between her thighs and her stomach. She smiled benignly as he passed.

He did something with his mouth that perhaps passed for a smile, but it was odd. As if he had been told to smile, but wasn't quite familiar with how. He kept his pace, walking the remaining four lots to the northernmost end of the island, then turning back and passing her again a few minutes later.

She smiled again, just to see that strange reaction. And . . . there it was. She thought she saw a small hearing aid, or secret service earpiece, and decided to snap a picture of him just for the hell of it. He was walking away from her by then, so he wouldn't know. She lifted the camera and snapped a series of his retreating back, catching the hint of his profile, then swung the lens out toward the ocean.

He turned his head, as if he sensed she was watching him, but he was far away by then. Even from that distance, she could see the tension in him—alert, hyperconscious.

In this bizarre little corner of the world, there were heads of state and politicians and, well, just plain rich people, who had personal security details. It wouldn't have been the first time someone was sending forward recon to make sure the beach was clear. Even so, Ellie often forgot that some of the richest people on earth lived all around her. When she and Rob had purchased the house, it had seemed sort of silly.

Palm Beach.

Just the two words alone evoked images of people with last names like Kennedy and Astor and Flagler. But when she and Rob saw the actual house, a humble little beach cottage, really, and the expanse of wide open Atlantic from every modest room, and the dilapidated wood frame construction and the real estate glut and, well, it just sort of all conspired to make it seem like a really good deal.

And one thing that Rob and Ellie had always shared was a deep and abiding affection for really good deals. They had never joined any clubs or societies or boards. They'd never gone in for socializing at any fancy charity events. They walked on the beach. They befriended their neighbors. They cooked on the grill. They liked to eat out occasionally at Chez Jean Pierre or Café Boulud, but mostly they were pretty reclusive.

Ellie enjoyed the other year-rounders who lived nearby, and soon realized they all craved a similar anonymity. Even though there were probably captains of industry to the left of her and kept women to the right, everyone retained a friendly, egalitarian pleasantness on their quiet street.

Whereas . . . this man in his black rash guard was something else altogether. Ellie looked down at the small screen on the back of her camera and pushed the button that skipped to the previous frames. She stared for a few more seconds at the images then looked up to compare the real thing. He was jogging away from her now, a brisk, no-nonsense pace that looked as if he could run twenty miles in Tripoli without breaking a sweat.

Ellie got up from her kneeling position, brushed the sand off her legs and turned back toward her house. Instead of going straight home, she decided to check in with her neighbors one lot to the north.

Isabelle and Fred Grumman were in their early seventies and had built the McMansion of their dreams in the early 1990's. Despite their questionable taste in colossal derivative architecture, Rob and Ellie used to joke, they were quite down-to-earth and friendly, always attentive, without ever being nosey. The ideal type of neighbor who tells you when your air conditioning handler is making a strange squeaking noise, but never calls to complain when you need the occasional blast of Nine Inch Nails to soothe your frayed temper.

Then, after Rob died, they had become downright protective.

After walking through their dune path, Ellie tapped at the immaculate wooden gate that said, "No Trespassing" on a little hand-painted sign. It was almost welcoming in its very warning. As if it said, "No Trespassing . . . but *you* can come in."

"We're here!" A man's voice called over the fence.

Ellie pushed the gate open then shut it behind her. "Hey, Fred. How are you?"

"Great!" he said, without looking up. He was standing across the patio, watching his grill with scientific intensity.

"What's the matter with your grill?"

"Isabelle's inside. She'll explain. Go on in."

Ellie laughed as she walked past him, patting him on the shoulder before sliding the glass door open and going inside.

Isabelle was standing at her kitchen counter slicing tomatoes.

"Hiya," said Ellie. "What's with Fred and the grill?"

"Oh, hi honey!"

Ellie gave a worried smile when the tiny, frail woman looked up from her kitchen task, but continued to slice. Concerned she might cut off her fingers if she looked away too long, Ellie added quickly, "Don't mind me. I just popped in to say hi."

Isabelle returned her attention to her cutting board and said, "Oh, Fred and that silly grill. As if the charcoal wasn't good enough, and then of course the propane, and then the propane had to be hard-wired to the main gas line, or hooked up or whatever, and now he has gone and bought some new-fangled infrared grill and he is trying to learn how to cook the steaks and you would think it required the skill set of a brain surgeon."

Ellie was laughing. "He looked very . . . dedicated."

Isabelle used the back of the blade to slide the tomatoes into a nearby wooden salad bowl. "Would you like to stay for dinner, dear?"

"No, you're sweet, but I think I'm going to just go home and curl up in front of the TV. But I saw a strange guy walking around just now and I didn't know if you knew if anyone was in town. I think Vickery's place is shut and so is the MacMillans'."

"I think we're the only two on the street until the end of August. Do you want me to call Steve?"

Everyone in this part of town was on a first-name basis with the local policeman who'd been patrolling the same beat for the past twenty years.

"No, I just thought I'd mention it in case you saw him again. He looked sort of military and I thought maybe someone famous was sneaking into town." Ellie gave a little wink.

Isabelle and Ellie were terrible peeping Toms, perching themselves up in Ellie's bedroom with binoculars to watch the Obamas or the Bushes or some other visiting dignitary walk the beach when they came into town to glad hand the big donors.

"You sure you don't want to stay for a glass of wine?"

"No, but thanks again. Oh, also, I'm going away for the weekend."

"Oh, where are you going?"

"Just down to the Keys for a couple of nights."

"To take some pictures?"

"Probably . . . but I'm also going with a new friend."

Isabelle had been washing the knife and the cutting board and setting them in the drying rack when Ellie spoke. The older woman turned slowly. "What kind of new friend? The kind who rides a motorcycle?"

"Oh, Isabelle, you're impossible. I hope it didn't wake you up, did it?"

Isabelle dried her hands on the kitchen towel, then kept it gripped in her hands in excitement. "Oh, Ellie! Is he handsome? Don't answer that! Of course, he would be handsome. But is he *irresponsible*?"

97

Ellie laughed because the way Isabelle said 'irresponsible' you would have thought it was the highest compliment one could pay to a possible suitor.

"Isabelle! You're terrible!"

"So he is."

"Stop! He is quite . . . lovely."

"Hmmm. Not sure that's what I would call a resounding vote of confidence. But I suppose something gentle and calming—"

"Oh! He's hardly gentle or calming! I mean—" Ellie blushed and lost her train of thought. "I certainly don't feel *calm* when I'm around him."

"Oh good!" Isabelle put the towel down next to the sink then turned back to give Ellie a quick hug. "Have fun in the Keys. We'll keep an eye on your place for you."

"Thanks. I'm leaving early Saturday morning and I'll be back at some point Monday."

"Damn it, Isabelle!" Fred came slamming into the kitchen with the two steaks on his wooden platter. "Oh, sorry to swear, Ellie."

"No worries. I think I've heard that one. I'll leave you two to sort out your dinner." Ellie winked at Isabelle as Fred proceeded to complain about the lack of char, and smiled to herself as Isabelle tried to remain calm.

"What did you expect, dear, there isn't any charcoal . . . "

Ellie slipped out the back door, walked across the short stretch of sand and made her way up the narrow winding path through the dunes to her back door.

Later that night, Ellie fell asleep after watching a movie and taking a long bath. She was woken up by the sound of her cell phone ringing, but was disoriented and didn't know if one hour or seven had passed since she'd fallen asleep. She looked at the screen. 10:39.

"Hello," she croaked, not recognizing the phone number.

"Hey, just thought I'd call to wish you a good night's sleep. Just, you know, at ten thirty nine. No reason. Just some random time."

Ellie smiled a warm, coming-awake smile. Hearing Luke's voice when she was in that transitional state from sleeping to waking was ridiculously sexy. "Mmmm. I like random-time calling." She turned onto her side and rolled her head deeper into her pillow. "Where are you? What number is this?"

"It's mine. I just left the cell phone store."

She smiled wider. "You went to the cell phone store?"

"Well, yes. It's the strangest thing, but I heard they sold cell phones there. I had convinced myself that I had no use for such an intrusive, inconvenient device in my new pared-down life, and then I found it was becoming highly inconvenient not having one."

"Mmmm. Inconvenient, huh?"

"Yes. Turns out there are times—very random times—I felt like calling you."

"I hope you got the unlimited texting plan."

"I did, but why?" he asked, feigning ignorance.

"Because I'm going to want to text you."

"Why wouldn't you just call me?"

"Maybe you're at work or the beach or whatever. And sometimes talking's overrated, don't you think?"

Luke coughed a little. "On occasion. I could see that there might be times when talking was unnecessary."

"Mmm. And then, there are other times I could just talk and talk." She was purring into the phone again. She made a big, delicious yawn followed by a satisfied little hum.

"Maybe this was a bad idea." His voice was a little strained.

"Why?"

"Because now I'm going to want to hear that purr and yawn at the most inconvenient hours of the day."

She hummed again, loving the feel of being half asleep and his voice in her head, almost as if he were in the bed with her.

"You're just a sleepy little lamb, aren't you?"

"Mm-hmm. I swam for a long time this morning, but I just can't seem to shake this nervous energy. What do you think it is?"

"I have my ideas."

"Do you?" she asked with a slow suggestive lilt.

"Yes. But I'm standing in the parking lot outside the phone store and I'd rather give you my ideas from the comfort of my own home. Can I call you back in ten minutes?"

"Oh, yes. I'd love that." Her voice was more awake now. "Turns out I have a few ideas for you, too."

His voice was a low growl. "Ten minutes."

"Okay. I'm excited."

"Me too. Bye."

She jumped out of bed and went into the bathroom. Taking a quick look at herself, as if she were going on some sort of impromptu date, she whipped off her gray UVA T-shirt and went into her closet to rifle through her lingerie. Wanting something really satiny against her skin, she passed over the lacy thongs and bras and dug deep into the drawer until she pulled out a long silk slip that she'd found at a vintage shop in Paris. Pulling it on over her head, she shivered in anticipation as it slid down over her hips with liquid ease. She stared into the drawer and contemplated a pair of underwear . . . sometimes she liked the feel of the fabric rubbing against her even more than skin and fingers.

She shivered again. In a few days it wouldn't be fabric or fingers, but Luke pushing into her. She shut her eyes and took a deep breath. Exhaling, she slowly turned out of the closet and shut the door behind her. She lit a candle on her bedside table and shut off all the lights. Then her phone rang.

She stared at the number and her bones melted inside her body, a warm, thick response to the mere idea of him.

Flopping into bed and sliding her finger across the screen, she said, "Hey you."

He was falling in love with this woman. It was as simple and terrifying as that. Never mind the turn of her hips or the swing of her long cinnamon hair, just her voice was enough to rearrange his organs.

"Luke? Are you there?"

"Yeah, sorry. I mean, God, just the sound of your voice and I'm pretty much wrecked."

He heard her shuffling in bed, the sounds of sheets and pillows rustling through the phone. "Really? Just my voice?"

"Don't even start with me." His voice came out more strident then he intended.

"Oooh. Bossy. I like it."

Oh God. He'd kicked off his work shoes when he came in the front door and he was sitting on the edge of his low futon, his legs crossed in front of him. "You like bossy?" he asked as he settled himself back onto his pillows and stretched his legs down the length of the Japanese bed cover.

She hesitated. "I don't know. I mean I liked it just then when you sounded bossy. I don't know if I like *bossy* as a thing. Do you have a red room or something?"

He burst out laughing. "No, I don't have a red room." She laughed along with him until they both simmered down, but he could hear from her breathy silence that getting sexy on the phone excited her.

Because he was a gentleman, he obliged her.

"Tell me what you're wearing. And touch yourself as you describe it to me."

"Oh, you know, I'm just . . . "

"And don't pretend you stayed in your old gray T-shirt. You changed into something soft and silky while I was driving home, didn't you?"

She inhaled and he felt his cock twitch in response. "Yes," she whispered.

"Are you wearing underwear?" It was such a simple straightforward question, almost amateurish. Almost.

But he was hardly the one in control—imagining Ellie alone in that big bed, with all those pillows and soft French sheets and nothing but a slippery sheath of satin between her and her throbbing—

"Yes," she whispered, her breath getting shorter. "I wanted . . . I don't know if I can talk like this, Luke."

"Sure you can," he said in his normal voice. Gentle and supportive. "It's just a different way for you to tell me what you want, but if you'd rather not, if it feels wrong . . . "

His voice trailed off when he realized she was humming her pleasure and he suspected she was touching herself while she listened to him talk and all semblance of his controlling the situation evaporated. "What are you doing?" he nearly croaked.

"You told me to touch myself . . . while we talked . . . and the sound of your voice is such a turn-on . . . "

He could have sworn he actually heard the pass of her tongue across her lips as she spoke. "Talk to me, sweetheart. Where are your hands?" As he asked about hers, he slid his right hand flat down his bare abdomen.

"My, um, my left hand is sliding over my hip and . . . " She moaned again.

"And?"

"And my right hand . . . " She lowered her voice. "I'm imagining my right hand is your hand . . . "

"Good." He undid the buttons of his jeans and pulled his cock free. "I'm imagining your hand is on my cock right now."

"Oh God," she whimpered. "Just like that. You just say the word *cock*?" But he could hear her desire had far surpassed her supposed shock.

"Yeah, just like that. I can say I've got my cock gripped in my hand and I'm closing my eyes and it's your hand I'm imagining, or maybe your lips—"

She made that little mewling sound again that made him want to rise over her and pound into her so damn hard she wouldn't be able to sit for days.

"Yes?" she asked. "My lips . . . go on . . . "

He laughed. A quick bark of pleasure. "I'm so glad you like that idea."

"Mmm. You have no idea how much I love that idea."

He heard her humming again. "Oh god. What are you doing now?"

She made a little smacking noise with her lips. "I'm just sucking on my fingers and imagining it's your . . . *cock* . . . "

He loved the way her voice caught on the word. "Will it feel good to have me in your mouth?"

"Mm-hmm."

"And your other hand is on your wet clit isn't it? Probably right through that silky fabric?"

She whimpered her agreement again and he could hear how her breath was ratcheting up.

"I'm so hard for you, Ellie. Can you sense it? How much I want you?"

She mewled again and he realized he was about to come—from the tiny sound of her sucking on her fingers and that little whimper of pleasure.

"Oh god, it's going to be so amazing—"

She cried out and he watched as his own release pulsed and shot in response to the sound of her breathy pleasure. He groaned into the phone, his eyes nearly rolling into the back of his head. "Ellie . . . " His voice was somehow strained and satisfied all at once. "Oh, god."

"Mmmm. That was delicious," she murmured in a throaty whisper.

He lay on the bed, half naked and wholly satisfied. "You okay?"

She sounded like she was falling asleep again. "Mm-hmm. So much better than okay. But now I'm sleepy."

"I wish I were there."

"Yeah, why aren't you?" She didn't sound accusatory at all, almost absentmindedly curious. As if she too had been wondering that very thing.

"I don't know. Some silly pact I made with myself to have a job and be responsible. To be normal."

"It wasn't silly. I'm glad."

"Good. I'm glad you're glad. You ready to go to sleep?"

"Mm-hmm. But I don't want to hang up. I love the sound of your breathing. Everything about you . . . " Her voice trailed off and the even breaths of sleep filled the air.

"You too," he whispered. "Sleep well, angel."

"You too," she whispered, already through a fog of sleep. "I'm so glad you got a phone."

"Me too. Bye."

"Bye," she repeated in an even softer whisper, but she didn't disconnect the line, and she could hear that he hadn't either. She felt like she was in high school. She just wanted to hear the sound of his breathing, to imagine a time, not too far in the future, she hoped, when he would be in the bed next to her after she came like that, and she could not only hear his breathing, but feel the warmth of it against her skin.

She missed that so much, the feeling of someone . . . *alive*. She felt the press of tears and whispered very low, "Good night, Luke," then disconnected the phone.

Oh god. She needed to talk to Lotta. She wiped at her slow tears and pressed the speed dial. Over the past three years, all of her post-traumatic-stress insomnia had been blessedly offset by the fact that her best friend lived three time zones away and the late-night phone calls were not late-night phone calls on Lotta's end.

"Hey. What's up?"

"Hey . . . " she croaked.

"Oh, no. Are you crying?"

"How can you tell that from me saying 'Hey'?" But she was hiccupping by that point so the aforementioned crying was now obvious.

"Did something happen with Luke? Was he a bastard? Doesn't he know that you are stupendous and—"

"Lotta!" Ellie was laughing (and still crying a little). "It's nothing like that. We're going down to the Keys for the weekend. He's great. I just—"

"What happened? Wait, let me put down all this crap and sit down."

Ellie listened and pictured Lotta setting down her bags full of organic vegan food (in environmentally responsible reusable tote bags) onto her reclaimed wood countertops. Then she heard the unexpected sound of a male voice in the background and

Lotta getting a kiss and muffling the phone to tell him she needed to talk to him later.

"Oh, God. Is Philip there?"

"It's no big deal. But yeah, of course, he's here. I mean, he's pretty much living here."

Ellie heard her cousin's indignant, "What do you mean by 'pretty much'?" Then a sweet shared laugh and then Lotta was back on the line.

"Sorry about that, I meant to say, *he's living here*," she said, almost giggling. She sounded happy in a totally unfamiliar, silly way. "He's gone into the other room, now. I promise."

"Oh man, you sound so happy lately."

"Did I not used to sound happy?"

"Of course, you are always, or always were, joyful and all that. But now you sound, I don't know, it sounds stupid, but you sound like you're frivolous . . . in love."

"I think I am. I mean," then with more certainty, "I am. I cannot quite get my mind around it, but I guess that's the point, right? Not getting your mind around it?"

"I think you're totally right."

"More importantly, what's going on with you?"

"Oh. You know."

"No."

Ellie exhaled out of her mouth in a long stream of air. "I just . . . Luke just called to say good night . . . "

"That sounds sweet . . . was it sweet?"

"Yeah, it was sweet all right."

"Ah. A little dirty phone sex before bedtime? I like it." She said *like* as if she were some sort of hustler.

"Stop!" But Ellie laughed and it felt good. It all felt good, actually. The coming. The crying. The laughing. She sighed.

"All right. Enough with the post-orgasmic sighs. What happened? What's been going on with you two since the murderous boar hunting trip—that you know I disapprove of in every way imaginable."

Ellie laughed again. "Tell me how you really feel."

"Fine. I will. Guns are not something that you can play with when you feel like it, Ellie. It's karma," Lotta warned. "Something's going to happen. I hate it."

"Oh you and your karmic warnings. The guns are all safely put away."

"Yeah right. Like the .357 you keep in your bedside table?" Lotta exhaled in frustration.

"We agreed to disagree about this ages ago. Drop it."

"Fine. But not fine," Lotta grumbled. "But fine. So tell me what happened when Luke made you cry?"

"Oh I don't know. He didn't make me cry. He's sexy as all hell. Just the sound of his voice is enough to get me all riled up."

"So far so good."

"And then, you know."

"Yeah, I got it."

"And then I said goodbye, but I didn't hang up, remember like we used to do in high school, you-hang-up-first-no-you-hang-up-first-no-you-hang-up . . . but neither of us said anything. And I was just listening to his breathing and I thought how I couldn't wait until he was really in my bed after, you know, and I could feel his exhale against my skin and have him . . . someone . . . *alive* . . . " Her breath caught and the tears came again.

"Oh, God, honey—it's so totally okay that you felt that, that you feel that."

"You think *everything* is totally okay!" Ellie tried to make it sound like a joke but it came out sort of screechy.

"Because it is! Or it usually is. I mean you're not hurting anyone. You're trying to get to know this guy, right? He knows about Rob and that this is all really tender for you?"

"Yes." Ellie tried to take deep breaths. "I am totally getting to know him. I mean I really do feel like I know him, even after only a couple of weeks. But I had this moment of feeling like I also wanted a warm body—any warm body—but I do want Luke specifically, I swear." Then her voice lowered, as if to herself, "I really *really* want him." Then back to her normal volume, "But I also miss—" She breathed again, a long exhale, that forced her to slow down. "—I miss having someone around. And I don't want to ever make him feel like I'm using him—"

"Okay. Stop right now. You are so *not* using him, Ellie. You have been in mourning—"

"Lotta—"

"What? You are so anti-death-vocab nobody even knows how to talk to you about it, even after all this time. Forget the semantics for a few minutes, will you please? And listen to me. You *are* ready, Ellie."

Ellie wept harder. "I'm so scared."

"I know you don't want to hear it, but I don't think you would have called me unless some part of you was ready to hear it. It's been three years since Rob died. You are allowed to move on with your wonderful, beautiful life. You are such a gift. You are attracted to this man. You called me the first day you laid eyes on him. There is something strong between you two."

Ellie's sobbing was getting louder and a bit more racking.

"Listen to me. It's going to be hard. Rob was so good. We all loved him, you most of all. But, *ach*, everything sounds trite and stupid, but it's trite because it's true. He would never have wanted you to be alone. Rob wanted to make you the happiest woman alive, remember?"

Ellie cried harder and pushed her face into the pillow to muffle the sounds.

"Oh, El. I wish I were there to curl up with you and watch a movie and eat popcorn in your bed and laugh." Her voice was soothing and sympathetic, and then all of a sudden she shouted, "Go away!"

"What?"

"Sorry. That was Philip coming back into the kitchen too soon. Sorry."

But then they both started laughing uncontrollably and finally settled back down after a few minutes of laughing and wiping away the tears after re-enacting ooh-sweet-fiancé-goo-goo-GO-AWAY!

"Oh, Lotta. You're the best!"

"Are you going to be able to fall back to sleep?"

"Yes. I think I've cried myself back into a state of pleasant exhaustion. Thanks, as usual for letting me get hysterical on your shoulder."

"Any time. You know that."

"All right. Maybe I'll call you from the Keys if I go for a walk alone or whatever."

"I seriously doubt I'll be hearing from you before next week, but if it makes you feel better to think so, then, sure, that would be great of you to call."

"Hey, what's going on with the wedding? Are you sure I can't do anything? It feels weird not to be all stressed about flowers and guest lists and catering like I was all those years ago."

"I promise it's all good. But you sound like my mother—who's completely confused that there aren't a million things to do. I called the inn and asked them if we could have a dinner for 24 people on September 15 and they were like, 'Sure.' Then I chose the menu off their website, ordered cases and cases of wine and champagne. Then we asked our friend Otto if he wouldn't mind bringing his cello to play a little something and that's about it. Am I forgetting anything?"

"Oh, Lotta. You are your mother's worst nightmare! Forgetting anything? Poor Sheila is probably lying awake at night worrying over the absence of monogrammed matchbooks, color-coordinated cocktail napkins, and a ten-thousand-dollar Vera Wang dress. You really are depriving her of one of her primary objectives in life."

"I know. It's cruel of me, but I promise I'm not motivated by spite. I couldn't imagine in a million years doing all that. But I did splurge on a dress." The independent-woman-voice had turned practically giggly. "Philip and I were walking around before dinner the other night and there's this beautiful tiny boutique that opened down the hill. This young designer guy just graduated from the Fashion Institute and hung out his shingle, and there was this creamy sexy silky spaghetti-strap dress in the window and the two of us sort of stopped and gaped at it."

"Oooh! How romantic!"

"I know! And then—" Lotta lowered her voice, "—and then Philip whispered in my ear that he thought I should wear that when we got married so he could picture peeling it off of me the entire time he was saying his vows."

"Oh my God. I think you'd better stop telling me these sordid tales of my cousin's perverted, sex-addled mind. I just don't see him that way. He's so preppy."

"Well, let's just say that's a bit of an affectation, shall we?"

"Lucky for you."

"Quite!"

"Okay. I think you have this whole wedding-planned-in-weeks thing down pat. Obviously, I'll take some photographs for posterity. But what about flowers? Can I do the flowers? I would love to come in a few days early and go to the markets in San Francisco with you then arrange big beautiful buckets of flowers everywhere at the inn. Can I do that?"

"Of course you can. That sounds perfect."

"Any color? I want to start imagining!"

"Oh, I don't know. Every color I guess . . . lots of passionate colors!"

"Oooh! I love the sound of that . . . coral reds and vibrant oranges and saffron yellows . . . I'm going to go look through some of my photos from Madras and get inspired."

"Are you bringing Luke?"

"I think I kind of want to. Is that okay?"

Lotta squealed. "Oh my god. I joked about it and now it's going to happen. Of course, it's *okay*. I'm so excited to meet him." She sighed. "That's the best news."

"Aw, thanks honey. Thanks again for everything. I always know I can call."

"I'm so glad. Go get some sleep and have a great weekend with Blue Eyes. Bye."

"Okay. Bye."

Ellie spent most of Friday going to a bunch of different grocery stores and packing up two big coolers with wine and food for the weekend. The inn where she'd booked them in the

Keys was pretty remote and she didn't want to have to drive fifteen minutes to deal with grocery shopping while they were there. The whole point was to feel completely transported.

Luke had called a couple of times during the day, to give her directions to his place and to confirm details, but they'd both been busy and signed off quickly, looking forward to the next day.

Friday night, Ellie took a long bath before slipping into bed and setting her alarm for six thirty.

She woke too soon, excited. After a while trying to get back to sleep, Ellie finally rolled out of bed and let her eagerness defeat her lack of rest. She decided to go for a swim to work off some of the nervous energy and headed out, unaccustomed to the deep pre-dawn darkness.

After forty-five minutes of swimming at a strong pace, Ellie paused at the shallow end of the pool. When she looked across the dunes to see the very first hint of dawn on the horizon, she had a momentary feeling she was not alone. She listened more intently to the sound of the wind rustling through the nearby dunes. A few fallen leaves from the large sea grape tree between her house and the Grummans made a scratching sound along the uneven coral tiles that surrounded the pool.

She sat perfectly still, crouched there like one of those freezing Japanese monkeys in a steamy mountain pool in *National Geographic*. Ellie had the same tingling sensations she'd had right before she made eye contact with that wild boar. She knew some creature was in those rushes, either watching her, or fearful for its own safety. Probably one of the foxes or raccoons that was always scurrying around the neighborhood, she thought, trying to calm her irrational fear.

She watched her step as she got out of the pool and then pulled the nearby towel quickly around her nakedness. She walked toward the house and nearly tripped on the step as she pulled open the sliding glass door. She went into the house and double-checked all the locks then lowered all the electric hurricane shutters.

Whenever she went away for more than a week or two, she liked to keep everything sealed up tight. It protected the artwork, primarily, but also served to let people know the place was closed for business, the alarm was on, and the cops were informed. But she didn't usually do it to go to the Keys for a couple of days.

This morning, though, something felt a little bit off.

Chapter 7

At seven forty five, after wending her way through the unpaved, sandy streets of a small, kind of ramshackle neighborhood (affectionately known as a county pocket), Ellie pulled into Luke's driveway. It was more of a parking spot, than a driveway, really. Luke's little house was so *him*: modest, immaculate, perfectly pared down. Exactly what it was meant to be.

Simple.

Ellie took a few minutes to look at the way the small white beach house looked so ideally situated: right on the ocean, tucked into a narrow lane, backing up to a great stand of overgrown Australian pines.

Modest.

She got out of her suddenly-too-fancy car and walked along the few coquina stones that served as a front walk, then knocked on the edge of the screen door. The front door was open and she started to look into the shadowy interior, then looked down at the vintage egret design that overlaid the screen door. Ellie was tracing the edge of the bird's head when she looked up.

"Hey," Luke said, standing a few inches in front of her, on the other side of the screen.

Ellie stood on the small porch and couldn't help the happy smile that spread across her face when she saw him standing there in a pair of shorts and no shirt. Through the screen, still in the shadows, he looked exactly like he had that first day she talked to him in the garage. He certainly hadn't turned any less handsome in the intervening weeks, that was for sure.

"Hi."

"Hi." He looked down at his half-dressed state. "You're a little early. I was putting the last few things in my bag and straightening up. Come on in." He pushed open the screen door and held it steady for her to pass by him into the house.

"No need to get dressed on my account," she said as she walked in. Almost as an afterthought, she paused to kiss the beautiful turn of his upper arm, on the soft underside where it was straining slightly from the awkward angle of holding the door for her.

His small intake of breath was all the welcome she needed.

Then she continued into the house, looking in every direction as if she were a real estate agent or property appraiser. "Wow! Great ceilings. Is that the original pecky cypress?"

Luke stayed at the door, recovering a shred of equanimity after that touch of fire on his arm, until he let the screen door slip slowly back into place. "Yes, it's pecky cypress. And Dade pine floors."

"It's really a great place. It looks tiny from the outside." She turned to look at him over her shoulder. "I mean, that's not an insult, it's a little house, right?"

He smiled at her worry. "Yes, it's a little house."

"But this ceiling in here is really something. And then what, one or two bedrooms?"

"Yeah, come here I'll show you." He reached out his hand to hold hers and oh how she loved the look of that, of him and his lovely, formal gestures. Even without a shirt on, he looked put together somehow . . . contained. He caught her looking at his biceps and she smiled guiltily, then put her hand in his and they continued down a tiny hall with three doors.

"Here's the bathroom . . . or shower room as they'd say in the U.K."

Ellie looked in at the vintage turquoise tile that ran about two-thirds of the way up the wall, and the matching sink and toilet. "Amazing. It's like a museum. I love it."

"Me too," Luke agreed, but he was staring at Ellie when he said it. "And then here's a tiny guest room, I guess, but I use it for storage." He gestured into a room that was neatly filled with a surfboard, a wetsuit, some fishing rods, and other beach paraphernalia. "And here's my room."

Ellie turned to follow him. "Oh, Luke, it's so peaceful." She looked up and saw exposed cypress beams like the ones in the living room—only they'd been stained a soothing gray—and then she looked down at the queen-sized futon atop several tatami mats.

In stark contrast to all that spare simplicity, an ornate Japanese quilt was folded neatly at the foot of the bed. Ellie walked over and knelt at the end of the bed to rub her hand lightly across it: intricate embroidery depicted peacock feathers and cranes and rivers and fairy tale misty mountains in rich sapphire and emerald and gold.

"This is so beautiful." Her hand stayed resting on the fabric, petting it lightly. "Let me guess, this is one of the things from your old life that made the cut?"

"Yes," he said. "I couldn't part with it. It was a gift from a very dear friend in Japan."

Ellie was nearly successful at suppressing the spurt of jealousy that came unbidden at the idea of some lover giving him this beautiful present.

"I lived with a family when I was studying there a few years ago. They gave it to me—and I couldn't give it up. The irony, of course, was that I'd gone there to study Buddhism and to finally rid myself of all my earthly shackles." He smiled and shrugged, as if not achieving enlightenment was one of life's little pitfalls. "But that's kind of the point, too, to become attached to the beauty of life, don't you think?"

"Definitely. I am so glad you never gave it up. It's too glorious to abandon. What if the next person who owned it didn't fully appreciate it? That would have been tragic."

"It would. Not to worry, I won't let that happen." He turned to his small black duffle bag that was almost full with neatly folded clothes and took out a black T-shirt and pulled it on over his head and then down, covering his lean muscled stomach. Ellie said a brief, silent farewell to his obscene abs, then looked up at his eyes, which were mocking her.

She gave him another sheepish grin. "It's a lovely view. And I'm sad to see it go. You caught me."

He walked the few steps toward her and pulled her up into a rough embrace, almost as if he were frustrated or angry. "I loved talking to you last night," he whispered close to her ear. "I've missed you, Ellie." He was pulling his hands through her hair and grabbing it in great clumps in his fists. "It's only been a few days . . . " He kissed the edge of her mouth. " . . . but I've missed your hair." He kissed her neck where it met her shoulders, then lifted her hair and kissed her nearer her nape. "I missed the smell of your neck." He kissed the edge of her ear then her cheek, then, *finally*! Ellie thought, he took her mouth in a demanding kiss.

She pushed herself up against him—wrapping her arms around his lower back, bringing her stomach against his, her breasts firm into his chest—trying to get as much of herself pressed to him as she possibly could. She felt herself opening to him. To Luke. Not to just somebody. But to this very specific, very delectable somebody.

She sighed. Out of relief or appreciation or gratitude, she didn't know; she simply sighed and welcomed him into her arms.

Luke felt the moment she gave herself over to it, to him. It was slight: the turn of her body, the pressing weight of her breasts, the press of her hands at his back. But there was nothing demanding or rushed or desperate—only the wonderful feeling of Ellie putting her body into his care. Putting her entire being into his care.

Some tiny alarm sounded deep in his mind. He'd failed in that department, more than once. His past record as a great protector was not clean.

"Ellie," he whispered, gently setting her away from him. "At this rate we might need to cancel the reservations in the Keys."

But she looked less urgent than he had imagined she would after that moment of shared fire. She looked beatific. Content.

"Oh, lord, Ellie." He inhaled slowly. "You are divine. Look at you."

"You are looking pretty heavenly yourself."

He tucked a strand of hair behind her ear then curled it around his index finger. "Let us go then . . . "

" . . . you and I . . . " She finished, then headed back out to the living room, calling lightly over her shoulder, "I'll get a glass of water then meet you in the car."

The drive down to the Keys was a snap. The Turnpike was nearly empty. Ellie hooked up her mp3 player to the car's sound system and played DJ while Luke drove.

She loved how he drove. It put her in mind of a man from another century driving a team of horses. He was alert, confident, in control, mindful. He used the car, but respected it. Loved it.

"What are you smiling about?" he asked, turning his attention briefly away from the two-lane highway. They had left the Turnpike a few minutes ago and were wending their way across Card Sound. Civilization slid away behind them.

"I'm smiling at how I am crushing on your manly driving skills."

He burst out laughing. "You're what?"

She felt like a fifteen-year-old girl. Expectant. Risible. Joyful. "I was thinking how handsome and adept you are at driving the car. You know, like a gladiator or a ship's captain."

He made an effort to keep his eyes on the road, but eventually turned and saw the blush of pleasure creeping up her neck and cheeks.

"Oh, Ellie." He shook his head slowly, his grip tightening on the steering wheel, then loosening. "I am none of those things."

"Well, of course not!" She swept away the looming tension as if it were nothing but a speck. "I'm only telling you what silly thoughts go through my girlish head."

What was she going to say? The truth? That she was starting to idolize him? That she was suffering from the world's most acute case of hero worship?

"Oh, I love this part!" she blurted, tearing her mind away from that dangerous territory. "This bridge always makes me feel like I am going to fly right off the top, soaring straight off into space, like *Chitty Chitty Bang Bang*."

The quick change of topic made her feel young and carefree again. She tried to force herself to remember Lotta's directive. Above all else, carefree!

Luke gave the engine a sexy rev as he began the steep approach. Ellie reached across and let her hand rest on the fabric of his shorts, stretched taut across his thigh. She wanted to keep it light, she really did. But he was so good, and she didn't see much point in pretending she felt otherwise.

Life was simply too short.

The Landings was more of a collection of houses that had been built in the midst of an old coconut palm grove than a typical hotel or resort. Each bungalow was a unique house, with its own kitchen and living room, and then one or two or three bedrooms depending on the size.

All told, there were only a dozen structures on the property, not including the main building that housed a small reception area, a nicely stocked honor bar, an intimate paneled dining room, and a library that was packed with what felt like a million well-worn paperbacks that were directly or indirectly about Florida and the Caribbean: Hemingway, John D. MacDonald, Marjorie Kinnan Rawlings, Carl Hiaasen, Susan Orlean, Elmore Leonard, Meg Cabot, Dashiell Hammett, Zora Neale Hurston, Ian Fleming, Roxanne St. Claire, Thomas Sanchez, Marjory Stoneman Douglas.

When Rob and Ellie had first happened upon this place, what they dubbed the-world-at-the-end-of-the-world, they knew they had discovered a hidden gem. When Ellie walked into that library, she thought they'd discovered a slice of heaven.

The owners, a British couple in their late-fifties named Denny and Joanna Billings, lived on the second floor of the Big House. Before the car came to a complete stop, the sound of their tires crunching over the crushed seashell lane having announced their arrival, Denny and Joanna were walking out of the Big House to greet Ellie and her 'new friend.'

"Oh, Ellie! Where have you been!?"

"What do you mean?" Ellie asked as she embraced Joanna in a warm hug. "I was just here in May."

"Well, that's simply too long between visits." Then Joanna turned to Luke as she kept Ellie's hand squeezed in hers. "Now introduce me to your new friend!"

Denny had finished introducing himself to and shaking hands with Luke and the two of them were standing with their hands shoved in their pockets, looking exactly like two unacquainted men are wont to look.

Ellie laughed at Joanna's coaxing tone and said, "Joanna Billings, please allow me to present Luke—"

In a barely perceptible move, Luke shook his head, a tic almost, that let Ellie know she was not to give the full rundown as it appeared in the family Bible.

She smiled wider, an expression that told him instantly his secrets were quite safe. "Luke McCormick. He moved to South Florida last year."

"Well, how wonderful. A Scotsman!"

Luke smiled at her knowing reference to his last name. "Ay, a Scotsman indeed," he said with a sexy Scottish burr lilting his voice.

"Denny, didn't we used to know some McCormicks in London? Other than the famous ones, of course," Joanna winked at Ellie.

Ellie continued to smile and made a mental note to pursue said-famous-McCormicks line of questioning when she was alone with Luke later.

"Leave the poor man alone, Jo! Let me help you with your things." Denny said, then proceeded to help Luke with the coolers and luggage.

He showed them to one of the larger three bedroom bungalows with double wrap-around porches that opened up directly to the wide, empty beach.

"Oh, Denny, this is way too nice! I reserved a one-bedroom. We can stay in one of the smaller ones!"

"Of course we're only going to charge you for the one-bedroom, Ellie, but it's only the four of us here this weekend, so why not spread out a little, eh?"

"Don't be ridiculous, of course I'll pay for it!" Ellie made Denny sound like he was the most absurd person she'd ever come across.

Denny looked at Luke and rolled his eyes. "Don't ever argue with that woman about finances. She's very hard to bend to your will." Then he spoke slightly louder to make sure Ellie could hear him as she wandered off toward the kitchen, "Especially when you're trying to do something nice for her!"

"I heard that!" she called back from the kitchen.

"Good!"

Luke smiled at their warm banter as he brought the second cooler to the kitchen.

Denny followed him into the small, practical room. "Okay, you two. Do you have everything you need?"

Ellie looked around at the familiar white wooden cabinets and well-oiled wooden countertops. "Looks great, Denny. I don't know how you keep it all up."

"Labor of love, of course. Nothing less."

"Of course." Ellie gave him a quick hug. "Thanks for everything."

"Do you want to have dinner with us one night? I caught some snapper this morning. Or at least come over for a drink. Say around seven?"

Ellie looked at Luke to confirm and then accepted both invitations. "Please tell Jo I'll bring a salad and some wine."

"All set then. Very good." Denny gave a quick wave and let himself out the screen door at the back of the small kitchen and stepped down to the path that led back to the Big House.

The slap-slap of the door as it fell back into place seemed to exaggerate the fact that Ellie and Luke were alone in the small kitchen. Ellie watched him as she leaned her lower back against the counter, the her fingers curled around on the edge. Luke walked a few steps toward her and she started to release her hold to reach out to him.

"Stay like that," he said, looking like he was going to devour her as he moved a few steps to come in close, but didn't quite touch her. Angling his shoulders, he bent to inhale the scent at her neck. She gasped when he rested one hand on the flat of her stomach, and the other caught at the back of her neck and tilted her face up to his. So. Slowly.

She was instantly in his thrall, but for some reason she couldn't help briefly thinking of her sex life with Rob—like their relationship overall, it had always felt so straightforward between them. They were golden. They were forthright. Touching. Orgasms. Talking. Laughing. It was all good.

But in this moment, she knew that sex with Luke was going to be something else altogether. Something profound.

Ellie felt a shiver of deep, almost frightening longing when he held her like that. Possessive. Protective. The way he was holding her made the heat in her center clench and ripple, and he hadn't even touched her there yet.

"Oh, Luke." His name escaped on a whisper of sheer ecstasy as he held her, then he was kissing her neck, sucking on the lobe of her ear, nipping at the soft skin beneath her jaw. When he grabbed the hair at her nape even tighter, she felt her muscles strain and give. Then he let his other hand reach beneath her T-shirt and caress the underside of her breasts.

The harsh tension pulling at her neck made the smooth, tenderness of his fingers against her soft, wanting flesh even more sensitive. The contrast—of his gentle back-and-forth-caresses around her heavy breasts (almost careless), and then the determined, fierce attention of his mouth (almost brutal)—was totally consuming and exasperating.

She arched into him and let her eyes roll back into a dreamy, transporting netherworld. Bliss.

And then he bit her earlobe, hard, at the exact moment he grazed the very tip of her breast with the softest touch. The paradox was maddening. She didn't know whether to beg for more (harder, faster at her chest) or less (slower, gentler at her ear).

A moment later he reversed the pleasure. He slowly licked at her ear, soothing that small hurt, and then unexpectedly pinched her nipple so hard she saw bright stars of some entirely new experience flash across the inside of her eyelids. He thrust one of his legs into the hot juncture at the top of hers, then pressed his strong muscled thigh against her throbbing center. She was overtaken almost immediately by the fierce, gripping waves of her orgasm.

Her body slammed into his.

He might as well have thrown her off a cliff. Just grabbed hold of her and hurled her into a storm of pleasure. Her eyes shot open and her arms flew up to grab around his neck, as if she were really free-falling off the side of a sheer drop. He captured her scream of astonished pleasure when his lips took hers in a thorough, powerful kiss—her satisfaction his to claim now.

She must have squealed or whimpered or made some sort of throaty sound of desperation.

"I've got you," he whispered, between more long slow kisses.

Finally, after the racking waves of pleasure subsided, she looked into his eyes.

"Are you okay?" he asked.

She bit down on her bottom lip and nodded, feeling as if she'd slipped past words and into some other world of mindless pleasure. Then again, it wasn't mindless: her body was still completely focused on being there with him, how they reflected off each other in some infinite loop of pleasure.

She started to shake her head slowly from right to left.

"No? You're not okay?"

"I . . . I'm almost beyond speaking . . . " she whispered. "I was just thinking that I'm sort of mindless, but then I thought *no*, so I shook my head no, because it's the opposite. It's totally acute. Every touch. Every nip. How good it feels to have you . . . to be with you like this . . . I thought it would be terrifying . . . after so long." She smiled and stared right into his eyes. "But it feels amazing."

"It does. But if we're going too fast—"

"No!" She laughed at how the word flew out of her. "No," she said more quietly, kissing him lightly on the lips then simply staring at him with that blissed out grin. What she felt was high and soaring and honest and not at all like something that needed to be held in check. She hoped her eyes could convey some of that, some of what she couldn't quite articulate, because even without words, it seemed perfect.

Luke stared at the glassy pleasure in Ellie's bright sea-green eyes, and tried to rationalize the delight that peered back at him. It's only sex. It's only lust. It's only . . . Luke bullshitting himself. He was totally in love with her.

He'd fought the wave of responding fire that had roared through his blood when she'd responded to him just now. Some part of his brain—he knew what part—was tearing to get out. He'd spent the past five years learning how to live a life of balance and stoicism. Before that, for five years after he'd left Kate, Luke had been reckless and stupid—sleeping with as many women as possible in order to prove to himself that sex could be meaningless, that the power Kate (and Desmond to a certain extent) had wielded over him was destructible. He'd needed to deaden himself to everything that reminded him of that insanity, especially physical intimacy.

But what he felt for Ellie was unstoppable, terrifyingly real, and undeniably intimate. He leaned his forehead against hers as he moved his leg gently away from between hers, and then loosened the fierce grip he'd forgotten he was still holding at the base of her neck. He toyed with silky strands of her long hair as it slid through his fingers, trying to ease both of them back to the present.

"Are you sure you're okay, sweetheart?"

"Mm-hmm." She hummed while fingering the hem of his shirt. "Are you?" She lifted her gaze to look directly into his eyes.

"I don't know . . . I mean, yes, of course, but . . . "

"Tell me." She rested her palm over his heart.

"I've been so closed off for so long—"

"I totally get that!" she interrupted, obviously trying to soothe his rattled nerves; the irony was not lost on him. "If it freaks you out," she started hesitantly, "this type of emotional . . . intimacy . . . or whatever, then you can . . . you know . . . I mean we can . . . we'll figure it out, right? But, just now, I felt like I had this glimpse of some raging part of you—"

"Oh, Ellie. I'm sorry—"

"—and I loved it," she blurted.

Their last words came out at the same time and then Ellie's low laughter followed. She grabbed at the hard muscles of his upper arms, as if to shake him back into reality. "I want you like that . . . that strong . . . that free . . . it was awesome."

"Ellie . . . " He tried to pull his gaze away from hers. This wasn't supposed to happen. Not with her. Not with anyone again. But especially not with her. She was pure. Beautiful. He had tried so hard for so long to detach, to free himself of all the psycho-sexual crap he'd dealt with in his marriage. Intimacy had been a path to misery—and with Kate that misery had been all tied up in their sex life. Yes, he'd been through years of therapy, but what had happened between them had cut so deep, Luke wasn't sure it ever really went away.

The memories assaulted him anew. The day he'd walked in on them—how Kate had let the sheet fall away from her full breasts, how Desmond had trailed one finger down her arm and stared at her profile as she stared at Luke, how she'd taken a minute to process that Luke wasn't going to shoot them right there on the spot. Kate's heated gaze was one Luke had never seen before—almost beatific. Glowing. He later came to understand she'd been radiating a feverish inner torment.

Kate had always told him sex was just a game, but that had only made it worse in the end, because it had never felt that way to him. And maybe that was both the problem *and* the solution with Ellie.

He took a deep breath and dragged himself back to the present. Maybe with someone who was actually capable of caring about him, who hadn't been so destroyed by the past—maybe then the aftermath of passion wouldn't leave him feeling empty and wretched.

Feeling sick.

Ellie watched him carefully. Probably trying to parse the different emotions that flickered across his face like a stippled silent movie: fear, shame, sadness, pain. There was a thread of *wanting* as well: a deep, banked fire, that he felt, that she must've seen.

"It's just me, Luke. Look at me," she pleaded quietly. "Whatever it is. It's okay. Even if it's not okay, or wasn't okay, it's okay now, right? Because it's me? It's us?" She brought her hands up to his cheeks.

He opened his mouth to speak, but nothing was there.

She continued softly, her thumb tracing his lips. "I certainly don't want to make you do anything that you . . . that makes you feel . . . oh, fuck, I don't even know what I'm saying. Just that I *love* how you make me feel, I guess, when we're both crazed with lust, or whatever." She tried to laugh but it came out like more of a croak.

Her smile was so hopeful. He wanted to see her like that, keep her like that. And he couldn't help feeling that she wouldn't look like that if he let her see that part of himself. He closed his eyes and she must've known that something just within reach was retreating away from them.

She exhaled slowly then forced her voice to buck up. "Okay, then. Let's unload the groceries into the fridge and then how 'bout a swim?"

He looked at her a moment longer. "Okay." And then he kissed her softly on the lips. "Thanks."

"My pleasure." She winked and slipped out of the circle of his embrace. "Let's get this put away and then check out the rooms upstairs before we head out."

She opened the first cooler and started unloading beers and orange juice and milk into the refrigerator. Luke shook his head then turned to put the non-perishable things into the cabinets over the counter where Ellie had been standing a few minutes before. He could still feel the heat emanating from where her body had been.

After a long swim in the sea, they made sandwiches and drank a couple of beers out on the porch, then Ellie got in the hammock that was strung between two nearby palm trees.

"They have an amazing library here, if you have any interest in local color. You should go check it out." Ellie held up a dog-eared copy of *Skinny Dip*, as the hammock swayed in a lazy rhythm. She was wearing a gauzy white cover up that did very little to cover her up, Luke thought ruefully. The blue ocean, the green palm fronds, the hot white sand, her red hair, the shadows of her breasts through the thin fabric of her top, all these disparate pieces swayed together, lulling him.

She watched as he stood on the porch contemplating her.

"Why don't you come lie down with me on the hammock?" Ellie patted the space next to her. "I won't bite."

He stepped off the porch and strode over. He had changed into a dry bathing suit after lunch and his bare stomach and chest reflected the play of shadow and sun beneath the palm trees. Ellie scooted over to make room for him and left one arm flung wide for him to rest his head on.

"Come rest for a while." she purred. Being a seductress was never going to be her thing, but it was still fun to try.

He looked suspicious and Ellie laughed.

"What? Do you think I am going to take advantage of you while you're asleep?"

He shook his head, then slowly lowered himself onto the hammock and settled his head on her soft upper arm. They adjusted their weights and positions to balance on the hammock, and then he relaxed completely into her.

She realized that she'd never seen him totally at ease when he was awake. He was usually too busy being adept and mindful. Within a few minutes, his steady breathing and the diaphanous murmur of the waves against the sand were the only sounds she heard.

She held her paperback open with one hand, then exhaled a contented sigh as one of his sleepy hands came to rest on her hip, and the hammock continued to swing at its easy pace. They stayed there for nearly two hours, in that quiet heaven, where only the two of them existed and everything felt safe.

Eventually it was time to get ready for dinner at the Big House, so Ellie kissed him awake and reveled in the burgeoning smile that spread across his face. He kissed her neck and then slowly opened his eyes. "Thank you."

She stared at him—at this powerful, barely contained man—and all she could see was tenderness, generosity, and humility. Now if she could just get him to see himself that way.

They headed back into the house and parted ways in the upstairs hall. With the two extra bedrooms, they had spread out, each taking a room of their own to shower and change.

Ellie was ready before he was, and went downstairs to the living room and picked up her book. She looked at him when he came down the narrow wooden stairs, ducking his head as he turned the corner landing. She smiled at how he moved, the angle of his shoulder, the dip of his neck, the strong tendons of his bare feet as he stepped, sure-footed down the stairs.

"I like you," she blurted.

He looked up from where he was walking and smiled back at her. "I like you, too." He came over to where she was sitting and kissed the top of her head and she felt a shiver run down the center of her spine, just from that little innocuous kiss.

"You want a beer now or should we go?" he asked.

Ellie put her book down on the small wooden side table that was really just a chunk of an old palm trunk that had been sanded and worn smooth. "We should probably head over. Let me grab the salad and the wine."

"Okay." Luke offered his hand and helped her from the deep armchair. She stopped for a second after she surged up, her face a few inches from his. Breathless. She leaned in and kissed him gently on the lips, then pulled away first, reluctantly.

"Best not to linger in your arms," she whispered. "I think."

She walked into the kitchen, the hem of her turquoise sundress swinging across her tan legs and the fabric around her hips moving with her stride. Luke rubbed his eyes and forehead. He stood in the middle of that simple, tropical room and tried to wipe away the encroaching desire. He felt it like something demanding that he ought to beat back. *She wants it, you fool.* She wants *that*, his restless, sexual self chided.

"Are you going to stand there beating yourself up all night or are you coming with me?" she called from the kitchen.

"I'm coming." He laughed as he said the words.

A few hours later they walked back from the Big House and their dinner of fresh fish, delicious green salad, and lots of crisp white wine.

Ellie felt light and buoyant, holding Luke's hand as they walked through the thick night. The gardenia bushes were in full flower and the exotic scents floated all around them.

"Isn't this great?" Ellie whispered.

Luke just squeezed her hand, letting her know he agreed.

"Did you have a good time tonight?" she asked.

He stopped in the path. She loved the way the silence and sense of isolation wafted around them, how they might have been on a deserted island.

"I'm having such a good time with you—so good I'm a little concerned."

"Oh, don't be. It's so gorgeous here, just feel the warm night air against your skin. Isn't it such a simple pleasure?" She rubbed the tips of her fingers delicately up and down his strong forearms, wanting to soothe him, but also wanting to touch him—*always* wanting to touch him it seemed. At one point during dinner, she'd had to sit on her hands to stop herself from touching him.

"Let's just focus on those, okay?" she suggested. "On the simple pleasures. Food. Sunlight. Water. Wine. The basics."

"Okay." The hard angles of his face reflected the changing moonlight, and the clear blue of his eyes shimmered when he turned his head to look up at the stars. "The night sky."

"Exactly!" Ellie gripped his arm and then held his hand. "The smell of that gardenia." They started walking toward their bungalow. "Your turn."

"The creaking of the palm trees."

"Yes!"

"The moonlight against your hair," he murmured.

"No!" She scowled like a disappointed school marm. "*Simple* pleasures . . . not anything to do with how good your hand feels in mine right now or how the smell of your skin makes me light-headed. *Not* those."

He laughed, and it carried through the trees and through the night as they walked into the back door and Luke set the screen door gently into place.

Ellie walked to the refrigerator and pulled out a bottle of water. "Want one?"

When he didn't reply she turned to see him staring at the back door. There was a hook-and-eye lock near the pitted metal doorknob. It seemed fairly ridiculous to secure it. Anyone could walk right in regardless.

"What's the matter?" She crossed the kitchen and stood next to him. "Do you want to lock the door?"

"It's not very safe here."

"We're in the middle of nowhere. Safe from what?"

"I don't know." He turned to look at her, and the look in his eyes nearly knocked her over, so full of deep, tender protectiveness.

"Oh, you're sweet. I considered bringing a gun, but then I thought it would be sort of weird coming here with a weapon in my bag. Maybe I should have?" But he wasn't coming up for her attempt to make a joke of it.

"I might stay up for a little while after you go to sleep." She could see he was going into soldier mode and that was the last thing she wanted.

"No!" He looked startled by her quick reply. "I mean, why? So you can watch over me? Don't be ridiculous. Come on. Let's go to bed. To *sleep*! Another simple pleasure. One of my very favorites. Sweet, innocent, restorative sleep."

She practically dragged him up the stairs. When they passed through the living room, he looked at the front door with a worried frown.

"Yes, anyone could walk right into that door too. Or they could climb through any of the windows, or shimmy up any of the porch columns and walk right onto the veranda outside our bedroom."

They went into the separate guestrooms to change. Ellie put on an oversized T-shirt and an old pair of boxers, brushed her teeth, and walked down to the larger room with the king-sized bed where they were going to sleep. Luke was rattling around in his bathroom (probably looking disappointedly at the absence of window locks). She muted the volume on her cell phone and set it on the bedside table. Old habits didn't die, even on vacation. She always slept with her phone within arm's reach. When she looked up from adjusting the pillows, Luke was standing at the foot of the bed.

"So, just sleeping right?"

"Just sleeping, you big baby." Ellie pulled back the bedcovers on his side of the bed in an exaggerated welcome. "Hop in."

He sat on the edge of the bed then finally swung his legs up and let his head fall slowly back onto the pillow. Ellie pulled the cool white top sheet over them, enjoying how it billowed and then settled onto their skin. "There, that isn't so bad, is it?"

Luke kept looking at the ceiling. "It's torture and you know it."

"Oh, stop being so dramatic. It's just sex. Or a lack of sex." She reached for the lamp and switched it off. The bright moon quickly offset the room's darkness.

Ellie snuggled deeper into the sheets. The night was warm and sultry, but she'd never been able to fall asleep fully exposed to the air. No matter how hot it was, she always needed that slight drape of comfort over her skin. "Can I hold your hand, or would that be incendiary?" she asked quietly, without irony.

Luke silently took her hand in his and brought her knuckles to his lips for a kiss, as if they were in a Victorian receiving line. Chaste.

"Mmmm. That's nice. Good night, sweet Luke. Sleep well."

And then, wonder of wonders, Ellie started to breathe in the unique scent of his skin and the fresh sheets and the ocean and that hint of gardenia and she somehow fell right to sleep.

Just after three-thirty a.m. her phone started vibrating. Her eyes opened slowly as she reached her hand clumsily around to stop the insistent buzzing. She sat up and answered the phone. Luke stirred next to her, but did not come fully awake.

"Hello?" her whispery voice cracked.

"Hi, Ellie. It's Steve from the PB Police—"

"Is everything okay?"

"Totally fine. I almost didn't even call, especially at this hour, but I just wanted to let you know that your house alarm went off. But it was probably a raccoon or something scratching its way into the garage again. I went over with my new partner Bob and there's no sign of any forced entry or anything at all. But I know how safety conscious you are."

Luke was awake by then and could easily hear the officer's voice. He rolled his eyes at Ellie's version of safety consciousness and she smiled back at him, then interrupted Steve.

"Thanks for calling me, Steve, I'm glad you did. You know you can always call me no matter what time of the night. And now that I have you on the phone—" She hesitated, kind of dreading that she had to say this part in front of Luke; the last thing he needed was to have his paranoia stoked. "Um, I saw someone a couple of days ago walking down the beach who looked a little . . . " She locked eyes with Luke. " . . . out of place . . . kind of military. Is there anyone with a security detail coming into the neighborhood this week?"

"Not at all. It's going to be really quiet for the next three weeks before the Mexican president visits. And they're going to be over on the lake side in any case."

"I'll call you next week. No worries. I'm sure it was just someone taking a long walk. Thanks so much again for calling. Bye, Steve."

"Bye, Ellie. I'll keep an eye on the place for you while you're away."

"Thanks. I'll be back Monday morning probably. I'll call you then. Bye."

She hung up the phone and slowly put it back on the table, turning her back to Luke and hoping (vainly) that he would have drifted back to sleep by the time she put her head back onto her pillow.

No such luck. He was furious. He was sitting upright with his back against the headboard, his legs pulled up, arms crossed over raised knees.

"So, you didn't think to mention some strange *military*-looking guy was sussing out your house—"

"He wasn't *sussing*! He was just taking a walk on the beach. He wasn't casing the joint or anything. But it's so quiet up where I live, especially at this time of year, that anyone seems out of place. Relax. He kind of reminded me of you, actually."

Luke shook his head as if he were dealing with a rank amateur. "What the hell is that supposed to mean?"

"I mean, I don't know, he was spare in his movements. I smiled when he passed and he looked . . . " Her voice trailed off and she turned her gaze out toward the ocean and the moon for a second, trying to remember. "Controlled. That's what made me think of you. His movements were really controlled. And then I thought I saw one of those little security coil things coming out of his ear when he had turned back south and was walking away from me."

"What did he look like?"

"Here I have a picture of him." She got out of bed and walked toward the other bedroom where she'd unpacked all of her things.

"You took a picture of him?" Luke was walking behind her. "Why would you do such a thing? What if he didn't want his picture taken and became violent—"

"Relax already! Jesus. It was just a snapshot, the silhouette as he was receding away from me. I was out there for hours taking pictures of this tidal pool—"

"Whatever. Just show me the picture."

Ellie stopped short, blocking his way into the smaller room where she had all her stuff. "Did you just 'whatever' me?"

"Did I what?" He was impatient and worried and wanted to see the picture already.

"You heard me. Did you just dismiss me with a *whatever*?"

"Oh, please. Are you going to get sensitive all of a sudden?" he snapped.

"I'm really mad at you right now, just so you know."

He loved how she could say it like that, without any malice. Just a fact.

Luke looked into the room and smiled at the crazy explosion of clothes on both of the single beds, creams and lotions on the small white wicker dresser, mismatched shoes on the floor, and two skimpy bathing suits hanging from the closet doorknob.

"Nice unpacking," he teased.

"Don't try to make small talk. I'm still mad. Be quiet while I get my camera." After she'd pulled it out of the tote bag, she sat on the end of one of the beds and started scrolling through the digital images.

Luke tried to sit next to her but she used one elbow to keep him away. "Back off."

He folded his arms and stood a few feet away, waiting for her to get to the photo. She slowed when she came to the series of tidal pool images, and started looking at them objectively, aesthetically.

"This one's pretty good, actually." Her head tilted to one side and then the other, analyzing the composition. "I might want to print some of these up on a larger scale and see how—"

"Ellie. Are you *trying* to aggravate me?"

"A little. Probably yes." She looked up at him and stuck her tongue out at him.

He burst out laughing. "How old are you, twelve?"

"I turned thirteen last week, thank you very much." She smiled a reluctant half-smile. There was no way she could stay mad at him for being concerned about her. But that "whatever." Ugh.

"Okay. Here he is." She gestured for Luke to sit next to her on the bed after all.

"Are you sure I'm allowed to sit down now?"

"You're on thin ice, mister. Sit."

He sat next to her and put one of his hands under hers so they were both holding the camera.

"Okay, go to the next one," Luke said slowly. He looked for about twenty seconds at the small screen. "Okay, the next." Another long look. "The next one." Then he breathed in. The picture that showed the profile filled the screen. "Can you zoom in on his face?"

"Sure. Here." She pushed a few buttons and the screen zoomed in, blurry, then the pixels reverted to stark clarity.

Luke tried to take the camera out of Ellie's hands, to get a closer look, but she resisted. She never let anyone hold her camera. Ever.

"May I look at it please?" he asked politely.

"Yes, but I . . . I don't like other people holding the camera. It's like my whole professional or creative life or something. Can't you look at it while I hold it?"

He looked at her again, and she felt a smashing desire to kiss him. He cleared his throat. "Sure. Sorry, I didn't mean to get grabby."

"And I didn't mean to be tightfisted. It's just a quirk."

"It belongs to you. You should be protective."

"Thanks," she said quietly, holding the camera toward him so he could see. "Do you think you know him?"

"Yes. I think I know him." The simple words were loaded. "I don't think I do. I do. Know him."

"What a small world?"

He smiled sadly at her levity, then shook his head.

"So . . . you don't think it's a coincidence."

"No, I don't." He kept staring at the image.

She finally broke the silence. "Who is it?"

"Desmond Cresswell . . . it's my ex-brother-in-law. Ex-best-friend. Ex-everything I've been trying to leave behind for the past ten years." He raked his hands through his hair and exhaled. "Let's go downstairs and make some tea . . . " His voice trailed off.

"Is he bad?"

"Yeah . . . he's bad." Luke gave her a small, sad smile and then his attention was drawn back to the camera. "May I?" She nodded and he reached over to press the arrow that scrolled back to some of the still lifes she'd taken of the tidal pool.

"These are amazing, by the way, not that I know the first thing about photography, but they're really beautiful."

"Thanks." She tried to see what he was seeing, to look objectively at the lines and colors and to perhaps get a glimpse of what appealed to him. "I like them, too. They're different from what I was doing before . . . " Her voice trailed off.

"Have you ever shown your work?" He kept scrolling and looking and it was easier to talk to him without him looking at her in that piercing way of his. She suspected he was purposely not staring at her for just that reason.

"Yes. But not since Rob died."

He let the ensuing silence be and she was grateful for that too.

Then he paused at one of her favorite shots—the light made everything jewel-like and the small orange shells were almost neon. "I love this one," he said softly.

"Me too." She rested her head on his shoulder and relaxed into him. "I love that you love it."

He turned and kissed her, a sweet hello kiss, nothing more. But it was everything, how close and gentle they were with each other. How much he wanted to protect her and free her all at once. "You'll start showing again when you're ready. Or not." He smiled and let go of the camera, so the full weight of it was back in her hands. It felt heavy. She'd actually liked the feel of him holding some of that weight.

She sighed like the silly lovestruck girl she was, then turned off the camera and put it back into its case. When she looked up, Luke stood waiting for her by the door to the hall.

"I don't really want to go downstairs and make tea." She got up and walked over to him. "Can we just go back to bed and talk there?"

"Sure. Come on." He stretched out his arm and she folded herself into him. He stood there hugging her for a few dreamy minutes, the cool wood floor against the bottom of her feet contrasting with the warmth of his embrace.

Eventually, he turned her toward the room where they'd been sleeping. They settled back under the covers and faced each other across the narrow expanse of pillows.

"So. Spill it," Ellie said.

Luke exhaled, then started talking slowly. "So, when I was eight my father remarried. He had three sons with his second wife. Their names are Ethan, Michael, and Trevor. Even before that, I was nothing more than a menace as far as Father was concerned. When he had his new young wife, that's when I was sent to live with my mother's side of the family. In Wyoming."

"I know about Wyoming. Who's the guy in the photo?"

"I'm getting there. He and I used to work for the same . . . company, I guess you'd say, and now he works for my half-brother, Ethan—or at least he did the last time I was in touch with either of them, at Kate's funeral five years ago. He's Kate's brother." The way he said it made Ellie's heart constrict; everything felt too close and complicated all of a sudden.

"Okay," she breathed out the word. "Why don't we start at the beginning? What happened when you moved to Wyoming?"

"So. My father had his new wife and soon his new family and I was not . . . a part of that. I think for a long time after that my father didn't even acknowledge my existence. I mean, of course his wife knew me, knew he'd been married before—they were all living off my mother's fortune for chrissake. I mean, it was his money, I guess, after my mom died. I get that."

Ellie didn't miss the bitterness and Luke's rapid effort to conceal it.

"But I was really just a nuisance. A reminder of a chapter that was well and truly finished. So they sent me—no, to be fair, they *asked* me if I wanted to go live with Uncle Grant on his ranch. But, just so we're clear, I don't think that's really the type of decision an eight-year-old boy should have to make, or more importantly, be forced to stick to . . . " *when he calls home in the middle of the night, crying for his Scottish nanny and his favorite Scottish food and his bed and his few toys*. He didn't see the point in giving Ellie that whole sob story.

But she must've seen the loss in his eyes. She brought her hand up to his cheek and kissed him softly on the lips.

"What was that for?" he asked.

"Just for you. For that little eight-year-old you."

Her tenderness made him sort of crazy. And then furious. He wanted to roll around in it, and then he wanted to tear her to pieces for pitying him.

She put her hands back together under her own cheek, in that way she did, as if she were listening to a long and engaging story around the campfire, which, Luke figured, she kind of was. "So? Go on."

"So Grant Allerton was this sort of stereotypically eccentric guy from the Northeast establishment. Recited Euripides. Knew baseball statistics from the bush leagues. And loved horses. When he got back from World War II he just sort of checked out of his whole Boston Brahmin upbringing. He bought a ranch near Sheridan and never went east of the Mississippi again. He's my mother's uncle, actually, but I always called him Uncle. He was the much younger brother of my grandmother—and she's the one who really rocked the boat."

"Oooh, good. Who was she? Some reckless flapper?"

Luke shook his head, but loved that Ellie could make his messed-up family seem somehow worthy of a racy novel. "Okay, let me see if I can get this straight for you . . . my mother's mother—my grandmother Alicia Allerton—went to France for her whatever-you-call-the-year-after-boarding-school when rich American women between the wars would go to Europe and learn about art and food and wine, and if everyone was really lucky, find some aristocratic, preferably titled, adoring husband.

"Alicia's problem was that she fell madly in love with a young winemaker in Bordeaux who had abandoned his family of high position and fortune—to start his own vineyard. To add fuel to the Brahmin fire back in Boston, he was Jewish."

"I feel like I should get popcorn. This is *really* good," she said.

"I'm glad you find the trials of a generation so amusing."

"I'm not amused in that way and you know it." She held her lips in a flat line. "I love hearing about where you came from and the people who made you *you*."

He took a deep breath and went on. Whenever she started a sentence with *I love . . .* he got a bit jumbled. "Anyway. So Alicia married against her family's wishes. She was disowned and then she and Gerard lived in Bordeaux in the 1930s and basically, according to family legend, they really loved each other and they were great. They built the wine business. They thrived. They had a son and three daughters, the oldest of the girls was my mother, Diana Rothschild."

"I figured that surname was going to be part of the punch line. So the young rebellious winemaker eventually made a proper go of it, huh?"

"Yeah, you could say so."

"Okay. So far it sounds like a bed of roses and all that."

"Things went a bit thorny in the 1940s, as you might imagine."

"Oh, I'm so sorry. I didn't mean to joke about it."

"It's all right. I mean, awful. But I know what you meant. Somehow they managed to survive during the war. I think the wine kept them alive. Giving it to all the troops—on both sides. I don't know if that ultimately makes them collaborators, but they stayed alive. Anyway, they made it through, and then in the late 50s and early 60s my mom and her sisters became these sort of It Girls in Paris. One of them married a wild, dissolute French publisher—and they had my cousin, Jérôme de Villiers. You'll meet him at some point."

"I think I've heard of him—isn't he some ne'er-do-well playboy or something?"

"Yeah, he projects a kind of wild, Euro-trashy image for the press, but he's great in real life. You'd really like him."

"If he's related to you, I'm sure I'll like him."

"I wouldn't be so sure about liking all my relatives. They're not all that great."

She rolled her eyes. "Fine. They're not all great. So back to your mom?"

"Right. So anyway, my mom was apparently all glam and big eyelashes and she had this wild independent spell in the fashion industry in the early 60s and then she met my father when she was modeling in London." He sighed and stayed silent for a bit. "He was this penniless Scotsman with a crumbling castle and an ancient pedigree—and they had this zany love-at-first-sight story. All her money and his, well, I don't know, his untitled nobility I guess. Apparently. I've seen pictures and what have you, but it's so impossible for me to imagine my father loving anyone but himself."

"Mmm-hmm. We're getting to the you-part. Right?"

"Yes." He smiled at her clamoring for his arrival into the story, into the world, then frowned a bit. "So then, the me-part. It seems sort of medieval in the re-telling, but I guess my parents were at their place in Scotland and my mom was eight months pregnant and she went into early labor and, well, it was bad. They got me out, but it was a mess, and my mother only lasted a few hours. My nanny always used to tell me how happy Lady

McCormick was that I'd made it. There are, or were, a couple of black and white snapshots of her holding me, that I vaguely remember finding in my father's desk when I was a boy. She looked dark and beautiful and exhausted, almost as if her job was done, and then she just sort of left the earth."

Ellie wanted to crawl all over him. She wanted to take him into her arms and wrap herself around him somehow. All that stupid talk when they'd first met, about how he'd never missed his mother because he'd never known her. She reached one arm across his chest and one leg across his hips, sort of pinning him to the mattress.

"And then it was, I don't know." He shrugged, as if he could shrug off the memories. "My father was pretty much lost. But not in a way that anyone could sympathize with him. When he was really going off the deep end, my mother's parents tried to get custody of me, to raise me in Bordeaux, but my father wouldn't hear of it and English law was in his favor. And of course my mother's vast fortune also went entirely to Father. It's not the money I really care about, or care to talk about, or whatever, but my father went sort of berserk with the finances after she died. He would alternate between living like a hermit, holed up in one of his estates in Scotland or Ireland, and then he'd go spend enormous sums on yachts or Venetian masquerade balls or dangerous trips up the Amazon."

"Oh, Luke." She squeezed him again.

"I know. How terrible for me to be dragged to Venice and Kenya and Corfu as a child, right? Such deprivation."

"Stop it. None of that matters to a little boy without a mother. Or a father, really, for that matter."

He pulled her closer. "You're right. It was pretty dreadful, from what I can recall. But once I got to Wyoming, it all turned out okay. Nobody there gave a damn about fortunes or fathers. I was just some scrawny kid with a weird accent who barely spoke normal English. I went to the public school in Sheridan. Uncle Grant let me start driving when I was ten; he said driver's licenses were another example of government getting too big by half. Grant also helped me stay in touch with my grandparents in France. After that first year in Wyoming, I always got to spend the summers in Bordeaux with them, so I had that connection to my mom's side of the family."

"Oh, that's so good. Are they still alive?"

"No, but my Uncle Michel, my mother's older brother, runs the whole wine business and he's always been really great about making me feel welcome."

"Oh, I'm so glad." She couldn't help envisioning summers in Bordeaux . . . with Luke.

He smiled knowingly. "You want to go there?"

She nodded sheepishly. "I like you for other reasons, but yeah, duh, I totally want to go hang out in Bordeaux and hear you yammer on in French and drink insane Pomerols. Who wouldn't?"

He kissed her forehead and she burrowed into his neck and smiled while she kissed him there. He sighed happily and she reveled in her ability to make him feel that, to make him happy. She took one last delicious inhale of him, then rested her chin on his chest and looked into his eyes. "So then what happened? How did you meet Kate?"

He shook his head to clear it, then continued. "So, I spent my teen years in Wyoming, dismantling and rebuilding every machine and engine on the ranch. The public school was okay, but I think it was Grant treating me like an adult ever since the time I arrived on his doorstep at the age of eight that really constituted my education. He spoke different languages to me whenever he felt like it. Greek. Chinese. He made me memorize and recite lengthy passages of Ovid and Aeschylus." Luke blinked at the memories. "I graduated from high school when I was sixteen."

The sound of his voice was wonderfully soothing and Ellie felt sleep returning. She looked at the clock and saw it was nearly five. "I'm really sorry about your mom." She spoke through a yawn.

"Me too."

"Tell me more tomorrow, okay, about the guy in the photograph? And summers in France. I want to hear about summers in France . . . " Her voice finally trailed off.

"I will." The last thing she remembered, he gently re-settled her back on her side of the bed, then he kissed her shoulder and reached across her nearly sleeping body to turn out the light.

The next morning Ellie felt lazy and languid. She opened her eyes slowly. She'd turned her back to Luke at some point in the night and rolled over quietly to look at him while he slept. His dark hair, just starting to gray at the temples, was in a sexy, tousled mess. She squeezed her flat palms between her thighs to prevent herself from running her hands greedily through that hair. She steadied her breathing and just stared at him. The firm cut of his cheekbones, the turn of his jaw. His lips were amazing, curved and even fuller in the relaxation of sleep.

She stared at the pulse in his neck and felt something kick hard against her chest. If she had wanted someone *alive*, as she had been saying to Lotta, she had certainly found him. He was so alive he was practically on fire. Ellie was beginning to believe that Luke had a heart that pounded harder than even he was willing to admit.

She'd loved hearing all of his family history and tried to imagine how the different physical parts of him had come together. Did he have his mother's nose? His father's eyes? His grandfather's hands?

The soft shafts of morning light were still gentle, but hinted at the fierce heat that would soon take over the day. Ellie wanted to capture that play of light and shadow across Luke's angular cheekbones. She slipped out of the bed and into the other room to retrieve her camera, switched off the shutter-sound, then tip-toed back to where he slept.

She was momentarily reminded of all the pictures she'd taken of Rob while he slept, when they'd been in India and she'd first started taking her photography more seriously. It was so much easier to figure out angles and depth and light and color when your subject was blissfully unaware. She succeeded in fighting back the bittersweet tears that nearly sprang free at the memory.

Ellie stretched her neck and looked up to the ceiling, letting her hair hang down her back, swallowing back the prick of emotion. She took a slow, cleansing breath, then began to look at Luke through her lens.

The wrinkles in the sheets, the light spray of hair on his sinewy forearm. His pulsing neck. She spent a while shooting close-ups of his neck and shoulder, with those intimate turns and corners of bone and skin. The camera kept her safe, created a barrier that prevented her from burrowing into those inviting little hollows of pleasure. She moved down his body, chastising herself for how badly she wanted to pull the sheet away from his waist.

He was sleeping on his side, so she focused on the turn of his hip under the folds of white linen. In the abstract it was very similar to a dune in the Sahara, she thought. Sloping, shadowy, mysterious.

She moved down toward the end of the bed where he had kicked one foot out from under the sheet, the very tip of his toe hanging off the edge of the mattress. She zoomed in on the bottom of his foot, reminded of Michelangelo's *David* and how much she'd loved the statue's feet—the strength and purpose and solid perfection of those Renaissance toes.

"What are you doing?" Luke asked, his waking voice gravely, as he wiggled his toes to get her attention.

"Thinking about the first time I went to Florence." She smiled and put down the camera on the dresser across from the bed, then turned back to look at Luke as he woke up. "Good morning to you."

He was rubbing the tough palms of his hands into his eye sockets. It looked like it hurt.

She walked over to his side of the bed and nudged him in a bit to make room for her. She put her hands on his wrists and took his hands away from his face. "Don't be so hard on yourself."

He let his hands rest at her waist. She started gently massaging his eyebrows with her thumbs, then his temples, then lightly along the bridge of his nose and back across his cheeks. "There, that's better."

She let the pad of one thumb trail across that lovely, full lower lip. The touch was both a temporary farewell and an invitation.

"Simple pleasures, remember?" he prompted.

"No. I don't remember that at all." She ran one finger around the curve of his ear then let it trail down his neck, remembering all the pictures and details she had seen there a few moments before. "I took a lot of pictures of this . . . right here . . . " Her index finger traced a line near one lean muscle that ran the length of his neck. She felt the frisson of pleasure that tripped through him at her touch, and her nipples hardened in quick agreement.

"Ellie . . . "

"Luke . . . I don't want to wait . . . I don't want to talk about it . . . what if you get run over by a bus tomorrow?"

"There are no buses here . . . " But he was touching her now, tentatively caressing her breasts through the thin fabric of her T-shirt with his thumbs. She had to bite down on her lower lip to prevent herself from crying out, but a strained little sound escaped her throat.

"Please touch me," she said. "Soft. Hard. However you want. I want . . . "

Then he really was touching her and her voice failed her. His thumbs were circling her nipples and he was staring through the fabric, at how her body responded to his attention.

She arched her back and thrust her chest toward him, letting her head tilt back in a state of utter abandon. She didn't care about anything it seemed. Modesty. Propriety. Manners. She didn't care about anything except his hands on her.

"You're so gorgeous." He leaned toward her and lifted the T-shirt at the same time, then brought his lips to the bare skin of her right nipple. She couldn't repress the cry of pure delight that flew from her mouth.

Her hands flew up to his neck, pulling him more firmly toward her. She bent over his head as he licked and sucked and taunted her. The heat that pooled in her core was a quivering independent thing. Demanding. Almost angry.

"Luke . . . stop . . . "

He looked up quickly, his lips moist and his eyes glazed. "What is it?"

"I mean, unless we're going to, you know—" She leaned in and kissed the corner of his mouth then retreated a few inches. "I feel like a teenager saying this, but unless we're going *all the way*, I want to stop. I have a pounding need to feel you inside me, and if we're just going to fool around, I think we should stop. Or else I'll just be frustrated the rest of the day."

He leaned into her again, letting this forehead rest against her chest, slowly lowering the cotton of her shirt back over her stomach.

Dammit! she thought bitterly. *I didn't mean for him to actually stop!*

"You're right. I need to be more prepared," he said.

For some reason that irritated her. "Honestly. Prepared for what? We're not doing an Everest ascent. It's just sex." She was frustrated by unfulfilled lust and the hottest man she'd ever laid eyes on was lying *right there*—so she might've sounded a tad peevish.

He looked at her sideways and she regretted her tone immediately.

"I don't think you and I will ever have 'just sex,' do you?" he asked quietly.

She shook her head. "No, I don't." But her brain was completely at odds with her wanting, eager body. She breathed out a heavy sigh, and then let her hand start wandering down his stomach, under the sheet, toward his hard erection. "But . . . "

He grabbed her wrist when she reached the waistband of his trim, fitted boxer shorts. "Please, Ellie. We both know it's going to be major, so let's just, I don't know . . . honor that? Okay? I'm going to need a little more time to get my mind around . . . everything."

"Grrrrrrrrr!"

"Did you just growl at me?" he laughed.

She growled again and shook her head at him, then smiled. "Okay, Mr. Honorable. I know you're right, but I'm still allowed to be frustrated. Let me make a big breakfast and get some physical satisfaction from food, at least." She got up from the bed and Luke let his head fall back onto the pillow with a theatrical drop. He covered his eyes and groaned.

"And by the way," Ellie continued blithely, standing at the foot of the bed, "it's totally unfair that you got to see me naked coming out of the shower that time and I haven't, you know," she looked meaningfully at his erection, "seen you."

He split his fingers so he was peeking at her through the opening in his hand, partially covering his face. "Seen me?"

"You know, in the buff. Naked!" She turned and walked toward the door.

"You want to see me naked?"

She halted and pivoted around to face him. "Duh."

"Aren't you afraid you'll be so overcome by mindless passion you won't be able to control yourself?"

"I think I'm up to the challenge." She crossed her arms to show how tough she was.

He smiled the best quirky, seductive smile Ellie had ever seen, moving the hand from his face and then slipping it slowly across the ridged planes of his bare stomach. She shook her head and stood there looking at his firm chest and toned muscles below.

"You want to watch me get off?" he offered, taking her completely off-guard.

Her eyes flew from where she'd been watching his hand roam across his abdomen, up to his eyes. "Uh. Yes? Is that allowed?"

He chuffed a laugh. "I don't know what the hell's allowed. I just want us both to be totally comfortable around each other. Seems sort of ludicrous, in hindsight, to put a number of days on when that will be."

She was watching his hand again. He was moving it provocatively—taunting her—touching the dusting of hair right above the waistband of his underwear with the tips of his fingers.

Her mouth was dry. Her mind was blank. "Yes . . . ludicrous."

"Ellie?"

"Mm-hmm?" She kept watching that hand and licked her lips.

He laughed again. "Okay. Here goes nothing." He lifted his ass and shucked off his underwear, settling himself back into the middle of the bed. He plumped up some of the pillows so his face was angled better to look at Ellie where she remained frozen by the doorway.

"You okay?" he asked.

"Great," she croaked. "Go on."

The sight of his strong fingers wrapping around his hard shaft made her whimper. Then he started a damnably slow rhythm. It was so beautiful to watch his patience, his even pace. She knew he was watching her, could feel his eyes on her, but she couldn't look away from that sure hand. She was turned on—obviously—but she was also desperate to see what he liked, the pressure he applied, where and how he touched himself.

She couldn't stop her tongue from roaming lazily across her lips, imagining her mouth taking the place of his hand. The thought must have ricocheted from her brain to his—at least she was pretty sure she hadn't said it aloud, but he answered anyway.

"I want that too."

Then his hand pumped harder and his thumb swiped at the pre-come at the peak of his erection and then he whispered her name, like he had on the phone the other night when they were fooling around, and after a few more pulls, she whispered his name and watched him spend on his stomach right as she did.

At some point during his exhibition she must have stopped breathing. She inhaled with a *whoosh* when her eyes finally returned to his and she caught the tender, satisfied expression in his bright blue eyes. He looked like a big cat after a long hunt, languorous and satisfied.

"Happy?" he asked with that lazy grin.

"Luke," she whispered again.

"I know. We're going to be something together, aren't we?"

"Yeah, we are." She shook out her hair and took another deep breath. "Okay. Wow. I think I'll go make that breakfast now."

"Sounds good. I'll be down in a minute."

"Okay." She wandered off shaking her head, as if she'd encountered a mirage and wasn't quite sure it was real.

They spent the rest of Sunday hanging out on the beach in a lazy stupor. Sometimes swimming, sometimes lying in the hammock, holding hands, having a few beers, joking, touching each other easily. Ellie loved being in her tiniest bikini and watching Luke's eyes cloud over. It was totally blissful. There was nothing in the world, no one but the two of them.

By mid-afternoon he'd dozed off alongside her on the hammock again, probably because he was up all night worrying about the absence of high-level security, Ellie thought. By five o'clock, very reluctantly, she started to prod him awake.

"We probably need to head back soon. Unless you want to get up really early and drive straight to work in the morning?"

His eyes were even more blue right when he woke up, if that was scientifically possible. Whether it was the reflection from the sea or the late afternoon sun, Ellie felt like those blue eyes were electric.

"I've never had an addictive personality," Ellie whispered, loving the feel of his warm, calm body in her arms, the sway of the hammock cradling them like two peas in a pod. "But you make me want to run away from everything and consume you until I'm drunk with you."

Chapter 8

He leaned into her and kissed her neck, then put his hand on her bare hip. He knew she was purposely torturing him by prancing around more-or-less naked in these tiny bikinis, but who was he to stop her? It was a sweet, sweet torture.

"I know exactly what you mean."

"Can we just . . . make out for a while?" Her fingers were trailing lightly through his hair. She leaned in and her mouth met his, almost cautiously. She whispered between brief kisses, "You don't even have to do anything . . . just let me . . . " She kissed down his neck to his chest, then leaned up on her elbow, causing the hammock to tilt at a perilous angle.

They both laughed as they nearly fell off. Luke sprang free with his characteristic coordination and strength, quickly turning to catch her before she went face down in the sand. They panted and smiled at the near miss, Luke holding her upper arms firmly to steady her. Then her voice went low, her breathing slowed.

"I mean it. I want you. Right now. Major. Minor. Serious. Frivolous. I don't care." She grabbed at his hair, feeling the hard strength of his skull beneath her hold, and pulled his mouth to hers, demanding satisfaction.

"You're sure?" he gasped between kisses. He groaned and reached his hands around to the curve of her bottom and lifted her up. She flung her legs around his waist and he carried her into the house. She kissed him with all the fire and abandon and desire that had been roiling between them since that very first look at the garage.

"I'm so sure. Are you?"

"Yes," he breathed at last, staring into her eyes, and knowing it was finally true.

She pressed her nearly naked body against the firm, hot strength of his stomach and chest. She wanted to be soldered to him. She kept saying stupid meaningless begging words, demanding words as they stumbled into the house. "Yes . . . do it! . . . please . . . dammit! . . . god . . . yes! . . . Luke . . . "

She vaguely heard the sound of a small spindly table by the front door toppling over when Luke must have shoved it out of the way as he took them through the front door with the force of an ancient invader. He carried her upstairs, his firm hands kneading her ass, keeping her maddeningly close to his powerful erection.

The sunscreen and sweat glued them to each other. When they got to the bedroom, Luke held her against him with the palm of one hand as he yanked the covers back off the bed, then settled her, suddenly gentle, down onto the center of the cool white sheets.

He stopped for a moment, staring into her eyes.

"Come *on!*" she said, a throaty, happy command.

He leaned in and kissed her.

She would have laughed out loud if such a thing were possible. She was so totally overjoyed. Her body was singing, rising up to his, gripping him, pulling at his bathing suit trunks.

She felt tears come to her eyes and he stopped to give her a little non-verbal check-in.

She smiled through the emotional mist. "They're from joy, I promise."

He lifted his torso away from hers for a minute, both of them smiling at how it felt like he was peeling himself off her. He stared down at the tiny black triangles of fabric that passed for her bikini top. "What is that anyway?"

"What?" She tilted her chin to see what he was talking about, her already-hard nipples tightening another notch at his focused attention.

He put the tip of his finger at the edge of the tiny top. "This. Is it meant to be a bathing suit?"

She arched her back and closed her eyes. "It's whatever you want it to be, as long as you get it off my body as quickly as possible."

He let his finger dip under the stretchy fabric, still warm from the heat of the day's sun and her skin. When his fingertip grazed her nipple she cried out.

"All right, then," he said matter-of-factly. "Let's get you taken care of."

He had the scraps of fabric off and his head settled between her legs before she'd even thought to open her eyes. He licked and kissed her hot center and within minutes a crashing orgasm whipped through her like a firebrand. She shrieked at the speed, power, and unexpected ferocity of her response.

"Luke!"

Somewhere in there, he must have also taken his trunks off as she felt the bare skin of his hip and thigh next to her calf and began rubbing against him. He was still holding her hips steady as the final aftershocks of her pleasure rode through her.

"So, was that it then?" Ellie asked with a pouty stare, looking at him down the length of her own body.

"Oh, my dear, that was just to take the edge off—to calm you down a bit. We're going to be here for a very, very long time."

In the past, she'd never really understood when people talked about toe-curling pleasure but in that anticipatory moment, Ellie felt her scalp tingle and her toes curl in the most delicious way.

"A long time, you say?"

He started to move up and over her body with a hint of delectable menace.

"Mm-hmm." He kissed his way up her stomach, then stopped to lavish all of his attention on her breasts. "A *very* long time."

"But what about you getting to work tomorrow?" she squeaked, her body already starting to hum again in response to his mouth on her.

He looked up at her with a twinkle in his eye. "Didn't I tell you? Bill left a message this afternoon on my cell phone that things were really slow at the shop. I don't need to go back in until Wednesday."

"*Wednesday?*" she managed to gasp out, as he pulled one nipple between his teeth, gently tugging, his eyes meeting hers in naughty collusion.

"Mm-hmm." His lips circled the tip of her breast and the vibration of his voice added even more pleasure. He released her with a little smack of his lips and smiled at her responsive gasp. "If that's okay with you, of course? If we stay here until Wednesday?"

After a beat, she realized he meant here, *right here*—in this bed—until Wednesday. Her mind fumbled and tripped to grab at all the luscious, naughty things they could get up to between now and *Wednesday*, and he saw how *okay* it was with her if they stayed *here* until Wednesday.

His smile was wide as she pulled his face to hers.

"I told you cell phones were the best invention ever! Can you imagine if we had driven all the way back for nothing?"

"You were right. Cell phones are the best." Then he looked at her with more meaning. "You're the best." He leaned in and captured her mouth in a plundering, demanding kiss and she felt the heat start to ramp up between them once again.

He pulled away eventually and looked at her more seriously. "Before we go on, though, sorry to be a killjoy, but what should we do for protection?"

"Protection from what?"

"Ellie!"

"Oh that! Neither of us has had sex in forever, right? I know I'm clean. Are you?"

"As a whistle." Then his face fell in dismay, and she had a moment of worry. "Although I always though whistles were pretty dirty, you know, what with all that blowing and saliva and that cork ball flying around in there."

She laughed and punched him in the shoulder.

He kissed her again then pulled back and looked at her more seriously. "What about a baby?"

Ellie swung her hand away in a dismissive gesture from where she'd been caressing his back. "I can't have kids. Fallopian occlusion. Just not meant to be I guess." She'd said those exact words many times over the years and had totally come to terms with them—the pragmatic truth of them—but in that moment she experienced an unfamiliar spike of loss. There would never be a product of this, of The Luke-and-Ellie Show. The brief emotion must have flashed across her face.

"Oh sweetheart, I'm so sorry."

"Don't be. It's all for the best, don't you think? In a way? I mean, if I'd had kids where would I be right now? At a soccer practice or a little league game?" She grabbed at his shoulder blades. "And I would *so* much rather be here with you."

But she could see he'd felt deep, sympathetic sadness and—for the first time in a long time—so had she. There would never be any physical evidence of what the two of them had together, not that she needed a child to prove how inspiring it was to find someone who made you feel like you wanted to stand on a street corner and yell at the top of your lungs that you were—

"Obviously I love you," she blurted. "I mean, I'm totally in love with you—" She sped through the words. "So, you know, there's that."

He looked down at her honest, vulnerable green eyes, the pupils like little hard magnets that seized him in a narrow tunnel of focus. He spoke softly. "I hate to say it lest it sound like a call and response or something, but I think I've loved you since the minute you squinted up at me from your car that first day. I held onto that clipboard like a medieval shield or something, to protect me from what slammed through me, from what you made me feel. Everything I thought I never wanted to feel again . . . or never could feel again." His entire body strained above hers, shoulders tense, legs firm.

"Oh, Luke. We're so lucky!" She smiled and all he could see was pure, undiluted innocence. "How could we be so lucky?"

"For now . . . " he whispered, ever cautious, but she obviously didn't want to hear it.

"Exactly. For right now. For this very moment. Which is all there is, right? Now."

He leaned in and kissed her. "Yes. Now." The words punctuated the kisses and she replied in similar one-word increments, meaningless and perfectly comprehensible all at once.

"Soon. Together. One."

He moved against her slowly, wanting to feel every inch of her skin along his. "You are the most carefree woman I've ever met."

She laughed and the roll of muscle and sound rose up through her and into him. "Just wait until you meet the rest of my friends and family. They think I am the most uptight, careful, controlling person ever."

While she talked, he began mapping her body, dipping his tongue into the curve at the edge of her breast, tracing his fingertip lightly over a sensitive spot where her thigh creased at her hip. "Go on. I love the sound of your voice . . . "

She talked about the farm in Virginia where she grew up and how she'd always been a tomboy and then she would gasp when he found a spot on her body that made her gasp.

"I like that spot too," he whispered, kissing and sucking on the silky skin behind her knee. "What were you saying about that boy in eleventh grade . . . "

And on it went.

"I feel like a queen or a maharaja or an odalisque whose only purpose is to be languid and responsive."

"Good," he said on a laugh. "I think that means I'm doing something right."

Ellie started rambling about random memories—how it had felt when she lost her first tooth, how much she hated her prom, how she had first masturbated in a shed behind the chicken coop because she was afraid to do it in the house. He hummed his encouragement and all the while he moved around her body, gradually making every bit of her . . . his. Her memories, her body. He was claiming all of it. Then something changed and she stiffened.

"What is it?" he asked. He was massaging her foot, pressing gently and then more firmly on different pressure points. When he pushed on one near the ball of her foot she whimpered.

"That makes me feel like I might burst into tears for no reason. Or for every reason."

He lightened the pressure.

"Now I feel like I might burst out laughing." She sighed into the feelings and they were both silent for a few minutes. "It feels wrong to talk about Rob when I'm in bed with you, but that's what I was thinking just then when I froze up."

He kept massaging her feet gently. "Then don't talk about him. I mean, I know you loved him. I love that you loved him. Or maybe even still love him. I don't think that takes anything away from us."

"You don't?" she asked, then moaned again as he worked his way up her calf.

"No. I think it's amazing," he said. "I'm jealous, but maybe not in the way you'd think. Not of what you had with him, but of how you are able to love people. Everyone you love, you obviously go all in. The way you talk about your friend Lotta, and how you are with your mother and father, and even how you talked about your childhood dog—you just put your love right out there."

Ellie closed her eyes and spoke softly. "Now you're making me feel guilty."

"Why? How?" He moved his hands further up her calves, rubbing deeply and then lightly, judging what she liked, what made her bend and moan, or what just made her feel good.

"I feel guilty because I think I would gladly throw them all over for you."

He stopped moving. The tick of the overhead fan marked the passage of time . . . two seconds . . . five seconds . . . ten seconds. She finally opened her eyes and looked at him askance.

"Scared you, huh?" she asked, a quick smile flashed and then she looked embarrassed. "Too much?"

He shook his head slowly, overwhelmed. "Not too much for me. Whatever you're giving, I'm taking."

"Oh god, I certainly hope so." She arched her back and slid her leg out of his grasp and trailed her foot along his thigh until she was touching his hard cock with the tip of her toe. He moaned at the contact. "You like that?" she asked, barely touching him, but the feather light strokes were causing him to catch his breath in time with her slow movements.

"Enough about me," she said in a smoky voice, then crawled up onto all fours and stalked to the end of the bed. "You've been methodical long enough. My turn." She gave him a gentle shove until he was lying back on the bed. She was on her knees between his spread legs. "Well, aren't you something?" She began slowly, rubbing the palms of her hands along his hard thighs. "Just relax."

He nearly coughed. "Easy for you to say."

She laughed and leaned down to kiss the head of his cock, circling him lightly with her tongue then taking him briefly into her mouth. She pulled away, maintaining that constant back-and-forth rubbing motion on his thighs.

"Ellie . . . " His voice sounded odd and tense to his own ears, almost angry.

"Yes?" she answered sweetly. "I thought you wanted to go slow?"

He exhaled through his teeth, then shut his eyes and began to control his breathing, relax his muscles.

"No fair! You're doing some sort of Eastern mysticism thing and totally checking out." She spanked the side of his hip, near his ass, with a playful, firm slap that demanded his attention.

His eyes flew open in a brilliant flash of shock and delight. "Did you just spank me?"

She laughed without a hint of guilt. "Yes. Did you like it?" She caressed the spot she'd just smacked. It was paler than the rest of him, where his bathing suit usually covered his skin and it was beginning to pinken from her swat.

"Yes, but don't make a habit of it," he said, pulling her up for a kiss, his hands reaching between her legs, her grip reaching for him. Then turning. She'd never known anything like it. It was so slow, such a gradual build—his hands, her mouth—the two of them coiling around and through each other, moving along the bed, delving into each other, performing some sort of finely orchestrated dance. At one point, he pulled her mouth to his, at another point his mouth was between her legs while her mouth was between his.

It was fluid and powerful and stunning. She was lost in the whirl of his movements—of their shared movements—and then he was inside her again, but not with his fingers. And it had been seamless, a continuation of all the touching and gliding and loving they had been doing all afternoon, for weeks really.

She tried to mark the moment, to have some sense of time; she thought it was night, but she wasn't really sure anymore. The time was Luke. The place was Luke. Her world had telescoped to this man. All of her senses were focused on him.

And, god, his focus was so entirely on her. When her eyes would flutter open between gasps of pleasure and kisses and licks of the beads of sweat that were accumulating in that beautiful hollow of his neck. In those moments, she saw that he was right there with her. Every thrust. Every slow penetration. He kept looking at her, holding her gaze as easily and completely as he was holding her hips. Slow, constant, patient.

He made her body into something entirely new, as if he could slow down the actual pace of her heartbeat. Slow it way down. So every beat. Every. Single. Beat. Belonged to them, and only them. In that place. In that now.

When she finally exploded beneath him—around him—it was more like a building imploding, or a star collapsing. Instead of an outward explosion, her orgasm felt like one of those fireworks that are deafening and abrupt. She was confused, filled with a tingling pleasure, held there for more ticks of the fan. She thought that was it.

"Now," he whispered, his hot breath against her ear like the pin being pulled from a grenade.

She detonated.

The weird unfamiliar inward orgasm—intense and powerful in its way—reconfigured all of its energy, coalesced, then shattered her with the most explosive release she'd ever experienced.

Their eyes never left each other as wave after wave of ecstasy pounded through her, as she cried out his name, and then he was exploding within her and in the midst of that conflagration the two of them held fast to one another.

"Holy hell." Ellie stared blindly at the crossbeam above the bed.

Luke chuffed a laugh.

They were both on their backs, panting and staring at the ceiling fan. On and on it turned, unaffected by the nuclear sex bomb that had just gone off in its midst.

"Seriously?" Ellie was nearly laughing also, through her heaving breaths. "You're like a goddamned sex god." She breathed hard. "No wonder you wanted to wait. That shit's not for amateurs."

"I think I tend to become a bit narrowly focused." His breath was settling back to normal, but she liked the way he was still a little winded.

"You think?" She laughed and it felt glorious. To be holding his hand and lying next to him on the crumpled sheets with the sound of the ocean and his breathing. It was heavenly. She was alive again.

They spent the next two days in bed or in the ocean. Denny knocked on the kitchen door one time to say he and Jo were going into town. "In case you want to go skinny dipping while we're out," he called. "Promise we shan't be back before five."

Ellie called down from the bedroom, "Thanks for the heads up!" She heard him chuckle as he walked away from the cottage. A few minutes later they heard the car crunching over the bits of shell and exiting the compound. Then the two of them flew out of the house, naked creatures running across the sand. They tumbled through the water, slick skin against skin, frolicking like the mad lovers they'd become, until they inevitably ended up back in bed.

Again and again, he brought her to those peaks. Again and again, they took each other through those slow endless paths to pleasure.

They would occasionally get up to make sandwiches or a salad or to grab more bottles of water, or a glass of wine, but then, not long after, it was like they simply had to hold each other. Sometimes they would read quietly for an hour or share passages aloud, and then a hand would wander. Or one of them would take a nap and the other's foot would end up along someone's calf and it always led to the same glorious celebration of sheer, simple vitality.

By Tuesday afternoon, Ellie wasn't sure she remembered what calendars and alarm clocks were ever invented for in the first place. As the days had spread into nights, nights to days, Luke was right there to share a thought or a kiss. Dusk rolled into dawn and they could look at the moon or the sunrise and turn on the radio and dance naked to Bing Crosby or The Weeknd.

"Can I have a sleepover at your house tonight?" Ellie asked shyly, as the sunlight shifted from late afternoon to early evening on Tuesday. They were lying entwined again, spent and slowly recovering in a tangle of one another's arms and legs.

"Sure. It's not very grand, as you saw. I can stay at your place if you'd rather."

"I keep thinking of that silk blanket and bedroll. I won't even be crazy sexy—"

He pulled her more firmly toward him in the bed as if to say that wasn't really a possibility.

"I mean, I just want to sleep under that beautiful cover with you—to feel the weight and texture of that, while I'm holding onto you—if that's okay."

Luke burrowed deep into the curve of her neck and the web of gorgeous red hair that awaited him there. "Oh, Ellie, please do. Keep holding onto me."

She gripped him harder to emphasize her point. "I'm not going anywhere."

Around seven o'clock Tuesday night the two of them finally pulled themselves out of bed, showered, packed up their gear, and headed back to Palm Beach County. They drove through the glowing summer night in a blissful, contented silence.

Chapter 9

Luke went to work Wednesday morning and left Ellie half-asleep in his bed. He hadn't felt this light or free in years. Maybe ever.

But he still hadn't finished telling her about Desmond and Kate and everything about his insane past . . . and the realization niggled at him. Soon, he promised himself. Later, another voice whispered.

He turned the motorcycle between the chain link fence gate that had been pulled back. Bill was already in the office. Luke parked the bike in the furthest parking spot, near the end of the row of garage bays where it wouldn't be in the way.

He strode back toward Bill's office to check in with him and see what he'd be working on for the day. He'd thought it would be hard to part from Ellie that morning, but everything, even parting from her, seemed just as it should be. She offered to cook dinner at her house that night and he'd happily agreed.

Luke pulled open the thin aluminum door to Bill's office feeling like all was right with the world, and stopped abruptly at the familiar face sitting across the desk from Bill.

"Well, look what the cat dragged in." The plummy British accent seemed even more grating somehow within the confines of the small office.

"Ethan."

Bill looked from one man to the other, checking for the family resemblance. The peculiar slant of their startling blue eyes, if nothing else, was irrefutable evidence of a blood tie.

"So, Luke," Bill began, "Your . . . brother . . . called a couple of days ago looking for you . . . and I told him you were . . . away."

"Thanks Bill. Sorry if he was rude. He makes a habit of that." Luke spoke about Ethan as if he were in another country, not sitting a few feet away—sitting with the same old casual arrogance, Luke saw.

"My apologies, Bill—" Ethan began, with all that syrupy, false familiarity Luke despised. "—if I was . . . demanding . . . but our family has been trying to track down this rascal for quite some time. Please pardon my forthrightness."

Bill stood up. "There's way too much going on in here. Luke, let me know if you need anything. The 325 in garage four needs a full tune-up. I told 'em it'd be done by three o'clock."

"No problem. This won't take long"

Bill looked again from one brother to the other and shook his head. "All right then." He nodded once toward Ethan in a silent, terse farewell. The door closed behind him and the plastic wood paneling of the small room vibrated around them.

Luke's eyes rested, unseeing, on a calendar with a beautiful buxom blonde crawling cat-like across the hood of a bright orange Dodge Charger.

"What do you want from me, Ethan?"

"What are you doing here, Luke? This is so *utterly* ridiculous." Ethan gestured around the tidy room as if it were a rat-infested tenement. The aristocratic lilt of his voice—the sibilance of that *utterly* carrying centuries of Etonian and Cantabrigian privilege—scraped along Luke's spine like barbed wire. This was how his father's sons were supposed to be. Not hardened ex-special ops grease monkeys.

"I don't have anything to do with you. Leave me alone."

"I would if I could, but your dying father has some absurd notion that he'd like to make amends."

Luke looked down at his own practical shoes. "I'm not sure I'm up for that."

"That's what I told him. You don't give a fuck about him or your inheritance or your family history. Just sign your portion over to me before he dies and he'll know that the inheritance is secure, at least. Otherwise, who knows what will happen? It'll all be caught up in the courts for decades, and everyone loses. I have the paperwork with me, in the car. You can't ignore him forever."

Luke had to command every bit of his will to refrain from punching this arrogant prig right in the middle of his aquiline nose. "I think you'd better go."

"That's your answer? I have to tell the old man something, damn it. I did not fly all this way for nothing."

"Where is he?"

"What? Who?"

"Where is Father?" Luke asked impatiently. "Is he in London?"

Ethan looked taken aback and then amused. "Oh, this is rich. Are you going to visit him in person? Show up after twenty years and be the prodigal son? Maybe you could run across a field of daisies into his arms."

"Fuck off. Do you want me to reconcile with him or not?"

"Actually, I'd prefer *not* because I don't want his final weeks or months to be disrupted by a load of cock and bull about how you were deprived of a family. We were always there, Luke, and you were always somewhere else, acting like we had robbed *you* for chrissake."

"You did rob me, you stupid ass." His fists clenched at his sides.

"I have never had any need to rob you, you idiot. In case you haven't picked up a newspaper or a magazine in the past fifteen years, I own one of the most successful international security firms on the planet. And it's not because my father's first wife was a Rothschild. Get over yourself!" Ethan yelled that last bit and it was obvious he immediately regretted it. He was standing now, his full height and broad shoulders mirroring Luke's almost exactly.

Luke smiled for a split second at how they must look: Ethan in a white linen suit, as if he had just come out of wardrobe on the set of *Our Man in Havana*, and Luke looking like the mechanic he was, in clean blue work pants and matching shirt rolled up to his elbows.

Ethan continued in a more controlled voice. "I'm too old for this shit. I have my own family and my own business and I just don't want to deal with Father's . . . regret . . . or what have you. Still, you have responsibilities. You can either abandon them formally or assume them. But these years of vague ambivalence really must come to an end."

Luke kept staring at his half-brother. Ethan wasn't a bad guy, not really. Just a product of his world, Luke thought. He tried to imagine any of their mutual colleagues from the Special Forces unit hearing Luke described as vague or ambivalent and he gave a little laugh.

"What's so funny?" Ethan looked like he could use some comic relief.

"I was just thinking that if you told someone like Desmond that I was vague and ambivalent he'd probably laugh in your face. Bitterly."

"Yeah, probably." Ethan gave a half smile. "About that . . . I hope he didn't frighten your girlfriend or anything. Desmond is a bit of a loose cannon at the moment, but we're monitoring him."

"Yeah, she doesn't know anything yet. Still, she's a photographer and took pictures of him. Pretty sloppy."

"Don't worry. He left the States a few days ago. I'm keeping an eye on him."

Luke took a deep breath. "Unsurprisingly, you keeping an eye on Desmond doesn't lessen my worry. In fact, it brings up a whole host of questions about why you are still in touch with him at all." He exhaled and let his shoulders relax. "And then I remember he is no longer my problem. He's all yours."

"Fine." Ethan sighed. "I guess I asked for that." Despite grave warnings from Luke, Ethan had foolishly hired Desmond as an independent contractor ten years ago. As far as Luke was concerned, they deserved each other.

The silence extended a few more moments then Ethan continued. "You still haven't answered me about Father."

Something about the strength or ease or quiet purpose he'd rediscovered since meeting Ellie gave him the courage to consider a reconciliation, or at least rapprochement. "All right, Ethan," he continued quietly, "I'll come to England to see Father. Are you flying back soon?"

"No. I think I'll stay in this godforsaken jungle and get my car fixed," he said with false compliance, then barked, "Yes of course I'm flying back as soon as possible. My jet's at the private airfield in West Palm Beach on standby. Why don't you bring your pretty friend? Maybe she'll soften you up a bit around Father?"

"She does have that effect on people. On me," he added. "Have you been tailing her?" It had irritated him that Ethan had been watching him, but it made him irrationally angry that he'd been tracking Ellie.

"Don't get mad all over again. We were making such progress." Ethan smirked, then sighed and rolled his eyes. "God damn it. Of course I've had her under surveillance ever since you two went out to Sam's. What'd you think I would do?"

"So Sam is the one who told you I was here?"

"Don't get mad at him either. He owed me a favor, a big one. And maybe it'll all be for the best. Did you ever think of that?"

"I don't want to assume all of Father's responsibilities." Luke had been trying for ambivalent disdain, but he came off sounding like an impudent teenager even to himself.

"Well, boo hoo for you."

"Oh, shut up. You know what I mean. In this day and age? It's bordering on despicable. Lord of the manor and all that."

"Then make it honorable, or sell it off in pieces. Give it away. I don't care. But just do something. Please. Before Father drives the rest of us crazy."

"All right. Let me think for a minute. I need to give Bill some notice."

"Are you bloody joking? You don't think he can find anyone else to fix cars? Please. Enough with the procrastinating."

"You are asking me to confront a lifetime of closely-held anger and frustration, you ass. Can you give me a day or two?"

Ethan smiled, as if he'd never considered he might eventually come to like his older brother. Apparently, stranger things did, in fact, happen.

"All right," Ethan said charitably. "Take your time."

"Thanks."

"But hurry up about it. My son's got a rugby match next week and I want to be there."

Ethan started toward the door and Luke stepped aside to let him pass.

"What's your phone number?" Luke asked.

They exchanged details and then Luke thought he might try his hand at being cordial. "Uh, Ethan," he started.

"Yes?" His brother stood half-turned with one hand on the doorknob, still glancing at his smartphone.

"Would you like to come for supper tonight? At Ellie's house. That's her name by the way. But you probably knew that already, didn't you? Eleanor Sinclair. You might want to thank her in person for breaching my defenses."

"Wait, what?" He looked up. "Are you actually asking me to break bread with you?"

"Forget it," Luke snapped. "If you're going to turn it into some sarcastic battle of the wills—"

"Not at all." Ethan held up one hand. "I'm not. I mean, sorry if that's how it came out. What time shall I meet you? And why don't I take you two out? Olive branch and all that."

"Let's just have dinner at her house. She's a great cook and, well, let's just do it there."

"Sounds good. What time?"

"Oh, I don't know. Why don't you come 'round about seven?" He gave him the address and watched in bewilderment, at himself mostly—at the relative normalcy of it all—as Ethan got into a dark-windowed limousine that pulled up as soon as he left the office. It had been idling in the shade across the street. How had Luke missed that?

He shook his head and went to work on the 325 in bay four, and to give his notice to Bill.

Luke called Ellie at lunchtime to see if it was all right to have Ethan for dinner.

"Wow! What a surprise. The way you talked about him it didn't sound like . . . well, of course. I'd love to meet him and have him for supper."

"Yeah, I don't know how much of a love-fest it will be. I have to confess I'm kind of using you as a human shield. I don't think he'll really light into me if there's a . . . lady present."

"I heard that hesitation before the word lady, you sorry excuse for a gentleman. Just because you've already seen me in every erotic position in the Kama Sutra doesn't mean that anyone else on the planet has! Cut it out with the suggestive little hesitations."

He was smiling at her feigned irritation. He loved that she was completely free when they were in bed, and curiously buttoned up the rest of the time. At one point while they were in the Keys he'd caught her humming *Anything Goes* after a particularly ambitious round of playful positions.

"All right, I promise to be utterly respectful and devoted to propriety at dinner."

But Ellie paused for a second, suspicious. "Is there anything else I should know about your brother before I meet him?"

"What? Like food allergies?"

"Very funny. No, I meant more along the lines of whether he's here to settle some biblical feud or are we really just having dinner? Is this cigar just a cigar or what?"

"I hope it's just a cigar. He's come to track me down to get me to visit my father—who's apparently near the end." Ellie inhaled to speak but Luke continued quickly. "But he's been near

167

the end too many times before so I'm not convinced. Anyway, I'm so biased with all my history of real or imagined antagonism from Ethan, I thought it would be good to, I don't know, see him through your eyes."

"What a nice thing to say."

"Well, I like how I look through your eyes, so I thought maybe I could sign on for the whole Ellie worldview."

Her stomach turned in a combination of happiness and nerves at the idea of Luke signing on for the whole Ellie *anything*.

"Okay. I was just on my way out to the store right now. This'll be fun. I can spend the afternoon cooking and making the house pretty. What time did you tell him to come?"

"I suggested seven, but I told him I needed to talk to you first, so whenever."

"No, that sounds great. Why don't you come a little earlier for a glass of wine just the two of us?"

"Sounds great. I'll see you a little after six."

"Okay. See you then."

Ellie hung up the phone and looked around the kitchen in a happy stupor. *She had a boyfriend.*

She picked up her cell phone and called Lotta.

"Hey!"

"Well hello cheerful Ellie!"

"I am cheerful. And you know why?"

"No. Tell me."

"I think I have a real, live boyfriend!"

"Oh, sweet Ellie. You sound like a teenager."

"I swear, I feel like one. We just got back from the greatest five days at Jo and Denny's place in the Keys. I mean, really great."

"Like, you broke the let's-wait-thirty-days-before-we-have-sex-pact kind of great?"

"Yeah. That kind of great."

"Oh my god really? Was it so fabulous? Did you two really get it on?"

"You are such a throwback! *Get it on?* Are you sitting in the Haight getting a henna tattoo . . . *get it on* . . . who even says that, other than Marvin Gaye?"

Lotta was already laughing. "What do you want me to say?"

"Preferably nothing. But if you must know, yes, we really *got it on*. And on and on and on and on."

"And on?"

They both started laughing uncontrollably.

Ellie settled first and started talking as she wiped away the final tears. "So, it turns out his brother is in town. Some guy named Ethan McCormick and he's coming for dinner tonight. I'm already being introduced to the family. It's almost like a little courtship."

"Ethan McCormick . . . why does that name ring a bell?"

Philip's voice warbled in the background. Ellie could hear Lotta put her hand over the phone and chastise her fiancé for eavesdropping. Then she moved her hand away and started speaking, half to Philip, half to Ellie. "Well, of course it's not *that* Ethan McCormick, Philip. Don't be ridiculous. Ellie's boyfriend is a mechanic in South Florida for chrissake. How could his brother be that despicable war profiteer? Go get your own friends and your own morning phone calls. Scoot! Go to work already."

Ellie was smiling at the happy banter of the soon-to-be-newlyweds.

"I swear. He is impossible. He hovers around me like a helicopter mom."

"Maybe he likes you?"

"Yeah, I think he does. Funny, isn't it?"

"It's so good. Anyway, I have to go to the grocery store and I figured I should keep you posted on my progress, since you're my life coach and all."

"All right then. Proceed apace."

"But, just out of curiosity, is that other Ethan McCormick American? The war monger one?"

"No, I think he's Scottish or British or whatever. But Philip's just being ridiculous. You know how he loves to pore over the *Forbes* billionaire list and all that capitalist crap."

Philip was apparently back in the kitchen, horning in on Lotta's call with the offending magazine in hand and opened to the page about Ethan McCormick.

"Okay, just to put this to rest," Lotta spoke to both of them, "Well, he does have quite sparkly blue eyes . . . probably a trick of the photography . . . "

Ellie's stomach started to clench.

Lotta continued, half skimming, half reading aloud, "Thirty-five-years-old, primary residence London, father of three, married to the same women for fourteen years . . . he probably cheats on her all the time . . . has two brothers, Trevor and Michael, and he owns a security company, nice euphemism," Lotta added with bitter derision, "that offers contracted services to military and diplomatic personnel worldwide. Who writes that shit? Seriously. Why don't they just write *mercenary* under his name?"

Ellie was dead silent.

"Ellie? No relation right? Your guy is Luke, right? No mention of a brother named Luke." Silence. "Ellie?"

"It's his half-brother."

"Oh. Well. I'm sure he's really nice in person then."

"Very funny. Just out of curiosity . . . how rich is he?"

"Only about three . . . billion. That puts him somewhere in the middle of this list."

Philip started talking again, but his words were still muffled.

"Philip just asked if he could come to dinner, too."

"If you two could get here in time I would love that. But as it is now, I think I'm going to have to fend for myself." Then Ellie's voice went softer. "I mean, is it a form of duplicity that Luke didn't tell me his brother was mega rich? What do you think? He's told me all about the family and the turmoil and all that. But I guess I kind of ignored the . . . scope."

"Of course it's not duplicity. This good Luke probably wants nothing to do with this very bad Ethan. Good boy, Luke! Go Luke!"

Ellie laughed. "But, I think they're trying to mend fences."

"Borders more like it."

"All right, you go get on your high horse and I'll go make dinner."

Lotta laughed too. "I'm not on my high horse—"

"You are too. You would never fall in love with the brother of an arms dealer—"

"Have you?"

"Have I what?"

"Have you *fallen in love* with him? I told you to be *careless*! This is your life coach talking. You have only known this guy for a few weeks—be careful!"

"Well which is it? Careless or careful?"

Lotta started laughing again. "I am not actually a fully-licensed life coach—you shouldn't really listen to me." Then her laughter died down a bit. "But do take care of yourself. I know you will. But, well, you know what I mean."

"Yes, I do. I love you, Lotta. You've always got my back. But you'll love Luke, too. He's got *my* back." Ellie's cheeks burned at the double-entendre as soon as the words had slipped from her lips, and her throaty pronunciation of that last bit totally gave her away.

"Oh, Ms. Sinclair. You are so naughty. I think I might have to hang up on you."

"I'll talk to you soon. Go away."

"All right, talk to you soon."

By the time six o'clock rolled around, Ellie was perfectly fine with the fact that Luke's brother was some crazy, filthy rich, gun-for-hire. What did she care?

She'd taken out her milky white French plates and light-blue linens and iced down lots of cheerful white Burgundy and there were enormous white hydrangeas in tall tubes of glass around the kitchen table and living room. She was in her element, whether an arms dealer was coming to dinner or not.

Luke tapped at the front door at six, but Ellie had already heard the muffled rumble of his motorcycle when he pulled into her driveway, so she was right there and practically ripped the door off its hinges when she let him in. She dove at him as if she hadn't seen him in weeks.

He gripped her head in that way she was coming to adore, the base of her neck totally captured. He dropped his small overnight bag on the floor and put his other hand at her lower back and then around the curve of her hip.

"Do we have time to run upstairs?" he whispered hotly.

"If we're really quick about it? Then, yes, we probably have time before I need to stick the roast in the oven." Her words were choppy and hoarse with desire.

He turned and locked the front door then grabbed her wrist and more or less hauled her up the stairs and into her bedroom. He undid his belt buckle and zipper on the way then practically tossed her onto the bed as if she were feather light. She laughed at the sheer joy of that moment of weightlessness—the abiding trust of it all.

Her breath caught when he kicked off his shoes and had his linen trousers and underwear off in a single, deft motion. He was so hard she started to laugh and scoot away from him, up toward the headboard, but he looked stormy and full of purpose and simply grabbed at her ankles until her legs were partially hanging off the end of the bed.

He moved his hands slowly up her thighs, pushing her sundress up until it pooled around her hips, and then he threw his head back with a great, deep laugh when he saw that she had nothing on underneath.

"Tsk tsk. You are wicked." He rubbed the palm of his hand over her smooth lower stomach and then between her legs, finding her warm and ready. He slid a finger into her and she bucked to meet him, and then he took his hand away, held her gaze and drove himself deep into her wet, welcoming hold. He held her hips gently and firmly—if such a thing were even possible—controlling the pace and intensity until she was crying out, begging him to ride her harder, faster and then he touched—exactly where she had centered all of her fervor—and she flung her head back and clenched her eyes shut, gasping in a great gulp of what felt like the last breath she might ever inhale on this earth. And then her entire being shattered into and through and around this incredible man.

She barely registered his own glorious release, which he somehow, perfectly, wove into her own rhythm, his own climax binding them to one another instead of taking either of them to another place.

He pulled away from her with controlled gentleness, settling her back onto the bed then crawling slowly up to lie alongside her. He reached out to rest his hand over her womb in a casually possessive gesture. Another tremor of residual pleasure fluttered beneath his touch.

"Oh, man," she whispered.

He stared at the ceiling fan and exhaled slowly.

She stared at his profile. He'd never taken his shirt off, but she could see clearly the rise and fall of his chest beneath the white fabric, still recovering from the exertion.

Ellie closed her eyes and leaned in to nip at the soft warmth of his neck. Then, with a final kiss she lifted herself up on one elbow. "So, I should probably get that roast in the oven." She looked at her watch and smiled up into Luke's eyes. "Perfect timing. Six fifteen!"

She sprang from the bed, shimmying the fabric of her dress back over her hips and thighs. She made a pit stop in the bathroom, then slipped on a pair of underwear, and nearly skipped out of the room and down the hall toward the stairs, whistling *Anything Goes*.

A few minutes later, Luke came into the kitchen looking perfectly put together, his hair combed back into submission, his shirt tucked neatly into his linen pants.

"You clean up very nicely." She shut the refrigerator and began putting together a platter of food. "I thought the fresh figs looked great, so I was going to do those with a little chèvre, wrapped in prosciutto, all roasted with a balsamic reduction. Does that sound good?" She was working at putting a dab of the moist, white cheese onto each piece of the quartered figs she'd prepped earlier, then wrapped them in the ham and set them all in neat rows in the baking dish.

She smiled up at him, waiting for his answer, her head slightly tilted to one side as her hands continued in their happy productivity.

He kept looking at those beautiful fingers and the sinew along the back of her hands. Strong, confident, knowing. Gentle. If anyone could save him, it was this woman.

"Luke?" she paused, holding her messy hands, covered in fig and cheese and grease, slightly away from her. "What is it?"

"It's you. It's just you." He came to her then and kissed the side of her neck and whispered, barely audible, "I love *you*, Ellie."

She looked into his eyes to make sure he was okay. "So, the figs were a good choice?"

He shook his head and kissed her again on the cheek, then turned to the refrigerator to grab a beer. "Perfect. As usual."

"Well, I wouldn't go that far, but I'll settle for pretty good."

"Fine. Pretty good. As usual."

She smiled again and took a few more minutes to finish the figs then put the dish into the second wall oven, below the oven into which she'd already set the pork roast.

"Would you mind opening one of those bottles of Burgundy out in the garage fridge for me? I'll take a glass and I want to put a little in the artichokes."

She was back in the refrigerator pulling out a platter of baby artichokes that had been trimmed and cut into long pieces. They were glistening in a light glaze of olive oil and garlic, coarse salt and pepper.

"Here." Luke handed her the opened bottle of wine.

She poured a generous splash of wine over the whole pan of artichokes, set the cool green bottle down on the white marble counter, then slipped the platter into the same oven with the figs.

She rinsed her hands in the sink and dried them on the cotton kitchen towel that hung from the drawer pull to her left.

"What else?" she asked herself aloud, then snapped her fingers. "The salad. Then I'm done." She smiled at Luke as she walked past him again, then gave him a small wink.

She put together a salad of fresh mâche, slivered jicama, and carrots. She whisked together a lemon and mint dressing and set it aside to toss right before she served it.

"I think that does it. I also made these great little individual tarte tartins that are totally easy. I can put those in when I take the meat out. Want to go into the living room?"

It was a few minutes before seven.

"Ellie . . . "

She looked around the kitchen and toward the round table where they'd be eating to make sure everything was neat and ready. "What?" she asked absently.

"Ellie."

She turned to really look at him then. "Yes?" She walked toward him and took the cool glass of wine that he held out for her, and put her other hand on his cheek, then she asked quietly, "Are you sure you're okay?"

"I think I'm a little nervous."

"Oh, honey. Why?"

"It's so old and ingrained. I don't know. It just seems awkward. I'm so happy to be here with you."

"Me too," she whispered, then kissed him softly on the lips. "You're a really good person, too, you know. We're all freaks with our families. Let's just have a nice night, okay?"

"I'll try."

The doorbell rang and Ellie looked at the wall clock above the sink. The second hand was swinging across the twelve; seven o'clock exactly.

"So punctuality runs in the family?"

"Yeah." Luke smiled as they walked together toward the front door. "We all tend to be very . . . prompt."

Ellie opened the door and schooled her features to be as welcoming as possible. She wasn't prepared for the family resemblance, especially around the eyes.

"Well, you're definitely related!" she blurted.

Ethan smiled and Ellie felt a moment of treachery. He was smiling in the same sexy way that Luke smiled, as if he were simply delighted to see her. And he was seriously hot . . . billionaire hot. Then she felt Luke's hand tighten around hers and shook herself out of Ethan's compelling gaze.

"Please come in," Ellie said a bit more formally.

"Ethan McCormick, Ellie Sinclair. Ellie, this is Ethan." Luke might have sounded natural to someone who'd never heard his voice before, but Ellie was already worried. He sounded, well, icy.

They all stood there staring at each other for a few seconds, then Ellie's laugh broke the tension. "Come in already!" She almost had to pull Luke out of the way to make room for Ethan to pass into the small entry hall.

"It's just a kitchen dinner," Ellie said as she started walking down the hall. "I hope that's okay. We're sort of casual around here."

She could tell that Luke did not like when she smiled at Ethan. At all. He probably knew he was being an infant, but it was impossible to ignore Ethan's powerful presence and the effect it was having on her. He was kind of a beast of a man. Ellie felt like she was in a prehistoric cave with two saber-toothed tigers circling around a carcass that would only satisfy one of them. Ethan was almost quintessentially male: confident, controlled, vital. Luke looked like he was reining in his rising adrenaline with great difficulty.

Ellie slapped the palms of her hands on the cool white marble countertop. "Okay! I was going to suggest wine, but I think we should do a few shots. What do you two say? You're not driving are you, Ethan?"

"Uh, no, I have a car and driver to take me back to my plane."

"Ah, plane, right." She nodded slowly then looked at Luke. "And you're certainly not going anywhere, mister," she said with a brazen wink that seemed to have quite the consoling effect on his frayed ego. "What's your pleasure gentlemen? Tequila? I have some great Herradura that a friend just gave me."

She looked up from the liquor cabinet at the two predators in her little Provencal-decorated kitchen. How in the world had she ended up in this situation?

Ethan spoke first. "Tequila sounds great."

Then Luke. "Perfect. I'll get the limes."

Ellie pulled out three little hand-blown shot glasses and took out some of her favorite Camargue salt. "Oh, this is going to be fun! I haven't done shots of tequila in ages!" Her enthusiasm was contagious and both men began to relax.

"I'm not certain I have ever done shots of tequila," Ethan said, obviously trying to loosen up, but with his British accent and inherent loftiness, he ended up sounding like a National Geographic announcer coming upon some heretofore-unknown indigenous tribal behavior. After a beat or two of silence, they all three started laughing.

"Fabulous! There's an entire ritual. It kind of makes the let's-just-get-wasted aspect of the whole enterprise seem less glaring. You're not just getting drunk, you are having an *experience*!"

Ethan smiled again, and then turned to see his perennially pissed off half-brother smiling in a completely unfamiliar way. Luke must have felt his brother's look, and turned, prepared to let his mask of a lifetime of bitterness return, but Ellie intervened again.

"All right, give me those limes, Luke. So, Ethan, just like in the movies, you lick your hand like this." Ellie looked at Luke when she wet the tender skin at the crook of her thumb and index finger with the tip of her tongue. "Then you put a little salt there, that's your *amuse bouche*, and then you just toss back the shot," which she did with a quick squint of her eyes. "Then suck on the lime. Lather, rinse, repeat. Easy as pie!"

The two men looked at her.

She looked up. "God you two are so stiff. Honestly. Luke, you next, here." She grabbed his hand, licked his skin, poured a little salt on it, then put the shot glass in one hand and the lime slice in the other. "Go!"

He did as he was told and she watched as the tang of smooth, strong liquor and cool, tart lime slid down his throat. She thought perhaps there was redemption in the world after all.

"Well done! Now you, Ethan." She was pouring his shot and without looking up said. "Sorry, but you'll have to lick your own hand. That's just a special treat for the regulars."

After three shots each, they were all pleasantly buzzed and had moved into the living room, Queen pounding in the background, Ellie sitting close to Luke on the sofa, Ethan standing and giving them a perfect, if cruel, impersonation of their father's bitter soliloquy when his horse lost the Epsom Derby in 1994.

They had switched to the white Burgundy and all of them burst out laughing when Ethan, in a perfect Scottish accent, finished with, "If the stupid animal had had the basic decency to run faster, I would have won!"

Ellie continued laughing as she went into the kitchen to check on dinner. "Everything's ready! Do one of you two want to carve the meat or shall I?"

They both stood looking at her at the far end of the kitchen island as she set out the hot dishes.

"Here, Luke. Come help me with this." He walked around and grabbed her from behind, kissing her on the neck.

"Cut that out. We're into the food now. No more nonsense. Here's the carving knife and the cutting board. I'll set up the salad. Ethan, would you mind getting another bottle of the Burgundy out of the garage refrigerator for me?"

"Sure."

She gestured toward the door that led that way.

After seeing that Ethan was out of sight, Ellie turned quickly to take hold of Luke's face in her hands. "Don't ever be jealous of me," she whispered harshly. "I only have eyes for you." She kissed him hard and fast. "Ever! Do you hear me?"

He was still holding the carving knife and fork in each hand, and nodded. "I'm sorry."

She heard Ethan's footsteps coming back down the short hall from the garage. "That's okay," she answered Luke brightly, as if he had cut the pork at the wrong angle or some other insignificant offense.

"Do you want me to open these Ellie? I brought two bottles . . . just in case."

Ellie was tossing the salad and setting up their three plates, composing each with a balanced display of several figs, several stalks of baby artichoke, and two slices of pork. "Oh, I forgot I picked up a mango sauce for the meat, and I need to put the dessert in." She opened the refrigerator and bent low to grab the jar of sauce and to get the tray of ramekins that held the desserts.

Luke paused to appreciate the gorgeous turn of her ass then looked over at his brother admiring the same view.

"Damn it Ethan! Don't do that!"

"What?" he asked, all innocence.

Ellie stood up, holding the tray and the mint sauce. She kicked the refrigerator door shut with her foot and handed Ethan the sauce. "Put that on the table, will you please?" When he was out of earshot she turned to Luke. "What did Ethan do?" She walked over to the oven and put in the apple desserts.

"Nothing." But Ethan was back, and smiling, and Luke was pointing the carving fork in his direction. "Nothing he's ever going to do again, right Ethan?"

But his younger brother was still smiling. "Sure. Right, Luke."

"That's enough pork. You can stop carving now. Here." She picked up two of the full plates. "Let's go sit down."

They got settled, Luke refilled their wineglasses, Ellie poured water into glasses, and served the salad onto the smaller plates near each place.

"So." Ellie raised her glass. "Here's to brotherly love, eh?"

The two men looked at each other skeptically, then at her. "Cheers," they both agreed.

The food was delicious, the wine superb. Ellie loved appreciative eaters and she wasn't disappointed with these two. Ethan acted as though he hadn't had a home-cooked meal in decades. Perhaps he hadn't, for all she knew.

"Really delicious. Really." He was lifting his glass to show how much he was enjoying himself. "So, would you ever consider a permanent move back to Scotland with Luke?"

Luke nearly spit out the wine he'd been swirling around in his mouth in a (now past) moment of ease and contentment.

Ellie looked at Luke. "Uh . . . we haven't really discussed—"

"I am *not* moving to Scotland, you asshole," Luke snapped.

Ellie was suddenly afraid no amount of tequila or high-quality white Burgundy was going to smooth away a lifetime of animosity in a single evening. "Luke," she said softly, resting her hand on his. "It's fine."

"No, it's not. He's the same smarmy little shit-stirrer that he was when he was six years old. All smiles and charm and then, bam! 'Daddy, look what Luke did!' I should take you out to the beach and beat the crap out of you once and for all."

"Oh, please cut it out," Ellie demanded quietly.

Then Luke was mad all over again because Ellie's lovely dinner had been reduced to one more in a string of botched family gatherings.

"I'm sorry, Ellie, I didn't mean to spoil your lovely meal," Ethan apologized.

Then Luke was really fuming because Ethan beat him to the apology and made him feel even more frustrated. But Ellie kept her eyes on Luke, stroking the back of his hand.

"Nothing's been spoiled. It's time for dessert anyway. Luke, come help me with the plates please." She tried to pull him from the table and out of his stew of age-old resentment. "Luke!"

He finally let his stormy, threatening look move away from Ethan and met her gaze as he stood up.

"Relax, sweetheart," she whispered in his ear, and kissed him sweetly on the cheek.

How did a man stay mad in the face of that tiny show of solidarity? He felt his shoulders begin to un-tense as he followed her toward the sink to wash up the dishes. He rinsed and loaded the few dinner and salad plates into the dishwasher while Ellie set up dessert. Ethan's cell phone rang and he went over to the far side of the living room to take the call.

The three of them were back at the table about five minutes later.

Ellie spoke first. "So, Ethan, please stop saying things that you know will piss everyone off. And Luke, stop being so easily provoked. Bon appétit!"

The two men looked at each other as if no part of that discussion was anywhere near being resolved, but the very least they could do was enjoy the steaming apple confection that had been placed in front of them.

"Oooh, I forgot the Sauternes!" Ellie leapt from the table and returned a few seconds later with a small bottle of sweet wine and three new glasses. "I have been saving this for a special occasion. Don't you two think this is *special?*" She smirked at both of them.

Luke reached out to move a piece of Ellie's auburn hair back behind her shoulder and smiled his agreement. "It is."

"Thanks." Then she turned to Ethan. "I have an extra tarte tatin . . . does your driver want some?"

Ethan looked across the table at Luke. "What do you think Luke? Would Schenk like to join us for dessert?"

Luke smiled, finally. "I do believe he would. But Ellie, no mention of your penchant for photography, okay?"

She looked from Luke to Ethan, then back to Luke. "Okay."

"And don't mention the man you saw on the beach, okay?"

"Um, okay. Why don't you two go get him and I'll set up his plate."

Ethan and Luke got up from the table and came back a few minutes later with what Ellie could only describe as a killer.

Then the other man smiled, a tight rictus of a smile similar to the one she'd seen on the beach last week, like he wanted to smile, he really did, but he had never learned how to do it. But the other man had looked lifeless, whereas this brute of a man looked very much alive.

"Hi, I'm Ellie Sinclair." She reached out her hand to shake his.

Luke introduced Schenk.

"Just Schenk?" Ellie asked.

The three men looked at each other and started laughing. Then the strong bodyguard nodded. "Yeah, pretty much. Everybody calls me Schenk."

"Well. Okay. Please join us for dessert . . . Schenk."

The rest of the evening passed at a much easier pace. Schenk gave both men a distraction from their own frustrations with one another. Ellie also got to learn more about the bare basics of how the three had all come to be friends . . . of a sort.

"I don't know exactly how many years we've known each other—do you remember, Schenk?" Luke asked as they sat outside on the deck around the pool.

Schenk was distracted by a rustling sound in the nearby dunes. He looked like a hunting dog on point. "This place is kind of vulnerable, Ellie."

"Well, since my three companions are so well-versed in the fine art of protection, I won't overworry."

Schenk shook his head, as if daft females were a territory he would never conquer.

"Don't worry—she's a crack shot," Luke added.

Schenk turned toward Ellie with renewed interest, not that his interest in her had ever really waned. He'd been like a puppy ever since he walked in. "Really? You know how to shoot?"

"A bit."

"She's just being coy. Ellie was the one who dropped the boar at Sam's place a few weeks ago."

Both Ethan and Schenk sat slightly forward in their deck chairs.

Ellie's eyes sparkled from the reflection of the pool lights. "Do you guys know Sam, too? That was pretty crazy, right Luke?"

"Yeah, crazy is one word for it." He was turning a glass of Armagnac around in his palm. "And terrifying."

Schenk barked a laugh. "Luke terrified? That I'd like to see!"

Luke stared into his glass.

Ellie had a shiver at the recollection of the moment the boar charged. "It was pretty intense, but I don't think Luke was afraid of the boar. He was afraid for me."

Schenk looked at Luke then back at Ellie. "Yeah. I could see how that might happen."

"Huge tactical error on my part," Luke said, before taking a slow sip.

"So, stop getting distracted by imaginary invaders," Ellie said. "Tell me how you all met."

Schenk looked at Luke, as if he needed permission to tell the story.

Luke lifted his chin. "Go on. Tell her."

"We met while we were working on a project together in Southeast Asia. In Thailand—" Schenk began.

"Oh, I love Thailand," Ellie chimed in. "We had the best time there, near Koh Samet."

Schenk looked at Luke for guidance, obviously unsure how to proceed.

"It wasn't really a holiday, Ellie," Luke replied.

She looked chastised. "I'm sorry, I didn't mean it like that."

Luke felt instantly guilty for being such a patronizing dick. "I'm sorry, El. It just, well, anyway, Schenk and I worked on the same team for a company that . . . facilitates international trade."

Schenk's smile was a thin line. "Oh, is that what they do?"

Luke smiled too. "Yeah. That's what I've heard they do. International trade."

Ellie still looked a bit dejected. "I suppose you can't just come out and say you're all retired spies, right?"

The three men looked at her. Ethan spoke first. "Who said anything about retirement?"

Ellie's head spun back to Luke and he hated the worry in her eyes.

"Don't listen to him, he's just trying to piss me off." Luke reached for her hand and smoothed his thumb over her knuckles. "I am not a spy. I have never been a spy. And I am utterly and completely retired from my former occupation. For the sake of full disclosure, many moons ago I did *interact* with the occasional spy." When he was finished he turned to Ethan. "And you stop being an ass, please."

"I'll try, but you know old habits and all that." Ethan took the final sip of his drink. "Well, on that note, I think we should head back to the plane." He stood up and Schenk rose to join him. "Want me to send the jet back for you next week, Luke?" Ethan asked.

Ellie thought she could actually hear Luke's teeth grinding before he replied, "I'll make my own way, thanks."

"Suit yourself. Just trying to save you a bit of dosh. No need to get all riled up again."

Ethan approached Ellie's chair and took her free hand to his lips in a perfectly executed courtly kiss. "My deepest thanks for a wonderful dinner, my lady." And again she had the feeling that she really was the lady of the house, or the manor, or what have you.

"Oh, Ethan. It was my pleasure. Let me show you out." She stood up, pulling Luke up with her. "Come on, let's show our guests to the door."

After the limo pulled out of the driveway and Ellie had finished waving into the retreating rear window, she dropped her hand unceremoniously and stared at Luke as if he were a complete stranger. "What the hell was that all about?"

"What do you mean?" But he couldn't look her in the eye.

"You know exactly what I mean. I don't care if he ruined your childhood or blamed you for the London fire. You're an adult now, do you hear me?" She was shoving one (lovely, he thought) pointed finger into his chest for emphasis. "And don't you ever behave like that around me again."

She stormed into the kitchen to clear up the last of the mess and to get a glass of water before heading up to bed. She wasn't sure if she was so mad she was going to ask him to go home, or if she was so mad she was going to ask him stay and make it up to her in bed.

Seemed silly to send him away when his penance might be—

She felt his stealthy presence come upon her at the sink before she felt his hands wrap around her from behind. His palms went right to her breasts . . . no gentle slide up from her waist or down from her shoulders. He growled in her ear. "I despised when you looked at him or when he looked at you. I hated when you would laugh at his funny stories. I hated how much he loved your food."

She reached forward and turned off the faucet before letting her head fall back onto his shoulder. Through rapidly shortening breaths, Ellie mused aloud, "I was just contemplating whether I should send you home or extract your apology—" He reached between her legs with one hand. "—in another way," she gasped.

"I like the idea of another way."

"Me too."

"I'm sorry," he whispered, kissing his way down the back of her neck. "I'm sorry," he repeated, letting his hand slide down the front of her dress.

Any irritation she'd been feeling was swept away in the combination of physical and emotional heat of him, on her, around her. She twisted around to look at him, then reached between their two bodies and cupped his erection in the palm of her hand, through the straining fabric of his pants. "Were you angry? Jealous?"

"Ellie," he growled. "Don't tease me."

"Maybe that's your punishment." She squeezed him harder and he moaned as he pushed against her palm. "I get to tease you."

His eyes narrowed. "Fine." His voice was thick with desire. "Tease me." He exhaled slowly and she felt his desire tighten right there against her fingers.

She licked her upper lip. "I think I'm going to like this."

He groaned into her and kissed her fiercely, letting all of his barriers down. She came at him, matching his urgency and force with every thrust of her tongue and press of her hips. They took each other right there on the kitchen floor, and they both cried out at the quick, violent pleasure of it.

Then, slowly, she removed his shirt, positioned his muscled arms taut above his head, and held him pinned beneath her. She began to work him over. She bit his nipples then licked them tenderly, maddeningly, until he was begging for more of the biting. She rode him, spreading her thighs wide and obviously not caring about the hard floor against her knees or against his back. Not caring about anything but him. Having him.

At the moment just before his next release—at the pinnacle of that wild animalistic instant when Kate used to snarl her disgust and make him feel the most abject, misogynistic shame—Ellie looked straight into his desperate soul and whispered, "I love you . . . I love you wild like this. Only you."

Then she arched her back and cried low and keening, as she flew into the abyss of pleasure along with him.

A few minutes later, his back sore and his legs stiff, he started to chuckle. She was draped over him and mumbled against his bare chest, "What's so funny?"

"First of all, I'm too old to have sex on a kitchen floor. And second of all, your punishment totally worked. I swear I will never be jealous again."

Luke called into work the next morning to see if he needed to come in and Bill said it was totally slow again.

"Really, Luke. I know you're trying to do the right thing by me, but it's such a slow time of year anyway. You won't be leaving me in the lurch if you need to move on. I've really appreciated having you these past few months—don't get me wrong, you do great work—but you're free to go with my blessing. I understand when family obligations come into play."

"Thanks, Bill. I really appreciate it. I think I'll take you up on that."

"No worries, man. Call me if you're ever back in town. Take care."

He clicked off the phone and walked back into the bedroom where Ellie was sound asleep. And probably would be for hours, he thought ruefully. They'd let loose on each other last night. All night.

She groaned and reached out one hand. "Luke?" she mumbled into the pillow.

He crawled back into bed and held her in a tight, protective embrace.

"Mmmm." She pressed herself closer into him. "I'm exhausted."

Luke laughed and gripped her tighter. "Yeah. I'm not surprised. I'm a little worn out myself." The sex in the Keys had been beautiful. The sex last night had been raw.

"I do feel sort of wrung out, now that you mention it."

Luke laughed again, and the vibration of his delight coursed through Ellie as if they were one person. In a way, she kind of felt like parts of them were starting to knit together. Not in any creepy soul mate way, but just . . . together. She hummed her pleasure and they both dozed for a few more hours.

When she woke up again, Luke was sitting up reading a paperback in bed next to her.

"Hey," he smiled.

"Hey back."

"You look nice and rested."

She rustled around until she was more or less sitting up. "I think I finally am."

"You sure?" He tucked a bookmark into place and set his book on the bedside table.

"Yes, I'm sure. It was the best kind of tired." She smiled, feeling a bit shy, even now, after all the grappling and crying out and, well, all of it. "But I'm also starving!" When she yawned and stretched her arms, she loved how Luke's eyes glanced across her body, in just the way his hands had touched her all night. Possessively.

"Good god, Ellie. You're tremendous." He pushed her back down on the bed beneath him, both of them laughing. "Let's go have a huge, fabulous dinner," he said between kisses. "What do you feel like? Something rich and dripping and French, or something spare and precise like sushi."

"Damn. Even the way you describe food is making me want you all over again. But I think I want French . . . lots of *foie gras* and perfectly trimmed vegetables and terrines and a bubbling *pot au feu*. Does that sound good? Let's go to Chez Jean Pierre and *indulge*." She pressed her hands against his cheeks and smiled in glee.

"Sounds great." He leaned in and gave her a brief kiss on the lips. "Do you want me to run a bath for you or are you going to take a shower?"

"You're sweet, but I think I'll do some laps and then shower outside. Want to join me?"

"Sure."

Chapter 10

Ethan McCormick sat in his private jet looking out over the silvery blue panorama of the sparkling Atlantic far below. He'd dreaded the reunion with his half brother and was mulling over how it had gone and how it might all pan out.

The actual meeting had not been nearly as bad as he'd anticipated. They hadn't laid eyes on one another in over four years. Still, no matter how much time passed between their confrontations or how thoroughly he tried to ready himself for their meetings, Ethan was never fully prepared for that moment of angry recognition when Luke first saw him. They were both so much like their father in appearance: the lean, hard lines of their cheekbones and the infamous gleaming blue eyes. But nearly all of the similarity died there. Or so Ethan had always thought.

He no longer resented that Luke had been set free, to live like a wild thing out in Wyoming for most of his childhood, while Ethan was hamstrung by convention. From the moment he was born, his father had treated Ethan as if *he* were the legitimate heir to the McCormick name and all that, ironically, entailed.

Yet, Luke would come to visit and even the very tone of his voice was a threat to his father's authority. Luke spoke like a quintessential American teenager who had no need of anyone's approval, respect, or even attention. For as long as Ethan could remember, his older brother had exuded an air of almost military self-possession.

When Luke had come to Scotland for a visit at Christmas one year, Ethan had been in awe of his seemingly effortless ability to, if not disrespect, at least dismiss their father's autocratic demands. Ethan had been seven or eight years old at the time, eager to impress or even be noticed by, this larger-than-life fifteen-year-old god.

Even when he reluctantly dressed in the formal clothes Ethan's mother demanded at dinner, Luke retained some inner rebellion, as if the young, arrogant cowboy was always simmering right beneath the surface of that immaculate white collar. Perhaps more impressive, Ethan thought, was Luke's ability to upset Vanessa McCormick, a woman no one else ever dared trifle with.

Everyone knew Vanessa's stance on the "matter of Luke," as she referred to her stepson. She had worked too long to rein in the wild, nearly debilitated man she'd fallen in love with, to let his upstart son from his first marriage stir up a bunch of needless worry of the past. "That never did anyone any good," she was wont to say. To her mind, she more than fulfilled her responsibilities as Luke's stepmother by including him in several holiday visits each year. She'd made certain that, as was his right by blood, he would inherit the castle in Scotland, along with one or two of the smaller properties, but she was deft and thorough in her transfer of any other moveable assets into trusts for her own sons, Ethan, Michael, and Trevor. She wasn't venal or greedy; she just felt justified in having been the wife to survive. She and her children had rights.

As they sat around the formal dining room on that long ago Christmas, being stared down upon by the painted penetrating eyes of every member of the McCormick clan since 1543, Vanessa strove to maintain her composure. Her three sons had been given special dispensations to eat dinner with the adults during their older brother's visit. Throughout his visit, the three younger boys had followed after him like ducklings, traipsing through the snow out to the stables at all hours of the day and night.

"So, Luke." Vanessa tried to sound affable. "Do you ride in an English saddle anymore?"

"Nope. Western all the time. I mean, if you're really working and rounding up cattle you can't have some prissy little seat."

Vanessa had one of the best prissy little seats in all of the United Kingdom, and well Luke knew it. "How often do you ride?" she replied, ignoring the insult.

"All the time, pretty much. Grant and I go out for an hour or two in the morning before I go to school, and then a couple of hours in the afternoon and early evening, just to check on the different herds and the fencing and that sort of thing."

Ethan watched in utter amazement as this *person* was able to walk the earth without giving his mother the respect she demanded from every other person in Christendom. His mouth must have been hanging open in wonderment, because his mother chose that moment to turn her formidable ire onto him.

"Are you catching flies, Ethan, or merely waiting for nurse to spoon-feed you?"

Ethan's jaw flew up into his upper teeth with a firm clap. He saw the older boy smile to himself as he shoved in another fork piled with peas and mashed potatoes and roast beef all in one big glob.

Ethan resented that little smile. He wasn't a baby, and when this *person* was not in attendance, he was also *the oldest*. And then along comes this . . . this . . .

"What do you think, Ethan?" Luke asked again.

Ethan refocused his eyes, but was unable to retrieve the thread of the conversation that had been taking place while he was busy stewing in a brew of his own filial frustration.

"About what?" he answered with a seven-year-old's idea of witty impertinence.

Luke smiled again. He liked this little guy. He was a total kiss-ass to his domineering mother, but he seemed to have a bit of real fire in there somewhere.

"About riding out tomorrow and roughing it in the gamekeeper's abandoned cottage in the Southern Forest. Just the two of us. Man to man."

Luke felt his father's stern gaze upon him, but refused to look in his direction. It had taken him years of practice—being bullied in Wyoming for being a parentless freak or a sissy who spoke with a Gaelic lilt that he'd worked tirelessly to erase—but it had paid off. Luke had succeeded in learning how to school his features so they revealed nothing. In fact, he congratulated himself silently, he didn't even have to look at his father unless he felt like it. Let his father stare. What did Luke care?

But when his father actually spoke, it was quite impossible to ignore him, no matter how schooled one was.

"Luke."

"Yes, Father," Luke answered, looking at him without quite meeting his eyes.

"I don't think December is the best time to go haring off to the Southern Forest on horseback, do you?"

Luke had intended it as a sort of bonding, brotherly adventure. But, like everything that transpired between Luke and his father, it went pear shaped. Ethan looked hurt that his father didn't think he was old enough or tough enough to handle a night of mid-winter camping, but rather than turning that hurt toward their father where it belonged, it looked as though the young stripling preferred to blame Luke for suggesting it in the first place, as if he had suggested such an adventure—something Luke got to do under the Wyoming stars any old night he felt like it—just to make Ethan feel small and worthless.

But now, Luke could tell, Ethan was in the damnable position of really wanting to go—and really wanting to defy his father—but not wanting to collude with the person who might be making fun of him. The boy's frustration at this dilemma was almost comically palpable. Luke smiled again at Ethan's steamy anger, in what he hoped was a burgeoning camaraderie, then turned to look at their stern father.

"Whatever you say, Father. I think Ethan could *probably* handle it."

Looking back, maybe if Luke hadn't inserted that *probably*, the two of them would have been best friends and built a new empire on the foundation of their mutual rebellion to their father.

Instead, Luke perceived arrogant disinterest in the younger boy's stormy gaze and simply gave in. "But if you don't think it's a good idea, Father, I am happy to defer to your wishes."

The man looked as if he had grave doubts about his firstborn ever deferring to his wishes unless they aligned entirely with his own original plans. And, almost immediately, looked as if he had doubts about the benefits of fostering any real friendship between Luke and Ethan. The last thing he needed was a joint rebellion within his petty fiefdom.

"I am glad you agree," his father paused to raise his eyebrows—because clearly Luke wanted to say that he didn't agree at all, but was merely conceding the point—then continued, "Ethan has no interest in slogging through the wet rain to sleep in a lean-to in any case. He will be performing the minuet he's been practicing these past few weeks in honor of your visit, and he needs to practice."

Ethan had loved music from the moment he could first recall consciousness, but that love was almost irrevocably tarnished when his father set it in direct opposition to a John Wayne adventure into the mysterious and far-reaching Southern Forest of their estate. And again, to Ethan's mind, it was Luke who was to blame for the odious comparison. A young boy mastering a Mozart minuet was no mean accomplishment, Ethan knew, but it felt empty and precious when he looked at it through Luke's disparaging eyes.

The petty resentments that were planted that day grew and flowered over the subsequent years into full-blown hatred. Luke could never confess the envy he felt for Ethan's smooth understanding of every social subtlety—the ease with which he moved through business negotiations, his marriage to the right woman—and Ethan could never admit his profound desire to eschew every shackle of his upbringing that had prevented him from ever once feeling a drop of the raw freedom that Luke radiated so naturally.

Perhaps they were finally being offered a chance to remedy some of the ancient misunderstandings. Vanessa McCormick had died four years before—the last time they'd all seen one another was at her funeral—so at least that particular splinter had been removed. Ethan respected his mother, but in hindsight he felt a pang of associated guilt for how carelessly she'd treated Luke. Of course Luke had feigned independence—he was a teenaged boy after all—but it was clear to the most obtuse observer that he craved the affection that only a mother, or even a stepmother, could have provided.

Now with their father so close to death, perhaps something good could come out of all the years of miscommunication.

The next day when he was back in his office in London, Ethan picked up the phone and dialed Luke's number.

"Hello," Luke answered, sounding wary.

"Hi, it's Ethan."

"Yes."

"So," Ethan persisted, "I just wanted to say thanks again for dinner last night. I'm sorry if I . . . "

Silence.

Ethan exhaled through his clenched teeth. This git wasn't going to give him an inch. He tried again. "If I spoke out of turn in front of Ellie—about you moving to Scotland—I mean . . . you two seem close . . . I thought she might know already."

On the one hand, Luke had to agree with him. Even though it had only been a few weeks, he also felt like he'd known Ellie a lifetime and he knew the two of them exuded a unified front. Jo and Denny had remarked upon it in the Keys; just that night at dinner in Palm Beach the chef and his wife had sat with them at the bar after the restaurant cleared out, and asked how it was possible Ellie hadn't brought her boyfriend in before. Was he visiting from out of town? Where had she been hiding him?

Luke had watched as Ellie's smooth skin reddened slightly at the innocent reference to her 'boyfriend.'

Now, well after midnight, she was curled up asleep on the couch next to him, as if she'd done so for years. He tried to give Ethan the benefit of the doubt. That had to be progress.

"Look, I appreciate the call, but I'm not sure we're ever going to be buddy-buddy. You're kind of an asshole."

"Well, the feeling's mutual. You're all Zen master and Mister Equilibrium for everyone else on the planet except me." Ethan's voice was strained and cracked a tiny bit at the end.

Luke thought it sounded like the voice of the little boy Ethan had once been.

Ethan took a deep breath. "Anyway, maybe we can just get to know each other, or whatever, without the burden of so many years of *sibling rivalry* on top of everything else. We could treat each other with, oh I don't know, common courtesy."

"Is that what it was to you?"

"What?"

"Sibling rivalry? Is that what it was?" Luke gently moved Ellie's sleeping head off his lap and walked quietly out to the back deck, sliding the glass door shut behind him so as not to wake her.

"Of course that's what it was to me. What else? Why, what was it to you?"

Luke looked out at the ocean and pictured Ethan sitting at his desk in London. "What in the world was I *rival* for? —"

"All what? Eton and Cambridge? All the constricting education and parental suffocation and expectations and—"

"You need to pause and think before you speak to me." This was never going to work. "I might need to hang up and call you back in a few minutes because you don't even listen to yourself—"

"Fuck you. You're so much holier-than-everybody. All thoughtful and concise—"

"Ethan." Luke's voice was low, but he might as well have been shouting for all the power behind it. "I had no *parents*. Are you really that much of an idiot? It's so fucking basic I wouldn't think I'd need to spell it out for you. Every holiday, every godforsaken visit to Scotland, it was like being taken to the goddamn zoo—like peering through the glass at the great apes: *this is what a family looks like, the pithy narrator in my mind would say, this is a father, this is a mother, those three are brothers. And you will never ever be a part of any of that.* And I've dealt with it. I know it doesn't seem like it to you, but I have."

"Luke—"

"Let me finish. Please. I *have* dealt with it. I haven't stayed away from Father out of bitterness or spite. I just have nothing to go on, you know? There's nothing *there*. It was all too much after Kate and I split, and I had to accept that I couldn't even make a family of my own. But it's actually really hard when you don't know, firsthand, what a family *is*, you know?"

Ethan was silent.

For once, thought Luke meanly.

Luke inhaled slowly then let it out, tried to let it all out. "I'm totally with you on this *common courtesy* plan, but it's going to be a little . . . slow, okay? I'm going to ask you to be patient. The problem is—" Luke laughed a quick, self-deprecating snort. "—and don't take this personally, but I see your face and I want to punch somebody. Like you, for a start."

Ethan started laughing and then Luke started laughing too.

"But don't take it personally!" Ethan imitated his brother's stab at being considerate. "Other than wanting to clock you every time I see you, it's all good!" They both started laughing again.

When they settled down, Ethan spoke first. "So, when do you think you can come over to London? Not to press. I just—I mean it would be good to see you and Ellie here. Do you think you're really going to stay in South Florida permanently?"

"I don't know. It probably sounds ridiculous but I think I'll just go where Ellie goes for the rest of my life."

"It doesn't sound ridiculous." Ethan was serious again. "None of us ever liked Kate, and that was just one more thing that got all twisted around, now that I think about it. You probably thought it was another example of all of us passing judgment on you or something, but she really just wasn't nice to you. Not that I'd know a nice person if I tripped over one, but Maria can tell that sort of thing."

The two of them laughed again, strange and unfamiliar, but so welcome. Luke took a deep breath and tried to listen to his brother's words without filtering them through the years of bitter prejudice. Ethan was right, and a weight started to slip off Luke's shoulders. "You were right. Maria was right. About Kate, I mean."

"Oh."

"Yeah. Oh."

"Well, all of that was just to say, following Ellie seems like quite the right thing for you to do. Please bring her to London, for the visit, or whenever, however it works out. I'd love to introduce her to Maria and the boys."

Despite all the problems and judgments Luke had passed on his brother's arrogance and foolishness and aggressive business practices, he could never fault Ethan's wife. Maria Costa had grown up outside of Rome and Ethan had had the good sense to pursue her mercilessly until she agreed to marry him.

"I think Ellie and Maria would get along," Luke agreed, then added, "Now, let's not push our luck with the whole brotherly love thing. I'm glad you called. And glad you tracked me down. I'll let you know how soon I can get over there. Ellie's best friend is getting married in California in a couple weeks and she's asked me to go with her. So after that, okay?"

"Sounds good. Call whenever. Stay with us if you want, or at a hotel, or whatever. But know that you're welcome to stay with us, okay?"

"Okay. Thanks for that. See you soon."

"Bye."

Ellie started to come awake as Luke lifted her off the couch to take her upstairs, then she tucked her head into the crook of his neck and took a deep breath. "Mmmmm."

"You feel good, too," he said.

"Who was on the phone?"

"Ethan."

"Mmmm. What did he have to say?"

"He wanted to thank you for dinner."

"And?" she asked sleepily.

"And mend thirty years of misunderstanding and treachery, preferably in five minutes or less."

Ellie gave a husky laugh into the fabric of his shirt. Luke loved the feel of her breath as it warmed his skin. He settled her onto the bed and then just stared down as her soft mussed red hair spread out around her face. She burrowed into her pillow and pulled the sheets up to her chin. She looked as if she were ready to drift right back into a deep sleep when her eyes opened slowly, glassy, and she spied Luke looking at her.

"What are you doing?"

"Staring at you."

She smiled and closed her eyes. "Okay." He marveled at how her contentment spread from her expression right into his soul.

A week and a half later, Ellie sat on the flight to San Francisco with that same smile. She wasn't really able to make eye contact with Luke without at least a slight look of mischief or optimism appearing on her face. He'd just caught her eye as a ridiculous trio of teenagers sauntered by, all of them nearly screaming into their cell phones and the two girls carrying enormous pillows.

Luke rolled his eyes. "What's with the pillows?"

She was almost too distracted by the whisper of his breath against her sensitive skin to really interpret the words. "I . . . uh . . . "

His face was still near hers so she turned to face him full on. She could stare into his blue eyes endlessly. Mooning, she supposed.

"Do you know?" he asked again.

She shook her head, because she had no idea what he was talking about. If she weren't so happy, she might have been more concerned about her precarious condition: the complete inability to concentrate when Luke was around.

"Are you even listening to me?"

"No." She smiled dreamily.

He leaned in and kissed her. He probably meant it to be something brisk, but she softened and arched into him, letting her hand fall to his lap in an unintentionally (sort of) provocative fashion.

She released a slight moan of pleasure then opened her eyes, only to see a little blue-eyed boy peering at them—with avid interest—over the headrest behind Luke.

Ellie pulled away quickly. Luke opened his eyes slowly to look at her. "Careful. Not much we can do between now and California if we get too stirred up." He grazed his thumb along her lower lip.

She widened her eyes then jerked her glance to the boy. Luke turned to see the little peeping Tom.

"Hey, man. What's up?" Luke let his hand fall slowly away from Ellie's lip.

The boy looked taken aback to be spoken to so directly, then figured he might as well meet like with like. "Just watching you kiss the pretty lady."

"I like your honesty, kid. What's your name?"

"William."

"How old are you William?"

"I am five-and-three-quarters years old."

William's mother had just finished her cell phone conversation in a rush before she had to turn it off. "William, stop bothering those people—"

"Oh, it's no bother," Ellie said over the top of her seat. "We were just getting acquainted."

"Oh, thanks. It's a little crazy traveling alone without his dad. Sit back down. Face forward, please."

The boy complied reluctantly, and right before his head dipped below the top of the seat, he gave Luke a small man-to-man thumbs up.

Ellie covered her mouth to prevent the laughter from barking out. "I can't believe you just got the equivalent of a fist bump from a five-year-old for making out with me."

"It's obvious to every male of the species that I am one lucky bastard."

Ellie leaned her head back into her seat and closed her eyes, reaching out to lace her fingers through Luke's. "Thanks for coming to California with me."

"Of course, I'm honored you want to trot me out. I'll try to be good."

She left her head resting on the seat but opened her eyes and turned to face him. "When are you *not* good?"

He shook his head a little. "Ellie, I've tried to warn you, I'm very bad in large social situations. I tend to be a bit . . . awkward."

"Really?"

"Really."

"I mean, I could see how that might happen, but you're also really intuitive." She blushed. "I mean . . . I think you're really attentive." She blushed again.

"Go on."

"Ugh. Seriously. I think of how you spoke to my friend at Starbucks that first day—with such focus and concentration. Or how when you came over that one night, you knew just what to say to my parents to put them at ease. You don't seem easily distracted." Her blush deepened and she looked at her lap, embarrassed. "Whatever."

"I hope I always make you blush like that." He reached one finger under her chin to bring her face to his again. "It makes me feel reborn."

She looked at him and wanted to weep for why this amazing man had not been showered with the love and affection she couldn't even contain. She brought her hand up to his cheek. "Then I will always blush for you, because I always want you to feel that way."

He turned and kissed the palm of her hand.

She spoke again in a more pragmatic tone. "But now, back to this social awkwardness business. What do you think it is? Are you too busy, you know, looking for spies?" She winked. "Or do you find it difficult to come up with topics of conversation, or people bore you, or what?"

"I don't know. Mostly large crowds just unsettle me. All that simultaneous talking and laughing and clinking of glasses and it feels like nobody is really listening to anyone. It just unnerves me. And then I'm exhausted. You know what I mean?"

"I hear what you're saying, but that's not how it's going to be with this group. My parents are going to be there, first off. And they already love you."

The four of them had gone out to dinner twice since the first time they'd met at Ellie's. Luke had impressed them that first night—even in a sweaty T-shirt—but in a pair of ironed trousers and a collared shirt at their favorite restaurant in Palm Beach, he'd totally sealed the parental deal.

She continued trying to put him at ease. "And Lotta is insanely interested in everything. When she's talking to you, she's one of those people who makes you feel like the world is about to self-destruct and you are the *only* person left on earth who can stop the bomb from exploding." Ellie stared at him in a wide-eyed impersonation of Lotta's 'interested' face.

Luke laughed and Ellie continued. "And there are only going to be like thirty of us there, so I seriously doubt there will be any of that weird superficiality."

He didn't look convinced.

"And if all that fails to be true, you can always just stand next to me and hold my hand and look at me and pet my back and whisper what you want to do to me in the room at the inn later. That'd be fine too." She squeezed his hand to assure him.

"I like the sound of that plan immensely."

They were quiet for a while, as the plane took off and reached cruising altitude. Ellie loved how the two of them could sit in perfect stillness. Their time together so far had been revealing and wonderful in many ways, but especially in that peaceful companionship.

Lotta had been thrilled when Ellie confirmed she was, in fact, bringing Mr. Blue Eyes to the wedding. Ellie smiled at the memory of their conversation and Luke caught the humor in her face.

"What are you smiling about?"

"Just how Lotta is taking credit for us."

Ellie savored the feel of Luke's thumb caressing the back of her hand. She kept smiling, eyes closed, then felt a wave of worry and opened her eyes and looked at him.

"Hey, I've been meaning to ask you, are you going to call your daughter while we're in San Francisco?"

His face folded in, his expression receding away from her.

Silence.

This was the problem with intimacy, she realized. On the one hand, she honestly didn't want to pry: he was his own person, with his own life, after all. On the other, if *she* couldn't ask him these things, then no one could. She'd sensed the subject of his daughter had been off limits. Ellie had tried to steer the conversation in that direction a couple of times when they'd been in the Keys, and then a few times in the past week, but to no avail. Luke was very adept at deflecting any topics he didn't wish to address.

"Will you tell me her name, at least?"

He looked across the aisle toward the escape door, as if jumping might be preferable to her interrogation.

Silence.

"It's a long flight," she said softly. "Are you just going to ignore me?"

"I might."

"Oh, come on. Even if you don't call her, what's the harm in telling me about her?"

"You're going to try to hurl us together. You're a fixer, remember?"

"Okay." Ellie sighed and couldn't hide a self-deprecating smile. "For now, what if I promise not to, you know, push you in that direction? I'm just curious. Can't you talk to me about her? At least a name?"

He looked down at Ellie's hand twined into his own and stayed quiet.

"Diana McCormick . . . Didi."

"Oh, how sweet! You named her after your mother?"

Luke tried to remain stoic, but something about the way Ellie made everything in life seem loving and *coordinated* left him confused and frustrated. He wanted to retaliate. "I only did that to piss off my father."

"No. No, you didn't. You did it to honor the memory of your mother."

"No. I was . . . I was not the nice person you think I am."

"But you are." Her voice held a vehemence he didn't recognize. She looked around the plane then lowered her voice to a whisper, "You are to me."

He smiled and brought her hand to his lips.

But she refused to be placated with a kiss. "I mean it—you are *not* that person, not anymore at least. Whatever changes you made when you decided to move on, or redefine yourself, or whatever—" She swung her left hand around vaguely. "—by doing that, you changed. You made the decision to change."

He tried to believe in himself with the same intensity that Ellie believed in him, but he doubted he ever would. He'd actually been there when he'd done a few unspeakable things, things that did not simply evaporate in the wake of an epiphany or a decision to sell all of one's belongings and move to a modest bungalow on the beach in Florida. To humble oneself.

He shut his eyes.

"So, what does Didi do?"

Luke smiled and then opened his eyes. "You're being relentless."

"Of course I am. That's why you like me, remember?" Her eyes twinkled with mischief and purpose—and he had to admit he adored her persistence. He felt the quick pull of sexual tension and exhaled slowly to prevent the wave of desire from getting ahead of him.

"Ellie."

"Luke."

"She's . . . I have no idea. The last time we spoke she was in her first year of college."

"In England?"

He soon realized that Ellie was going to peck and badger him until she got the bare details of Didi's existence, so he might as well provide them quickly, rather than letting a drawn out assault ruin the whole flight.

"Didi finished boarding school in the UK, then went to California for university. She wanted to become a teacher the last I heard."

"When was that? At Kate's funeral, right?"

"Ellie . . . please . . . "

She gripped his hand with a tight, brief, encouraging squeeze. "It's just me. Just tell me."

He released a long exhale. "Fine. Yes. She was at her mother's funeral in London, of course. I thought there might be a chance for us to, well, at least connect there. I was totally wrong. She stared at me across the coffin as if I'd pulled the trigger. Even Ethan thought I was getting the raw end of the deal that time." Luke gave a short, bitter laugh.

"So what happened at Kate's funeral?"

He hesitated. "We all met up in London. Kate died there. So, anyway, I was working an office job in China at the time. I flew to London; Didi was already living in San Francisco by then. Anyway, a very angry nineteen-year-old woman and her heartless thirty-nine year-old father at an unexpected funeral did not make a pretty picture."

"So, have you seen her since then?"

"No."

"Oh, that's just so sad." Ellie looked as if she might cry.

"Listen, she's entitled to *not* want to see me. I was not a good husband nor a good father."

"I just don't believe it. You have so much love—"

"For you."

"I don't see how that's possible. You're considerate. You're careful. There's no way that can just be for me."

"I don't know if a hostile young woman who's just lost her mother can see that. I think she would have preferred to see me despising myself, or at least weeping."

"You didn't cry?" Ellie had just finished blinking back her own emotion.

"It's not really my bag. I'm not a crier."

"But . . . she . . . you must have loved Kate . . . once . . . didn't you?"

Luke looked away across the aisle again. Anything to get away from this conversation.

"I don't know if I ever did, love her, I mean." Then he turned to her. "Certainly nothing like what I feel for you."

"Oh."

"Yeah. Oh. I've dealt with the guilt and the mourning, I guess you'd call it. But Kate was really lost to me very soon after we got married. Maybe even before. She was really messed up, but I never knew until it was way too late."

"Well. Maybe it's not too late for you and Didi."

Luke nodded doubtfully, but he loved how Ellie was able to spread a protective, emotional shield around him. She wasn't being naive. She just wanted him to be happy. Safe. He supposed this was what it felt like to have someone love you. It was an unfamiliar sensation.

Ellie pressed on. "The thing is, with your daughter, you need to be making overtures to see her. You need to remind her that the door is always open. You need to remind her a lot. What a waste it would be if years went by, years of unnecessary estrangement, because you were trying to give her space when she really needed you to be more communicative, not less."

"I know what you're saying, but—"

"But what?"

"But nothing. You're right. I'll leave her a message if you like."

"It's not a matter of what *I* like—"

"Please. I know your intentions are good, but they're still *your* intentions. I've carved out a very simple, orderly life, because that's how I can deal with it. It's never just one phone call to my daughter. You'll see. Or one trip to London. Or one trip to San Francisco. Everything just explodes into a bunch of uncontrollable pieces—"

She started laughing then put her free hand up to his cheek again. "Oh, my sweet Luke. You are so deluded." She kissed him gently. "Life is always exploding into a bunch of uncontrollable pieces all around us, whether we can deal with it or not."

"I know." He kissed her back. "I won't overanalyze it. I'll leave her a message when we land."

"I'm glad."

He smiled and stared at her lips, then back into her eyes.

"Don't look at me like that. I'm glad for you, not for me, you rat!" She gave him a little shove.

He shook his head and his smile broadened.

"Okay. I'm glad for you and for me for having convinced you. Is that better?"

He kissed her on the cheek and put his mouth against her ear. "Have a care. I believe you will always convince me."

Chapter 11

They landed in San Francisco and made their way out to the rental cars. As they walked across the large lot, the September temperatures were strangely cool. Ellie had visited Lotta many times over the years and she'd never fully understood the deep affection so many people had for the city. It always seemed too cold when it should have been warm, and too sunny when she'd planned for rain.

"I love it here," Luke declared.

"That's so funny, I was just thinking how it's like a bestseller that everyone adores and I stand at the back of the room not really understanding its mass appeal."

"Really? I can't believe it. Look around. Everything is so photogenic. So crisp."

"I guess I'll need to see it through your eyes. Or through my camera lens."

They were driving into the city to spend Wednesday night with Lotta and Philip, then the four of them were going to drive up to Elk in tandem Thursday afternoon. The rest of their families were arriving Friday.

Luke accelerated onto the Freeway in the expensive rental car he'd insisted on paying for.

"Why in the world should you pay for this car when you're here all weekend as my guest?"

"Because you reserved a Neon or some damn thing and I wanted this ludicrously overpriced convertible. It would be sort of petty of me to do a spreadsheet breaking down the cost of the Neon versus the cost of the Mercedes and then pay you the difference, so let me just do this."

Ellie stared out the window. "Do we need to talk about money?"

"What about it?"

"I mean, I've invited you here and I want to pay for everything. We're not going to split the hotel or any of that."

Luke reluctantly turned his attention away from the road. Ellie had come to realize that he hated having conversations of any real depth while he was driving. He did not see his time behind the wheel as a passive role from point A to point B. He was *driving*.

He turned his eyes back to the road. "This is ridiculous. Of course I'm going to pay."

"Why is it ridiculous? Do you feel like because you're a man—"

"Oh, here we go." He kept his attention firmly on the curving highway in front of him.

"What do you mean *here we go*?"

"You sound exercised. That's all."

Ellie tried to breathe—or to steady her breathing. She took a deep breath and spoke in a voice that had always served her well in private equity negotiations with older, sexist investment bankers. "Okay. Let's start over. Hi, I'm Eleanor Sinclair. I am financially independent and I'm not interested in entering into any relationship that does not honor that financial independence."

Luke smiled.

"In addition, I will not tolerate sexist assumptions that prevent me from paying for certain things, or everything if I feel like it."

Luke was silent. No longer smiling.

"Well?" she snapped.

"Oh. Were you finished? I couldn't tell. That particular voice sounds like it's accustomed to speaking in lengthy paragraphs. Lengthy *uninterrupted* paragraphs."

She felt a burning heat in her nostrils that usually foreshadowed blind rage. That cartoon with the red smoke coming out of the bull's nose suddenly made perfect sense. "There's no need to be patronizing—"

"Really. Good. Because that's exactly what you're being."

"What? Me?"

"Why would you assume that it's because I'm a man that I want to pay for things? I don't want to get into some decades-old battle of the sexes. In this at least, I was merely treating you like a guy, or a girl, or a person, or whatever. We're traveling companions. In this type of situation, I'm accustomed to paying my fair share."

Ellie fumed and continued to look out her window, not seeing any of the wheat colored hills that rolled past as their car swept across the beautiful peninsula toward the city.

Luke relaxed his shoulders. "Look, I'm also financially independent. I'd even venture to say I'm extremely rich, if it didn't sound so pompous. I know it might appear, well, *odd* that I was working for a minimum wage when we met, and living a rather Spartan existence, but that was all a conscious decision, you know. I have . . . plenty."

"But . . . " Ellie started to speak then didn't really know which direction she wanted to go. Just tell him her net worth and be done with it? How did this get so contorted? It was impossible to know the right way.

Luke watched her mental calisthenics. He wanted to smile, but was afraid she would think he was making fun of her. "Just relax. I can pay for some stuff. You can pay for some stuff. Or if you want to pay for this trip and then I'll pay for the London trip. However you want to handle it. Just so you aren't worrying about it. I have my own money. You have your own money. Just like I have my own house and you have your own house."

For the first bit of that little speech, she'd been happily lulled by that just-relax part, hmm, your-own-money, yes, exactly, and then that your-own-house business didn't sound very promising. *At all.* Eventually—Ellie was already starting to hope—they would be permanently cohabitating. So that separate-house analogy was, if not specious, at least short-sighted.

Would he want to combine their finances when she invited him to move into her place? Obviously, they weren't going to move into his place. It was barely big enough for him alone. Did he foresee keeping his own place indefinitely? A private refuge of sorts? Would they always be separated like that? Is that what he wanted? Did he need that?

Ellie debated with herself about how far down this rabbit hole she really wanted to go. It felt sort of creepy and neurotic even to her. She could practically hear Lotta's voice in her brain yelling, "Don't be so controlling! Go with the flow! If he says he has his own money, then leave it alone! Quit getting ahead of yourself!" She started chewing on the cuticle of her thumb.

She tried to go with the flow, she really did. But she wasn't Lotta. "Well, I mean, do you think you want to have your own house forever?"

She felt the air around them go perfectly still even though the wind was whipping everywhere. He kept looking at the highway. "Do I need to pull over so we can have a really deep, life-altering discussion, or are we still talking about the rental car?"

Ellie didn't know whether to laugh or cry, what came out was an awkward combination of both. "No. Yes. Just the rental car. We're good." She sounded cheerful enough, but wiped at her eyes as if a speck of dust were lodged there.

A few minutes later she clicked open the GPS on her phone and double-checked the directions to Lotta's place, serving as his co-pilot and thus avoiding any dangerous forays into any further deep, life-altering discussions.

Lotta's apartment was a modest duplex in a walk-up in the district South of Market known as SoMA. She'd bought it soon after moving out west after graduation from UVA. Everyone had thought she'd lost her mind, especially her mother, Sheila Jamieson. Crack phials and old hypodermic needles had littered the sidewalk the first time Sheila flew in from her pristine townhouse in Georgetown. Lotta had called Ellie in New York and the two of them had laughed so hard at their mothers' reactions to their so-called lifestyle decisions.

At the time, Ellie and Rob were living in a big loft in a walk-up on the Lower East Side of Manhattan, before there were any hip restaurants, late-night bars, or indie knitting shops. Ellie's mother had come up from their farm outside of Richmond, stood in the kitchen for five minutes without removing her snug-fitting tan leather gloves, and suggested they repair to The Colony Club with all due haste.

But now, a dozen years later, Lotta's place was at the center of a thriving, artistic neighborhood replete with bakeries, art galleries, music stores, and bodegas. Ellie and Luke each carried their own bags up the narrow interior staircase to the second floor. Ellie knocked on the door and almost immediately heard the shriek of joy—"Ellie!"—accompanied by the pounding of excited footsteps.

Lotta pulled the door open with crazy enthusiasm and grabbed Ellie into her arms. "Thank *god* you're here. I'm so damn glad to see you!" She released her hug slightly and started to pull Ellie into the bright, open-plan loft.

Ellie resisted her with a tug, and then Lotta caught sight of Luke. Ellie tried to see him the way he must look to Lotta, pulling off his aviator sunglasses, white oxford shirt rolled up his strong forearms, khaki safari jacket.

"Oh my!" Lotta's eyes sparkled as she took in Luke from head to toe. Then she turned to Ellie. "His eyes really are *that* blue."

"Luke McCormick," Ellie said with a loving glance in his direction, "this is Carlotta Jamieson. Lotta, this is Luke."

He reached out his hand to shake hers and Lotta dove at him. "Are you kidding me?" she yelled into his ear. "I'm not going to shake your hand, you idiot!"

If he hadn't seen her near-tackle of Ellie a few moments before, the two of them might have tumbled right back down the staircase. As it was, he had a second to brace himself and hold his position. Ellie was laughing over Lotta's shoulder as she watched Luke's intense awkwardness. She suspected no one had ever greeted him with quite that level of fervor. He was adorably uncomfortable.

"That's enough. He's not really into all that grabbing."

Lotta gave him a wink and a little pat-pat on his upper arm after she finally released him, then turned to re-enter the apartment. "That's not what I hear," she whispered as she slid past Ellie.

Ellie burst out laughing again and dragged Luke into the apartment.

"Don't worry. She's the only one who will attack you . . . standing up at least." Ellie winked.

Lotta was calling to them from the far end of the apartment. "I moved the guest room down here last year, to give people more privacy."

Luke had pulled Ellie into a quick passionate hug after that wink, and Lotta returned to the main living area to find them caught up in a steamy kiss.

"Jesus, people! Your room is only a few feet away!"

Luke released Ellie from the full embrace, but kept his hand resting at her lower back.

Ellie spoke through a breathy laugh, "It was a long flight."

"Oh my." Lotta sounded exactly like her genteel, diplomatic mother. Then she put one hand on her hip and turned to Luke. "Do you speak or just stand there and smolder?"

For a split-second Ellie thought Luke was going to give her the cold shoulder, then his face broke into a stellar grin. "Both. As the company dictates."

"Well, isn't he a saucy dish? Come on you two, enough banter, let's get you settled. Then I'm going to need Ellie all to myself for a few hours."

"Sounds good. I'd love to go for a run while you two are at it, if you could point me in the right direction."

"Oh, god, is he a jock too? Can he keep up with you in the pool, El?"

"Yeah, pretty much."

"Let me call Philip. He'll be able to tell you a good route. What do you usually do? Something insane like a quick ten miles?"

He smiled and stayed quiet.

"Damn you people. Honestly, I run for the bus and I feel like I'm going to keel right over." She grabbed the telephone off the kitchen counter and hit the speed dial while she talked. "Hey, it's me. Yeah, me too," she said in a more intimate tone. "Anyway, Luke . . . yeah, Ellie's Luke—" She rolled her eyes toward Ellie. "—uh-huh . . . yeah . . . Yes! Let me get a word in! He wants to go for one of your quick ten-mile runs. Where should I send him?"

She started straightening some magazines on the coffee table and gesturing to the guest room for Ellie and Luke to dump their bags while she finished the phone call.

"Okay, let me ask him." She pressed her hand over the phone. "Philip said he'd love to run too—ugh, you are so male, fine—he didn't say the word *love*, he wanted me to clarify that, he said he was going to go for a run today. He'll be home in about an hour if you want to wait and go together."

"Sure, that sounds great."

Forty-five minutes later, Luke sat staring at his cell phone, trying to muster the courage to call his daughter. Ellie and Lotta had gone off to check out the flower markets after swooning over the wedding dress and nailing down some of the other details.

Ellie kept saying, "Seriously, Lotta, who are you?" And then the two of them would start laughing all over again. Luke pretended to read his book in one corner of the room as he listened to Ellie assuage Lotta's remaining concerns.

"No one will ever notice that . . . oooh, you're so clever . . . I never would have thought of that . . . oh, that's the sweetest thing I ever heard . . . "

He'd realized, as he listened to her soothe and temper her anxious friend, that he loved Ellie completely. He loved the way she was supportive and joyful and never took anything away from other people's happiness to fuel her own. It was as though she truly believed there was more than enough happiness in the world to go around.

"Is it a funny book? I'd heard it was sort of grim." She'd come to say goodbye, and leaned his shoulder.

"The book is miserable. I was just thinking of you while I pretended to read it." He kept both hands on the paperback lest he pull her down onto the couch on top of him.

"You're so bad." She kissed him at the pulse along his neck. "But try to be good." Then she was gone.

Ellie made him want to be good, to be the type of person who made amends with his estranged daughter, he thought, as his finger hovered over the numbers he'd punched in after finding Didi's number right there online. He closed his eyes and pushed the call button, then brought the phone to his ear.

She picked up after half a ring. "Hello."

"Oh. Hello."

"Hello? Who's calling please?"

"Hi, Didi, it's . . . " He didn't want to say *it's your father*, in case it sounded too autocratic, or like Darth Vader. He might've contemplated an opening salvo before dialing, he chided himself. He always felt unprepared when it came to Didi. "It's Luke . . . your dad."

"Oh."

"I . . . I'm in San Francisco and I know it's been a couple of years—"

"Yeah, more than a couple. Why are you calling me?"

He exhaled and tried not to react to her anger with more of the same. "Well. Because I'm nearby, and because a friend told me that *of course your daughter wants you to call her*, that deep down everyone wants to be reunited with their parents, or at least have resolution. I told her I didn't think that was necessarily true—I doubt it's true in my case, with my own father, I mean—but I respect this friend's opinion so I thought I'd just call and say I

was in town if you wanted to meet for a coffee or something."
Silence. "Or not. No pressure. I don't want to impose on your
time or anything—"

"Slow down," she interrupted. "Uh . . . I don't know what
to say. I—"

"You don't need to say anything. It sounds like it's not a
good time. Never mind. You can always call me, this is my US
cell number now, so you've got it, just in case. So never mind—"

"Wait!" She sounded almost amused. "Just stop for a
minute. Stop telling me what to mind or not to mind or whether
or not it's a good time for me. Give me a second, okay?" She
exhaled in a self-monitoring way that made him feel like he was
listening to himself. "I think I might want to see you," she said.
"Or maybe talk to you at least. I'm in the middle of something at
work. I can fill you in on all that, too—I'd like to. I ended up
graduating early and I was recruited into a really great position."

Luke had a momentary, appalling sensation that she'd been
recruited by an intelligence agency, then tossed it aside as
ludicrous. She was a peace-loving, French major from Stanford.
Impossible.

"Okay," he answered slowly. "I mean, *great*." His voice was
finally revealing his burgeoning enthusiasm. "That would be *really*
great." Something deep in his chest constricted and released.
"We're going to be up near Mendocino for the weekend but I'm
happy to come back into town early on Sunday, if that works for
you."

"Sunday would be great. Why don't we meet for brunch or
lunch or whatever? Do you want to bring your friend? I'm living
with someone, too. Maybe we should all four meet up. Safety in
numbers and all that."

And that slight hint of an easing, or humor, made all the
difference. "That sounds really great. Want to pick a place now?
Just in case I'm out of cell phone range or whatever?"

"Sure. Let me think. Why don't we meet at one o'clock at
Bar Jules on Hayes? I'll make a reservation."

"Okay. And if you want to call me before—or talk or
whatever—you have my number now. So call anytime. Okay?"

"Okay . . . Dad . . . Luke . . . I don't even know what to call you . . . I'll see you Sunday."

"I'm really looking forward to it."

"Oddly enough, so am I. Thanks for calling. Really. See you then. Bye."

"Bye."

Luke kept the phone pressed to his ear as the dead line clipped and faded. He was still sitting there listening to nothing when the front door bolts slid open and a tall, aggravated, preppy-looking guy walked in.

Luke stood up as he set the phone on the coffee table. "Hey, you must be Philip. I'm Luke."

"Hey man, I just got rear-ended. This neighborhood is a fucking nightmare. The things we do for love and all that." He strode across the loft and shook Luke's hand. "I'm so glad you and Ellie are here."

"Me too. Nice to meet you."

"Let me change out of my work clothes and we can go for a long run."

"Sounds good. Thanks." Luke had already changed into shorts and an old T-shirt and was ready to go. "Take your time. I don't think Lotta and Ellie will be back much before midnight if that so-called punch list is anything to go by."

"That punch list is my nemesis!" Philip called as he went into his bedroom.

A few minutes later, the two men had hit a brisk pace and were making their way out of the neighborhood and across the bridge to Berkeley. Luke was grateful Philip wasn't the type to launch into all sorts of choppy conversation while they ran. They kept mostly silent for about an hour, when Philip finally cried uncle.

"All right, you win!" He panted and stopped to rest his hands on his knees and catch his breath. They were about ten blocks from Lotta's apartment. "Dude. You're a machine. Let's get a beer."

The two of them walked for a while, then sat at an outside table in front of a pub. "So," Philip began. "You know I'm Ellie's cousin, right?"

"Yeah. I heard that." Luke felt like this might be the beginning of the family grilling portion of the trip. "I've met her parents a couple of times—I think I passed muster."

Philip took an appreciative sip of his Sierra Nevada and put the bottle down on the table, making sure to set it exactly in the center of the coaster. "You've definitely passed with flying colors as far as my aunt and uncle are concerned." He took another sip of his beer. "So, you're Ethan McCormick's brother?"

"Half. We have the same father, different mothers."

"Cool. I do venture capital for a lot of computer companies that specialize in high-level security. I've been following his progress for a while."

"Yeah. He's been pretty successful."

Philip laughed. "Yeah. Pretty."

Ethan's net worth was public information. He was splashed all over every billionaire list from *Fortune* to the *FT*. Luke had made a habit of ignoring all of it. "We kind of lost touch for a while, though I think we're in the midst of mending fences."

"Hmm." Philip took another sip of beer. "And what about you? What type of business are you in? Early retirement in Florida? Ellie was a little cagey when I asked her."

Luke smiled. "I'm not after your cousin's money, if that's what you're worried about."

He laughed as he reached for his beer. "I tried to tell my mom that you were probably worth a lot more than Ellie's IPO golden parachute, but our whole extended family is pretty star struck when it comes to Ellie's financial prowess. She and Rob made a lot of money for a lot of people—a lot of us. She's got some devoted fans."

"Trust me. I'm her most devoted fan—but it's nothing to do with her finances."

"I believe you. Just letting you know the naysayers are out there and they'll be poking around this weekend. My dad is especially suspicious. Ellie's his goddaughter and he's incredibly protective. You might want to come up with a story or an alibi or whatever. Are you Ethan's older brother or younger?"

Normally, Luke would have bristled at the interrogation, but he thought of Ellie and relaxed. These people loved her. He was going to have to get used to it. "Older. My mother died shortly after I was born. Ellie knows all the details. In any case, Ellie's going to come with me to London in a couple of weeks to meet my ailing father. There won't be any way to hide my aristocratic, moneyed background from her then."

Philip quirked his lips. "Aristocratic? *And* moneyed? How sad. Inherited a shitload of property and prestige? Poor you."

Luke met the smile with one that was only slightly more jaded. "Yeah, poor me." He lifted his glass and raised it to Philip, then took a sip. "So, do you have any investors interested in a thousand acres of craggy, non-arable land in Northern Scotland? It's ideal for fending off Saxon invaders."

Philip burst out laughing. "Get Rees Jones to design thirty-six-holes of destination golf and I just might."

"I don't really see that happening, but you never know. And to answer your original question, I worked in Asia as a military consultant for nearly twenty years, and now I'm more or less retired. But I usually just tell people I was a businessman. It's easier."

Narrowing his eyes, Philip stared more intently. "Sounds dangerous."

"Not anymore." Luke shrugged. "It had its moments."

They finished their beers and walked back to the apartment. As Philip opened the door, Luke was surprised to hear the throaty laughter of Ellie and Lotta coming from the living room, the two of them already back from their supposedly endless string of errands.

Ellie clapped her hands together and leapt up from the sofa. "Look who's back!" She wrapped her arms around Luke's waist and looked into his eyes. "I missed you," she whispered as she gave him a gentle kiss on the cheek.

He tried to prevent the heat that flared in his gut whenever she held him like that—loose and greedy all at once—but it was impossible. She smiled devilishly as she felt the answering tremor run through him and then she turned to Lotta and Philip who'd settled onto the sofa. "Luke and I are going to go get changed for dinner. We'll see you in a bit."

"Yeah, you do that." Lotta laughed. "You go get changed for dinner."

They all laughed as Ellie practically dragged Luke into the guest room and shut the door behind them.

"I'm a sweaty mess." His voice was a low warning.

"I love a sweaty mess."

"They're right on the other side of the door."

"I can be quiet."

"Really? Why have I never witnessed that?"

She smirked at the taunt. "Try me."

"Okay. So you won't make a sound—not even a whimper?"

"Not even a whimper." She stood a little straighter, letting him know she was up for the challenge.

He came closer to her then, slowly, and ran his hand up under her lightweight cotton skirt. She bit her lower lip then released it with a gasp.

"See?" she whispered through clenched teeth. "Totally quiet."

"Mmm-hmm." He reached higher up her leg as he guided her away from the door. Soon they were across the room with her back against the wall, between the two windows that faced out onto the street. It was early evening and the sun was setting, the slats of light coming through the partially closed blinds and the sheer fabric curtains.

Luke knelt down.

"That's not fair—" she whispered through a gasp when he pulled at her underwear and kissed her exposed flesh.

"You said totally quiet. And I trusted you." He kissed her again and she felt the jolt of pleasure that was becoming so familiar, but still not something she could actually prepare for.

He heard her slow hiss (he loved knowing that it would've been an unrestrained full-throated cry if they'd been at home). He licked and nipped at her sensitive skin, and held her hips hard against the wall. Eventually, he reached around to grab at her ass and massage her in ways she adored. He paused occasionally to gauge where she was on the trajectory of her arousal. It was glorious to watch her contain her reactions. He stared as she bit her lip, closed her eyes, and concentrated on her breathing—hard, through her nose.

"That was just to see if you could take a little bit. Get ready to bite your tongue." He watched as her fists balled tighter, the skin across her knuckles straining white. He pushed her skirt higher over her hips and devoured her, loving her body, her soul, her every reaction to him, how the two of them knit together. And finally, her loving, giving, and almost-quiet surrender.

As she began to wilt over his shoulder in her quivering state, he swept her up into his arms and set her gently on the bed.

After spreading a light blanket over her, he turned to go. "Wait . . . " Her voice was slurred with pleasure. "What about you . . . don't you want to . . . ?"

"I'm going to jump in the shower. You have a little rest and then we'll pick up where we left off once we get back from dinner."

"Okay."

The last thing he heard was her contented sigh.

The next morning, the four of them drove the three hours up to Elk. The inn was perched on the edge of a cliff over the ocean, with a spectacular view from the gazebo where Philip and Lotta would be saying their vows. They had dinner together that first night—the quiet before the storm, Philip warned—and then nearly forty guests began arriving the next morning. Ellie's parents were thrilled to see her with Luke, as were so many of her relatives. He was Such An Unexpected Surprise.

For the past few years, everyone in Ellie's extended family had been justifiably concerned. Luke represented a new beginning for her, and they all welcomed that in theory, but the old protective feelings were still strong. In the end, it had been Ellie who'd been unprepared for the onslaught of love and all the probing questions that came with a family's loyalty. She and Luke stayed by each other's sides the entire weekend, with her relying on his support far more than the other way around.

He kept her tucked into his side, and she loved the way they leaned into each other or laughed together at her cousin's bawdy jokes, or how he held her close and firm when they danced.

They spent their nights with the cool, fresh air coming in through the open windows of their seaside cottage. The sounds of surf and wind swept around them as they made love.

When they woke Sunday morning just after dawn, Ellie almost felt like it had been their wedding, rather than Philip and Lotta's. Something had solidified between them. Nothing spoken, just a settling-in-place of a few more pieces. They were a couple. Her family liked Luke and he was learning to soften a bit when people asked him about himself. She'd laughed when her uncle had given him the third degree about his *intentions*.

"Oh my god, Uncle Larry, you've got to be kidding me? Maybe *I* have dishonorable intentions?" Ellie had joked. "Did you ever think about that?'

He'd just stared at her in shock. "No. I never thought about that. And neither should you, young lady!" She somehow managed to keep a straight face, but she and Luke had laughed about it later that night, with Luke repeatedly calling her *young lady* while he did some lovely, dishonorable things to her body.

"I think I'll go down to the beach one last time." Ellie said as she finished getting dressed and brushing her teeth Sunday morning. "Do you mind?"

"No, I'd love that."

"I'd like to go alone, if that's okay. Just to say goodbye."

She'd told Luke how the memories of Rob had been swirling around her for much of the weekend and he respected that. But she could see it still hurt. It hurt him because she knew he wanted to make sure she never experienced any hurt ever again. He pulled her into a hug. "Of course. Take your time." He kissed her quickly, nothing passionate. "I'll be here."

She walked slowly, taking care as she went down the steep wooden steps to the misty shoreline. She stood there and the tears simply came. She cried for the loss of Rob, and the memories the two of them had created and shared in so many beautiful places like this. Then she wiped her eyes after a time and breathed in all the violent, crashing surf, all that natural cleansing and sifting of the sands and the earth. She remembered what Luke had said about feeling reborn, and she felt the truth of it wash over her. Her new life with Luke was never going to replace the life she'd shared with Rob. It was simply her *new* life. Her *next* life. This life.

Feeling a shiver of awareness, Ellie turned and looked up to the top of the cliff. She saw Luke there, looking far out to the horizon. He wasn't hovering or invading her privacy. The way he watched over her made her feel a spreading warmth through her heart: he gave her space and protection in equal measure.

Waving to get his attention as she turned back to walk up the long, weaving steps, she felt like she was finally moving forward in her life. When she reached the top step and he opened his arms to her, she pulled him into a gruff bear hug. "I think I'm going to be okay," she whispered into the fabric on his shoulder.

"You're going to be so much more than okay."

Soon after, they bid their goodbyes to everyone and set off to get back into town in time for lunch with Didi.

Chapter 12

"It doesn't seem fair that I flew all the way out here—supposedly to stand up for my best friend and my cousin—only to be distracted by you the entire time," she mused aloud as they sped south along the winding coastline.

"Merely *distracted?*" Luke was clearly enjoying the Pacific Coast Highway. The car was hugging the curve of the continent and Ellie enjoyed the moments of brief, confined terror when the car would swing toward the ocean far below. Then Luke would steer the wheel with sexy assurance back into the banked turn.

"Would you prefer devoted? Delirious?" she offered.

"Mm-hmm. Yes."

She laughed and kept looking out her side of the car toward the Pacific. "You're totally having a Zen moment with this car and not even listening to me . . . "

"Mm-hmm."

Ellie smiled and simply enjoyed the firm pull of the car. They were going straight to the restaurant to meet up with Luke's daughter, and Ellie started to get a little nervous about the whole meeting as they got closer to the city. She hadn't pushed Luke to share more about his past, but it hadn't been easy. Between what little she knew of his daughter, not to mention that mystery man on the beach in Florida, Ellie had to congratulate herself on her restraint.

"So," she asked after another lengthy silence. "Are there any red-flag topics?"

"What?" The roads were starting to be more congested with Sunday drivers, and the past few hours of flying along the coast were already starting to feel like a memory.

"Any topics of conversation that I should avoid when I meet Didi? And what's her friend's name?"

"I have no idea."

"What do you mean?"

"I have no idea who her friend is. I have no idea what she's doing for a living. I am as clueless as you are."

"Why didn't you ask her?"

His face came as close to a scowl as Ellie had ever seen it. "It wasn't the most easy-going conversation. I think I did pretty well, all things considered."

"I'm sure you did. I'm sorry. I didn't mean to be shrewish. All will be revealed."

"Or, knowing Didi, very little will be revealed."

"Is she secretive or private or what?" Ellie didn't bother adding, *like some people who shall remain nameless.*

"I don't know how to describe her. Yes, she's some of those things, probably. But it's more, you'll see. She's a very careful person."

Ellie tried not to laugh. "Hmm. I wonder where she gets that from?"

"Very funny."

"How else is she like you . . . or Kate?" Ellie knew there was a complicated, probably sordid past that Luke had shared with Kate, but she didn't know the details.

"We all used to joke she was Kate on the outside, and me on the inside."

"Well, that's a good thing, right? Given that Kate was beautiful?"

Luke turned to look at Ellie when he'd pulled the car to a full stop at a red light. They were getting close to the Golden Gate Bridge. "How do you do that?"

"Do what?"

"Always find the good thing." He shook his head, as if her whole being was a marvel to him. "Didi's going to love you."

"Oh, that doesn't matter."

"Of course it does. It matters to me."

She placed her hand over his where it rested loosely on the gearshift. "I meant it's more important that she love *you*."

The light turned green and Luke retrained his attention on the road. He shook his head one more time.

They pulled up in front of the restaurant two minutes before they were due to meet Didi.

"Seriously?" Ellie said over a short laugh. "Even from three hours out you can plan your arrival down to the minute?"

"I like precision." He shrugged with boyish self-consciousness.

"And I like that about you," Ellie winked. "Shall we go in?"

Luke took a deep breath. "I want to tell you everything—"

"Oh, you don't have to. I didn't mean to pry before—"

"No, I really want to, but it seemed wrong, somehow, to unload all my crap when we'd just met. And then this weekend was all about you and your family and celebrating all of that." He turned off the car. "But mostly I don't want to burden you."

"Loving you could never be a burden." She leaned across the narrow armrest and kissed his cheek. "We'll have plenty of time for everything else, but right now we need to go meet your daughter. It will be great."

And, surprisingly, it was great. Didi was a striking young woman. Ellie stuffed her momentary jealousy right into her mental trash bin where it belonged. *Kate on the outside*, some lingering adolescent part of her mind had whispered. The young woman wasn't just beautiful—she was *stunning*. Didi's eyes were dark and penetrating, from her mother perhaps, but when Ellie looked closely, she saw they were a deeper version of Luke's arresting blue. The combination was mesmerizing.

225

She had very long, straight black hair that hung in a beautiful, silky sheet down her back. It shone and caught the light when she stood up to say hello.

"You must be Didi," Ellie blurted before they'd even reached the table.

"I am, yes," she answered (carefully, Ellie thought, just as Luke had described).

"And I'm Ellie. Eleanor Sinclair, but please just call me Ellie."

"Okay." She was measured, so much like Luke had been when she'd first met him. "And this is Jamie Folkes. Jamie, this is Ellie and my father . . . "

And then silence.

"—Luke," Ellie filled in, when it seemed that Didi had forgotten her own father's name.

"Yes. Luke." Didi smiled, and that changed everything. Her smile transformed her from a rather repressed, serious-looking academic, to a goddess of some kind, an Olympian. She had presence. "Is this table okay?" Didi gestured at the table where she and Jamie had been sitting. "Or we can sit outside if you like?"

"No, this is great. Perfect." Luke was nervous and sweet in his effort to be accommodating.

"Oh. Good. Okay." Didi turned to get herself resettled in her seat and Ellie saw a few colorless scars along the inside of both arms and quickly looked away, but Jamie had seen her looking and he lifted his chin a tiny bit. Their loving-outsider-status was established in a split second.

After that, the four of them ended up talking easily about everything and nothing. Ellie talked about photography and how they were going down to Carmel later to visit one of her favorite galleries, spending the night, and then flying back to Florida Monday afternoon. Jamie talked about his work at the music department at San Francisco State and how he and Didi were going to travel to Japan the following December to attend a series of concerts that he'd been invited to conduct. Didi talked about her job, but only in the most abstract terms. She said it was "challenging" or "rewarding" or "complicated." Luke mostly nodded in agreement.

"So what do you guys do for fun?" Ellie asked, when their food arrived.

The other three looked at Ellie as if she had a couple extra heads.

Didi smiled. "Yeah, we sound pretty serious, huh?"

"No! I mean, I didn't mean it like that," Ellie hedged. Luke took one of her hands into his under the table. "Well, you know what I mean. San Francisco's always been a bit of a mystery to me. I never know where the hot gooey center is."

Jamie laughed. "You know, when I first moved here from New York I had the exact same feeling. Like where is everyone going, and where is the subway, and the taxis and the bustle? But it's got a great rhythm once you're here for a while. Don't you think, Didi?"

"Yeah, I mean I miss London sometimes, the vastness and the variety, but there's only one London, right? Speaking of London, how's Uncle Desmond?" She turned from Ellie to look at Luke.

A pulse of energy snapped through Luke's hand in hers, almost a flinch. *Is he bad?* Oh Jesus, Ellie remembered Luke's reply to that question. *Yeah, he's bad.*

"We've not been in touch," Luke answered too quickly. "Since your mother's . . . since I saw him at your mother's funeral."

A slow, powdery quiet descended over the four of them.

"Oh." Didi inhaled. "I just figured . . . you guys used to be so close."

"Yeah." Luke was nervous, Ellie could tell, but he probably looked less so to a stranger, or even to his estranged daughter. Maybe he even appeared normal. "Past tense."

"So what happened?" Didi pressed.

"Just grew apart, I guess." Luke was gripping Ellie's hand so hard under the table it was starting to hurt, but she didn't move. And Didi wasn't buying the vague answers.

"There's more to it than that, isn't there?"

Luke exhaled slowly and loosened his grip a bit. "He was always much closer to your mom," Luke tried. "He and I disagreed about a lot, especially there at the end." Luke lifted his chin slightly toward Jamie. "I don't know if you want to get into it now. In front of everyone."

Didi's back stiffened. "Yes, actually, I would like to get into it. Jamie knows about Mom . . . and you. So why don't you tell me what really happened with you and Uncle Desmond?"

Even hearing her refer to him as *Uncle* Desmond made Luke want to slam his fist onto the table and yell that Desmond was no kind uncle deserving of her respect. Then he felt the slow, gentle stroke of Ellie's thumb against the tender skin of his wrist. He took a deep breath before he spoke. "Well, you know, about ten years ago, when your mother went back to London, and you started boarding school—"

"Yeah, I remember," Didi added softly, but with more than a hint of irritation.

"Well, Desmond and I had a pretty major disagreement, and your mother was upset. The three of us could never really get on after that."

"He was totally loyal. He was with Mom right up until the end." Didi said it matter-of-factly, but the unspoken accusation hung in the air: *And you weren't.*

Luke could feel how Ellie had to almost physically restrain herself from joining in the conversation, her desire to protect him nearly palpable.

"Yeah," Luke said slowly. "He was with your mom when she died. And I guess I had some major trust issues around that."

"Wait one damn minute." Didi said, suspicious and angry. "Are you trying to imply that Desmond had something to do with Mom's death? Because that's bullshit. He was great to us after you left."

Luke felt the bile rise up in his throat. If Desmond had ever touched Didi, Luke would rip his throat out. He should probably rip his throat out anyway.

"What do you mean he was *great?*" Luke didn't even bother trying to conceal his disgust.

Ellie squeezed his hand under the table again, trying to keep him calm. His voice was starting to strain like it had when he lost his patience with Ethan. It was a low, threatening tone and did nothing to foster the very incipient trust that Didi had been starting to show.

"Oh, forget it," Didi snapped. "You're just getting all whipped up into your typical blind fury. Let's just get the check." She turned to get the server's attention and her sweep of black hair fell over one shoulder.

Jamie whispered, "Come on, he's trying to talk to you."

"Whatever." She gestured more adamantly for the server.

Ellie kicked Luke under the table.

"What?" he said aloud.

Ellie rolled her eyes.

Luke inhaled then turned back to face his daughter. "Look, Didi, if you want to have this conversation, here, like this—we can do that. You're an adult."

Didi shifted in her seat and began to look uncomfortable for the first time since they'd arrived. Maybe she didn't want the truth so badly after all.

"Well?" Luke asked. Ellie squeezed his thigh to let him know he was veering toward confrontational again.

"Well what?" Didi answered uneasily.

He modulated his voice to be more calm. "Do you want to hear the truth about what happened—with Desmond and your mother and me—or not?"

The restaurant sounds started to crystallize all around them. Jamie took a sip of his coffee then looked over the rim at Didi. Luke had to admire the way Jamie treated her, silently letting her know that he was there, no matter what, but never interfering.

Didi took a deep breath, still resisting. "You mean *your* version of the truth."

Luke repressed another spurt of anger and felt an encouraging squeeze under the table from Ellie. He straightened a sugar packet a couple of times—lifting it up, putting it down—

then raised his eyes to Didi. "Yes, Diana. *My* truth. The truth I saw with my own eyes."

When he called her Diana, she sat up a little straighter. Maybe it was just some old trick of being called out by a parent, that voice of authority that never really goes away no matter how grown-up we think we are. But it worked. Didi didn't look like she wanted to react or rebel. She looked like she wanted answers.

"Yes," she said more quietly. "I would like to know."

The check arrived and the conversation stopped again.

Ellie grabbed the leather holder. "I'd like to pick this up," she sang. "Why don't I go pay at the register and you two can have a little time alone," she said, looking at Luke and Didi.

"That sounds like a good idea," Jamie agreed, taking Didi's hand in his and giving her a quick kiss on the cheek. "I'll go wait outside with Ellie, yeah? You okay?"

Didi nodded. "Yeah, I'm okay."

Ellie and Jamie got up from the table and went to the register to deal with the check.

After the other two had left the restaurant, Luke stared across the table at this young woman who looked so much like his former wife. He tried to breathe. "I'm not really sure where to begin."

"Tell me what happened. Just say it straight out. Why did you and mom split?"

He looked around the restaurant, not for an escape, really, but to scan for danger. Old habits.

"I'm right here, Dad."

And that *Dad* was all it took. Luke rubbed his face and began telling her in the most basic terms what happened.

"Your Uncle Desmond sexually molested your mother—his own sister—for years." It just came out. Flat out.

Didi stared at him. At first he didn't think she'd heard, then he watched the pupils in her eyes. Again, old habits. She was going into shock. "Like when she was a child?"

Luke nodded slowly. "And later."

As her mind began sifting through what his words meant, her face blanched.

"Oh my God. Is he my—" She looked horrified and sad and confused and then furious. "Did he get Mom preg—"

"No, Diana." Luke interrupted and grabbed her hands across the table. "God, no. You're my daughter." He almost laughed at how much she was his daughter—the hard lines of her face, the self-defeating strength. "You know that, don't you? On some deep level?" She was starting to cry and pulled one of her hands out of his grip, then used her napkin to cover her face. When she was done patting her eyes, she looked as if nothing had happened. And in that moment he knew with certainty that she'd undergone intelligence training.

"Where are you working, Diana?"

She shook her head once, letting him know she was not at liberty to say.

He looked down at his empty coffee cup and shook his head, squeezing her hand one last time then releasing it. "What goes around . . . "

She reached for him this time. "I'm good at it, Dad."

"I know. We were all good at it. That doesn't mean it's the right thing to do. Your mother was the best at it because cultivating lies was how she lived her life, how she survived"

"It's not like that, I promise. I can't say much, but I'm not out in the field. Yet. And if it comes to that, I'll be careful. I promise."

Something about the way she made that promise opened Luke's heart. Everything about this brilliant young woman terrified him. Starting with her brilliance. So much like her mother, but he forced himself to remember she was not her mother. She wasn't irreparably damaged and fragile and, consequently, vengeful. She was her own person, damn it. She wasn't cursed.

"I didn't mean to get sidetracked," he said. Then he smiled with a bit of sadness. "Or maybe I did. Are you seeing a therapist? Do you have someone you can talk to?"

She nodded. "I do. But can we talk a little bit more about it?"

"Of course." He wanted to comfort her, but, ironically, he didn't know her well enough. "What do you want to know?"

Then—just like he would have done, he thought ruefully—she started interrogating him. She wanted dates, details. How he'd met Desmond in Thailand and they'd become best friends at the age of twenty: misfits, smart, quick, ready to do things that other people were not willing to do. How Luke met Kate and they'd fallen in love: she'd been visiting her diplomat parents in Tokyo and Desmond had been so happy for them—how they'd become the three musketeers.

God, how happy Luke was to finally have his own family, after his messed up childhood.

Then Didi asked how Luke had found out about Desmond and Kate. There was still that reedy hope in her voice . . . maybe it was hearsay, malicious gossip.

He swallowed. "I walked in on them."

It didn't really get much simpler than that, he realized. As complicated as it all was, that part was . . . simple. "You were ten and I fought like hell to get custody but there was no way I was dragging that shit into court and your mother knew it, but at least I got her to promise, no matter what, that Desmond was never to come near you."

Didi's face was hard as steel. He knew that face just like he knew the one he'd seen in the mirror that morning. She wasn't going to cry about this again, certainly not here.

He sighed. "So . . . I let her have you. The courts ruled in her favor—she was a fantastic mother and no one was going to say otherwise—and I didn't think you'd appreciate me kidnapping you, even though the thought frequently crossed my mind."

They spoke a bit more about her time in England, and how she hadn't seen Desmond much during her teenage years, except at a few family functions with her grandparents from that side of the family. "It was only after I left for California that mother mentioned he was back in England . . . " Her voice trailed off when she realized what she was saying, that Kate had indeed been trying to keep Didi—if not herself—safe.

It was excruciating, all of it, but in the end, it was such a relief to both of them. That the truth no longer had the power of its secrecy and shame.

"Thank you," she whispered finally.

"Oh, please don't thank me," Luke said. "I'm so sorry. There was never a right way to deal with this. Or at least none that I was able to see clear to. Your mother wanted to be with you—don't ever doubt that she loved you—and after a time I knew you wanted to be with her too. Even now, please be careful, okay? Please be careful around Desmond, if you ever do see him. He's not well."

Didi stared right into Luke's eyes. Like looking into a mirror. "I understand."

Luke's heart pounded and his eyes widened. "Did he ever—"

It was her turn to assuage him. She reached for his clenched fist. "No. But . . . I just didn't feel safe around him. I remember how he used to look at me over my last Christmas holiday, my freshman year, before Mom died. She was drinking a ton by then, there at the end, but I was grown and had my own understanding—of when things felt weird or whatever. And I just called a friend and made plans to go out." She looked like she was going to cry again, then inhaled and took control of herself. "I shouldn't have left mom alone—"

"Stop." His voice was harsher than he meant, and maybe even a bit militant. "I mean, I've gone down that hypothetical road and, trust me, you need to just . . . not go there. It was all between them. I'm so, so sorry. I should have fought harder to keep you with me."

She barked a laugh. "I remember when you tried. A bunch of times. When I was fourteen, do you remember? You were my mortal enemy. Abandoning Mom. Killing people for a living."

Someone from the next table nearly choked on her eggs benedict, and Didi smiled and lowered her voice. "We're screenwriters," she said conspiratorially. The woman nodded and smiled with relief.

Luke scowled, but deep down he was glad she knew the truth now.

"Private security," Didi corrected, but she caught Luke's eye and he felt another layer of duplicity slip away. She'd always known.

He took a deep breath. They'd been talking for over an hour since Jamie and Ellie had left the table. "I think this is a pretty good beginning . . . a new beginning for us. Don't you?"

She smiled briefly and nodded once. "Yes. A very good, new beginning." She reached for her long scarf that she'd tied to the back of her chair, and then began looping it around her neck. "Speaking of new beginnings . . . Jamie and I are expecting a baby."

"What? Oh, Didi! Congratulations!" Luke felt like something hard and mean and old had just shattered into a million pieces inside his chest. Destroyed. Freed. "Oh I'm so pleased for you. I mean, I'm assuming you're happy about it?"

She shrugged, but her smile of love and happiness shone through. "Totally inconvenient actually. But love comes along." Her smile widened. "I told Jamie I was surely going to be a shit mother and he assured me I was wrong. And if I'm right, he promised he'll be superdad. So, I guess we're good."

"I really am delighted for you both."

She smiled and stood up. "Yeah, we're pretty delighted too."

They walked out of the restaurant together. It wasn't going to be perfect, nothing ever was, but it was one of the most glorious second chances Luke could have ever hoped for.

Ellie and Jamie were sitting comfortably on a bench just in front of the restaurant, exchanging sections of the Sunday *New York Times*, as if they were old friends . . . or a couple. Luke had a moment of chilly self-awareness: he was old. Comparatively old, at least. And Ellie looked young. Especially sitting there next to Jamie—a tall, lean, young, intellectual-looking kind of guy on a sunny afternoon in San Francisco. They could have definitely been a couple.

Then Ellie looked up from the paper and her face was instantly awash in love for *him*, for Luke. A blind, trusting sort of joy suffused her expression. He leaned down and kissed her quickly on the lips.

"Hi." She stood up and put the folded newspaper down on the bench. "I'm glad you two made it out of there alive."

Luke slid his arm around her waist and pulled her in close. She caught Didi looking at them with a hesitant smile. It was a start, thought Ellie.

"All right." Luke kept his arm possessively around her waist and turned to face Jamie and Didi. "We need to get down to Carmel pretty soon. I'm so sorry we can't spend the rest of the afternoon together."

Ellie stepped out of Luke's embrace and gave Jamie a quick hug. "It was really great to meet you. Good luck in Tokyo and please come visit us in Florida, if you're in the mood for Cuban coffee, spinner sharks, and ficus hedges." Then she turned to Didi and hugged her too. She was resistant, Ellie thought, exactly like her father. These people needed to be loved right out of their own stiff skins.

"Call anytime." Ellie reached up and put a strand of hair behind Didi's shoulder that had flown loose when she and Luke had walked out to the street. It was a momentary, unplanned intimacy. Didi looked like she might recoil, just from the unfamiliarity of having someone touch her, then her lips curved up.

"Thanks, Ellie. It was really great to meet you. You keep an eye on the old man, okay?" Didi flicked her thumb in Luke's direction, as if dismissing him, or trying to make a joke out of the mere idea that he might need protection. But there was a hint of real concern, and maybe the beginning of something akin to love.

"I'm going to."

A few seconds later Luke and Didi hugged. Awkwardly. Ellie imagined it was how blowfish or porcupines might hug. Then the four of them lingered there on the sidewalk, not wanting to part. Eventually, they said goodbye one last time.

Jamie and Didi stood in front of the restaurant holding hands and waved goodbye until Luke and Ellie had walked across the street, started the car, and driven away.

The drive to Carmel was a warm, golden version of their cool, clear morning drive from Elk. The surf was relentless and dramatic as the white foam of break after break crashed against the rocky shore below. And, Luke marveled, he was in love. And his love for Ellie seemed to make life *possible*—especially everything to do with his family that had seemed utterly *impossible*. Eventually he would tell her about Kate and Desmond, and all he'd shared with Didi, but for now he just wanted to fall back into the comfort of her, of how he felt when it was just the two of them.

They got to the gallery in Carmel right before it closed. An older woman was just starting to pull down the vintage-looking roller shade with the little white covered ring at the bottom of the string.

"Oh, there you are!" the woman cried, after pulling open the glass door and coming out to the sidewalk to greet them.

Luke thought she looked exactly like Ellie would look in thirty years: elegant, wise, and full of cheer. The two women hugged and then, while still holding hands, Ellie introduced Luke. "Luke McCormick, this is Sandra Ascher, Sandra this is *Luke*."

All throughout the wedding weekend, Luke had loved the way Ellie introduced him to everyone, as if he were the most wonderful treasure. *Luke*. She presented him like a gift to the world. *Look what I found!* She wanted to share (but not too much sharing, her firm hold seemed to say). Here he is for you to meet, but he is *mine*. He adored her possessiveness.

Sandra led them in, and then locked the front door of the gallery. She invited Luke and Ellie into the smaller room at the back. A round, white Saarinen tulip table with four chairs and a large white metal flat file were the only furniture. The three of them ended up sitting there for two hours, Sandra opening a bottle of white wine, showing them some new work from a few local artists. Then she asked Ellie if she'd brought any of her work to show, if she was finally ready to show again.

Luke looked from Sandra to Ellie with an inquisitive look. "Is this business or pleasure?" Luke had thought they were just coming to have dinner with an old friend.

"Yes, Ellie," Sandra pressed. "Which is it?" Then she turned to Luke, "I've been waiting years for her to say 'business,' but she's so resistant. Maybe you can talk her out of her own humility. It's so tiresome." She gave Luke the wink of an accomplice.

Ellie reached into her bag and pulled out a thumb drive. "Here you go, you taskmistress. Take a look."

"Hooray!" Sandra leapt from the table to retrieve a laptop from her office then sat back down, rubbing her hands together with anticipatory relish. "Hand it over!"

She slid the drive into the side of her slim computer and clicked. Luke watched at an angle as the first set of images came up, from that day on the beach, when Ellie had been looking at the little tidal pool. He turned to her and reached under the table to take Ellie's hand in his, loving the look of tender hope on her face.

"Oh, Ellie, honey," Sandra said. "These are so beautiful. Please let me sell some."

"I don't know. I'm still such an amateur—"

"Luke! Help!" Sandra practically launched at him. "Tell her! Please. Look at these." She turned the screen fully toward him and the image bewitched him. It was the same arresting image that had captured his attention when they'd been looking at the pictures on her camera a few weeks ago.

"See?" Sandra jarred him out of his thoughts.

"Yeah, I see." He turned to Ellie. "They're beautiful, darling."

"It's just a picture . . . " She looked unaccountably shy and he wanted to take her into his arms and lift her up, like a dancer or a skater, to raise her up to the sky.

"It is not *just* a picture," Luke countered. "It is filled with so much vitality . . . it's practically throbbing."

She actually blushed.

"And I didn't mean it like that you strumpet." He muttered with a hint of a Scottish brogue.

Sandra burst out laughing, a deep, happy, graceful sound. "That settles it then! It is vital. I want to sell these Ellie. We can start gradually if you're really reluctant, but I'd love to begin with a dozen from this series. I don't know about the one with the figure on the horizon."

Ellie looked guiltily at Luke, as if she hadn't intended for that shot to be in the group. "That one's not supposed to be in there anyway. Just delete it."

"Oh okay. No worries. It works better as a thematic show if we keep it . . . oooh—!" she interrupted herself. "What have we here?"

She'd reached some of the images Ellie had taken in the Keys, the shadows and angles of the palm fronds abstracted beautifully. Luke felt as though he could hear the scrape of the leaves emanating from the screen, as the three of them stopped, frozen and staring.

"Yeah, I like that one." Ellie said softly, with a tentative smile toward Luke. She had taken it while he'd been asleep in her arms, the hammock perfectly still beneath their warm, close bodies. He felt the wave of recognition in her look, the warm tide of love and joy washing over him as he looked at her, then back at the image.

Sandra turned the screen back so she could give more images her critical attention. "Can you leave this with me Ellie? There's just so much here. I need to really look." She paused again and a small grin flitted across her face. "They're so rich. I don't know how else . . . " She kept clicking. " . . . perfectly beautiful . . . knowing . . . mature somehow . . . " She clicked past a few more images then snapped the lid of the computer shut and rested her palms flat against the top, protectively. "This is a trove. Please think about it and then we can figure out what you want to do." Sandra had a victorious gleam in her eye.

Eventually, the three of them left the gallery and walked to a nearby restaurant for dinner. They drank a little bit too much of the very good wine. Sandra picked up the bill, then walked them back to the inn where they were staying.

"I'll be in touch in a few weeks," Sandra said as they were parting. "After you two get back from London."

"That sounds great," Ellie hugged her close. "Thanks again for dinner. It was such a treat to get to see you."

"You too. Take care of each other." Sandra turned to Luke and gave him a hug as well.

They spent the night in Carmel then made their way up to the airport first thing Monday morning for their flight back to Palm Beach.

Chapter 13

The following week, when they were about two hours into the nine-hour flight from Miami to Heathrow, Luke lifted their clasped hands to his lips and she turned to look at him. They were in the first class cabin settling in after the light supper and a glass of wine. Ellie was fretting.

"You looked serious just then, what were you thinking about?" he asked.

"Just you."

"Then you should have been smiling in that slightly open-mouthed, blissful way that means you're *thinking* of me."

Her eyes twinkled at the innuendo. "I sometimes think about you in other ways." He frowned theatrically. "But only sometimes," she added quickly.

"So what were you thinking then?"

"Just how you'll tell me everything about yourself when you're ready."

He looked down at their joined hands resting on the armrest between them. "I am . . . you know me better than anyone . . . in the world . . . ever."

She felt the warm spread of love through her chest when she heard his words. "Me too. To you. But there are details, you know, about your life and your family, that you haven't shared—"

"Ellie—"

"And I'm not asking you to," she interrupted quickly. "I mean, that's probably why my face was looking serious. I don't want to pry you open. I don't ever want you to feel like I'm doing that."

His expression turned thoughtful. He looked at her face in a way that made her feel like he was memorizing every millimeter, like he was scanning her into some internal computer. "You don't need to pry. You're in already. I simply don't know how to talk about it. I wish you could just know it all already without my having to tell you some things."

Ellie paused for a few seconds. "I know the feeling. But maybe your telling is the best part of it, of how I want to learn it. I mean, I could have investigated you or, you know what I mean, asked around." The corner of her mouth turned up a bit. "But that's what I meant about not wanting to pry it out of you. You'll tell me when you want."

"But I do want to. It's just long and boring."

"Not to me. It's new and gripping."

He kissed the back of her hand again. "So where should I begin?"

"I guess we sort of left off in Wyoming, when you were telling me about living with your Uncle Grant and moving to California to go to college." She straightened the blanket on her lap and snuggled down into the seat with a little anticipatory motion. "So, go on."

He let his head fall back onto the headrest and closed his eyes for a few seconds to collect his thoughts. He spent the next three hours speaking quietly and thoughtfully about the circuitous route that had taken him from an engineering degree at Cal Tech to working for a strategic consulting firm in Tokyo. To Thailand where he'd met the dynamic Desmond Cresswell. They'd become fast friends . . . and a few months later, Desmond had introduced Luke to his beautiful sister Kate.

Ellie tried to stay calm for this part. She knew it was coming, of course, and he'd been so open and good about all *her* feelings of loss and remembrance for Rob. She couldn't very well put her fingers in her ears and hum a babbling tune to drown him out when it came to beautiful, brilliant Kate. But she wanted to. A little bit. So apparently Kate had been in British Intelligence: independent and compelling and glamorous in a way that made Ellie feel like a piece of dry toast in comparison.

"Ellie?"

"Yeah?" she whispered.

"Don't do that." Luke put his hand on her cheek.

"What?"

"You know, feel like you need to understand what drew me to her. Or how you are different from her." He reached for her hand beneath the blanket and she breathed. "It was so long ago, and I don't mean that in a sweep-it-under-the-carpet sort of way. We were young and running as fast as we could through life and that's what brought us together. But those are terrible things to build a life on—shared frustration with one's background, trying to escape something we didn't even understand. Do you want the details or not?" He squeezed her hand.

Ellie sat for a few minutes. She loved how she could actually stop and think with Luke. She knew he'd wait for hours for her answer, if she needed that much time. She finally exhaled slowly. "Yes, of course I do. But I'm still a *girl*, you know what I mean? So don't make her too sexy or clever, okay?"

He shook his head slowly then kissed Ellie with firm conviction, his lips hard against hers, and the connection grounded her. He turned slightly and whispered into her hair, the heat of his breath tickling her ear and sending a delightful shiver down her spine. "You are the sexiest, cleverest woman I've ever met." He kissed her neck. "But more than any of that, you are the most loving person I've ever known. And that matters more to me than anything."

"Okay," she whispered back. "That was good. Go on." His eyes were a tiny bit glassy, hinting at the desire that ricocheted between them. "Keep talking and stop looking at me like that," she said, "or I'm going to need to get up to splash cool water on my face."

"Good," he growled near her ear. Then he pulled away a few inches and took a deep breath before continuing. "So anyway, we got married within six months, had Didi right away—check, check, check, Kate used to say. We were both twenty-one. Impossibly young. But somehow we trundled along for nearly ten years . . . " His voice trailed off in dismay.

"Oh dear," Ellie said without thinking.

"Yeah. It was bad." He lowered his voice and told her the details about Kate and Desmond.

All she could do was cry and keep murmuring, "Poor Didi. Poor Kate." Over and over. She felt the sadness in her bones, the sickness crawling along her skin. Apparently Desmond had started sexually abusing Kate when she was a young teenager, and the two of them had never really stopped. For the first ten years of her marriage to Luke, Kate had sworn she and Desmond had kept away from each other, but Luke could never be sure. The fact that Kate had been so brainwashed into thinking it was "their little secret" and "perfectly fine" made any reconciliation impossible. The grooves of their incestuous connection had worn too deep.

Luke's faith in families and their supposed loyalty had never been strong. When he walked in on Desmond and Kate in bed together, his tenuous faith had vanished.

Ellie finally dried her eyes and rested her head on his shoulder. Nearly everyone else on the flight was asleep. "I'm just so sorry." She kissed his neck.

"So am I." He exhaled slowly. "But, now, you can probably see how I'm sort of amazed by you?"

She smiled into the soft fabric of his shirt. "Not really. But I guess I'm sort of okay. We're sort of okay."

"We are so much more than okay." He kissed the top of her head. "Now let's get a bit of sleep before we land."

When they touched down at Heathrow, Ellie was completely disoriented. Luke had kept her snuggled up and made sure her sleep was uninterrupted by the passing flight attendants, so when the wheels hit the tarmac with an abrupt screech, she jolted awake as if the plane had fallen from the sky.

"It's okay." He took one of her hands and rubbed it.

Ellie was wild-eyed and confused. "What happened?"

"Honey, it's me, Luke." He reached up and caressed her cheek, until recognition dawned.

"I was so gone. I must've completely passed out."

"You did, lovely."

She looked into his eyes and thought she might melt into him. "You're really the sweetest person."

Luke shook his head.

"I mean it," she said. "I feel like you're always looking out for me—and not in a confining, suffocating way—just a wonderful, supportive way." She leaned in and kissed him on the lips.

As Ellie pulled away from the intimate moment she noticed that Luke's eyes had briefly swept over her shoulder to scan a passenger who'd stepped off the plane.

Ellie turned to see what or who had caught Luke's attention. The stranger was already out of sight.

Luke turned Ellie's face back toward him with a gentle pull at her chin.

"Do you know him?" she asked. "Oh Jesus, it's not *him* is it?"

He shook his head in a slow no, but Ellie wasn't convinced. She leaned into his ear and whispered, "Okay, okay."

"Start collecting your things," he said. "Time to put your game face on and meet the rest of my crazy family. I'm sure Ethan's got all the troops at his house for our arrival."

Ellie rubbed her eyes, wishing she could take away all the anxiety that Luke had built up around this visit to his father and brothers, then she set about putting her shoes on and collecting the magazines and book and reading glasses and other items she'd spread around her during the flight.

They passed through customs separately. Ellie had to go to the non-EU passport holders' line, then found Luke again on the other side of the row of customs agents. They had both packed light, trailing their practical black wheelie bags, so they passed quickly through baggage claim and out into the bright area filled with waiting chauffeurs, tour organizers, expectant parents, and excited loved ones.

Luke was looking up to see which direction they should head for the taxi stand when a deep voice called his name. Luke and Ellie turned together to see Schenk standing, like a smiling gorilla, on the other side of the metal divider. Luke walked slowly toward him and reached out to shake hands.

"I won't even ask what you're doing here."

"Hi, Schenk!" Ellie said brightly and leaned in to give him a kiss. He blushed and Ellie burst out laughing. "Are you so unused to being kissed?"

The large man looked like a bashful cartoon character, staring foolishly down at his immaculately polished shoes.

"We are perfectly capable of getting a taxi to the hotel, Schenk. Why did Ethan send you?"

"You're staying with him."

"But I already declined that invitation." Luke's irritation was obvious.

"Look, I don't want to get in the middle. It wasn't an invitation. He told me to pick you up and here I am. I follow orders. You know that."

Luke shook his head and smiled despite himself. "Yeah, I know that." He turned to Ellie. "What do you think? Should I fight him? I really wanted to get to that hotel room this morning." A sexy impatience edged its way into his voice.

Ellie smiled a broad, complicit smile. "Me too. But a little waiting never hurt anyone."

"Speak for yourself," Luke muttered as they headed out of the waiting area and into the bright morning sun.

Schenk led them to an immaculate, glistening maroon Bentley.

Ellie whistled low under her breath. "Nice car, Schenk."

"I try to keep it in good condition." He looked at the car with pride.

Luke shook his head, as if this whole trip was going to be a nightmare. Schenk opened the trunk and took Ellie's luggage and put it carefully in. He reached to take Luke's bag out of his hand and Luke stared at him with naked fury.

After he made sure Ellie was out of earshot, he said, "You're not my butler so you can cut it out." Then he slammed the telescoped handle back into the luggage frame and tossed his bag in the trunk next to Ellie's. "You can be all that in front of her if you want, but I'm pretty sure I saw one of Desmond's pals getting off the flight and don't think I'm unaware of the real reason you're here."

Schenk's look was serious. "Ethan worries. You can't blame him. And it's not like you don't have your own share of adversaries."

Ellie was waiting in the back seat of the car as the two men talked quietly, hidden from view behind the open trunk lid. "Then why does he want me to stay in his house? I would much rather stay in a hotel and fend for myself than be blamed for drawing anyone's attention to Ethan or his family."

"He doesn't see it that way. He prefers to keep everybody close."

Luke reached up and shut the trunk. He looked from Schenk's face to see Ellie through the oval glass at the back of the car. She turned her head over her right shoulder to catch his eye.

She must have brushed her hair and reapplied her lip gloss while he'd been bickering with Schenk—she looked fresh and welcoming. He wanted to run away—again—for fear of dragging her down into the morass of his life. Then she lifted her hand and curled her index finger with two small, inviting flicks. He rolled his eyes and walked toward the passenger side door, hating to admit (to himself at least) that he'd probably drag her straight to hell rather than spend even a few minutes out of range of that beckoning glance.

Luke settled into the back seat and pulled her close up against his side, resting his hand between her warm thighs.

Schenk had kindly left the soundproof privacy barrier up between the front seat and the back.

Ellie reached forward with a laugh and tapped on the divider. Schenk's voice came low through the intercom.

"Open that silly partition, Schenk! It's ridiculous!"

Luke closed his eyes for a split-second after catching Schenk's look in the rearview mirror. Obviously, Schenk could see Luke didn't think privacy was at all ridiculous.

As soon as the divider slid down, Ellie started a cheerful line of questioning and happy conversation with her new favorite killer. Luke let his head fall back onto the headrest and decided to catch a few winks as he tried to ignore Ellie's absentminded caresses along his thigh.

She touched him all the time now, he realized. When she was talking to him about an idea that inspired her she'd reach for his upper arm to grip him in enthusiasm, or she'd trace his cheek for the briefest second if he was telling her something he hadn't even realized was meaningful. She grazed his lower back as she passed by him in the kitchen; she patted his ass when he bent over to tie his shoes. He stilled her roving hand under his, restraining her before she wandered unwittingly into seductive territory.

"Sorry," she whispered into his ear. His eyes were still closed and he smiled.

"That's okay." He opened his eyes half-mast. "I just want to doze if you and Schenk are going to keep jawing. And you know I can't if you're . . . petting me."

She leaned in and kissed his cheek. "I'll try to control my roving hands."

"Thanks." His eyes closed again and he was asleep in a few seconds.

Ellie loved how he could turn his sleep on and off like a faucet. She didn't want to imagine the military or other training that allowed him to do it. She thought of young doctors in medical school who were notorious for taking seven-minute naps when they were on call. She tried to think it was something like that.

The morning traffic was a snarling mess. They didn't arrive at Ethan's house for another hour and a half.

"Here we are," Schenk announced when they finally got there.

Ellie looked up at the narrow lane where the car had come to a stop, and the long, low red brick building that seemed to stretch the length of the block.

"Where are we?"

Luke was instantly wide-awake and alert. "It's Ethan's bunker—I mean home."

"It looks charming." Ellie turned to him. "Stop being churlish."

"Okay. I'll try—for your sake."

Schenk opened Ellie's door and she stepped out onto the sidewalk. Schenk dipped his head to see if Luke was going to get out the same side, but Luke just growled and opened his own door and walked toward the trunk to get their bags.

Ellie turned as the front door of the house swung wide and a tall, brown-haired woman stood framed in the opening. "You must be Ellie!" She stepped down the front steps, barefoot, and grabbed Ellie in a warm hug. Then she pulled back enough to hold Ellie's upper arms and assess her like a picture. "You're even more lovely than Ethan said."

Ellie looked down, embarrassed and a little worried that Luke would get all twisted about the idea of Ethan describing her loveliness. "Oh, thank you . . . and you're Maria?"

"Aaah! Yes! I'm Maria Costa, Ethan's wife."

"It's so nice to meet you." Ellie started to reach out her hand to shake.

Maria laughed and it seemed to fill up the entire street. It was a deep, sexy, ironic laugh. "Put your hand away! I have already hugged you!"

Ellie smiled, feeling sort of immature and lost, but thinking she wouldn't mind feeling that way if Maria was her new best friend and would let her sit at the grown-up table with her.

Maria's voice had a throaty resonance and her black eyes sparkled with humor and intelligence. She reached up and touched Ellie's cheek briefly. "Just lovely . . . like a Rossetti painting with all that beautiful red hair." She spoke, as if to herself, then turned her full attention to Luke. "Ah, the return of the prince."

Luke set down the two bags that he wouldn't let Schenk carry, and took Maria into a firm embrace, lifting her slightly off the sidewalk. "How are you, *bellissima?* You were the one I missed."

Maria was gorgeous after all, but did Luke have to—

She arrested the thought and smiled at herself. Raw jealousy was completely unfamiliar. With Rob she'd always been, well, *With Rob.* They'd been together as long as anyone could remember, and Rob wasn't one for making grand *bellissima* compliments to other women in any case.

Luke caught her quizzical look over Maria's shoulder and released the other woman as soon as he realized what was clearly passing through Ellie's mind. He smiled broadly as he let go of his sister-in-law's hand, and crossed the small distance, taking Ellie into a ferocious embrace that almost knocked her off balance. "See how it feels?" he grumbled into her ear. Then he kissed her on the lips with terrific abandon, right there on the sidewalk.

Schenk picked up the two bags and followed Maria into the house as the Italian woman crooned loudly enough for Luke and Ellie to hear, "They must have had a very long flight, eh, Schenk?"

Luke finished kissing her then gave her a few extra kisses along the turn of her jaw and the column of her neck. Her voice was already rough with passion. "Don't you think we need to freshen up before lunch? Maybe a quick nap?"

He pulled her up the steps and shut the door behind them. Ellie hardly noticed the extraordinary luxury that greeted them in the entry hall. Renaissance paintings were subtly lit along the walls, a deceptively simple Jacobean bench was placed beneath what looked like a small Da Vinci etching to the left.

"I think Ellie's a bit tired from the trip, Maria," Luke said. "May we rest then join you for lunch?"

"Of course." Maria clasped her hands. "Let me show you your rooms."

Maria led them up the central staircase and began a quick tour-guide-like description of the layout of the house. "So, Ellie, the front part of the house, as you see, is quite old and long and narrow and dark but we added on lots of bright modern areas back here. As they turned at the landing Ellie gasped at the contrast. Great walls of glass, probably three stories high, opened out onto a private garden that looked like an Umbrian plot right there in the middle of London. Tall, slender cypress trees near the corners gave a loose formality to the space, then wild flowers rioted in lush beds of herbs, shrubs, and statuary.

"Oh, it's so beautiful."

Maria stopped and looked at Ellie's face, warm with enthusiasm, then caught Luke's eye. Maria nodded at him meaningfully then turned back up the stairs.

"I told that wretched husband of mine that if he made me live in this grim northern land—in the middle of a crowded city no less—that I wanted free rein to create my own sanctuary. He is very generous when he gets what he wants." Maria winked at Ellie.

Luke continued holding Ellie's hand as they went up the final flight of stairs.

"So, I've put you up here on the second floor—or it would be the third floor in America, wouldn't it, Luke?"

"Yes."

"The boys are on holiday with their school mates so you'll have more privacy here."

And protection, Luke thought to himself. He knew that the entire house was a study in the latest security devices, the best that Ethan could get his hands on. Despite Maria's breezy, *Barefoot Contessa* demeanor, Luke knew she was quite well aware of the internecine dealings in her husband's world. He also knew she was quite adept at handling a gun and protecting herself if need be.

"Here we are." She swung open the door to a creamy yellow guest room. The king size tester bed was draped with splendid yellow embroidered silk, and the walls were papered in an inviting, subdued pattern of branches, birds, leaves, and fruit that made the large space feel intimate and comforting without feeling crowded.

"This is gorgeous. You are so talented," Ellie said with enthusiasm.

"Oh, don't be ridiculous," Maria laughed. "The only decorating talent I have is writing exorbitant checks to Colefax and Fowler."

Maria told them lunch would be served at two o'clock in the garden. She showed them the dressing room and bathroom, the telephone system, and how the intercom worked if they needed anything from the kitchen or elsewhere.

"See you in a bit." She was half-way out the door, then paused and looked back. "And thank you for not putting up too much of a fuss about staying here, Luke. I of all people know how controlling your brother can be. But, just, thank you."

"Our pleasure," Luke answered.

The door closed and they listened as Maria's soft footsteps receded down the hallway then farther down the staircase.

Ellie exhaled slowly. "It really is beautiful here." She looked around the room again and then back into Luke's eyes. "Right here," she added, as she pulled him into a deep wet kiss.

He nudged her onto the bed and pulled down her summer skirt and tugged off her shirt, while she groped at his clothes and they tore into each other, as if it had been a week instead of a day since they'd fused their bodies together.

After they pulled down the comforter and sheets and tossed the decorative pillows on a nearby chair, Luke groaned with the relief of her naked body against his. The heat, the texture, the comfort, the excitement. The *life* of her.

Luke's bare skin against hers felt like heaven. After everything he'd told her on the plane, she'd been desperate just to hold him against her. She squirmed and rubbed herself wherever she could, wishing there were more of him, more of her. More of them.

He scraped his nails down her stomach, leaving a trail of raw desire in his path. She whimpered at the sheer, coarse pleasure of it. She was whipped up into a frenzied pitch in a matter of minutes. She scratched his back, raked his hair. They both flew at each other, hard and demanding, giving, over and over, until they broke into a thousand intermingled flying pieces.

Ellie gasped through the hot tears of joy and exertion that were now a regular part of their lovemaking. As she slid gradually toward a promising, satiating sleep, she tried not to acknowledge the near-terror that shook her when she contemplated a world without this man—and his warm, strong body in constant, reassuring, passionate proximity to her own. She relished the feel of the cool sheet as he settled it over their bodies, and then she slid her back and hips into the warm curve of his abdomen.

Two hours later, when Ellie woke, Luke was still breathing in even steady waves of deep sleep, but she could feel his stiff length against her lower back. She turned slowly; he rolled a half-turn onto his back, then resettled into the rhythm of his sleep. She moved gradually, slowly straddling his hips and sliding down onto him with delicious stealth. A fabulous half-waking grin spread across his lips. She kissed one of his nipples then draped herself over him as she very gently, very slowly brought him fully awake.

And took them both to another renewing pleasure. They languished in bed for a short while after, and then bathed and made their way down to the gardens at the back of the house to join the family for lunch.

Ellie carried her camera, hoping Maria wouldn't mind if she took a few frames of some flowers and statues that she'd seen through the glass wall on their way upstairs. She and Luke turned into the garden and were surprised to see Maria accompanied by Ethan and two other men who—by the looks of them—had to be Luke's brothers. Ellie felt the wave of nervousness that passed though Luke's body as if it passed through her own.

She looked into his eyes and tried to channel as much confidence and love as she could; Ellie squeezed his hand. "Just treat them like you'd treat me," she suggested.

He gave her a dark seductive look.

"Not like that!" But she smiled back at him. "How you treat me when you're not kissing me," she whispered.

"And how's that?"

"Gently."

By then they were a few feet from the large, outdoor table. It looked to be some sort of ancient slab of stone that had been carried across continents. Lovely, sea-green water glasses and wine glasses and glimmering silverware and pressed linen napkins and hand-painted ceramic plates contrasted with the almost pre-historic looking surface.

"Ah, there you are! Don't you look *refreshed*!" Maria's accented Italian voice left nothing to the imagination and Ellie couldn't repress a shy blush.

All three men stood when Ellie approached the table, one more handsome than the next. Ethan came around the table first, and took Ellie into a warm, friendly embrace. "Welcome." He pulled quickly away when he spied Luke's stormy expression.

"Ellie," Ethan continued, "please allow me to introduce my brothers." He gestured first to a man in his late twenties or early thirties, his hair loose and messy and sporting an old T-shirt that made him no less attractive. "This is Trevor, the youngest."

"You don't always need to say *the youngest*. We're not at Hamleys meeting Father Christmas for goodness' sake." Then he turned his sparkling blue eyes to Ellie. "It's a pleasure to meet you at last. We've all been extremely curious about the woman who could tame Luke." He leaned down and kissed her cheek.

Luke shoved him away with mock brutality, then they smiled at each other and Luke gave him a one-armed hug. "Good to see you, rascal."

"You too. It's been too long. I dashed up from France as soon as I heard you were coming into town."

"Thanks, we appreciate it."

Ethan continued with the introductions. "And Ellie, this is Michael."

Michael McCormick reached out his hand and shook Ellie's in his large, strong fist. He had more brawn than the others, which made him more lovable somehow. He resembled Luke more than the other two, in the way he looked at her—serious and gentle all at once. More like their father, perhaps.

When Michael released his hold on Ellie's hand, he quickly turned to Luke and almost toppled him, grabbing him in an enveloping hug. "I've missed you, brother."

Luke patted him on the back, as if he found the deep show of emotion difficult to process.

"All right everyone," Maria interjected. "Trevor, you sit here to my left, Ethan to my right, then Michael, then Ellie across from me." She smiled and winked at Ellie. "We ladies are thin on the ground so we need to spread out. Then Luke between Ellie and Trev. Sound good?"

They all found their places and settled in for what turned out to be two hours of fantastic Italian wine, course after course of cold meats, roasted vegetables, home-made pastas, tender cod, grilled chicken, more wine, cheeses, fresh exotic fruits, and tiramisu the likes of which Ellie had never encountered. Just before dessert, Trevor and Ellie switched places so Ellie and Maria could stop trying to converse across the length of the table.

"The chocolate in that sauce was beyond—where did you get it?" Ellie enthused.

"It's Valrhona—there's a shop up on the Marylebone High Street that has it. We can walk up there tomorrow."

Ethan looked briefly at his wife, then back into his coffee cup.

"Don't worry darling, I saw that," Maria said. "We can have Schenk drive us if you'd prefer."

"I'd prefer."

Luke caught the exchange and stared at Ethan as the two women resumed talking about their favorite chocolates and their favorite desserts.

"What's that about?" Luke asked, making no effort to hide his irritation. "They need security to walk out the front door? Should I accompany Ellie while I'm here?"

Ethan was obviously insulted that Luke had implied that he, Ethan, would delegate something as important as his own wife's personal safety. The hum of pending tension began to throb between them. "No." Ethan exhaled. "I'd just prefer if they go in the car."

"Why?"

"Because." Ethan stayed quiet for a few beats. "If they have parcels then they can transport them in the back of the trunk."

"Mm-hmm." Luke took a very skeptical sip of his espresso.

He felt Ellie watching as the storm brewed at his end of the table. She chimed in, "Oh Ethan, I love to walk. We don't need to tie up Schenk and the car. I mean, how much chocolate could we buy?" She laughed, trying to lighten the mood.

Luke smiled tauntingly at his brother. "See? She loves to walk."

Maria patted Ellie's hand where it rested near hers on the table. "Sometimes Ethan prefers if we take the car, when things at work are . . . " She looked at her husband and gave him a half smile. " . . . particularly stressful."

"Oh." Ellie looked confused and a little hurt that she was being cut off from the truth of the conversation. And Luke hated Ethan that much more for it.

"Yeah. *Oh.*" Luke lobbed toward Ethan, then took the last sip of strong coffee and pushed the small cup a few inches away from him.

Now Ethan really was fuming. Maria pressed her hand over his, silently begging him to hold his temper, but it was too late.

"You know what, Luke, you can take your attitude and stick it—"

"Whoa!" Trevor put up both palms, creating an imaginary wall between the two older brothers.

"Hey." Michael said simultaneously, putting one kind, but firm grip on Ethan's upper arm. "Steady."

Luke knew his smile was an adolescent taunt, but he was enjoying himself. "Let's have it out, Ethan. If Ellie is ever in danger because of you, I'll slit your fucking throat—"

"Luke!" Ellie snapped. "Cut that out!"

The other four people turned to her and watched as Luke mentally backed down and reached out to hold Ellie's hand on the bench next to him.

"What?" he asked, trying for innocence.

"Ugh!" Ellie shook her head, then turned to Maria. "He's impossible. I'm sorry he has no table manners."

"I'm sorry, Ethan," Luke said with genuine contrition, realizing at last that he'd been sliding into stupid ancient patterns. "I didn't mean to get riled. Old habits and all that."

The three brothers stared at him in complete amazement.

"Did Luke just apologize?" Trevor asked with a theatrical gasp. "This is up there with Halley's Comet in terms of rare events." Not that any of them would have ever admitted it, but on all of his teenage visits, Luke had terrified the three younger boys. He was never malicious or cruel—sometimes they probably wished that he had been, because at least then they might have known what they were up against.

What had been far worse was never knowing what would set him off. They'd all treaded lightly for fear of igniting a fit of temper that could last for days. At the very minimum he'd stew for hours, and always after meeting with his father. Those were usually followed by brutally arduous horseback rides to clear his head or blazing through entire boxes of ammunition on solitary target practices behind the storage barns.

Eventually, usually right before he had to step into the car that would take him to the airport and back to America, he would grumble something vaguely self-deprecating to his brothers about how he was not much fun to be around.

A real-time apology? Unheard of.

Trevor looked at Ellie. "Do you have a license?"

"What? What kind of license?" She rubbed the back of Luke's hand where she held it on her thigh.

"A license to practice sorcery. Magic? Enchantment?"

Luke looked at his lap, embarrassed.

The three brothers looked at Ellie with renewed interest. "Seriously," Michael added, "I don't think I've ever heard Luke apologize."

"Ever," Trevor added.

"For anything," Ethan threw in for good measure.

"Oh. Come on you guys. You're totally exaggerating." Ellie kissed Luke on the cheek. "He's such a lamb."

Ethan choked, really choked, on the sip of water he had just begun to swallow. Maria leapt up and began to pat her husband on the back. His face was bright red and he had his napkin up around his mouth.

"Are you all right, darling?"

He lowered the napkin and continued laughing hysterically. Maria punched him on the back. "You're terrible." But she kissed him on the side of his temple before she went back to her seat next to Ellie.

Luke turned to Ellie and spoke softly. "I tried to tell you. You're the only person who sees me like that. I mean, I'm not complaining, but it's best you know the real truth. I'm a brute." She knew he was trying to make light of the whole, sweet, family fiasco, but she also saw the thread of deep gratitude that swam behind his eyes. She leaned in toward his ear so only he could hear. "How I see you is the real truth."

He looked up at the sky, stretching his neck and tamping down the desire that always snapped between them when they leaned into each other like that. He exhaled, relaxed his shoulders, and took a sip of water.

"So there you have it," Luke said, as if he were giving the closing remarks at a slam-dunk trial. "I'm a lamb."

All of the brothers burst into spontaneous laughter, raising their glasses and cheering one another on as the two women looked at them and shook their heads.

"Infants," Maria muttered.

Chapter 14

The next day, Ellie and Maria rode up to the high street to shop and have lunch. Schenk hung around them, hovering in linen shops and jewelry stores and at the chocolatier's, about as inconspicuous as the *Hindenburg*. When they were ready for lunch, even Maria had had enough.

"Schenk, darling," Maria began. Ellie could see he was completely flustered when she turned on the Italian charm. "You're so good. Now please be a dear and bring all of these things back to the house for me, would you?"

"Well, Ethan asked me to stay—"

"I know, I know. And you've been marvelous. Divine. Now just drive us to Galvin, see that we're happily settled, drop the things at home, then come right back to fetch us in two hours."

"Two hours? Ethan will be—"

"—fine with it," she finished for him. "I'll call him right now and tell him. I'll butter him up." Maria winked and Ellie watched in amazement as Schenk went from burly protector to shy schoolboy.

"Well. Okay. If you're sure. I'll be back at three o'clock sharp. Yes?"

"Perfect," Maria cooed, and then just to really torture the poor man, she leaned up and gave him a soft, grateful kiss on the cheek. "You're a prize."

"Cut it out," he mumbled as he walked back toward the car, carrying the rest of their packages.

Ellie turned to Maria. "You're so evil!"

"I know. But I'd had just about enough of him breathing down our necks. Weren't you sick of it?"

"Yes, of course I was, but he's so sweet about it."

Maria slipped her arm through Ellie's. "The sweet highly-trained contract killer—"

"I know but—"

"There is nothing sweet about him—"

"There is too—"

"And you need to stop pretending that you don't know what's going on around here."

Ellie's smile faded. "Well. You don't have to be mean about it. I just think it's sweet when he turns all mushy and pliable in your hands."

"Oh. I didn't mean to hurt your feelings." Maria softened her tone. "I'm sorry. Ethan says I'm terrible about that. I just tell people what I think—pffft—" Maria snapped her fingers for effect. "And then I have to sweep up the mess later. I'm sorry, really."

"No. It's no big deal," Ellie said. "I just like to see the best in people. I always have. It's probably a fault—"

"No! No! It's not a fault at all. It's a lovely part of who you are. But, you know the truth, yes?"

Ellie looked patiently at this elegant, opinionated, glamorous woman, waiting for her to elaborate. "Yes. I understand what Ethan does, what Luke used to do."

"Good. Because these are big, strong men we're dealing with. They will turn quickly and easily into beasts if we let them." Maria patted Ellie's hand beneath hers. "But we won't let them, yes?"

"Yes." Ellie tried to regain her mental footing, but she felt at a disadvantage. Maria obviously knew every nuance of her husband's life—professional and personal—after nearly twenty years together. Ellie realized she was really just getting to know Luke. She'd been so busy falling in love with him, getting to know the emotional, tender heart of him, that all of a sudden she was confronted with the reality that she'd only known him a couple months. She felt slightly ridiculous as they walked into the cool bustling interior of a chic French bistro.

The maître d' recognized Maria immediately and began fawning over her. Ellie supposed it wasn't fawning necessarily, since his adoration seemed entirely genuine. They spoke in rapid French and Ellie listened as if the breath of a lover traveled over her skin. She loved everything about the language: the sound of the words but also how evocative they were, of the food, the culture.

"*Allons-y!*" the beautifully suited, dark-haired Edouard said as he gestured for them to follow him to a secluded table near the back of the paneled dining room.

They sat at the table for a few minutes looking at the menu and the wine list. Ellie started to feel comfortable again. She could only know Luke for as long as she'd known him, and there was no point in second-guessing everything.

"Shall we split a bottle of wine or is that too much?" Maria asked while she scanned the list.

"Too much what?" Ellie asked with mischief in her eyes.

"Just so!" Maria agreed as she looked up and signaled the sommelier. He came right over and Maria asked for a white Burgundy that Ellie had been dying to try for ages, but had not been able to find in the U.S. She must have hummed her approval aloud, because Maria was looking at her as if waiting for her to continue.

"How do you survive in Florida?" Maria pronounced the state's name like floh-ree-dah.

Ellie wasn't entirely unused to this kind of weird cultural insult. "I live quite well actually. What do you mean *survive?*"

Maria looked at Ellie with an assessing gaze. "Because you obviously love wonderful food and wine and city life and *the action*, I suppose, so it seems odd to me that you would choose to live somewhere so quiet."

The wine arrived and the sommelier performed the ritual removal of the cork, placing it carefully on the table, pouring a small amount into Maria's glass, waiting expectantly for her positive response, and then expressing his puffed-up pleasure at her approval. He poured a full glass for each of them, and then turned and slid the bottle into the waiting silver standing ice bucket before retreating back to the bar.

"It's not so quiet," Ellie picked up the thread of the conversation. "My parents are there and I travel a ton. It's a really nice home base. You would love it, I think. The ocean is glorious and my home is really quite . . . homey." Ellie smiled then raised her glass to toast Maria. "To the beautiful, sophisticated, charming Maria Costa McCormick. May this be the first of many shared bottles."

"Well, I'm not supposed to drink to myself, *certo*, so here's to you—perhaps the *next* female McCormick to come along in many years, eh?"

Ellie felt the heat rise up her neck at the implication that she and Luke would be getting married. Maria put down her glass and pressed her point. "You and Luke speak of marriage, yes?"

Ellie hesitated; it felt slightly treacherous to discuss her relationship in such a casual way. Ellie's temporary silence must have given Maria the impression that Luke and Ellie had never spoken of a future together.

"No?" Maria looked appalled.

"No . . . I mean, yes, of course, we speak of . . . the future. But we've only known each other for a couple of months. It's hardly the time to discuss marriage."

Maria's eyes went wide, then narrowed with shrewd knowledge. "Ethan proposed to me the first night he met me."

"And was forced to do so many times after, or so I heard."

Maria smiled. Far from being offended that her life story had been bandied about over tequila shots as part of the

McCormick family lore, she appeared perfectly pleased to have been the center of someone else's discussion. "It's true. It's best to make a man beg. So he knows his own mind, of course."

Ellie smiled at the convoluted logic that put begging into the same philosophical plane as self-aware enlightenment.

"Interesting." Ellie took another sip of wine, then ordered her lunch when the waiter came. After he stepped away, she exclaimed that she could eat a horse, but that she needed to wash her hands first.

She excused herself and headed toward the back of the restaurant to use the ladies' room. Five minutes later, Maria had finished checking her email, sending a text to Ethan, and calling home briefly to make sure the chef did not put the cheese she'd just purchased in the refrigerator; she wanted to serve it soft later that night.

After another five minutes, she was starting to tire of craning her neck down the length of the corridor that led to the bathroom, and then smoothing her napkin on her lap. She began thinking that Ellie was not quite as easygoing as she appeared if she needed all this time to wash her hands and apply fresh lipstick.

When a total of fifteen minutes had passed and their appetizers were sitting forlornly in front of her, Maria tossed her napkin on the banquette, grabbed her purse and strode down the narrow hall to the ladies' loo. She started to chastise Ellie before she was halfway through the door, "What in the world is taking you so long—"

Maria froze, staring at the contents of Ellie's purse where they lay strewn across the bathroom floor. There had obviously been some sort of struggle. She closed and locked the bathroom door behind her and reached into her purse to get her cell phone.

She made sure not to touch anything or disturb what might be evidence. Ethan picked up after half a ring. She never phoned him at work unless it was an emergency. So, basically, she never phoned him.

"What is it?" he snapped.

She whispered in case Ethan decided to take care of things without involving the police. "Ellie's been taken."

"What? Speak up, darling. I can't hear you."

"Ethan!" She was still whispering, but with a shrill, strained voice. "Someone has taken Ellie. She got up to use the loo, then about fifteen minutes went by and I came to check on her and her bag is here, tossed on the ground, money, passport, everything still here, and she's gone—"

"Fifteen *fucking* minutes!" Ethan roared. "You waited fifteen fucking minutes before you went to see if she was okay? Maria are you—"

"Ethan!" This time she yelled in earnest.

"Sorry. Okay." His voice was strained but relatively under control. "Here's what you need to do. No police. Pick up all of her things. Wipe down the bathroom for prints. Do you have any wet wipes with you, or anything you can use quickly?"

"Yes, there are some here." Someone knocked on the bathroom door. "One minute please," Maria called out cheerfully.

"If you can put her bag into yours or hide it somehow, try to do that. Otherwise, just—"

"What?"

"What are you doing?" Ethan asked. "I can hear you moving around."

"I'm doing what you said to do," Maria whispered angrily. "What do you think I'd be doing? Jesus, Ethan."

"I'm sorry. Okay. I'm calling Schenk now. He's probably already waiting out front for you. I'm going to call the maître d' and tell him you're horribly embarrassed but you seem to have locked yourself in the WC. That way, if that innocent person who's knocking at the door is perhaps not so innocent, you'll have a clear exit."

"Oh, god, Ethan. Luke is going to kill you. Or me. Seriously."

"We'll figure it out. Hang in there. A minute and a half more. Schenk is nearly there. I have to hang up, love. I'll meet you at home. We'll deal with everything from there."

"I love you. I'm so sorry."

The phone was dead.

Only a few seconds had elapsed when Maria heard the cheerful Gallic intonations of Edouard as he approached the other side of the bathroom door.

"Oh! I am so sorry madam," he crooned to the other person in the hall. "It seems our friend has locked herself in." He used his key to open the perfectly functioning door. Relishing his moment on stage, he rattled the knob with concern and then shook his head. "We will have this looked at immediately, but I am sure it is safe for you to use it." He spoke to a petite blonde woman who looked to be in her late twenties.

Maria passed close in front of the other woman as she entered the bathroom just as Maria was leaving. She didn't look like an accomplice to a kidnapping, but Maria had learned years ago that *nobody* looked like an accomplice to anything, especially people who were accomplices.

Maria gave her one more quick appraisal, then turned to Edouard and put her hand lightly on his forearm, letting him escort her from the restaurant and straight into the waiting Bentley.

She waved regally as the car pulled out into traffic, then, when she was sure the restaurant and its proprietor were out of sight, she punched the smooth, beige leather upholstery next to her thigh and swore a string of Italian epithets. Schenk looked into the rearview mirror with guilt and a touch of anger.

"Don't even start with me, Schenk. Save your I-told-you-so's for another time. *Mea culpa*, all right. Luke is going to have my head!" She punched the seat again for emphasis.

They were back in Mayfair and in the house within ten minutes. Everyone was on high alert; Maria could tell the minute she walked in the front door. Everyone it seemed, except for Luke.

"Back so soon?" He strode down the large central stairwell, all congeniality. "Did you two stock up on bonbons and baubles?"

Maria stood perfectly still.

Luke stopped before he reached the bottom step. "Where is she?"

"Luke—"

Before Maria even registered that he had left the stairs, he had crossed the entryway and had his hands on her shoulders, shoving her hard against the wall, beneath the Da Vinci etching. "Where is Ellie? Tell me!"

"We are going to find her, I promise—"

Clearly slipping into a blind rage, he brought a hand to her throat and she thought for an abstracted split-second that he might snap her neck right there in the hallway. Her head was turned at an odd angle and she saw the Da Vinci out of the corner of her eye; she stared at the six-hundred-year-old masterpiece and thought vaguely that it was ridiculous to have it hanging there in the front hall. Her lungs started to burn and her eyes began to throb when the front door swung open and Ethan kicked Luke's legs out from under him.

Maria gasped in a huge lungful of air and watched in horror as Ethan brought his leg back as if he were going to kick Luke in the kidneys as he lay there on the cool marble floor.

"Ethan! No!" she screamed, diving at him. She wrapped her arms around his neck and tried to retrain his focus on her face and away from the man on the floor. Ethan kept straining to look over her shoulder, to see if Luke had tried to get up yet, presumably so he could punch him in the face when he did.

Luke dragged himself to the bench, but stayed on the floor, resting his head between his knees. When he spoke his voice was as thin and taut as a piece of filament. "If anything happens to her, Ethan, I *will* kill you."

"Why wait? Let's kill each other right now, you fucking psycho. How dare you put your hands on my wife—" Ethan tried to move Maria out of the way, but she held him against her chest and kissed his neck, begging him quietly to simmer down.

"He was upset, he's upset," she explained. "I just walked in, he wasn't going to hurt me—"

"He had you in a choke hold with your feet a few inches off the floor!" Ethan croaked a terrible bark of a laugh. "You're probably right, it wouldn't have hurt a bit! He would have just cracked your spine like a twig."

"Stop it!" Maria's voice was returning to normal after a few more swallows. She opened the front door and pulled Schenk in. He'd been standing guard on the front step, unaware of what was happening a few feet away inside the house.

His gaze swept from Luke on the floor to Ethan standing behind Maria. "This doesn't look so good."

Ethan turned his rage to Schenk. "What the *fuck* were you thinking? You are so *fucking* fired you idiot sonofabitch."

"You're hired," Luke said from the floor. "That way I can kill you myself."

Schenk looked from one brother to the other.

Luke rose slowly then spread his arms wide. "How do you want to handle it, Ethan? Who's going to run this? We can sort out killing each other—and which one of us gets to kill Schenk—after we find her."

Ethan's phone began to vibrate in his pocket and he pulled it out and stared at the familiar number. "It's Desmond."

Luke shook his head and stared back down at the floor. When Ethan began speaking in low, confidential tones, Luke caught Maria's eye. "I never would have hurt you. Please believe me. I'm so sorry. I just—"

She crossed the few steps and put one arm around Luke. "I know you wouldn't. We're on your side. Just keep remembering that, okay?"

Ethan looked up from his phone call, furious. Maria was patting Luke's cheek in that quintessentially Italian way, as if she were his Mafia boss giving him a quick pep talk before they hit the streets. Ethan turned off the cell phone and shoved it into his pocket. "Let's go downstairs."

The next two hours were the longest of Luke's life, made up of a whirl of negotiations, threatening phone calls from Desmond, and violent outbursts between Ethan and Luke that were only barely contained by Maria and Schenk.

Chapter 15

Desmond Cresswell had been one of Ethan's first hires when he'd expanded his business into deep cover and black ops security fifteen years ago. Luke had tried to warn his brother that Desmond was far worse than a loose cannon, more like a finely tuned, psychotic cannon. But Ethan McCormick prided himself on his ability to hire and manage what many would consider *volatile* employees. He saw Luke's warning as a challenge, or even petty sibling jealousy.

For a while, it all worked. Luke quit the international security business altogether, selling out his share of the consulting firm in Tokyo after his divorce, and then working at a desk job in Beijing for a small computer firm. Under the radar.

Meanwhile, Ethan had convinced himself that a very generous compensation package, frequent vacations, and a long-term pension that included a house in a quiet, remote, tropical location would be enough to keep Desmond and similar employees on a leash. After several years of accompanying nuclear devices across hostile deserts or transporting the occasional unwilling *client* from one government location to another, most of those employees were perfectly happy to check out. And for nearly fifteen years, the formula had worked.

Until now. Until Desmond.

When they'd first met, Luke had liked Desmond immediately. He was funny and smart and bitterly sarcastic. Desmond was naturally brutal, completely unattached emotionally. He was perfect for the job.

He was also, Luke found it hard to admit even now, fun to work with. Despite the impression that high-level security work was a thrill a minute with high speed car chases and safecracking, it was usually days and weeks of sitting around—planning, plotting, and waiting—followed by several brief hours of action.

Desmond was an interesting person to be around in all those days and months of tedious preparation. He read everything from comics to Kant. He listened to music that ranged from medieval chants to Katy Perry. And even way back then, when he and Luke had been getting up to all kinds of trouble, when Luke knew any sane person would burn out within ten years, Desmond had said he never wanted to retire. His sister was the brain, he'd said, and he was the brawn.

When everything went to shit, and Ethan hired him despite Luke's grave warnings, Ethan didn't really take that into account. For years now, Ethan had been trying to figure out what to do about Desmond. He tried bringing him into an office position in London, but he was arrogant and ill-suited to working with others, most of whom he referred to simply as "the idiots." Ethan then transferred him to Mexico City, thinking he could run the more contentious Central and South American divisions. Mix a little action in with his bureaucratic inaction, Ethan had thought at the time.

The problem was Desmond refused to delegate. He always wanted to be a part of every operation . . . to the point of breaking down the front door and making sure every last person was successfully extracted.

Finally, after Kate's death—when Desmond really started to fray—Ethan offered him a severance and compensation package that would have made a mogul blush, only to have Desmond laugh and tell him he'd made more than that in one day when he'd cornered Russian oil futures back in 2004.

Raking his hand through his hair for what felt like the hundredth time, Luke looked across the worktable and asked his brother, "So, was there a precipitating event? Did you try to fire him again, or what? Or is he just trying to settle an old score with me?"

Ethan hesitated. "I tried to have him taken out," he said quietly, without looking up from his computer screen.

Everyone in the room fell silent. The basement of the McCormick's mansion in Mayfair was a combination panic room and center of operations. Luke shook his head. "You've got to be fucking kidding me? You tried to *kill* Desmond Cresswell?" Then Luke burst into hysterical, humorless laughter.

Ethan stood in front of a row of plasma computer screens and rested the fingers of his right hand in a tense arch on the tabletop. His face was grim and angry, but everyone knew it was directed more at himself than anyone else. "Yeah. It was ill-considered. I know that now."

"So now what does he want?" Luke asked with controlled detachment. He had forced himself, within minutes of realizing who had taken her, to remove Ellie entirely from his mind. The few times he'd allowed himself to actually think of her, he'd been unable to see or think or hear what anyone was saying, so he'd had to wander off and collect himself before coming back to the discussion.

At this point, he was able to narrow his focus to the task at hand by pretending that Ellie was swimming laps in Palm Beach—that he was on some assignment that had nothing to do with her—and he would see her when he got back.

Because, unless he played those mental tricks with himself, he wasn't quite sure what he might do. As much as he hoped and believed that he would never hurt Maria, or anyone else that happened to be standing by, there was a moment there in the upstairs hall where he wasn't entirely certain he could have stopped himself from killing someone—or destroying something—if Ethan hadn't come in. The most base rage and fear had flooded through his body when he saw Maria standing there alone in the hallway, and he knew in an instant that something had happened to the only person in the world who had the slightest idea of what or who he was. The only person who loved him.

And someone should have to pay for that sort of thing.

He shook his head again and tried to refocus on the plan that Ethan had set in motion as soon as they'd settled in the basement two hours ago. They were going to use Luke as the bait and try to extract Ellie while Luke dealt with Desmond. They were now waiting to receive the latest floor plans for Desmond's home.

"So Desmond is here," Ethan was using a large touchscreen computer on the wall to Luke's right to show where in London Ellie had been taken. "He's obviously thought of every eventuality related to his location, so we need to have you go in this way, right in plain sight."

Luke felt his skin crawl when he imagined Desmond alone with Ellie. In his more giddily optimistic moments he pictured Ellie making the man a delicious quiche and serving it to him with a bottle of Chablis, laughing with him about how needlessly serious and overwrought he was, and how much fun it would be if they all rented a villa in the south of France next summer. Then he remembered how sick Desmond really was—and the type of sick vengeance he was probably after—and all thoughts of giddy reconciliations vanished.

When Luke had filed for divorce Kate had begged him not to disclose her relationship with Desmond. She was right in assuming it would destroy her career—all of their careers. But the sickest part of all, what Luke could never really get beyond, was the fact that she had actually referred to it as her *relationship with Desmond.*

He'd begged her to seek counseling, or to at least admit that it was destructive and that she was being victimized by a brother who was seven years older than she was, and who had obviously been serially abusing her since long before she was old enough to consent.

She insisted their relationship was consensual, and even went so far as to suggest it was too complex for Luke to understand. So, years later, whether or not Kate willfully put the bullet in the chamber and placed the barrel to her temple, or had simply played Russian roulette with Desmond one too many times, it was still murder as far as Luke was concerned. Desmond Cresswell had been slowly killing his sister since the first time he abused her when she was a little girl.

And now he had Ellie. Luke felt his skin become icy cool, as if he were stepping into a metallic suit of close-fitting body armor.

"Enough planning," he said. "Let's be done with this."

Schenk, Maria, and Ethan stopped talking and turned to Luke. He suspected that his eyes had turned to emotionless steel and that he looked exactly like what he was: a man quite calmly resolved to kill another.

Ellie came awake in a slow, groggy haze. Her eyelids felt sticky and sandy.

"Hello, Eleanor."

The blood in her veins turned to a frigid current, like the slowed black streams in winter that ran behind her childhood home in Virginia. She kept her eyes shut, wishing that voice away with childish, vain hope.

She was blindfolded and strapped to some sort of table. She still had her clothes on, she realized. That was something.

"Aren't you going to say hello?" the voice prompted.

His voice was perfect. Or perfected. He had the hint of a delightfully plummy British accent, educated but not snobbish, but his vowels were mostly flat, American. He sounded like someone you wanted to be friends with. Someone you might meet at a bar when you were traveling abroad, and then spend hours talking to about everything you ever thought of. He sounded exactly like Luke.

He untied the blindfold and Ellie kept her eyes closed.

"Hmm. After seeing how you were with Luke, I thought you'd be far more . . . animated."

Ellie tried to immerse herself in some other mental state. He knew Luke. He sounded practical. She opened her eyes.

She was in a normal-seeming, if minimalist, windowless bedroom. The walls were painted a simple, modern gray with no moldings or decoration where they met the white ceiling. She turned her head slightly and saw she was lying on a narrow cot covered in smooth gray sheets. It reminded her of summer camp.

"Funny the things that pop into one's head, isn't it?"

She closed her eyes again, hoping she could shut out the sound of him along with the sight of him.

"Go ahead and shut your eyes if you like, it will only make my voice more compelling."

Her eyes flew open in rebellion, lest he think she was savoring the sound of his thrumming words. Then she closed her lids halfway, lest he think she was opening them to suit him.

"Everything you do from now on will be done in reaction to me, Eleanor. Just enjoy it, darling."

She felt a profound disgust as her body responded to the seductive words. He sounded so much like Luke, it was as if her body was missing him so much that it would accept this sham substitute. She'd been physically turned off for so many years after Rob's death that her passion with Luke had turned her into a walking, talking, physically receptive being.

For the past few months it wasn't just sex that stimulated her, but everything. Food, wine, the ocean, sand, wind, music, fabric. How could she turn that off? She couldn't. And this cruel man knew it. She was able to distance her mind from her body at least; she could float above herself if he touched her.

The irony was that, in the random moments when she had contemplated the horror of rape—in awareness seminars in college, when she had lived in New York City and had taken a self-defense course with the NYPD—she had always convinced herself it was an act of mindless violence. There was nothing sexual about it or, rather, there was nothing sexy about it. The real terror for Ellie at this moment was that her body was responding, starting to warm to the familiar voice. Pavlovian. She hated herself more just then than she'd ever thought possible. One scalding tear leaked out of her right eye.

"Don't worry. I'm not going to touch you."

She exhaled in relief.

"Well, not with my hands at least."

She shuddered as she felt the cool metal of the barrel of a gun trail up her bare calf. A small whimper of terror escaped her and she instantly despised the weakness. She breathed back more tears and kept her head turned away from that voice.

"Not that you wouldn't like some skin to skin contact. Your hips are practically arching toward me as it is. But we can't have any of my DNA mucking up our delicious plans, now, can we, beauty?"

She felt a quiver of desire between her legs and wanted to claw away his words, to destroy her despicable physicality. She tried to pull her hips further into the bed, caving into herself. He continued to trail the gun all along the lines of her body, the cool metal and the warm voice washing over her. The sick bile of disgust warred with the physical reality that he knew exactly what to say and where to touch her to arouse her sexual response. The tears were like fire against her face. She wished they could burn her skin right off.

The few times she opened her eyes, if only to rest the muscles that kept them clenched shut the rest of the time, she saw his expression—of concentration mingled with lust and desire. She didn't know how long it went on, but each second felt like an hour, the minutes as long as days. When she felt the barrel of the gun penetrating her body, her mind simply fractured and spiraled into shards of loathing and pure, if impotent, rage.

She pulled at her wrists with a jerk in a stymied attempt to cover her ears. There must be a way to mentally force oneself to stop hearing, her mind scrambled. To stop feeling. Buddhist monks or Indian mystics or Aboriginal shamans had found ways to do it. She tried to visualize her cochlea and Eustachian tubes and canals, the veins that brought blood to her ears, she pictured all of that occluding, closing up, willfully failing. She pictured herself crawling into her deepest, quietest place. She sidled up against terror and mourning. She crouched there in her mind.

And thought of Luke. And how he might save her. But he never came, and the gun was everywhere, and the voice was everywhere, and she couldn't hold on for Luke, or herself, any longer.

She finally—many minutes or hours later, she was never sure which—simply abandoned her psyche altogether.

Chapter 16

Ethan opened a nondescript-looking closet door. The fluorescent lights inside flickered then held steady, revealing row upon row of neatly displayed firearms. Handguns, rifles, antique shotguns, automatic weapons, machine guns, a few AK-47s.

Luke pushed his way past Schenk and Ethan and started to pull a variety of pieces into his hands, contemplating them one at a time, weighing them in his palm for heft and balance. He picked up a Beretta 418 then put it back. Then a Luger. Then a Colt .45. Then he settled on the Walther PP: compact, accurate. He picked up two of the automatic rifles and slung one over each shoulder in case he got the chance to take a shot at long range. He saw a couple of knives on the far wall. "Do you have any holsters?"

"Of course. Over there to the left, bottom drawer." Ethan pointed.

Luke walked toward the back of the room and pulled out the drawer. He strapped on a holster for the handgun that wrapped around his back and fit snug up against his ribs. He put a knife holster around his calf, lifting one of his pant legs, and buckling it into place.

He looked up to see Schenk and Ethan going through similar preparations.

Luke patted himself down to make sure everything was secured in place then walked out of the narrow aisle and collected ammunition from a large case near the door. "I'll meet you all in the garage. I need a minute alone."

Fifteen minutes later they were parked in front of a large, immaculate row house in the Maida Vale neighborhood of London, on a lovely tree-lined street called Hamilton Terrace. The early evening light cast everything in a beautiful soft indigo that was completely at odds with how they were all feeling and what was probably taking place inside Desmond's house.

"Well, he's done quite well for himself, hasn't he?" Luke's bitterness implied that Ethan had underwritten every ill-gotten farthing.

Luke's control was slipping far too easily. He knew rationally that Ethan had never been more than a pawn in Desmond's sick, convoluted life plan. Ethan was no more responsible for Desmond's twisted psyche than anyone else, himself included.

Luke turned to Ethan. "Look, I'm sorry. I'm sorry about Maria, and sorry about trying to blame you for everything. Whatever happens, I'm sorry. I just . . . " His voice trailed off to nothing.

Ethan narrowed his eyes, as if trying to pass final judgment on his older brother once and for all. "I get it. You love her. It's obvious. You can blame me if it makes you feel better."

"That's the thing, it's not making me feel any better. And if we don't find her soon I'm not sure I'll be able to feel anything at all ever again. It's like icy water is rising up around my ankles and if I don't get to her soon, it might just rise right up over my chest . . . and I'll never . . . "

Ethan stared at him. "It's all going to be all right. Honestly, Desmond's totally touched in the head, but he's not without his . . . aspirations. You'll find a way to get to him. And in the meantime, we know the house layout now and we'll find her. He—well, I don't want to upset you, but we all know he probably wants her very close by."

Luke shook his head in silent disgust. "I know." He paused for a few more seconds. "I'm going in." He stepped out of the car and fit his earpiece more snugly, making sure it was entirely invisible in his ear canal. He spoke quietly to make sure Schenk and Ethan could hear him as he walked away. They all confirmed they were on the same frequency.

Luke walked up the nine steps to the freshly painted, shiny black front door and gave the large silver knocker two quick snaps.

The door was opened almost immediately by what could only be described as the Desmond interpretation of a butler, namely a behemothic bodyguard. The man looked down his long (broken) nose at Luke.

"May I say who is calling?" he intoned in an abominable approximation of aristocratic English.

"Just tell him I'm here and cut the crap."

"Wait here." And with that the thug shut the front door in Luke's face.

Exactly seven minutes passed until the door opened again—at precisely six o'clock, Luke noted—and Desmond stood in the dimly lit entry. "Well, it really is you. I thought you'd try to gas me out or fire bomb me. Too afraid she might be here in the house, huh? Smart move. Come on in."

Desmond gave a quick, taunting wave to Ethan and Schenk who, he'd correctly assumed, were sitting there behind the blacked-out windows of the SUV. "Nice that you've mended fences with the family and all that. You can thank me later. Though I have to confess, I never took you for the sentimental type—which I now see was a tactical error on my part."

Luke followed him into the living room of the sparsely but elegantly furnished house. "Where's Ellie?"

"Oh, come on. We haven't seen each other in years. Since Kate's funeral, remember? Let's catch up a bit before we get down to the boring particulars of our negotiations. Or our new *arrangement*."

Luke knew she was right here in the house. He felt it as soon as he'd crossed the threshold. He had his bearings, having studied the floor plan of the house back at Ethan's. He knew there were at least two levels below ground, soundproof, bulletproof. "Everything proof," Ethan had added bitterly as they'd examined the blueprints that afternoon.

"Desmond, there's really nothing to catch up on. I want her back. I'll give you whatever you want. This whole operation is messy. This isn't your style."

Desmond's face went dark and ferocious, then calm and bland in a matter of seconds. "Please refrain from telling me what is or is not *my style*. You have no idea who I am or what I'm capable of. I stood by and watched you take your pathetic spiritual journey; I was always holding out hope that you were not this whining little excuse for a man. Kate and I always tried to show you your stronger self, but you just couldn't hack it. You and your pedestrian morals. The three of us together could have been unstoppable."

Luke had heard this whole part before. He was so far beyond caring what his dead ex-wife and her psychotic brother thought of him. "What do you want? Kate is gone. I'm sure there are plenty of women who would play those games with you."

"That's where you were always so wrong, Luke. They were never games. What Kate and I had was real, damn it. You were such an idiot not to appreciate that. But, I have to hand it to you. You've always had great taste in women. And now, it seems, you've done it again. You always were a good scout. Ellie looks like she might be teachable."

Luke felt the blood drain right out of his skull to be replaced by an arctic wave of hatred and adrenaline. "You must stop taunting me or I will simply shoot you in the skull."

"Now, see, that is something I always liked about you. Simple. Direct. Honest. Why couldn't you just be that way when it really mattered? When we were both with Kate?"

"*We* were never with Kate, you sick fuck." Luke knew he walked a fine line between tempering Desmond's palpable insanity and controlling his own roiling temper.

"Yeah, you go and tell yourself that." Desmond was fixing himself a scotch, dropping one ice cube at a time into an expensive, heavy, cut-crystal glass. He waved one hand in a casual, dismissive gesture that encompassed the room. Luke tried to clear his mind, to be ready to act, and he found himself wondering why the furniture was upholstered in a completely impractical, very expensive-looking white silk.

He waited for Desmond to continue then finally had enough. "Where is Ellie?" he repeated

"Oh, not to worry. I've taken care of her *needs*. She's very responsive, isn't she? Do you want a drink?"

"No. Where is she?" Luke ignored everything except the fact that she must still be alive.

"Stop asking me. It's annoying." Desmond turned from the drinks tray with a peevish sigh. "Just know the obvious, that if anything happens to me, that gorilla who answered the door has very strict orders to slice her throat. He's on the next frequency up from you and Ethan and Schenk, by the way. If you want to touch base." Desmond smiled and lifted his heavy cocktail glass in a salute.

Ethan had created a shared frequency that Desmond could not hack, at least not in the short time that the operation would take, so Luke wasn't worried about that, at least. "What do you want?"

"Ah, that's the real question, isn't it?" He looked thoughtfully out the window. "I want Ellie. I like her and I think I want her. In fact, I don't think so, I know so. So, it's not really negotiable, you know, because I suspect you don't really want to just hand her over. But there it is." Desmond shrugged, as if he was at a restaurant deciding between a merlot and a pinot noir, and had just settled on the merlot. I think I'll have the merlot . . . I think I'll have Ellie.

Luke felt himself sinking slowly into the other man's morass of insanity, when he heard Ethan's voice come into his earpiece. "We're on the closed frequency, Luke. We heard about the gorilla. We're coming in the back. Keep talking to Desmond. We've checked the heat signals and there's only the four of you in the house."

Again, all the words distilled down to: *Ellie is still alive.*

Desmond shook the ice in his glass and quirked an eyebrow. "So. Do you want me to kill you now or do you want me to watch you fuck her first? I can now see the whole three-of-us happily-ever-after thing is not going to work long-term."

Luke thought he might throw up right there on the polished, perfectly restored parquet floors. "Yeah, I think I'll pass on the three-way. But I'd like to say goodbye, if you'll grant me that."

"I don't know. I'll have to think about it." He shook his glass in a meditative twist. "How's Didi?"

"Fuck you."

"She looked great the last time I saw her."

"Fuck you." Luke was starting to see the little incendiary jabs before they came, bolstering himself against Desmond's taunting.

"You two looked happy in San Francisco. That was sweet."

Luke exhaled. "Desmond. I cannot sit here while Ellie is somewhere in this house suffering."

"She's not suffering. In fact, I think she liked it. The pressure at her wrists. The restraints. Does she like that, Luke? Tell me how hot she runs." He raised an eyebrow in what appeared to be genuine interest, as if he were taking over the training of a prized filly, and wanted to know her proclivities, her quirks.

"Please stop it." The please was a mistake and Luke knew it; Desmond despised weakness.

"Stop what? Asking you to be honest? Because no one else has the balls to demand honesty of you. Your fawning brothers and desperate, dying father? It's pathetic. You used to appreciate how honest Kate and I were. All three of us."

Deep down, Luke knew this was what would be coming— this twisted vision that Desmond held of something that had never existed, with Kate and Luke and Desmond twenty years ago in Tokyo—of somehow doing that with Ellie. When they were all best friends and Luke hadn't known the truth.

Luke took a deep, slow breath, silently begging Ethan or Schenk to report back that they had somehow, miraculously, slain the beast that was guarding Ellie. He tried to let the seconds linger.

Desmond's pupils dilated, letting Luke know someone was speaking to him in his earpiece. He was far too professional to reveal anything he didn't want Luke to know, he'd probably been getting minute-by-minute updates from Cro-Magnon man for the past twenty minutes. It was more like he was pretending to be a busy corporate raider who had to take another call; he might as well have held up a single index finger to let Luke know he'd be able to talk to him again in just a minute.

Then he spoke quickly. "No. Absolutely not. Just let her piss the bed." He turned back toward Luke as if he were in the midst of potty-training a puppy. "Apparently, Ellie has to go to the bathroom and is trying to get my man to undo her restraints."

Luke felt his stomach heave. He stared at Desmond as if he'd never seen him before. Luke's earpiece came to life with Ethan's breathless report that Ellie had "neutralized" the guard but they were double-checking the wiring on one of her restraints. He could hear her voice in the background. It was done.

But she'd had to murder that guard. Luke would never forgive himself for that.

He continued to stare blankly at Desmond, giving no indication whatsoever that he'd had any communication.

"Ethan and Schenk have probably found her by now, huh?" Desmond said softly, staring into his swirling expensive scotch. "It's going to be a stupid mess if they try to undo those restraints without this." He pulled a small device, about the size of a Zippo lighter, out of the trim pocket of his perfectly cut trousers.

Luke sat there wondering if the man in front of him had ever been sane, or if he'd always been quite mad. Military precision required a lack of ambiguity that many people confused with heartlessness. Luke knew that. When Desmond and Luke had orchestrated the toughest extractions in Libya and Afghanistan, that level of pure, emotionless precision was exactly what had made them a great team. Schenk's deadpan voice came through Luke's earpiece again. "The restraints were complicated but Ethan knew the devices. All clear. We're all out. Repeat, all clear. Kill him."

Luke felt a shiver of anticipatory pleasure. The joy of killing Desmond. He would hate himself later for that frisson of excitement, he was sure, but in that moment he stared into the man's eyes and pulled the Walther PP from the snug holster under his arm and fired it directly between his eyes. He never looked away from Desmond's gaze. Luke watched with cold disdain as Desmond's dead hand released the small silver device and a muted explosion could be heard below ground, somewhere beneath the lovely private garden, Luke thought dully.

"Luke, get out here." This time it was Ethan's voice. "Ellie's not responding. She's in shock. What the fuck are you doing in there? If Desmond's dead, get the fuck out of there."

"Yes I'm here. Desmond's dead."

"Now, now, now! Get out, you idiot! Now!" Luke took one last look around the strangely meditative room, wiped for prints, and looked dispassionately at the slow spread of dark blood that was starting to soak the white carpet around Desmond's skull.

"We're in the car in the back alley. What the fuck?" Ethan's voice yelled into the earpiece.

Luke started to run through the house as he listened.

"Get out now. Ellie's blood pressure is dropping."

Smoke was beginning to waft through the ventilation system as he found his way out of the house.

Ellie was lost. She wanted it to stop. People were grabbing at her and demanding things of her and probably planning to abuse her again, like the man with the velvet voice and the gun and she didn't want to react. But she did react, didn't she? To the second man. She didn't let the second man touch her. She got his gun and she shot him. No, no. She would never kill another human being. But she had, hadn't she?

Then she simply slipped away.

Luke opened the back door of the SUV, leapt quickly onto the seat, and pulled the door closed behind him. He smacked the back of Schenk's head over the driver's headrest. "Drive, asshole."

The car pulled instantly into traffic. Luke turned his attention to Ellie's collapsed body leaning into Ethan's embrace. Luke reached for her and pulled her gently into his lap, positioning her head into the crook of his arm and wrapping her in a blanket Ethan handed to him.

Luke cradled Ellie like a small child, crying and murmuring into her hair as Ethan filled in some of the details. Ellie had been standing over the dead guard when they broke into the detention room in the second sub-basement. Her eyes had been wild as she swung the gun toward Schenk and Ethan, her left hand still attached to the metal bedframe with a leather strap and several multicolored wires.

Suddenly, Ethan looking even more infuriated when Luke caught his eye in the rearview mirror. "How the *fuck* did Desmond get that explosive device? That's not even out of our R & D department. I'm going to have to fire my whole fucking company."

Ellie's face had an unnatural gray pallor; the skin around her eyes was papery. Luke kept rubbing her arms and shoulders. He swore to himself that he was never letting her out of his grasp again, as he kept talking to her softly, intimately. They pulled into the garage at Ethan's a few minutes later. Schenk must have broken every possible traffic code getting from Maida Vale to Mayfair as quickly as he had.

Luke opened the car door and carried Ellie's limp form into the house. Without pausing, he continued up the stairs two at a time and reached their bedroom. He kicked the door shut behind him with a vicious slam then set Ellie down on the large king-size bed as delicately as he could.

He ran his hands along her entire body, checking first for breaks or fractures, then pressing different parts of her abdomen to check for internal bleeding or signs of organ distress. He felt around her spine and skull, his thumbs and strong fingers making sure there was no blood or bruising on her scalp and neck. She was as lifeless as a doll when he turned her over onto her stomach, one arm flung wide. He began to feel his own heart rate increase in frustrated worry. He wanted to beat something or kill something or beat the life back into her, but she just lay there like a flimsy, destroyed thing, even though nothing appeared to be physically wrong with her.

He felt the warm trail of tears on his cheeks and wiped at them with disgust. He unholstered the guns and knives that he'd put on not even an hour before, and set them on a small chair across the room, near the fireplace. He slid off his shoes and set them neatly alongside one another.

The air conditioning kept the room at a cool, institutional temperature; he wondered if he should open some windows and let the evening air of late summer trail into the room. Instead, he crawled up onto the bed and stretched his body the length of Ellie's. Even though she was totally unconscious, her body stiffened as if his physical presence was unwelcome. He reached his arm around her shoulders, as he'd done every night they'd slept together for the past few months, thinking the familiar position might soothe her on some subliminal level. She reacted, but it was with a quiet whimper, as if she were in the midst of a terrible, frightening dream.

Luke rose up on one elbow and pulled her onto her back so he could see her expression. Her eyes were shut but there was nervous movement beneath the lids. Her brows were furrowed in defiance, but the terror was obvious. He tried to shake her awake, trying to keep his voice smooth and steady. Calm.

Instead of soothing her, his voice seemed to make her more distraught. She pulled at the sheets then, as if realizing her arms were free she started scratching at Luke's face and chest, trying to pummel her way out of the fog of her nightmare.

"Ellie!" he yelled, all hint of soothing nursemaid gone from his voice.

Her eyes flew open and she looked at him without a trace of recognition. Pure terror. He held her hands firm at the wrists, to protect himself perhaps, but more to protect her from any wild self-destructive reactions. He had one leg across her hips, the way she loved, and she began kicking her own legs in a primitive, brutal struggle to escape.

"Ellie! It's me! It's Luke!" He freed her instantly, feeling like an idiot for wanting to comfort her in a way that probably reminded her of how she'd been confined by Desmond.

She started screaming right into his face, as if he wasn't even there. "Luke!" she screamed over and over, looking everywhere but into his face, mere inches from her own.

Maria came whipping into the room, her mass of wild brown curls flying around her face. "Luke," Maria told him. "Get away from her. Now!" She looked like a fierce female warrior from some ancient Roman play. "Now, I said."

Luke was reluctant to let go of Ellie for fear she'd hurt herself, but Maria was there in an instant, soothing her with soft, feminine words. Ellie turned toward Maria like a child turning toward her mother. Maria gestured with a quick, firm toss of her head for Luke to leave the room. He walked slowly toward the door, looking back one last time as Ellie gripped at Maria's shirt and sobbed pathetically into her chest. He stared as her back was racked with sobs and then her head turned slowly toward him. When Ellie caught sight of him she began to howl anew with piercing, terrified screams.

Maria turned to see that he was still in the room and began to rant in a voluble, spitting Italian that would have made a dockworker blush, and then finally repeated in English, "Get. Out."

Luke shut the door with slow resignation and slid to the floor in the hall. He pressed his ear to the painted wood panel, trying to make out the placating words that Maria was using to subdue Ellie and bring her down from the frantic pitch that Luke's presence had obviously triggered.

A few minutes later a maid came up carrying a silver tray with a pitcher of water and a small blue container of prescription medication.

"La donna asked me to bring something to calm Miss Ellie."

Luke stood up and got out of the way to let the Italian maid pass. He opened the door for her, but then she shut it quickly with her hip, not allowing Luke even a peek toward the bed.

He listened, his forehead resting against the door, as Maria cajoled Ellie into taking the sedative. She spoke in soft French that seemed to be far more effective than English or Italian. The maid came out a few minutes later. About thirty minutes after that, Maria finally emerged.

Just as Luke started to speak, she lifted a single finger to her lips to silence him, then pointed to the floor, gesturing for him to follow her downstairs. They went to the lower ground floor kitchen. Ethan was in the far corner watching a small flat panel television that was showing an early evening news story about a random house fire in Maida Vale. There was no mention of a shooting. Only that there were two casualties.

"Do you mind?" Ethan pointed to the television, asking Luke if it was okay to leave it on.

"Sure. Go ahead and watch it. I'm sure you have it all in hand." Luke turned to Maria. "What's going on with Ellie?"

Maria had been working in the NATO Defense College in Rome when she and Ethan first met. Before that, she'd pursued a career in medicine, completing her degree and almost simultaneously deciding she could never spend her life within the walls of a traditional hospital. She applied for a position in the Italian military, much to her aristocratic parents' dismay, then spent three years working in the NATO hospital in Kandahar. Luke suspected she knew exactly what was 'going on' with Ellie, as much as she looked like she didn't want to be the one to come out and say it.

"It's not good. She needs professional help. Quickly."

"But, you're a professional! I don't want her in a hospital—"

"Luke," she reached out for his hand. "I haven't worked in a field hospital in over fifteen years. She's suffering. She's totally traumatized. *She killed that man, do you understand?* I don't even think she recognized me just now or knew where she was. She's just grateful I wasn't a man. I want to get her to a doctor who can give her a full evaluation and see if we can—"

"I don't want her moved."

Maria rubbed her temples. "Look . . . I can call a specialist and of course she is welcome to heal here after—"

"No after. She stays here. That's non-negotiable. Call the best doctor and have him come here."

Maria shook her head. "But she might need a more professional setting, just for a while."

Ethan looked at them over his shoulder occasionally, then returned his attention to the BBC. Luke covered his face with his hands and rested his elbows on the stainless steel kitchen counter. He spoke through his fingers. "Don't think I don't see you over there in the corner Ethan."

Ethan got up and walked over to where the other two were sitting. He put one hand around his wife's back and rested the other hand carefully on Luke's shoulder. "All things considered—"

"I know." Luke looked up, his vision blurry with tears. "We did it. We got her out. She's alive. I know. And we got him, damn it." His head sank back down. "But . . . I just don't know what I'll do. If she's not okay. I don't blame you. I don't care about any of that anymore. As long as Desmond's gone and Didi is safe. And Ellie is safe. But . . . "

Ethan rubbed his hand against Luke's shoulder with brisk encouragement. "She's tough. You said so yourself. She's just—it was creepy in there. We still don't know what happened, either with Desmond or the guard. I don't think he raped her—" Ethan looked at Maria.

"I examined her, Luke, after the sedative had taken effect, and there was no physical evidence of anything . . . forced. But we can get a rape kit if you think she'll want to be absolutely sure."

Luke turned his head toward Maria, then Ethan, his look asking for the details he dreaded. "Where was she being held?"

Ethan spoke first. "It was basically a holding cell—single cot, metal frame bolted to the cement floor—the usual. When we blew in she had just shot the guy who answered the door when you went in. Physically, she was fine. I mean, she was in shock, obviously, as you saw, but she was fully dressed and unharmed as far as we could tell. Not a scratch on her. We need to let her talk to someone, Luke."

"Fine. Yes. Get someone quickly." Luke turned to Maria. "Okay?"

"Okay," she agreed, but she shook her head as she walked out of the room and pulled out her cell phone.

When it was just the two of them in the kitchen, Ethan continued. "She might not remember any of it. She might not *want* to remember any of it. Sometimes it's gone forever; sometimes it never goes. You know all this."

Luke sighed and covered his face again. Yeah, he knew.

There had been two assignments in particular that he'd completely wiped from his memory. He recalled the general elements—where he was, how they'd broken in, the extraction— but there were portions of time, twenty minutes here, thirty minutes there, that were utterly, permanently lost. He'd also heard of soldiers with post-traumatic stress who'd lost way more time than that. Days. In one case, weeks—both before and after the event.

Luke tried to get his mind around what that would mean for him and Ellie. Could he make her fall him love with him a second time? Would her personality even be the same? He'd been friends with one guy who'd suffered so much on one assignment that—even though he remembered Luke and their friendship, and even thought fondly of the time they'd spent together—he'd finally confessed that he just didn't like being around Luke anymore. Something about him was too upsetting. "When I see you it just makes me think of how I used to be, and it's frustrating and confusing. Sorry, man." From a former colleague, it was depressing, but Luke had been able to chalk it up to military life, process it, and move on.

With Ellie? "No fucking way."

Ethan pulled his hand away. "What is it?"

"I'm not down with the wait-and-see plan." He stood up and started walking out of the kitchen. "I'm not going to let her go. She stays here, damn it. We get the best psychiatric care. End of story."

Maria was back in the kitchen by then. "Dr. Lawrence will be here at nine o'clock tomorrow morning. She's the best I know here in London." She watched as Luke turned toward the stairs. "Where do you think you're going?"

"To be with Ellie."

"I'm not sure that's the best strategy right now. We need to let her mind rest, just like you'd let a broken bone heal. Please."

"Fine." Luke moved his shoulder to shake off Maria's hand. "I won't go near her, but I'm not going to sit by and let her withdraw into some safe world that doesn't include me. I don't care if she gouges my eyes out, I have to be in there with her. I can't, Maria. I just can't . . . " His voice cracked and Maria pulled him into a hug at the bottom of the stairs.

"I know, Luke. We know. Just be careful."

"I will." He climbed the stairs back to Ellie.

Chapter 17

Luke walked quietly into the bedroom and shut the door gently behind him. Maria had changed Ellie into a light summer nightgown and tucked her under the covers. Her auburn hair was in a loose tangle around her head, as if she'd been thrashing a bit before settling into a drug-induced sleep. Luke went into the bathroom and stripped before stepping into a scalding hot shower. He stood there under the pelting water, trying to let every shredded emotion of anger and hatred and revenge and self-pity slide down that drain along with the dirt and sweat and terror of the most miserable day of his life.

He dried off and changed into a white T-shirt and loose pajama bottoms. He turned the air conditioning off and opened the two windows that faced out over the back garden. The night air wafted in, reminding him, and Ellie he hoped, soothingly of Florida. He breathed in the soft air and stood in front of the window for a few minutes. He walked quietly across the room and stared down at her, not knowing how best to comfort her. He didn't want to alarm her with his touch, but he didn't want her to wake up alone and frightened either.

He opted for a compromise, lying down on the far side of the bed without getting under the covers or disturbing her.

Pulling an extra blanket over him, he turned to look at her profile.

The late night air coiled around them. Ellie hummed with a familiar satisfaction. She took a deep breath, as if she were inhaling Luke's scent and then her body settled deeper into sleep. At least she wasn't trying to rip his face off, Luke thought optimistically as he tried to fight off sleep. He must have dozed eventually because he woke with a jolt of alarm when Ellie sat up in bed and stared down at him with a bit of wildness in her eyes, but nothing like when he'd first brought her back. More like how she usually woke up—disoriented.

He held perfectly still. "Ellie?" he whispered softly.

She shook her head, looking down at herself, then touching the backs of her own hands. "Am I safe?"

"Yes, you are."

She stretched out her arms and looked at the backs of her fingers, and then the palms. "My hands look strange to me. I don't recognize my own hands. Isn't that weird?" She looked at him for an answer, then shook her head in wonder. "Where are we?"

He wanted to reach out and touch her lower back so desperately, but he was afraid he'd startle her if he initiated any physical contact. "London. At Maria and Ethan's house in Mayfair. Do you recognize anything?"

She looked around the room, her eyes blank, then she gazed down into his eyes. "I recognize the smell of you. You smell nice. And your eyes." She smiled shyly.

"I think you smell nice, too," Luke tried.

But she didn't like that. Her brow furrowed and she looked mildly irritated, shaking her head a little and staring at her hands again.

Then she turned back to look at him more carefully.

He'd left the bathroom light on and the London night sky was relatively bright, so they were both able to see each other in the dim glow.

"Don't tell me your name," she said. "I want to try to remember it on my own."

Luke felt his heart crush under an ever-growing pile of emotional bricks. Devastation. But here he was in her bed. She must know. Some part of her must still know. "Okay," he whispered.

She reached out, timid. Her hand felt soft and exploratory against his cheek. "I think you love me very much."

"I do," Luke whispered. "So much."

"I have a terrible headache." Ellie dropped her hand from his face, the moment lost. "I think I need to go back to sleep now. Will you stay and watch over me? I'd like that." She rested her hands under her cheek—like she always did—and stared at his face a few inches away. "Like a sleepover."

"I'll be right here the whole time. You get some rest."

Her eyelids started to get heavy. "Thanks. Whoever you are." She added that last with a winsome smile and a small pat on Luke's shoulder, then retracted her hand back beneath her cheek and fell quickly into a deep, even sleep.

Luke stared at her face for what felt like hours, his fingers desperate to trail along the edge of her jaw or the turn of her brow. He watched as her dreams caused her face to transform, at moments full of worry and dread, and then, occasionally, a sweet, restful peace.

He finally fell asleep and woke when he heard the early morning birdsong of dawn wafting through the open windows. Terrified to discover he was alone in the bed, he stood up quickly and saw Ellie sitting over by the empty fireplace, cross-legged on the floor. Bits and pieces of her life surrounded her: clothes, wallet, computer, camera. And all of the weapons Luke had foolishly left sitting on the table at the far side of the room when he'd returned with her last night.

When she looked up at him, this loving stranger, her long hair cascaded over one shoulder. Even her hair felt unfamiliar. "Good morning," she whispered, her voice still strange to her own ears. She stared at him a long time, trying to process the whirl of emotions that surged up through her, nearly drowning her in a sea of contradictory particulars. Love, comfort, hints of terror at his strength, a deep yearning, a spike of fear, anger. All of it warred silently within her. She took a deep breath and patted the floor next to her. "Come sit by me . . . Luke."

She knew who he was. She knew where she was. When she'd woken up an hour ago, those two gifts, at least, had been hers. But that was as far as it went; it was as though a glass curtain had come down between her and the rest of the world—she was on the outside looking in and communication was impossible.

Gauging her response to him, she knew she didn't want him to touch her, but she also felt better when he was close. He walked toward her across the elegant room, and even in a simple white T-shirt and a pair of blue drawstring pajama pants, with rumpled morning hair and a unshaven jaw, he looked like some sort of medieval lord protector. When he sat down on the floor beside her, she inhaled the warm, comforting scent of him, feeling as though he were a devoted beast come to guard her. She felt like he was Saint Jerome to her injured lion: powerful and tender all at once. Or maybe he was the injured lion.

She shook her head. "Have you ever seen that painting by Fra Lippo Lippi of Saint Jerome removing the thorn from the lion's paw?"

"Yes. I know it." He looked at her with far too much depth, too much knowing, and an eagerness that made her uncomfortable.

"Please don't look at me like that." She turned her face away.

"Like what? I'm sorry. I won't—" He started to reach out to touch her upper arm, out of habit probably, then pulled it back and rested his hands loosely in his lap. "Sorry. Just tell me. Whatever you want."

"It just feels too intense. I like you." She smiled at how empty the words sounded when she said them aloud like that. "I mean, I think I love you . . . or loved you at one time . . . am I right?" She watched how the words spread relief and sadness through him.

"Yes." His voice was so small, so hopeful.

She couldn't look him in the eye. All of his hope started to give her a headache. "But I feel . . . " Her voice drifted off and she looked out the window as the gray light of dawn started to turn to something warmer, more golden. "I feel . . . diaphanous or something—I don't know how else to describe it. Sheer, transparent and very, very weak. But maybe not broken." She turned back to face him. "I know I'm strong, somewhere deep inside—"

"You are. You're incredibly strong—"

She patted him on his knee. "Thanks. But I also feel," she gestured up and down in front of her abdomen, "full of trap doors and pitfalls and—and when you look at me like that, like you did just now, intensely examining me, or looking for the old me, or whatever, it makes me feel like I'm going to topple right into one of those black holes." Her hand was still resting on his knee and she stared at it, trying to feel him for the first time, but it was impossible. She could sense they had a history; she could feel it passing between them, even in a touch as simple as that. But it was too much. She pulled her hand away. "Just give me time, you know, to sort things out."

He smiled and his blue eyes caught hers and she smiled back. "Of course. A friend of Maria's is coming over this morning to talk to you. She's a doctor . . . who can help you sort through . . . some things . . . "

"Thank you," she replied. "I need that." She could tell he wanted to touch her, but he wouldn't unless she asked him to. And then she was flooded with gratitude to realize deep down that his love and patience were apparently infinite.

Ellie broke the moment and directed his attention to the open computer in front of her. "Check this out," she said with more cheer, as a spreadsheet of numbers and stock call letters trailed up the screen. "So, here's something fun. Look how rich I am!"

He laughed. "Yes, you're rich." But he wasn't looking at the screen, he was looking at the turn of her shoulder where the simple cotton edge of her white lawn night dress curved toward her back. She pulled at it self-consciously and frowned.

"Sorry," he added quickly then gave his full attention to the computer. "Yes, you were—you are!—very adept at investments and that sort of thing."

"I remember all that. I remember you, Luke. I do."

"I'm so glad."

"But after we arrived in London . . . was it just a few days ago?"

"Yes. Just a few days. This is my brother's house. He lives here with his wife Maria, and their two sons."

"I know that, too. I remember lunch with your brothers out in the garden, but after that, it's a bit of a blur." She looked out the window again and then back at the computer. She highlighted one line in particular. "I don't want to invest in this anymore."

Luke looked more closely at what she'd highlighted, then marveled as she tapped in what must have been a seventeen digit account number and an even longer password.

She must have sensed his wonder. "Yeah, I've always had a thing for memorizing long strings of numbers. Luckily that's all still in here." She tapped the side of her head, then clicked on the stock she wanted to sell and set up the trade order.

"Maybe you should speak to your broker or an investment advisor before—"

She looked up at him. "I think I *am* the investment advisor." Quirking her lips, she returned her attention to the screen. "I'm completely sure about this. I want to reallocate a few things."

He watched in stunned silence as she prepared to sell over two million dollars worth of a superbly performing firearms manufacturer.

"Ellie—"

"What?" she chirped as she hit another sell order.

"That was one of your best performing long-term investments."

"I know, but I'm just not into it anymore. Good time to get out."

He looked across her lap and saw that she'd disassembled all the guns he'd left there, each one lined up like it was in a display case, with a little row of bullets or cartridges alongside it.

"Yeah." She followed his glance. "I obviously know how to use them. But I . . . they make me really uneasy. Can you get them out of here, please?" She didn't quite make eye contact.

"Of course, it was stupid of me to leave them lying around. I'll get rid of them right now." Luke walked over to the telephone and clicked on the intercom to the kitchen. He asked one of the maids to come retrieve a few items from their room. Two minutes later there was a polite knock at the door and Luke handed over the passel of weaponry. The lovely dark-haired woman didn't even look surprised when she took the two automatic rifles, two handguns, and holstered knives that Luke had put into a canvas tote bag. She might as well have been carrying a bundle of laundry.

Ellie's cell phone rang soon after Luke sat back down beside her.

"Oooh. I wonder who that could be," she smiled as if it were a game. "Hello?"

Luke watched as she fielded the call.

"Yes, this is Eleanor Sinclair. Yes, I just sold those shares. Oh, okay. Thanks for checking. Okay. Thanks again, bye." She turned to Luke and gave a little shrug. "Well, I suppose it's nice to know people are watching out for my interests."

Next, she looked down at the collection of items from her purse: credit cards, passport, drivers license, wallet-sized snapshots, and keys that she'd laid out in neat rows on the floor beside her. "My life looks really organized. I checked all the credit card accounts. Looks like we had a good time in California and the Florida Keys, didn't we?" She looked up to meet his eye.

Luke thought of how good a time they'd had *together* in those places and nearly wept. "Yes," he whispered. "We had a really good time."

She patted him gently on the shoulder as if she were the one consoling him, which, he thought, maybe she was. "It will all work out. Don't worry. I'm starting to remember that I'm the optimist in this operation." She gestured toward him and back toward herself

He wanted to kiss her so badly, she must have felt it like electrical pulses flying off him, but he could also tell she knew he wouldn't do anything without her invitation. He kept his focus on the creamy yellow lattice pattern woven into the carpet where they sat next to each other, lest she see the desire in his eyes.

Ellie reached for his chin and turned his face to hers with a calm, assessing manner. His eyes were brimming with unshed tears. "You have the most wonderful eyes." She wiped away the single tear that broke free. "I won't hurt you . . . I know we . . . we're connected . . . I really feel that . . . "

He reached up to touch her cheek and she shut her eyes as if she needed to brace for it. He let his hand drop.

She sighed and opened her eyes. "But for some reason I really can't have you touch me—especially like that—with that kind of tenderness. I know it seems like that's exactly what I must need, since I'm so confused and adrift. But, I mean, you can say no, of course, but I hope you'll just stay with me for a while."

"Oh god, Ellie. I'll never leave you. No matter what. It's inconceivable. Whatever happens. I don't have to touch you if you don't want it. Ever. Please trust me on that. Whatever else happens."

She let her hand come away from his face and rest in her lap. "Good. That makes me feel good. Safe, you know?"

"Yes. I know."

They sat quietly for a long time after that, with Ellie fingering different pieces of her former life. Because he already realized that's what it would be: *her former life.* A snapshot of her with Rob in India, her health insurance card. Luke made himself comfortable, pulling a throw pillow down from the loveseat and lying down on the carpet, then curling up his knees slightly. Close but not touching.

Ellie finished putting the contents of her wallet back in place, and then set it all back into her handbag. She looked around the small area in front of her and picked up her digital camera. She held it in her hand and appeared to be relieved she knew exactly how to operate it, how to skip ahead through the images, the intricacies of how the shutter speed worked. She'd paused at a particular image when Luke caught her glance.

"I love your feet." She turned the back of the camera toward him so he could see the black and white image she'd taken that early morning in Florida.

He looked from the camera to her eyes.

"Very nice," she added. "Just like Michelangelo's *David*."

"That's what you said when you took the picture." He watched as her face bloomed with the memory. "Does it feel like you remember that, or just me saying it?" He regretted the pressing tone of his voice, but he wanted to know.

She turned her head at a curious angle, looking at the screen again, trying to see the picture with fresh eyes. "No. It feels real. I totally remember it." Then she turned to him and he felt a thin, but glorious, ray of hope lance through him. "It was a quiet morning, we were talking like this. And then you—" Her eyes narrowed. "It was sexy."

He smiled despite himself. "Yeah, it was. But we don't need to focus on that part. Don't get ahead of yourself." She smiled down at him and he almost reached for her, instinctively, but he stretched out his arms and legs instead. Then he stood up. "I'm hungry. Do you want something to eat?"

They lounged around like that for days. Ordering food to be delivered up to the room. Talking or reading. Dr. Lawrence coming each morning and evening to speak to her alone. Once or twice Maria came in to check on them. She liked Maria. But Ellie had no interest in leaving the safety of that room. Or the safety of Luke.

She loved the look of him, all firm and sure and kind. At the end of a week, she had her first desire to go beyond their cocoon. "I think I want to cook. Do you think Ethan and Maria will mind if I use their kitchen?"

"No," Luke smiled and reached his hand down to help her up from the floor, where they'd taken to sitting each morning since that first day. She reached up and took his hand, then stood up quickly and held onto him for a moment longer, looking at their joined fingers.

Her stomach gave a little flip of pleasure at his warm touch, then her brain sounded some terrible internal alarm. At least she'd had a few seconds this time. Maybe one day she'd get a whole minute. Or two.

She tried to pull her hand away but he held her, not captive, just wanting to know. "What happened just then . . . what did it feel like?" He released her hand.

"I felt something . . . wonderful . . . and then it disappeared." He looked so good, so genuinely concerned about her, she hated that she couldn't dive into all that comfort, but she was so terrified; it was going to take much longer than a few good nights of sleep to sort out. "I felt our love, I guess." She smiled. "But then something clanging and horrible rang through my brain, and now I just feel . . . worried. And more than a little frightened. And my heart is beating faster than it should. Dr. Lawrence said the wonderful feelings will gradually get stronger."

He rubbed his palms against the fabric of his jeans. "I understand. I'm sorry. I miss you, that's all." He smiled with an adorable, guilty look. "I promise I'll be patient. I love you completely, Ellie. Not to scare you or . . . you know. Just, so you know."

"Thanks. I mean, I know that's a bit of a weak rejoinder, under the circumstances, but I mean it truly. I am really thankful that I woke up that first day—or half-woke—" She laughed bitterly, then continued softly, "to find someone kind and gentle there beside me."

"Yeah, that's me." He stared at her for a few more long moments. "So." He clasped his hands together. "Are you ready to go down to the kitchen?"

She stood there for a little while longer, looking around the serene room and a part of her hoped, foolishly, that she might stay there forever. The treetops of a lovely garden framed the window. The morning air was beginning to glow and crackle. It was a charming, lovely place to be emotionally waylaid. She took a deep breath. "Yes. I'm ready." She reached for his hand and he took it. Nothing electric or passionate, just a sure, guiding hand when she most needed one.

After that, they all sort of tip-toed around her for many days, with Luke trying not to cross any real or imagined boundaries and Ellie trying to process as much of the present and the past as she could without slipping into that place of brief piercing terror or worse, the slow, crawling sadness. Most mornings, she and Luke were the first to arrive in the kitchen. The cook knew that Ellie enjoyed making breakfast, so she set out a big bowl of eggs, some fresh bread, and set the coffee pot to brewing.

One morning, as Ellie was whisking eggs and Luke was pouring coffee, slow tears started rolling down her cheeks. Luke came from across the room to stand by her within seconds.

"What is it?"

"I don't know. Just loose feelings I guess. I don't know how else to describe it." He handed her a paper towel and she smiled as the tears kept coming. "Things are starting to come apart. In a good way, I think."

"It's totally all right if you want to cry into the eggs. Whatever you want to do or feel, you're totally safe. It's probably good, right, to let it all out?"

She gave him a watery smile. It might be perfectly safe for him, but it didn't feel at all safe for her. "It's like I have all these emotions—gratitude and terror and love—" She looked at Luke. "But everything is unmoored and swirling around in here. Does that make any sense?"

A huge man walked into the kitchen and Ellie moved behind Luke, instinctively seeking the protection of his body.

"Hey Ellie!" Suddenly she knew it was Schenk talking in his usual jovial, papa-bear way. But she was also afraid of him.

Deathly afraid. "I can't believe you're up and at 'em already," he barreled on. "I took the week off, but I'm back now, to take Ethan to the office."

Luke shook his head, probably trying to fend him off.

"Oh. Sorry. Didn't mean to come in with guns blazing."

Ellie's brow furrowed deeper, her worry increasing.

"It's okay. It's just Schenk," Luke said quietly. "He's with us. He's good."

She shook her head in a slow no and moved further behind Luke's back. "He's dangerous."

Ethan and Maria entered the kitchen a few seconds later, talking about their sons and the upcoming midterm break. They stopped speaking when they came fully into the room and sensed something was up.

Maria spoke quietly to Schenk, explaining that it would probably be for the best if he didn't come into the house for a few more weeks. Schenk looked like a forlorn puppy being punished for something he didn't do.

"Okay." He waved to everyone. "Hope you feel better soon, Ellie. See you all later."

Luke rubbed the knuckles of Ellie's hand. "It's okay. He's gone. But he's a great guy. You really like him. Liked him."

"I do like him," she said as she exhaled, feeling the terror abate. Then she turned to face Luke. "But he was carrying."

Maria, Ethan, and Luke froze.

"What makes you say that?" Ethan asked carefully. "He certainly wasn't showing one, was he?"

"No. But he did have one, didn't he?" Ellie asked, clearly irritated that Ethan was trying to undermine her certainty.

"Well, yeah, he did. But it was totally concealed and I'm sort of in that business and I was just curious *how* you knew."

"Oh." She looked down at the floor then up to Luke, finally turning back to Ethan. "I don't know. I just *knew*. Maybe physically his left arm was a tiny bit away from his body? Or maybe he stood a little bit more heavily to his right? Maybe?" She shrugged. "I just knew. And I hate guns."

Luke smiled at that.

"Is that funny?" Ellie asked with an almost snobbish tone to her voice.

"In a way. You own lots and lots of guns. But that will all sort itself out. Obviously, you don't like them *anymore* and that's perfectly fine."

She sighed. "I know I must seem like a hypocrite, but I actually don't own any guns anymore. I had my parents go over to my place in Florida and empty the safe. I'm totally gun-free."

"That's great," Luke replied, but there was still a ton of stress in the air.

"We're just all getting used to . . . whatever this is." Maria said, with a pleasant, all-encompassing wave of her hands.

"Thanks," Ellie said. "Now. May I cook you all something for breakfast?"

"Oh that sounds lovely," Maria said.

"I think I'd like to make a frittata." Ellie let go of Luke's hand and walked over to the large double-doors of the stainless steel refrigerator. She pulled out cheese, onion, red pepper, scallions, and butter. "This is such a lovely kitchen. A great house."

"Thanks. We love it too," Maria said. "Why don't I set the table out in the garden and the four of us can eat out there?"

"That sounds great." Ellie stopped for a few seconds.

"What is it?" Luke asked.

"I feel like something is missing." Then she snapped her fingers. "Music! I love to cook with music."

"You do. I'll go get your phone." He wanted to kiss her on the neck before he left the room, to have her stretch her head and toss her hair out of the way, the way she always did, offering that lovely tender skin.

Instead, he forced himself to veer away from where she stood at the counter, already beginning to chop the vegetables.

They stayed at Ethan and Maria's for nearly three more weeks, as if it were perfectly normal to live in a guest room in the middle of London, indefinitely, until further notice, never leaving the safe boundaries of the townhouse.

Toward the end of the last week, Ellie declined the sedative that Maria had been giving her each night to help her sleep. Luke had stayed with her all those nights, fully clothed, sleeping a few layers of linen away, but always nearby if anything should startle or upset her. The night she chose to forego the drug-induced sleep, she reached for Luke's hand as she was dozing off. She looked like she was arming herself, like they were about to embark on a roller coaster ride.

"Here goes," she said with a jaunty enthusiasm she obviously didn't feel.

"I'll be right here no matter what."

She closed her eyes and started to drift. Each night she'd been physically exhausted since she'd been using the lap pool in the sub-basement of the house, swimming for hours to quiet her mind and tire her body. As she fell asleep that night, she kept holding onto Luke's strong hand.

About thirty minutes after she'd fallen asleep, Luke heard her small moan of worry. He wasn't sure whether he should wake her and try to jog the memory free of the dream, while it was fresh in her mind, or leave her be. He let her go a little bit longer. Her worried expression was replaced by an angry scowl that made him oddly hopeful. If she were fighting Desmond, or the devil, in the dream, maybe she could fight her way out of the terror of the abduction and back into the relative safety of the present.

In her dreams, it was always Luke. It was like some psychedelic episode in a movie where every character turns to face the tortured protagonist and they all have the same mask of the same face. In the recurring dream, Luke was her rescuer and her abductor and her lover and her attacker. She woke up many times throughout that night, sweating and panting as if she'd been running miles at a full sprint. And he was always there, the *real* Luke, she would remind herself, the kind, loving, attentive, patient Luke. But in those first waking moments, it was all convoluted and he was all of those other menacing people, too.

She'd talked to Dr. Lawrence about it and they were working on lots of ways to separate the trauma of what had happened from the loving relationship she'd had with Luke, but it was still all tangled up together. In the middle of the night, she woke with the frantic pounding heart again. She tried to steady her breathing, then turned to face Luke across the small distance where they lay on separate pillows.

"He sounded exactly like you," she whispered.

Luke shut his eyes, remembering how when they'd first met, Desmond and he were always confused for one another on the telephone, how even Kate would mistake one for the other when they called. The thought later sickened him when he realized the terrible nature of Kate and Desmond's history.

"He kept telling me that you were friends," Ellie continued quietly. "He made it sound like you . . . " Her breath caught. "That you didn't mind what he was doing to me . . . planning to do to me . . . " Her voice was so small and quiet, as if saying such horrible things aloud might bring them back to terrifying life. Tears streamed down her cheeks into the pillowcase.

"Oh, Ellie." He didn't know what to say or do that didn't involve taking her into his arms and kissing her, that didn't involve physically protecting her with his own body. There weren't enough words in English to explain the perverse, duplicitous nature of everything Desmond must have said to her. "It was all lies."

"I know." She swallowed a sob and let the tears run. "But he was so *compelling*. And he sounded so much like you. Exactly like you." Her tears turned to racking sobs. "He *was* you. I responded to him, Luke. My body responded to him." She tried to gulp in air and looked like she might start hyperventilating.

Luke couldn't bare to be separated from her a second longer. He risked pulling her to him, wrapping his strong arms around her shoulders, as if he were buffering her from everything and everyone else in the known world. "This is me, Ellie. This is the real me. Feel every ounce of my body, every muscle. I love you so much. I will never hurt you. Please feel how different I am from him. Touch me and look at me and remember." He was speaking in hot, harsh tones against her hair, into her ear, as her body wracked and sobbed into his. She had her hands pressed up to his chest between them, but she wasn't pushing him away, she was grabbing onto him. Holding on.

He felt the first tentative touch of her lips against the turn of his neck as she cried. "I missed you so much," she said between sobs. "I kept thinking you would save me. I kept waiting for you. I tried so hard to wait for you. And then he was doing terrible things to my body . . . touching me with the barrel of the gun . . . it was so vile . . . he did terrible things to my mind . . . and I just had to shut it all away . . . you didn't come in time . . . "

"Oh god, I'm so sorry, Ellie." He was crying now too. "It's just impossible to say how sorry I am—"

"No." She pulled away a few inches to look into his eyes and almost smiled, a gleam of victory in her shining eyes. "I took care of myself, didn't I?"

He smoothed his palm down her back and held her close. "Yeah, you did. But . . . "

"I know . . . but then there's the weight of *that*, too. I get it. But I also think knowing that I ki-killed that man, deep down I know I can take care of myself. Can't I?"

He nodded and whispered. "Yes. You can. You're so strong, Ellie."

"And you did come in time. You all did." She kissed his neck again and inhaled. "You still rescued me—rationally I know that. But I mean, mentally, emotionally, whatever, I broke in there—I couldn't hold on any longer."

"Of course you couldn't. No one could. He—it doesn't matter now. You are safe. He's gone now. He is totally gone."

"Did you kill him?" She asked without any emphasis, her tears coming to an abrupt halt.

"Yes."

She let her head fall against Luke's chest, listening for the beat of his heart. The rhythm was soothing and familiar. "I know it's wrong to feel it, but I'm so glad."

After that night, pieces gradually started to fall back into place. Luke was there throughout the nights, and rarely let go of her hand during the days unless she was cooking or swimming laps, and even then he would usually stand nearby, just to be close. He started swimming laps when she did, and she didn't seem to mind the company. He tried to ignore the fact that they hadn't stepped out into the "real world" for weeks. Then, about a month and a half after the abduction, she reached for him.

Luke was swimming with her, ultimately unable to keep up with her grueling pace. Of course he could have beaten her in a sprint, but when she was going for distance, she was unbeatable. He rested his elbows against the edge of the pool, standing in the shallow end with his back to the wall as he waited for her to finish her laps.

At the end of her final lap, she touched the wall near where he waited, then rose up slowly, the cool water cascading off her hot skin. She'd told him the hours of daily exercise provided her with a wonderful break from the constant buzz of internal dialogue that dogged her. She scraped her palms along her wet hair, slicking it along her skull and sluicing the water down her back.

Luke had given up trying to look away. The tension along her neck and collarbones, the pull at her shoulders and upper arms. He was ravenous to touch her, but they had reached a provisional plateau where he was allowed to look at her wolfishly as long as he didn't actually make physical contact. After the night he'd held her through her first retelling of her terror, he hadn't held her since.

Her skin pebbled as the cool air caught the moisture.

He looked down into the pool so he didn't frighten her with his desire.

"It's getting okay. I know it will be okay. One of these days. I mean, I really am starting to feel how much we're meant to be together. Like that. Physically. A part of me, a really big part, a warm expanding part, wants to touch you, only . . . there's still an *only*."

"I know. I meant it when I said it won't ever matter. It can be never if that's what you want. But God how I love to look at you. The way the water trails off your shoulder, the way your hair curves over the angle of your back. It's not lascivious, really." He smiled. "I mean, I guess it might be a little." He held up his fingers to illustrate a little bit between his index finger and thumb. "But it's more that I just can't resist the sight of you, you know?"

She looked at him with a hint of genuine desire. "Yeah, I know." She came toward him, walking through the shallow water, then trailed her index finger along his neck and collarbone.

His eyes closed in some kind of blessed relief. She loved that he just received her touch and didn't demand anything of her. She moved a few inches closer—letting the water sounds and their breathing override those other cruel words and that miserable voice and that gun—letting all of it break into a million pieces and lose its power. She stepped closer still, as his eyes remained shut, and she rested her palm against his cheek, her thumb moving in a slow loving caress across his face, tracing his eyebrow, then his lower lip, then the curve of his ear and then back to his warm, strong neck.

"Oh," she gasped quietly. "I really love you—I feel it now—it's so strong."

He stood there, perfectly still, just letting her reacquaint herself with him. She put both palms against his face as if she were a blind woman feeling him for the first time. She closed her eyes as well, letting the pads of her fingers trace him everywhere, along his neck, down to his shoulders and along his beautifully muscled upper arms, then across his chest, the distinctive abrasion of his chest hair sending a lovely, comforting current through her fingertips. She rested her hands on his chest for a few long moments, feeling the steady, reassuring beat of his heart through his firm, warm skin.

Ellie opened her eyes for a few seconds, to really see him. His lips were slightly parted, waiting for her, she thought. Then she had the first real spike of desire, of wanting to drag her tongue along that innocent lower lip of his. She wasn't sure she had the courage, but he was so patient, so available, she leaned into him, slowly, so slowly, then touched her lips to his. Her tongue trailed hesitantly across his lower lip, learning him. Re-learning him.

His tongue reached out to meet hers and she had a flash of panic. He withdrew, instantly sensing her wariness. He opened his eyes and asked, "Should we get out?"

"Not yet," she whispered. She loved the warm rise of peace and love that seemed to be coming up around her, so she tried to release any stray pangs of worry or doubt. She let her fingers trail up his neck into his moist hair. The short, taut pull of his thick brown hair in her hands felt like an anchor. She tugged at him, feeling more urgency, and slowly drew him in to place her lips on his again.

This time when she kissed him, she wasn't sure if she could ride the wave of painful images that fractured across her mind, flooding her like a migraine of overwhelming snapshots and memories. But she rode it. She wanted him, his patient, loving self. She wanted all of him. And as Dr. Lawrence always said, "There's no way around, only through."

She pulled at his scalp, taking his head a few inches away from hers, and jarred him a bit. He opened his eyes in slow ecstasy.

"That was wonderful," he whispered.

She smiled, taking it as a compliment. "Thanks. For me too." She licked her lips as if she were contemplating her next move.

His arms hung lank at his sides.

"Do you want to touch me?" she asked quietly.

"You know I do. But take your time. I don't want to . . . set you back."

"I think I want you to," she whispered.

"Can we go upstairs?" he asked. "I'm freezing." The admission broke the tension and she laughed and agreed.

"Yes. Absolutely. Upstairs."

His fingers tingled in adolescent anticipation, as if he'd never touched a woman's skin before in his life. He reached up and let the pads of his fingers skim her silky shoulder.

She took his touch, at first, with a shiver of shock, then she eased into the feel of it, opening her eyes wide to process that it was Luke, after all, and no cruel phantom. After she'd told him that his voice was the worst reminder of her trauma, he'd become nearly mute; he was especially so now, when she allowed him to experiment with these types of burgeoning intimacies.

He gradually let the entire palm of his hand rest on her shoulders, checking with a look to make sure she was still okay. After a few seconds he squeezed her shoulders and she smiled a familiar, encouraging smile. He continued down her arms, rubbing her, touching her toned muscles along the curve of her biceps, then continuing down to her forearms and her wrists.

Luke pulled her wrists toward him; knowing how she'd been bound there made him, in some perverse way, want to reclaim that tender skin in particular, the part he'd kissed so many times before—to erase her body's memories of the torture and restraints. He lifted first her right wrist, then her left, to his lips, kissing the pulse point of each with careful attention.

Her eyes closed in bliss. A little breath escaped her lips as he let his tongue trail across her sensitive skin. They kissed and touched like that for nearly an hour, but they never took their clothes off or moved to the bed. Eventually, Ellie put a stop to it. It was enough to have a beginning.

"I'm famished," she laughed. "Let me jump in the shower and then I'll make you a big breakfast." He was beyond adorable, his lips thoroughly kissed and his eyes shining with that dreamy pleasure.

"Okay," he whispered.

Ethan and Maria came into the kitchen around ten, having slept late on Sunday morning. Maria heard Ellie and Luke laughing, then saw them sitting at the stone table in the garden, clearly enjoying the morning and the food and one another's company. Maria could see, even from the distance across the kitchen and out through the tall French doors, that Ellie's eyes were shining with a new, beautiful glow. She was recovering her confidence a little bit more each day. Or perhaps recovering something even more.

Ethan poured them two cups of coffee and added lots of cream and a little sugar the way Maria liked it. She took the cup from his hand and kept looking at the couple in the garden.

"What is it?" Ethan asked, following the direction of her gaze.

"She's changed."

He looked at Ellie while he sipped his coffee. "How so? She looks the same to me. Too dependent. Look how she's leaning toward Luke, still relying on him to protect her."

"Yes, but look how his hand is resting on her leg, how relaxed she is."

"I hope you're right, because she's going to have to leave the house soon. Or at least Luke is going to have to."

Maria turned to look at him. "Why?"

"I got a call just now while you were in the shower—Father is declining. It looks like the end is really close. Luke needs to see him."

Maria looked back out to the garden. "Ellie will love your father."

Luke laughed at something Ellie said and she turned to kiss him lightly on the cheek. Maria froze, then watched as Ellie also stopped, obviously having not planned the gesture and clearly taken aback at her own unconscious show of affection. Luke patted her hand gently and she shook her head and smiled. She looked happily startled by having initiated the intimacy.

Maria pushed open the French door and called hello. "So what are you two doing up so early and bright-eyed?" She looked meaningfully at Ellie.

Ellie returned her smile. "We just finished swimming some laps and then I whipped up some breakfast. There's plenty left if you or Ethan would like any."

Maria felt a warm wave of relief sweep over her. The old Ellie was really there, her former assurance perhaps a tiny bit undermined, but her eagerness, her quintessential sparkling joy had really returned. Maria walked to the far side of the table and sat down next to her. "You are looking particularly glowing this morning."

"I am *feeling* particularly glowing this morning." Ellie looked at Luke's hand still held firmly in hers, then back up to Maria. "And I suspect that means I probably need to leave the safe confines of this walled garden, doesn't it?"

Maria nodded enthusiastically, but before she could say a word, Luke spoke. He turned quickly to look at Ellie, cutting off his conversation with Ethan mid-sentence. "No you don't." He turned to Maria. "Why would you say such a thing?" He couldn't hide his irritation. They'd all agreed that Ellie could stay as long as she needed to, forever if necessary. He was girding himself for a battle of wills with Maria, when she took the wind out of him by simply shrugging her shoulders and looking at Ellie.

Luke turned back to Ellie with a questioning look in his eyes. "You want to?"

Maria got up to get her breakfast, and signaled for Ethan to join her, giving Ellie and Luke a familial version of mealtime privacy.

Ellie looked over Luke's shoulder, up toward the top of the twelve-foot limestone walls that were covered in climbing vines and ivies. Then she let her head tilt all the way back to take in the wide, free morning sky.

"I think I'm ready. If you'll stay with me every second . . . then I'm ready." Her eyes were half-closed, her neck stretched taut in an invitation that Luke could no longer ignore. He leaned across the few inches and kissed the side of her warm neck, pulling back quickly to check her reaction. Her eyes had flown wide and he checked her pupils to make sure her excitement was joy, not terror. She reached up her free hand as if she were going to caress his bottom lip, then let her hand drop away when she looked around the table and remembered where she was.

"Soon." Luke whispered.

Maria and Ethan returned with their plates and Ethan told them about their father. They talked for most of the morning, until Maria and Ethan left to drive out to the country see one of their sons in a rugby match.

After they'd said goodbye and Ellie had cleared the table, she asked Luke if he wanted to go back upstairs. "For a nap."

She laughed as Luke pulled her behind him, practically hauling her up the dark servants' stairs at the back of the house. The two of them tumbled into their room, Luke pushing the door shut with his elbow as his arms wrapped around Ellie's strong, narrow waist. He lifted her a few inches off the ground, so her eyes were above his and he gazed up at her with pure adoration.

He kissed her neck again and felt the delicious softening of her entire body against his, the lovely surrender, the release of fear, worry, residual terror. He carried her over to the bed and settled her onto the still-unmade sheets with a mischievous gleam in his eye.

Ellie propped up on her elbows, rubbing her bare feet and ankles together in happy anticipation. Her hair was a sexy, jumbled mess, having received no attention since she'd toweled it dry at the swimming pool. Her chest was rising and falling in a rapidly increasing rhythm, breasts straining beneath the thin fitted fabric of her old green T-shirt. Luke could have stood there for days, just taking her in. Ellie. His Ellie. Back at last.

He crossed the room, pulling off the T-shirt he'd put on after swimming, and then stretched his body beside hers, along the full length of hers. He whispered in her ear, "Do you want me to talk or not?"

She turned to curl herself up against him. His skin was awash with tingling pleasure, the long break without her touch finally over. "I want us to do whatever we feel," she started. "I'll probably get scared or spooked or whatever, but I definitely want this. I want you." She couldn't even look at him when she made the declaration. She said it into the tickling hairs on his chest, then kissed him there. He gasped, her touch so new and so welcome; he was afraid to do anything to break the spell.

"I remember it all now," she uttered between kisses, trailing her lips down the hard ridges of his firm stomach, letting her tongue trace some of her favorite muscles. "I remember how much I love it here." She let her tongue trace the turn of the muscle across the front of his hip and then pulled at the waistband of his shorts with her teeth.

"Oh god." Luke murmured.

"I think this whole reacquainting myself with all the things I remember might take quite some time." She pulled his shorts down the length of his legs, letting her fingernails pass suggestively along the taut muscles of his thighs and calves. She tossed the shorts aside without letting her gaze leave his. Her palms began rubbing his legs, pushing them slightly open to make room for herself there in the cradle of his thighs. "I think I might like you to lie there and take it for a bit. Are up to it?" She cupped him in the curve of her palm, then let her fingers turn and grip him, loving the feel of that warm, tender skin and how it contrasted with the straining power within.

"I'll do anything you want," he moaned.

She rested on her knees, leaning back onto the heels of her feet, never releasing her hold on him, just savoring the powerful energy that coursed between them. Releasing him reluctantly, she leaned back to take off her shirt and bra, arching her back and stretching her abdomen, watching him, feeling his eyes all over her like a warm wind. She shivered at the tactile power of his gaze on her.

"I think I could come just from you looking at me like that." She spoke with a throaty, seductive power, holding her warm shirt in her hands, partially covering her chest.

He lay there, coiled up tight, waiting for her. It was glorious.

Ellie shook out her hair, closing her eyes to feel the soft play of strands along her back, then threw her clothes lightly across the room. She leaned forward on her knees, then stalked up the length of his body like a hot, hungry predator.

"I kind of want to tear you to shreds." She dragged her nails along his stomach, remembering how he had often done the same to her. She watched as his skin reddened in the wake of her touch.

"Do it," he hissed and she looked up to see his eyes nearly closed.

"I feel like I might want to be rough," she confessed in a hoarse low voice. "Desmond was horribly calm—stealthy and silky—and I hated it. He made it all disgusting and wrong."

Luke's head turned, trying to hide from her. She moved quickly to get her face near his. "What is it?" she asked, pulling his face so she could see a slow tear down his cheek. She kissed it away.

"I know it's not about me," he whispered miserably. "But I can't help feeling so responsible, so ineffectual—"

She slapped him, hard, across the face. His pupils dilated instantly as if he might slap her back, just because that was his body's natural instinct—to strike back. She held his face in a firm grip between the palms of her hands. "Look at me. Listen to me. You killed him, for chrissake. It doesn't get any more *effectual* than that. It's over." She kissed him once—hard and final—then pulled back again. "If I talk about it or him or what it was like for those abysmal hours, it's only because I want it *out* of my head. That's all. I'm not dwelling on it, I don't want to analyze it—or him or his insanity—none of that is *mine*." Her thumbs started smoothing his cheek where she'd struck him. "And it's certainly not yours." She leaned in and kissed the reddening skin. "I'm so sorry I hit you."

"It's okay." He turned his head to kiss the palm of her hand, then slowly licked her skin there. The tiny motion was all it took: Ellie's heart slammed into her ribs and she dove at him, devouring every inch of his beautiful body, remembering and, more importantly, creating new, fresh memories. Creating a present.

She toyed with his nipples, she scratched and pawed at him wildly. At first she took the lead, riding him hard, kissing him with messy demanding kisses, bending him to her will. The first time she came, it was a purely physical release. A crash. A slam. A blow. She was on top, pounding into him, fucking him, and her climax was just like that. Fundamental. Rudimentary. Satisfying like food or water to a starving man.

Then gradually she started giving herself over to other glorious releases. The power of their passion brought them both through to another side, a fiery trial that left each of them utterly renewed. More than once she cried out, or sobbed, letting every emotion—the rage, the joy, the impotence of her captivity—come out through the glory of their lovemaking.

Ultimately, she was freed of the terror. And he was freed of the guilt.

Chapter 18

Later that afternoon, the house phone on the bedside table next to Ellie's head started to ring. She reached for it with a languid extension of her arm. Luke's head was resting on her stomach, a delightful, reassuring weight.

"Hello?" she answered quietly.

"It's Maria. I am mortified to interrupt you, of course, but it couldn't be helped."

Ellie must have tensed unconsciously, her flinching stomach muscles bringing Luke awake. She smiled as his loving blue eyes slowly opened and he awoke with a slow curve of his lips and turned to kiss the smooth skin of her lower belly.

"It's okay, we were just resting. What's up?"

Luke leaned up on one elbow and began kissing the turn of her hip.

Maria continued. "Well, Ethan and Luke's father is really very ill and Ethan feels we all need to see him, preferably today."

"Oh." Ellie didn't want to leave the heaven of this bed. She reached for Luke's hair and trailed her fingers along his scalp. "Shall I pass the phone to Luke?"

"No, that's not necessary. We're going to go see him in about an hour. Just be downstairs if you want to come. Otherwise, we totally understand."

"Hold on one sec." Ellie covered the mouthpiece of the phone and whispered to Luke, swatting him away from his incipient journey down her body. "Maria says they're going to see your father in an hour, that it's rather dire. Do you want to speak to her?"

Luke sat up and took the phone from Ellie.

"Hey, what's up?"

Luke listened, then hung up the phone a few minutes later.

Ellie widened her eyes as he resettled himself next to her on the pillows, arms behind his head, staring up at the pleated yellow canopy above the bed.

"Well?" she prompted, poking him in the ribs.

He smiled and kissed her neck, glad he hadn't left any red marks there when he'd kissed her—hard—a few hours before. "Do you feel up to it?"

She reached over and ran her fingers through his hair, smoothing the disheveled pieces back into place, massaging his scalp a bit more, and loving the grateful groan of appreciation it elicited in him. "I feel up to it." He looked a little skeptical. "I do," she said with more conviction.

He paused for a few seconds. "Speaking of *I do*," Luke started, then sat up a little straighter. "Will you marry me?"

Her hand froze at the turn of his ear. She was suddenly aware that they were lying there like a couple of nudists, her long, tan limbs intertwined with his, one of his hands roving aimlessly across her hip.

"Just like that?"

"Would you prefer me on bended knee? Oh never mind," he quipped, too quickly, brushing her off. Stiffening.

About to be affronted that he'd give up so easily, she looked closer, then saw what flashed across his eyes. The poor man was terrified.

She almost laughed, but didn't want to hurt his obviously tender feelings. "I would be honored to be your wife." She turned and kissed him long and lovingly on the lips, resting the palm of her hand against his chest, over his strong beating heart.

320

He kissed her and she thought she heard a small "thank you" whispered between kisses.

An hour later, they were in the back of the Bentley on their way to visit the patriarch of the McCormick brood. Maria and Ethan were facing forward, Ellie and Luke facing the rear, the four of them riding in the large back seat of the custom-made bulletproof car. Schenk was in the driver's seat.

Ellie had spilled the news about their engagement as soon as she'd reached the front hall and saw Maria and Ethan standing there.

"Where's the ring?" Maria asked with aristocratic disdain.

Ellie turned to Luke with her best impersonation of a lofty lady's air. "Yes, darling, where is the ring?"

He brought her hand to his lips and kissed the finger that would soon be wearing an engagement ring. "I think we'll be able to rustle one up when we get to Father's."

Ellie, eyes twinkling, turned to Maria, "Oooh—a family heirloom, no less!" The two women left the house amid a bubbling sea of laughter, leaving the two men to follow in their wake.

Maria and Ellie were sweeping down the front steps when Ellie stopped short. She felt a brief swell of panic. Luke came up next her and wrapped a firm arm around her waist. Maria kept skipping down the stairs, Ethan close on her heels.

Ellie took a deep, fortifying breath and continued slowly down the steps, pressing Luke's hand against her hip. "It feels very open and exposed out here," she whispered tightly into his ear.

"I know, sweetheart. You'll get used to it. Stick with me." He gripped her more securely. "Come into the car. You'll love my father. He charms everyone—except me, it seems."

She looked warily up the length of the innocuous, narrow, tree-lined street and forced herself to see it for the simple city lane it was. No lurking menace. No threats.

She breathed slowly out of her mouth. "Okay. I'm okay."

"You are. You're better than okay, remember?" Luke held open the door to the car and placed his hand on the small of her back as she bent to get in.

A few minutes later they pulled into the circular driveway behind a private wall and black wrought-iron gates that slid closed after they'd came to a slow stop in front of a large, porticoed front door. Ellie peeked out the window to take in the scope of the Georgian mansion, then felt Luke's body go rigid.

Ethan and Maria got out first. Luke hesitated.

"He wants to see you most of all," Ellie encouraged.

"I know. It's just been so many years."

She reached up and traced his lips with the tip of her finger. "New beginnings and all that. Remember?" Their entire morning had been spent leaving offerings at the altar of new beginnings, promising everything, pledging their troth with their bodies, manifesting their love, affirming the possibility of everything. "Even in this. Especially in this. Come on."

She pulled him this time, loving that she could begin to support him as he'd supported her these past weeks, that the ebb and flow of their relationship was starting to right itself.

Ellie tried not to gape as the butler opened the door to the mansion. The wide front hall was papered in beautiful French silk panels, faded turquoise backgrounds with delicate hand-painted scenes of classical architecture, peacocks, follies, vistas, lakes, streams, strolling couples under parasols. As the front door shut behind them, Ellie let her eyes adjust to the subdued light.

A classical marble bust that looked like it would have been at home in the British Museum was in a small niche in the wall to the left; a spindly, expensive looking bench in a French style with hints of faded gold leaf was to the right. Luke clasped Ellie's hand, whether to encourage her or fortify himself or both, she didn't know.

"It's beautiful," she murmured quietly.

"It was a wedding present from my great-grandparents to my mother."

She had been looking at the bust when he uttered the words. "It's a lovely sculpture."

"Not just the bust," he corrected. "The whole house and all the contents. McCormick men are notorious for marrying up."

"I hate to let you down," she said with a sly wink. "But I fear my parents won't be quite so generous."

He leaned in and kissed her on the cheek. "I'm sure I'll think of something you can do to sweeten the deal." He trailed a finger along her cheek, just as he had that first day after he'd helped her put on the motorcycle helmet.

"I remember that," she whispered with a conspiratorial grin. "Good."

They followed the butler up the expansive marble staircase that ran through the center of the hall then split at the landing. It was similar in feel to Maria and Ethan's home, but on a far grander scale. Ellie felt like she'd been staying in a mere cottage all these weeks, and was only now entering the main house.

They continued up to the first floor, the four of them walking in a silent procession behind the elderly servant. Ellie could almost feel the change that was taking place inside Luke and Ethan, their postures becoming more erect, their spines stiffening. Years of being told to stand up straight, Ellie thought ruefully.

The butler knocked quietly on a large set of double oak doors and the five of them waited. Ellie almost started to giggle as the image of the tiny green man from *The Wizard of Oz* pulling back the curtain popped, unbidden, into her mind's eye. Luke felt the spurt of energy and looked at her to make sure she was all right.

"It's nothing," she whispered with a guilty smile, trying to mentally prepare for the seriousness of the visit.

A male nurse opened the door a few moments later.

Ellie's first impression was that the luxurious suite was totally unlike any sickroom or deathbed scene she might have conjured. The room was bright and cheerful, the midday sun streaming in, splendid shafts of lights crossing the French carpet of faded rose and beige and brown. Huge fresh bunches of floppy pink peonies were set out on shiny mahogany coffee tables and end tables. A sparkling decanter of fresh water with a matching glass caught and refracted the light at the bedside table.

The upholstered furniture looked comfortable and well-used. A deep-seated leather reading chair near the fireplace looked like it would never lose the shape of the man who had spent a lifetime reading there. The loveseat opposite from it was covered in a pretty moss-green chintz that matched the long, pooling curtains at either side of the four, large sets of French windows that faced out to the deep, private back garden.

The bed was the only thing that felt heavy and overwrought. It was a massive four-poster, probably walnut, that had been finished to an almost-black patina, with each post carved in an intricate pattern of leaves, birds, nests, and branches. Ellie had never seen anything so beautiful.

The butler stayed near the door as Maria and Ethan led the way into the room. Ellie and Luke followed a few paces behind.

"Hello, Papa. I've brought Luke." Ethan was standing near the edge of the bed, hands behind his back as if he were a footman announcing the arrival of a stranger at a ball.

Ellie wondered why no one touched, why no hand reached out to hold the dying man. Every one of them seemed so isolated. The white-haired man looked small in the enormous bed, but he pushed himself up and Ellie saw that he was formidable, even near death. He turned his eyes—Luke's eyes, *exactly*—toward Luke, who stepped slightly forward. "How are you, Father?"

"Better for seeing you," the man finally replied. And then he turned slowly to look at Ellie. His voice cracked slightly, probably from lack of use. "And who are you?"

Ellie felt Luke begin to rankle then smoothed his knuckle with her finger and pulled her hand out of his grasp. She walked boldly over to the bed and took the old man's veined, weak hand into both of hers. He looked startled, and then pleased.

"My name is Eleanor Sinclair, but please call me Ellie. It is such a pleasure to finally meet you."

"Aren't you lovely?" He sighed and settled back against the large pillows.

"Thank you." She looked fleetingly at Luke. "I'm soon to be your daughter-in-law. Luke and I have just become engaged." She leaned in and whispered in the old man's ear, "So go easy on him."

She pulled back and watched as the decades of paternal anger, pride, loss, and devotion warred across his face. When she began to pull her hand away, thinking she had overstepped her bounds, she felt the fading but sure grip of his hand holding fast to hers.

"Sit here with me," he ordered. "And Maria, you too. I need beauty around me now, no more of these angry young men. You two lads go sit over there by the fireplace and let me remember what it was like to spend time with good-looking women."

Ellie smiled as she and Maria settled into the two chairs next to the bed. He never let go of her hand.

"So what do you see in my son, then?" he asked brutally.

"Oh, everything!" Ellie replied with undisguised adoration. "He's gentle, protective, funny—"

Luke's father raised a skeptical eyebrow at that. "Funny, eh?"

"In a very dark, dry sort of way, I grant you."

"What else?"

She lowered her voice so only Maria and he could hear. "And he's got those dreamy eyes of yours, so how could I resist?"

The old man's laugh was so out of use it sounded more like a rumbling cart. Ethan and Luke looked up from the magazines they were pretending to read to see what had caused such a rare event.

"Turner!" Mr. McCormick barked, after his unaccustomed mirth had settled. The butler slid across the room as though he were on some sort of motorized conveyor belt.

"Yes, sir?"

"Bring me the blue leather case from the safe in my dressing room."

"Yes, sir."

325

Luke gave Ethan a questioning look. Ethan shrugged his ignorance and returned his attention to *The Economist*.

A few minutes later, Turner placed a leather case, about the size of a large shoebox, onto the embroidered silk counterpane. Luke's father huffed a bit as he pulled himself more upright, and released Ellie's hand to bring the box onto his lap. He opened it slowly.

"You two whelps might as well come over and see this." He lifted his chin toward his sons. "It's mostly yours after all."

Ethan and Luke rose from their seats across the room and looked exactly like a pair of adolescent malcontents: hands in pockets, expressions shifty. Ellie looked at Maria who rolled her eyes and Ellie shook her head. If it weren't so serious, the whole exchange would have been comical.

"I tried to keep track . . . to keep it fair . . . " He looked up at Luke, for the first time really, and held his gaze.

Luke said nothing, so his father simply nodded and turned his attention back to the box. "Everything in the black velvet pouches belonged to Luke's mother. Everything in the maroon belonged to Ethan's mother."

There was a pause as pouch after pouch was laid out on the bedspread. The old man's scratchy breathing began to betray his illness. "Ethan, I'm sure you'll be responsible and generous with your two brothers. Please be fair-minded when you divide the spoils."

"Yes, Papa."

Luke hated being on the opposite side of the bed from Ellie. He needed her touch far more than she needed his, apparently. She was perfectly at ease in this room that held a torrent of hideous childhood memories for him. Those early years of being summoned by his father, inspected like a little soldier on parade. Looking back, it was strange to think how young his father was at the time—only in his early thirties, trying to make his way as a young widower with a wild-eyed boy in tow. But they could have been partners in crime, his father could have loved him a little.

Luke shook the dreaded, yearning refrain from his mind when he realized the rest of them were staring at him awaiting his reply. "I'm sorry, my mind wandered." He smiled toward Ellie and she got up from the chair where she'd been sitting and walked around the foot of the bed to lace her arm through his and kiss him lightly on the cheek. "Your father asked you to choose my engagement ring, love."

He was so overcome he wasn't sure what was happening. He had an almost psychedelic misapprehension of his father's kindness, he was that sure he was mistaken. "I don't understand."

Ellie looked at him closely. "Luke. An engagement ring."

His head turned to his father. "Which one did you give my mother?"

His father was surprised, then pleased, by the direct question. "Well, let's see. Yes, that would make the most sense, wouldn't it?" He started fumbling with the ties at the pleated edge of the different jewelry pouches.

Ellie intervened as the others stood there in some sort of odd shock—Ethan and Maria were quiet, probably out of respect for Luke, or their father, or both; Luke was just plain useless.

"Here, let me help you with that." Ellie climbed up onto the bed and sat cross-legged next to him. She shot Luke a look that said, quite clearly, *just because you all treat him like some untouchable doesn't mean I have to.*

"Oh, look at all this!" Ellie cried happily when sparkling gems began to tumble out—ancient rubies set in heavy gold; rivers of pearls; a glittering diamond bracelet.

Luke's father took one ring into the palm of his hand and seemed to let the long-ago memories wash over him. The stone was a piercing blue aquamarine, very close to the color of his eyes; it was round and surrounded by a small spray of diamonds, the whole arrangement set high on a white gold band.

"Yes, that was her favorite," he said quietly. "We were in Biarritz and she saw it in the shop and said she had to have it because it was exactly, well, she claimed it reminded her of my eyes." He looked at Luke, then at Ellie. "It's not the most valuable, of course, so perhaps you'd rather—"

Ellie nearly dove at him. "No! That's the one. No question!" She turned her head to look over her shoulder. "Right, Luke?"

Even after all these years, the resentment still flared that *all* the money that bought *all* the jewels had been his mother's to begin with, even though—yes! of course!—she'd left it all quite willingly to her young husband, as both law and love had dictated. Every gift that her father supposedly gave was really courtesy of his mother, or his mother's parents at least. Somehow it still rankled.

His father had always been able to read his thoughts. Illness and jewels and charming fiancées did nothing to curtail that ability. "Let me have a few words with Luke, alone please." He smiled at Maria and then, with a bit more seriousness, at Ethan. Ellie started to get up from the bed.

Luke pressed her shoulder. "Ellie stays."

"Fine with me," the old man barked back, then glanced at Ellie's face and all his bitterness simply melted away. "I mean, that would be fine." He patted her knee in a grandfatherly fashion.

Maria, Ethan, Turner, and the nurse all showed themselves out, leaving Luke, Ellie, and Mr. McCormick in a weighty silence.

"Come sit in these two chairs." Luke didn't move at his father's command. "Please." The old man added, more tired than irritated. As Ellie pulled herself off the bed, her soon-to-be father-in-law said in a loud, stage whisper, "He's such a stickler!"

She smiled and patted the dying man's hand. "He is, but in a good way. He'll never let anyone boss me around." She slid off the bed and turned to take Luke's hand in hers and they sat in the chairs Maria and Ellie had been sitting in.

"Try to let me just get this all out," Mr. McCormick began. "It's so utterly boring knowing I might die at any minute, and that there will be histrionics."

Luke kept his face stony. Ellie couldn't help but love the combination of world-weariness and humor. The man was about to die for goodness' sake.

"Very well." He stopped to breathe deeply, as if he might need to stay underwater for quite some time. "I know you always felt robbed—robbed of your mother," his voice cracked. "I was lost for those years. I was unfit. I looked at you and all I saw was her face. Still do, I suppose. Your intensity, your openness, even your humor." He looked at Ellie and winked. "Even then, devilish humor, just like Diana's. Black humor." He breathed again, a bit more ragged, and looked out the window toward the treetops. "And I failed you."

Even that Luke resented. The fact that at the final hour his father was going to come across as some sort of broken hero, damaged by the profundity of his love for his first wife. *Bullshit*, was all Luke could think. He was seething. Again, Ellie's calming hand was resting gently on his thigh, grounding him.

"And I was so wracked by guilt," his father continued haltingly. "The doctors had warned us she wasn't really built for childbirth. Tilted something or other. But she was so adamant. So stubborn. Like you. Intractable. She was going to have a baby, damn it. She wanted more of me, she'd said. Hard to believe, I know. I suppose we never know why the people we love deign to love us back. But she was determined."

"You could have refrained." Luke was furious as he spoke through clenched teeth.

Ellie turned on him. "You stop that right now. Show some respect. If not for your father, then for your mother at the very least." He felt as though she'd slapped him. Again. She softened and continued, "I'm sorry, love. But really, just listen. Let him get it out already."

Mr. McCormick took another deep, struggling breath. His exhaustion was starting to get the best of him. "All right, I'll save the more romantic parts for when Ellie comes to visit again." He smiled at her. "Which I hope will be often."

"Of course, I'd love that." She answered with her customary enthusiasm and Luke wanted to smash something to bits. "Go on," Ellie encouraged.

"The main point that I've never been able to convey, through arrogance or bitterness or what have you, is that I never touched a penny of your mother's fortune. Of *your* fortune."

"Horseshit!" Luke ground out through clenched teeth.

His father closed his eyes and Ellie thought for a dread moment that he'd actually up and died just like that. Then he lifted his head off the pillow and opened his eyes slowly, staring hard at Luke. "She loaned me one hundred thousand pounds the day we got married. She wanted to just give it to me, everything really. She was sick of the responsibility and the weight of it all. I refused to take it as a gift. I paid interest, I have the documents."

Luke looked at the antique weave of the carpet between his shoes. He didn't want his father to be redeemable. The repercussions were too dire. A lifetime wasted.

"And then I invested all of it with a group of hippie computer friends in the sixties. My angry father thought I'd lost my mind, but since he was the one who'd squandered the entire McCormick fortune to begin with, I didn't pay him much heed. McCormick fathers are notoriously heavy-handed." He chuffed a small laugh at the irony. "In any case, after your birth, and the loss of your mother—" His voice cracked and he started coughing.

Ellie quickly poured him a glass of water and helped him drink it. Even after so many decades, Ellie sensed how the pain of that loss still resonated through the old man's bones. Luke was a fool. She decided to save her verbal lashing for later, and smiled at Mr. McCormick instead, eager for him to continue. "There you go," she said as she handed him a tissue to dry his lip. "Would you rather we come back tomorrow?"

"No, dear." He smiled at her then looked at Luke. "After her death, all of her considerable assets were put into trust for you—"

"That's not true—" Luke snapped.

"It is true, damn it. You would never listen to me, and you would never believe me. Even when I wanted to explain everything to you—when you turned twenty-five and should've claimed your inheritance—you refused to hear me out and refused to take what was rightfully yours." He sighed and tried to catch his breath. "We will revisit that." He let his head sink deeper into the pillow and stared out the window. He looked exhausted.

Ellie patted his hand. "We don't have to go through all of this right now. You'll be here tomorrow."

"Nice of you to think so, but the doctors aren't so optimistic." He winked at her.

She loved him for that wink. It was exactly something Luke would have done. As if to say, we're all going to hell, but hey, not much you can do about it this late in the game. "So go on, then," she prodded.

"So," Luke's father continued. "I had been left behind my whole childhood. Parents in Cuba and Rio and Hong Kong, and there I was, years of my childhood holed up in that dreaded pile in Northern Scotland, and I swore I would never do that to you, Luke. But it was all wrong. You were never really *with* me. You were—I can't even describe it—you were always a little apart. And then I met your stepmother and she could see how torn up I was about you and I suppose I let her separate us."

Ellie was holding Luke's hand with fierce encouragement, silently begging him to offer the slightest hint of forgiveness. The old man had failed in so many ways, as a parent, as a husband, as a man, but hadn't we all? Ellie wanted to shake Luke and make him see how his own relationship with his daughter could have gone the same way, through the foolish belief that his own child would be better off without him.

"Do you still have the picture of her holding me?" Luke asked quietly.

Ellie froze.

The old man released a hiss of air through his slightly parted lips and reached behind Ellie to open the small drawer of his bedside table. He pulled out an old silver frame that folded together. He held it out for Luke to take.

Ellie watched the old man's shaky grip. Luke hesitated. Finally, he took it out of his father's hand, and slowly opened it. Inside were a pair of black and white photographs. The first showed a woman, Luke's mother obviously, in a gorgeous slinky ball gown that shimmered down the length of her tall, slim figure. It was a strapless sheath of some elegant fabric that should have made her look like a siren, but she was mugging for the camera and lifting her arms in the air in mock victory. Ellie wanted to know her.

The other picture was the one Luke had secretly discovered in his father's desk all those years ago. His mother looked exhausted from the ordeal of his birth, but even her exhaustion was beatific. Her hair was pulled away from her face with a simple, wide white band, her black hair falling loosely over one shoulder. The way she held that baby—Luke!—made Ellie want to sob right there. The same ring that Ellie now felt between the fingers on her left hand sparkled on the woman's hand where she kept the baby protectively in her arms. She was looking straight into the camera, straight at Stephen McCormick, really, and Ellie did begin to weep.

It was all there in her expression. She knew she wasn't going to make it, but she was so proud of herself, so grateful for having made this perfect baby. Ellie leaned into Luke's neck and wept into the fabric of his shirt, gripping her hands around his waist awkwardly.

"May I have this?" Luke asked.

"I'd like it for a few more days, but of course, after that, it's yours. This house, the houses in Scotland and Ireland. It's all yours."

"I don't care about any of that."

His father winced a little.

Luke apologized quickly. "I mean, I care, I will take care of it all. I'm sorry, Father. We've both been fools. I just meant, these images mean more to me than any of those other things, or mean something else entirely. I don't know."

"That's fine." His father said the simple words with a relief and gratitude that far surpassed their apparent simplicity. He meant it in the old-fashioned sense of the word. Those were fine feelings, good and true.

Ellie wiped her eyes with one of the tissues from the cardboard box that was covered in lovely embroidered white linen on the bedside table. The three of them sat in silence for a few more moments, then Ellie joked through her froggy voice, "Well, that was easy."

Luke's father smiled. Luke stayed somber, but he looked at his father with a new emotion, perhaps the beginning of some small hope.

"Now, I'm well and truly exhausted so you two must leave me." The old man had returned to his formal bluster. They were being dismissed.

"Here, let us help you get this cleared up," Ellie said as she gestured to Luke and the two of them walked to the other side of the bed and put all of the jewelry back into their proper pouches and then into the larger case. Luke picked it up and carried it back to his father's dressing room.

While Luke was gone, Ellie leaned forward and kissed Luke's father on the cheek. "So, about my visits, what's better for you? Mornings or afternoons?"

"Both, if you can spare them," he replied, patting Ellie lightly on the cheek.

"Excellent! I'll be here tomorrow at, what shall we say, nine-thirty or ten?" Ellie offered.

Luke had returned to the bedroom and stood close by Ellie's side.

"Well, I wake up at five usually—" the old man offered.

"Me too!" Ellie clapped her hands. "Why don't I come for breakfast? I love to cook. May I make you some breakfast and bring it to you around seven?"

"That would be lovely, my dear." He kissed the back of her hand in a formal parting gesture. Ellie stepped away and left Luke standing by the bed. Her poor fiancé looked completely unsure of how to proceed.

"Goodbye, Father." He reached out his hand and they shook. "I'll just put this back." He returned the pictures in the silver frame to the bedside table drawer. "See you tomorrow."

"Oh. You're coming too?"

Luke thought his father was dismissing him anew, after all that, and the wave of cold alienation started to rise once more. Then Luke caught the spark of irony, the latent smile on his father's lips. "Mmm, I thought I'd tag along. Ellie and I tend to stick together."

"Good. Very good." Then the old man shut his eyes and slipped into a gentle doze almost before the other two had left the room and closed the heavy doors quietly behind them.

Shortly after that first emotional visit, Luke and Ellie ended up transferring—like well-heeled Bedouins of Mayfair, Ellie had joked—from one guest apartment to another, leaving Ethan and Maria their privacy and moving into Mr. McCormick's home until further notice. The mansion was enormous and their presence was nothing but a wonderful blessing for the old man.

When he passed away in the middle of a dulcet, rainy November afternoon, Ellie was sitting quietly by his bed reading, Luke across the room at the fireplace drafting some ideas for updates to the castle and grounds in northern Scotland. At the time of his death, all of his effects were in perfect order. He'd had ample time to meet with each of his four sons to speak plainly about his hopes and aspirations for each of them, as well as the generous settlements he planned to bestow.

After the funeral, the four brothers met to discuss the realities of managing their father's estates. He and Ellie took responsibility for the mansion in London and the castle in Scotland, where Luke had been born. Ethan took the country estate closer to London, in Wiltshire, which included a beautiful manor house and farmland. Michael inherited the vast property in Northern Ireland, which featured a very lucrative horse breeding operation that he'd already been overseeing on his father's behalf for many years. Trevor received a large swath of lands and a sprawling hunting lodge along the borderlands of England and Scotland, south of Dunbar.

Epilogue

Two Years Later

Ellie looked up from the pile of images that lay scattered around her on the worn wooden floor, trying to decide which pictures she was going to show in her next exhibition in Carmel. She'd converted the large green drawing room into her studio and general personal mess area. Rapidly approaching squeals echoed down the ancient corridor, the happy clatter a wonderful counterpoint to decades of Highlands silence. Luke's home— their home, Ellie amended—McCormick Castle, was now a little boy's paradise.

Parapets and dungeons and dusty wardrobes and dark meandering stone stairwells. She watched, smiling, as black curls and bright blue eyes flew into the room in a joyful flurry and she held her arms wide as the unsteady two-year old boy turned, breathless, through the open doorway and ran in her direction.

Didi and Jamie were spending the summer in Scotland, along with their son, Johnny, the now-panting, squirmy jumble in Ellie's arms. The three of them had arrived from San Francisco a few days ago to spend two joyful months with Ellie and Luke in the craggy, beautiful hills.

After they'd reconnected in San Francisco, Luke had encouraged Didi to come to London to visit her grandfather, to meet him properly, before he died. Didi had warily complied.

Fostering a connection between Didi and her grandfather was only part of Luke's motivation, of course. He was suddenly alert to any opportunity that would afford him more time with his no-longer-estranged daughter.

These summer visits had provided unfettered time for father and daughter to become accustomed to one another's company. Luke had never been linked to Desmond's death, but he suspected Didi may have known something about it. They never spoke of it.

Luke's father had been thrilled to have yet another beautiful woman at his bedside, especially one who bore such an abiding resemblance to his beloved first wife in both name and appearance. His late-in-life adoration of his daughter-in-law and granddaughter had been responsible, according to his GP, for many extra weeks of life.

As more footsteps sounded in the hall, Ellie grabbed up the little boy in her arms and fell back with the momentum of his running tackle-hug. They were rolling around on the floor when Didi and Luke came running in a few seconds later, laughing and gasping from the exertion.

Ellie sat up and shifted Johnny in the basket of her crossed legs, then felt him shiver with delight as his mother and grandfather stalked into the room to capture him at last. He reached up and wrapped his chubby, sticky arms around Ellie's neck and into her long red hair.

When Luke and Didi were only a few feet away, Johnny laughed and grabbed Ellie tighter. "No! Ellie's home base, you can't get me when I'm with Ellie." He gave her a wet kiss on the cheek to prove his point.

"I think you're quite right about that," Luke agreed lightly, but he caught Ellie's eyes as he said the words, and conveyed the gratitude of a lifetime in that deep, simple exchange. "No one can get you when you're with Ellie."

Acknowledgments

This book makes me incredibly grateful for so many people in my life. Big thanks to Allison Hunter, Anne Calhoun, Janet Webb, and Mira Lyn Kelly for very early feedback (three years ago!); thank you to Miranda Neville for giving the manuscript a thorough once-over during our lovely time in England; thank you to Lisa Maxwell for spotting that one thing that shall remain nameless; thank you to my editor, Miranda K. Pennington, for your insights and direction; thank you to Amber Shah of Book Beautiful for creating a cover that perfectly conveys the longing and hope I tried to infuse into the story; and a whole cannon of glitter thanks to Alexandra Haughton for her expertise and enthusiasm—her savvy optimism constantly reinforces my faith in storytelling.

I also want to send out lots of love to the world's best beta readers: Peg, Kirsten, Louise, and Teri. And most especially, humble gratitude to my husband and children who continue to endure the vicissitudes of life with a fabulist.

About the Author

Megan Mulry writes sexy, stylish, romantic fiction. Her first book, *A Royal Pain*, was an NPR Best Book of 2012 and *USA Today* bestseller. Before discovering her passion for romance novels, she worked in magazine publishing and finance. After many years in New York, Boston, London, and Chicago, she now lives with her family in Florida. You can usually find her on Twitter @MeganMulry.

www.ingramcontent.com/pod-product-compliance
Lightning Source LLC
Chambersburg PA
CBHW051328250626
47155CB00007B/2502